I0593468

RUTHLESS CLAWS COMPLETE COLLECTION

MAGGIE ALABASTER

TRIGGER WARNING

NOTE: This book contains one non-con scene and forced sterilisation.

IVORY

RUTHLESS CLAWS BOOK 1

This is for all the lickable guys out there. We see you. We drool. Do you have to be so fucking delicious looking? Dammit!

CHAPTER
ONE

The garage stank of grease and fear.

Cars, or pieces of car, were spread all over the workshop. Dark stains covered the concrete floor. The smell of oil was embedded in the walls.

Terror wafted in exquisite waves from the man standing in front of me. His eyes were full of it. They had been since I walked in the door.

And I hadn't said a word.

It was Jake who spoke. Call him my second, my right hand man, whatever you want. He was one of the very few people in the world I actually trusted. In our line of work, trust was rare, but critical. Give it to the wrong person and you're fucking dead. There's no in-between.

Jake raised an eyebrow at the trembling man. He appeared calm and cool, but his bright blue eyes pierced souls and broke down lesser people. He wouldn't just smile while he was ripping out your throat, he'd make you smile too. "We hear you've been selling artefacts."

Silas Wheeler looked from Jake to me, then to two bodyguards who accompanied us.

Ben and Kyle stared back, unblinking, matching expressions of indifference on their faces. He would get no help there. Silas already knew he was a dead man. Unless he could somehow talk his way out of trouble.

Good luck with that, I thought.

His tongue darted over his lips. I could *see* him thinking desperately. This was one of my favourite parts. When people knew they fucked up and were screwed, but they squirmed anyway. Once in a while I let them live. Usually not. Worms weren't worth the hassle. Still, I would hear him out. I was nothing if not fair.

"Some artefacts might have come my way," he admitted. "I was, um, going to let you know. I'm a busy man. You know how things are." He gave a short, high laugh. He almost, *almost* convinced himself he dug himself out of the shit.

The doubt in his eyes was both obvious and delicious.

He continued, "I'm trying to keep this place running, more or less by myself. I thought when my nephew finished school, he would come and work for me. Ungrateful *prick* decided he's too good to dismantle cars."

Jack nodded. "It's so hard to find good help these days." To those who didn't know him, he seemed amenable, chill.

I saw the barely contained violence behind his smile and in his eyes. Lowlife slugs like Silas served their purpose, but he despised them as much as I did. People without the spine to admit when they fucked up. It wouldn't stop us from killing him if he did, but at least he might earn some respect from us first.

Silas nodded vigourously. "It really is. Young people today." He shook his head. "I don't know what the world is coming to. Am I right?" He looked at me. Apparently he hoped I would be a softer touch than Jake.

I gave him an ice cold, measured look, and he glanced away.

Hells yeah, dumbass. Nothing about me was soft. Especially not my heart. Assuming I actually had one.

"So, about those artefacts," Jake said. "The rules are the rules. You could have shut down for an hour or two. Sent word. Picked up a phone and texted. Hells, even sent up a smoke signal." His voice got more and more dangerous as he spoke.

And Silas got more and more nervous. "I *meant* to. I swear. Next time—"

"Next time," I echoed. "How many *next times* have you had already? Two? Three? We've been more than fair in giving you second chances." Several, in fact.

He served his purpose as a way to dispose of cars and cash. But I made it clear to everyone in the city of Sydney, and the rest of the state, that the sale of all magical artefacts came through me first. They weren't a common commodity, but they were fucking dangerous and I didn't want them in the hands of my enemies.

Several times, I had stopped a sale, or bought the artefact myself so I could lock it away in a safe somewhere. I knew there was a possibility people would funnel more artefacts into the area, hoping to make money from me. Whatever. I would rather have them than have those things floating around in the ether.

"You've been more than generous," Silas said. His eyes flicked from side to side, obviously looking for a lifeline from someone. He even looked pleadingly at Kyle and Ben, but they were my men. They worked for me. Whatever I ordered them to do, they would. I trusted both almost as much as I trusted Jake. They would do nothing to help Silas.

"Yes," I agreed. "We have."

Silas looked back at Jake. He assumed the last word would come from him. That because he had a cock, he must be the one calling the shots.

So many people thought that.

They were fucking wrong.

Jake looked at me. "Ivory?"

I nodded my head. "He was useful, but he overstepped too many times. If I let him keep doing that, then others will follow." I gave Silas a brutal smile. "We can't have that."

Silas stammered, "I'll make it up to you. I can..."

"You had your chance." I nodded to Jake. "End him."

Jake grinned. "With pleasure." He gestured to Kyle and Ben. All three started to strip off their clothes and put them aside carefully.

Silas shook his head and stepped back toward the door. He put his hands up to either side of him. "Please. I'll do anything. I swear, I won't sell any more artefacts. I just... Needed the money. *Please*."

In a handful of moments, Jake went from a ripped, heavily tattooed naked guy in his mid-thirties, to a magnificent, snow white wolf. Kyle and Ben were a second or two behind, neither less magnificent than Jake.

Silas' face was almost as white as the three wolves who stalked around him, toying with him. "Oh gods, please no." To his credit, he hadn't pissed his pants. Yet.

Jake stepped around him lightly, as if prolonging the anticipation, or looking for the right angle to strike.

Silas murmured. The stink of fear increased a thousandfold. The smell was sweeter than fine perfume.

It was as arousing as fuck.

In the blink of an eye, Jake struck. He leaped at Silas before the man could take another step away. He clamped his jaws on the man's throat and tore it away. A shower of blood fountained from the artery in his neck. Before I could move, it rained hot blood down over my cheek and the front of my dress. It felt like someone had jerked hot cum all over me.

The feeling, the smell—I was more aroused than ever.

The guys all leaped on Silas now, tearing him apart like three dogs playing with a toy.

By the time they were done, blood added to the stains on the floors and walls. And their muzzles. Silas' head was still more or less intact. There was no point sending a message if people didn't know who we'd dispensed with.

I let the boys have a little bit of fun pushing the head around with their noses like they were playing with a ball, then cleared my throat.

"I think he's dead enough."

Jake rolled the head to my feet. I glanced down. Silas lay looking up at me with glassy eyes. I resisted the urge to soil my shoes by kicking him away. Instead I watched Jake shift back and grab a rag to wipe the blood off his face.

"Sometimes I think you have too much fun doing that." I scratched the blood on my dress with a long, black fingernail. It was going to need dry-cleaning.

He grinned. "Only when they deserve it." He tossed the rag onto a workbench, picked up his clothes and started to pull them back on.

I watched for a moment with a twinge of regret, then turned away. "This place belongs to me now. Get the paperwork sorted. Find someone to run the place. The nephew maybe. Make it clear he's working for us, not himself." If he didn't like it, tough shit. If you screw with me, you get screwed.

"On it, boss," Jake said.

I turned back as he was doing up his pants. He scooped his shirt up off the floor. I noticed none of his clothes had blood on them. I also noticed he was taking his time putting his shirt back on.

He raised an eyebrow at me. "You smell good," he said.

I snorted. "You did that on purpose." I waved at the front of myself.

He grinned and picked up the rag he'd used to clean himself. He tossed it to me. "Would you believe it was an accident? You can clean it off if you like."

I threw it back at him and hit him in the side of the face. "That thing is dirtier than I am."

Jake caught the rag and tossed it back to the worktable. He missed. It fell on the floor with a plop.

"You don't look like you mind too much." He offered me his shirt. "You can change into this if you want."

I looked at the faded grey band T-shirt which dangled from his fingers. "I'll pass. I can change when we get back to Crimson."

He shrugged and pulled on his shirt.

While it was over his head, I *might* have taken a good long look at his abs. They looked rock hard. Every centimetre was covered in ink. A black dragon surrounded by skulls lazed across his stomach, distorted here and there with the lines of his muscles. An eagle with wings outspread soared over the dragon. A mountain rose behind it, grand like something out of a fantasy movie. I knew how many hours went into the work, but it was the body behind the art that made my breath catch.

I averted my gaze. He and I— that was a line I couldn't cross. I knew he wanted to leap over it given the chance, but it would fuck up our working relationship. How could it not? Sex changes too much. He knew that as well as I did. It didn't stop him from flirting every chance he got. And it didn't stop me from admiring him.

I watched Ben's tight, hard ass as he stepped toward the garage's small kitchen to wash his face. I immediately felt like a hypocrite for keeping Jake at arm's length. Sleeping with my bodyguard once in a while was a whole other story from sleeping with my work partner, right?

I sighed. Jake and I were different. So much more was at stake if we ruined things between us. Ben was just a smoking hot, protective distraction, that was all. Chalk and cheese. So I told myself.

I noticed neither Ben or Kyle had blood on their clothes either. Just as well. Jake got away with looking scruffy because that's who he was. As for everyone else who worked for me, I expected them to look the part. Black trousers and white shirts. Many of them toed the line by wearing a T-shirt like Jake. I let it slide because most of them were all muscle and tattoos and a girl liked to look, even if she didn't touch. Usually.

"What if this nephew isn't interested in running the place?" Jake asked. He tugged his hem into place and checked his face in the closest reflective surface. That happened to be a rear view mirror which sat on the work table. "From what Silas said, he didn't seem too keen. Want me to be persuasive?" He cocked his head and looked hopeful.

I drummed my fingernails on my thigh. "Hunt him down first. See what he has to say. We won't have too much trouble finding someone to run the place." I had a list running through my head already.

"Okay. As long as it's not me." Jake scrubbed the tip of his finger on his cheek.

I took the mirror from him and looked at my own reflection. I looked like I just killed someone, instead of *having* them killed. "I hadn't thought of that. There is no one I trust more to take care of my assets." I gave him a deadpan look.

He didn't buy it for even half a second. Fucking man knew me too well. All the more reason I should keep him close and not piss him off.

"You'd miss me too much if you relegated me to this dump," he said.

"Now I know how you feel about the place, I'll keep that in mind for the next time you give me the shits," I said.

"I'm safe then." He had a cocky look on his face. "Because that *never* happens."

I barked a laugh. "Not in the last two minutes, no."

He smirked because he knew that was total bullshit. I let him get away with way too much.

"I know you love me," he said. His blue eyes lingered on mine for a moment, until I looked away.

How I felt, or didn't feel, didn't matter. I had to stick to that hard line, no matter what the cost.

I didn't need to look to know he was frustrated. I sensed it. It had been a bone of contention between us for so many years. We should bury it and be done with it. Only, I knew he wanted to bury his bone deep in my pussy, not the ground somewhere.

"I'm heading back to Crimson," I said, my voice cool and businesslike. "Get on to the cleanup here. Do whatever you have to do to his head to let people know what happens to them if they fuck with me."

"You should invest in a display cabinet," Jake said lightly.

His tone didn't fool me. I knew if I let him put me up on the work table and fuck me silly, he would. Part of me wanted him to. The gods knew I was horny enough. It would be safer to fuck Ben, or even Kyle. It wouldn't change anything, including Jake's feelings for me. But the workbench was dirty and so was I. The smell of fear was gone. The smell of blood faded as it dried. The excitement of having a man killed in front of me had worn off. I filed the memory in the back of my mind for another day.

"A cabinet full of heads," I mused. "That would get full pretty quickly. Cocks would take up less space."

"That depends on the cock." Jake grinned, back to his usual sardonic self.

I laughed softly. "Who do you know who has a cock the size of a head?"

His grin widened. "Well, I don't want to brag."

I rolled my eyes. I walked right into that one. But I could go one better. "Does that make you a dickhead?"

He chuckled. "Probably. I've been called worse. By you. This week."

"I don't know why you put up with me," I said honestly.

Before he could respond with another declaration of love, Ben appeared out of the shop office, a box in his hands. "Boss, I thought you should see this." The slight frown lines around his eyes were the only sign he was concerned. Considering he was usually a stony statue of absolute calm, that meant a lot. His expression softened when he looked at me.

Ugh, him too? I appreciated the admiration. It was the added complications I was worried about.

"What is it?" Jake asked, all serious now.

Ben placed the box down on the worktable. "It looks like the kind that's usually used to contain magical artefacts. I thought it best not to open it." He would know. He was orphaned as a child and raised amongst witches. Not a happy childhood, from what I could tell. On the rare occasion a witch needed to be killed, he was usually the first to volunteer. Maybe he just had a death wish. Witches were more trouble than they were worth. Luckily they tended to avoid me.

I glanced at Jake. He nodded. None of us had magic, so there was little risk to us in opening it. Artefacts didn't tend to work by themselves.

Since there was a first time for everything, Jake opened the box carefully. Inside was a row of stones, all black but with streaks of various other colours. Two were round, two were oval-shaped and three were shaped like doughnuts. A couple were semi-precious stones.

"Wild guess: these contain magic of some kind," Jake said.

"More than likely," I agreed. There was probably a small fortune sitting inside that box. We wouldn't know how much until we had a witch look at them. "Kyle, take them to Rachel. See what she has to say about them." Rachel owned a small magic shop not far from here. She was about as reliable as a witch could be. I paid her well enough for that.

Jake snapped the box shut and handed it to Kyle. "Lucky thing we came here today. We probably put a stop to somebody's shenanigans."

I nodded. "Ben, keep searching the office and see what else you can find." If there was that much sitting out in the open, there might be more hidden away.

He nodded smartly. "Yes boss." He looked relieved I hadn't chosen him to take the artefacts to Rachel. Given his aversion to witches, I thought it better to keep him away from her. One or the other might otherwise end up dead. That would put me in a bad mood, and no one liked to see me like that.

"Does this feel weird to you too?" Jake asked.

"Being alone with you in a garage full of chopped up cars and people?" I asked. "It's pretty weird."

He flashed a brief smile, showing a dimple in one cheek. It would be better for everyone if he wasn't so fucking attractive.

"That wasn't what I meant," he said. "We knew Silas was dealing artefacts, but seven of them, right where we could find them?"

"You think someone set him up?" I asked. "He admitted what he did."

"I know," Jake said slowly. "But it has Alastair Dagen written all over it. If he was trying to provoke you, it worked."

"Silas wasn't the smartest paranormal in the city, but why would he die just to piss me off?" I drummed my fingers on my thigh.

"Why does anyone die to piss someone else off?" Jake asked rhetorically. "Presumably he has a family they threatened. There isn't anything the Onyx Ridge pack wouldn't do to get under your skin. Or your fur. Especially Dagen."

This used to be black wolf territory, before I took it over. The only thing more cranky and aggressive than a black wolf is a white one. I wouldn't let them get in the way of what I wanted. Dagen vowed revenge, but he had yet to be more than a flea that needed to be scratched off once in a while.

"Let him try," I said. "Sooner or later, he'll realise he can't win and he'll fuck off, his tail between his legs."

"I guess you're right," Jake said. He didn't look convinced.

"Of course I'm right," I said. "When am I not right?"

"Only when the other person is wrong," he said.

"Exactly." I nodded. There were many reasons why I needed him around, including to stroke my admittedly healthy ego. "I'll see you back at Crimson."

He hesitated. "I'll send Ben with you. He can come back here after."

"I can take care of myself," I reminded him.

"If Dagen is trying to start something, I don't want you out there alone," he said firmly. "Either I go with you or Ben does. Or you wait here while I call someone else to—"

"Fine." I threw up my hands. "Ben can play nursemaid if it makes you feel better. Don't forget who is the boss around here. I own this town."

"Yes, you do," he said. "Unless you get yourself killed."

"I have no intention of dying anytime soon," I said. But his worry was infectious. It had me on edge.

The drive back to Crimson was short. I let Ben come as far as the underground car park, before I sent him and the car back to the garage. His knowledge of magical artefacts was too valuable to let him sit out for too long. I was as safe here as I was anywhere, even without him following me around. He wasn't happy about it, but unlike Jake, he didn't argue. I knew I liked him for a reason.

My heels clicked as I walked to the private elevator. This was one of only two in the building that would take me up to level ten. The only other place the elevator would stop was level six, and that was empty. Anyone who wanted a meeting with me was taken there first and checked over thoroughly before they were allowed up the rest of the way.

I stepped inside the car and rode it straight up to level ten. The moment I stepped out the sliding doors, two of my men nodded in greeting. Dressed like the rest in dark trousers and white shirts, their presence there must be Jake's doing. Sometimes the guy was fussier than a mother hen, but I couldn't help appreciating him. It was nice that someone gave a shit.

I gave them a nod in return and ignored their scrutiny. They would never give me their opinion or ask why I was covered in blood, but they were obviously curious.

I walked past the door to the main office, into the room past that. I slipped inside and closed the door behind me.

The large apartment had a stunning view of Sydney Harbour and was fitted out with all the luxuries my extensive bank accounts could buy.

I didn't actually live here, since it was common knowledge the nightclub was the cornerstone of my empire. Ivory Claw, or the Ivory Claw Pack, started here. I dropped the word 'pack' from the name of the organisation when it became obvious I would need more than white wolves to keep it running. The nightclub was one of my favourite places to be, and a base for a lot of my operations. I lived in the apartment for the first year or so, back when it was little more than a rundown building in the city with a killer view.

The moment I got a real foothold in this town, I moved somewhere else. If anyone was going to come after me in a big way, they would attack Crimson. That made living here impractical and dangerous. Only Jake and some of my security knew where I really lived. In spite of that, I spent a lot of time here, and made sure it was clean and maintained. The apartment was especially handy at times like this.

I stripped off my clothes and put them aside for my maid to deal with. They might sit there until her next day of work, but she asked no questions even when my clothes were caked with dried blood.

I grabbed my phone, checked my messages and shot off a couple of replies before I got in the shower.

The sight of Silas's blood trickling across the white tiles and down the drain was gratifying, but brief.

I washed my face and hair and I wondered about the nephew.

Was it cars he wanted to avoid, or trouble? How much did he actually know about what Silas got up to? For all I knew, he was in it up to his eyeballs, but he could be as clueless as hells. If he knew nothing, it might be better to keep him out of it. I would reserve judgement until Jake found him.

I turned off the water and wrapped myself in a thick, plush towel that smelled subtly of lavender. My favourite scent after blood and fear. Okay, and testosterone.

I stepped from the bathroom straight into the walk-in wardrobe. If anyone else was to come here, they might assume I lived in the apartment. Every centimetre of my wardrobe was stuffed with something. Dresses, skirts and blouses hung on all the railings. The shoe rack was full of heels, boots and the occasional pair of flat shoes. The drawers were full of jewellery.

It was a fraction of what I owned.

I flipped off the towel, left it on the floor for the maid and pulled on a matching black lace bra and G-string.

A long, wide mirror hung off the wall. The reflection in its surface was of a woman who was fit, but not dainty, with generous hips, long legs, brown eyes and full breasts.

My white hair was almost dry already. According to my mother, it was black until the first time I shifted. When I changed back from a white wolf to a person, my hair stayed the same colour as my wolf. Apparently it freaked the fuck out of my parents, but it never changed back. It was my father who teasingly called me Ivory, both after the pack name and because of my hair. The nickname stuck.

I brushed my hair and dug into the table beside my bed before I selected my favourite—white—vibrator. My body was still humming from watching Silas die, and being showered with his warm blood.

I walked over to the couch in front of the window and sat with my back against one of the arms, my legs stretched out in front of me. The irony of where I was wasn't lost on me. The bottom floor of Crimson was an ordinary bar. The second floor was a strip club. The third floor was a place where lovers went to have sex in front of whoever else was there at the time, like a giant orgy. The fourth and fifth floors were a brothel. Yes, the business was so lucrative it needed two floors. And yes, many of the brothel workers were male and would be only too happy, and skilled, to fuck me until I couldn't see straight. A lot of the women too.

One of the downsides to owning the place was the feeling too many people would talk if I indulged in the pleasures of Crimson. Once in a while, I ventured down to watch the stripping or the fucking, but that was all I did. Watch.

You know what they say. It's lonely at the fucking top.

I know, cry me a fucking river. I had more money than I knew what to do with, and most people did exactly what I told them when I told them to do it. Even if I told them to kill.

What can I say? Even the rich and powerful need orgasms once in a while.

I set the vibrator to a light throb and pulled the gusset of my panties aside. I sat back a little more and rubbed the thrumming vibrator over my clit, just lightly at first. It sent a delicious shiver of pleasure right to my core.

I let it ghost over my clit and folds for a minute or two, until my thighs started to quiver and my pussy was wet.

I parted my legs further and slid the silicone dick slowly inside myself. The clit stimulator hummed against my sensitive nub. I quivered a little more.

Slowly I slid the toy out, and in again, teasing my clit and my g spot. I slipped my other hand inside my bra and lightly ran the tip of my finger around and over my nipple.

I was already panting through my nose. I closed my eyes and turned the vibrator up to a heavier throb.

I slid it in and out faster, then stopped to spoil my clit for a minute or two.

I was so engrossed in pleasuring myself, I almost missed the sound of the door opening and closing. I managed to keep myself from jumping out of my skin, but my eyes flew open.

Jake stood leaning against the closed door, arms crossed over his chest. He watched me with one raised eyebrow. And a tent in his pants.

Instead of stopping and acting like I did something wrong, I locked my eyes with his and kept working my clit and my nipple. I watched him watching me as I came, moaning and bucking against the humming vibrator.

I leaned my head against the arm of the couch while I came down, then slid the toy out. I drew my gusset back into place and put the vibrator down on the coffee table next to the couch.

"Shouldn't you be on cleanup?" I stood as though he hadn't seen me pleasuring myself and I wasn't dressed in a bra and panties.

"Clean up." He shrugged one shoulder and walked over to the coffee table. He picked up the vibrator and licked his tongue down the wand, which was probably still warm and slick from being inside me.

While I shook my head at him, he went on licking all the way around it, smiling the whole time. Finally, he put it back down on the table.

"There. All clean. Delicious too." He glanced at me up and down, obviously not just referring to the taste of me.

"I knew someday you would be useful for something." I made a face at him but at the same time I tried to keep a smile back. No one else I ever met would do something like that. No one else would get away with it either, and he knew it. Not even Ben. Sometimes we danced *way* too close to that line.

He gave me an ironic bow. "I live to serve."

I snorted. "Sure you do. What was so important you had to come in here without knocking?"

"I did knock," he said. "When I didn't hear an answer, I thought you might need help. Turns out I was right."

I rolled my eyes and waved at him to get on with whatever he actually came here for. While he spoke, I headed into my wardrobe and grabbed a blouse.

"I thought you would want to know I found the nephew." He at least had the sense to stay out of the wardrobe.

"Okay." I pulled on the blouse and did the buttons up. I took a second to contemplate Jake's timing. He couldn't have known what I was doing, and I believed him when he said he knocked. I was distracted. Too distracted. He could have been an assassin.

He also could have turned and crept back out the door. If he waited five minutes, or ten, I would have been done. If he was anyone else, I would be sure his body was floating in Sydney Harbour before night fell. Instead, I realised I *liked* seeing him watch me.

And that terrified me. I could not, would not walk across that line, no matter how much I wanted to. In the long time we've known each other, there were other men, apart from Ben. Quite a few of them. None of them ever meant anything, and Jake never seemed to mind. When the dust settled, I always circled back to him. It was like a dance, but only he and I knew the steps or the song that went with it.

"Where is he?" I asked. I took a skirt off the hanger and stepped into it. As I slid up the zipper, a tiny part of me acknowledged that I wished Jake was sliding it *down*.

I pressed my feet into a pair of black heels and walked back out of the wardrobe. In heels I was almost as tall as Jake, which is why I wore them.

"I'm not sure where he is right now," Jake admitted. "But I know where he's going to be tonight."

"It's not like you to be so cryptic." I stepped over to the kitchen and turned on the coffee machine.

"Isn't it? I'll have to work harder at that." He went to the cupboard and pulled out two coffee mugs.

"How about you don't," I said. "I don't like to be kept guessing all the time. But you already know that about me." What *didn't* he know about me? We had both seen each other naked more times than I could count. Hazards of being a shifter. He knew most of my secrets. Those he didn't know probably weren't worth knowing. Or at least weren't worth remembering.

"I do know that," he agreed. "I also know you can be patient when you need to be."

"Yeah." I waited and worked in the shadows for years before I was able to strike back at Barnaby Dagen and the whole Onyx Ridge pack. "It's been a while since I've needed to be patient. These days I can pay people to be patient for me."

He chuckled and made us both coffee. "Who says money can't buy happiness?" He looked at me over the rim of his mug. His thoughts were as transparent as the window behind him. What was the point of money if he couldn't have the one thing he really desired?

I looked away.

"El—" He was one of the very few people who knew my real name, much less got away with using even a part of it.

I shook my head. "What about this nephew?"

"Elodie... " In the corner of my eye, I saw him reach out a hand towards me, then lower it again. He sighed. "He'll be here tonight. At Crimson."

I turned back in surprise. My mouth formed an O. "Silas must've been in more debt than we realised."

"It's all on his computer. I forwarded you a copy. He was in a shit load of debt to Alastair Dagen." He gulped his coffee and made a face at how hot it was.

"It must be significant if this nephew would come here tonight." I blew on the top of my coffee gently. "It's not something anyone should do lightly."

"It's something someone would have to be desperate to do," Jake agreed gently.

I glanced down at the dark hardwood floor. "Yeah. I assume his alternative would be to be in debt to Dagen for the rest of his life?"

"And the lives of his children," Jake agreed.

"It's that much?" I asked.

"Not for you or me, but if all you have in the world is a chop shop, then it would be virtually impossible to pay all of that back." Jake sipped his coffee, which must have cooled enough by now.

I nodded. I remembered the days of living hand to mouth all too well. Sometimes it didn't matter how hard you worked, you would still always live that way. I was one of the lucky ones. Or one of the ruthless ones. Maybe both.

"I guess I know what I'll be doing tonight," I said. "You want to tag along?"

"I was going to wash my hair, but that sounds like a much better idea." He grinned.

"Good." Only now I was picturing Jake naked, with water and suds sliding down his body. I pushed away the thought. I needed to focus on more important things, like what I was going to wear tonight.

Jake must have read my mind, because he asked, "Do I have to wear a suit?" His lips curled at the idea.

"When you put it that way, yes," I said. "This is a Crimson event. You should have a suit ready for it."

"I do," he said. "But usually something comes up every time we plan anything like this. Last time it was that stupid motherfucker who tried to pass himself off as one of us."

"Right. He ended up part of the concrete in the foundations of one of our buildings, didn't he?" I asked. I couldn't possibly remember the way we disposed of everyone.

"That's the guy." Jake gulped down the last of his coffee and put his mug on the counter top. "The time before that it was the Onyx Ridge pack stirring up trouble."

"And this time we need to go because this nephew of Silas' is deep in debt to Dagen. It's never a dull moment around here." Once in a while, I could use a little boredom. Just for an hour or two.

"Run the biggest criminal organisation in the state they said. It'll be fun they said," Jake joked.

I laughed. "Who said that? I only did this because the Onyx Ridge pack murdered my parents and took over what they built. All I did was take it back."

Of course, Jake knew all of that. He smiled sympathetically. "You could have had a nice, quiet life. Become a teacher or a police officer."

I laughed harder than before. "Police officer? Wouldn't that be ironic?" I had a bunch of them on my payroll. The rest were oblivious. Or pretended to be.

Jake chuckled. "I would let you arrest me."

And we were back to that again.

"I don't think I could arrest you," I said.

"Because I'm so handsome and charming you would let me get away with anything?" he asked teasingly.

"No. Because you're an arrogant motherfucker. I'd shoot you on sight and save myself the trouble." I swallowed my last mouthful of coffee and put my mug down beside his.

He grunted. "You're a hard woman, El."

"I know," I said. "That's why I should probably fire you and make you go off and find a nice girl and a decent, legitimate job."

He barked a laugh. "You like me too much to inflict that kind of torture on me."

That was half the problem. I should push him away harder than I did. He deserved better than to pine after me and hope to once in a while walk in on me with a vibrator in my pussy. He should meet someone. She didn't have to be a *nice* girl, if that wasn't what he was into.

What the shit was I thinking? If he liked *nice* girls, he wouldn't be into me. If I wasn't such a selfish asshole, I would force him to stay away from me. The truth was, I liked having him around.

"We should start getting ready for tonight."

THREE

"Are you ready yet?"

This time I heard Jake knock so I was ready for him to enter. I wasn't ready for how stinking hot he looked.

He wore a perfectly tailored dark suit that fit so well it could have been painted on. Under that was a crisp white shirt and crimson and red striped tie. He had just enough scruff on his chin for that designer badass look. Although most of his tattoos were covered, the ones on his wrists peeked out from his sleeves, hinting at what else was there.

While I drank in the sight of him, he did the same to me.

He let out a soft, low wolf whistle, no pun intended. Okay, yes it was.

"No one else will be looking at anyone but you," he said smoothly.

"What? In this old thing?" I put my hands out to either side and did a turn, showing off my long, white shimmering gown. The neckline plunged low enough to show a barely decent amount of cleavage. The back plunged even lower. It covered my ass by about a millimetre. Just below the base of my neck was a tattoo of a wolf's head, surrounded by flowers. I liked to be part wolf, even in human form.

A split in the side of the dress showed a lot of thigh. White stilettos completed the outfit.

"If you wore shorts, a T-shirt and thongs on your feet, people would still only look at you," he said.

I laughed softly. "Is that a challenge?"

He chuckled. "Only if I thought you'd take me up on it. If we're going to go there, let's go one more. I dare you to go naked."

I leaned over towards the mirror to apply my lipstick. "Are you hoping I'll say yes so you can go naked too?"

He stood behind me so I could see his reflection grin. "When have I ever had trouble being naked?"

"Never," I agreed. "But that's not the impression we need to make tonight."

He snapped his fingers. "Okay. We'll save that for another night."

I grabbed a tissue and dabbed my lipstick. "How many do we have coming to our little event?"

"Attendees or... Special guests?" he asked carefully. He watched my expression in the mirror.

I made a face at him. "Both."

He nodded. "About two hundred attendees. Eleven special guests."

I knitted my eyebrows. "That many?"

Jake shrugged. "Times are tight."

"I guess so." I straightened up and turned to face him. "We shouldn't be fashionably late. They'll start without us."

"They wouldn't dare. I told them you're coming." He put a hand on my arm, just above my elbow. "Are you okay? I know these things bring back memories." His eyes bore into mine like he was trying to see into my soul.

"It wasn't all bad memories," I reminded him. "I'll be fine. We just have to focus on what we have to do tonight. This is all about the nephew."

Jake nodded slowly. "In that case, can I ask another question?"

I arched one shapely eyebrow at him. "Can I stop you?"

He looked thoughtful. "Technically, yes, but you'd have to have me killed. I need to know the answer to this. It's important."

He made me nervous, until he said, "How the fuck is your gown staying on?" He looked at me sideways, then the other way.

"Magic," I said jokingly. The truth was, my dressmaker was a genius. He managed to make clothes that looked incredible, and stayed in place with stitching in just the right place on my shoulders or waist.

"Is it sticky tape?" he asked. "Can I find out?"

I patted him lightly on the chest. "It's not sticky tape, and no you can't. Come on, we'll be late." And if we didn't leave now, I might change my mind about crossing the line with him. Besides, my gown cost six thousand dollars. I should at least wear it for an hour or two.

"Anyone who comes after you is late." Jake opened the door and waved for me to step through first.

"On the contrary." I swept through the doorway and into the corridor. "Anyone who comes after me is a gentleman."

He chuckled. "Touché. For the record, I would never do that."

I looked at him over my shoulder. "I know." I pressed my hand on the palm pad beside the elevator door. It scanned my hand and turned green. The elevator doors slid open.

I pressed the button for the sixth floor and the doors slid shut. Neither of us minded enclosed spaces, but we both knew if anyone was going to attack Crimson, this would be a shit place to get stuck.

Fortunately, we reached the sixth floor without incident. We got out and crossed to the other elevator which led down into the rest of the night club.

Jake used his palm this time on the palm pad, and pressed the button for the second floor.

The elevator doors slid open to a scene of bustle and noise. This floor was usually reserved for the strip club, but tonight a sign read 'closed for private event' hung on a velvet rope in front of the doorway.

Entry to this event was exclusive and by invitation only.

One of the security men on the door unclipped the rope before we even got there and stepped aside. He gave us both a respectful, but slightly anxious nod, before looking me up and down appreciatively.

I ignored him and stepped past.

Jake placed his hand on my lower back. His demeanour changed immediately, visibly. He went from the chill, amenable, even approachable guy, to the cold, hard alpha male of the Ivory Claw Pack. One of his fingers rested just below where the back of my dress ended, under the shimmery fabric, his fingertip on my ass.

Typical alpha male possessive shit. It was a move everyone would expect. That was one reason I allowed it. That and I liked the way it felt.

I lifted my chin and scanned the room, my ice queen persona firmly in place.

Everyone here was dressed in formal, expensive-as-fuck suits and dresses. Many of them were wolves, but I caught a scent of what might be a tiger or some other big cat.

All eyes were on Jake and I as we walked through the room to the chairs at the front reserved for us.

I heard somebody mutter, "Ice bitch," and the muscles around my cheeks twitched. If there was anything that would get you dead around me, it was using the word bitch as if it was a bad thing. I wasn't oblivious to the nickname, but whoever used it was either bold or stupid.

Jake's finger pressed into my ass cheek, letting me know he'd heard it too. He would deal with it later.

"Ahhh, how nice of you to grace us with your presence." Alastair Dagen stepped away from the group he was talking to and gave me a sardonic bow. He looked me over like he wasn't sure if he wanted to fuck me or kill me. Maybe both. I don't think he cared which order those events took place. He was a sadistic fucker who seemed to get worse by the year.

"The infamous El— Ivory, and her favourite lapdog." His apparent misstep was purposeful, to remind me he also knew my real name, and exactly where I came from. "Have you come to buy? Or sell?"

I didn't give him the satisfaction of getting angry. The virgin auction was a part of my past, and the way I got to where I was now. I reminded myself it wasn't his fault I was that desperate. It was his parents who murdered mine and took everything they built. In retaliation, I had his parents killed. I understood his burning need for revenge, because I had lived it for so many years. Unfortunately for him, I had no intention of letting him be successful.

I laughed. "I could ask the same of you. If you're so hard up for a fuck, I'd be happy to let you have a free hour in the brothel." And if, or rather, when he raised a hand against my staff, I would have an excuse to cut his throat.

He chuckled, but his dark brown eyes narrowed. "Always such a charming host. That's why I had to accept your invitation to be here this evening. Who else in town holds a better party? Besides, it gives me a chance to decide what decor I'm going to replace when I own this place."

I would have retorted that him owning Crimson would be over my dead body, but that was the point. *Good luck with that, assprick.*

"Would you like a drink?" Jake asked him. "I hear the whiskey is especially fine. On the house, of course."

Alastair curled his lip at Jake. "You first, lapdog."

As wolves, none of us could eat or drink anything that was toxic to canines of any kind. That included alcohol and chocolate. At least we could drink coffee and tea, although in smaller doses than humans or other paranormals. It was a small price to pay for being a wolf.

Jake turned to me. "I'm starting to think he doesn't like me." Truthfully, Alastair had as much reason to like Jake as he had to like me. He was by my side every step of my way back from beaten down omega to alpha female and head of an organisation that dwarfed the scope of the Dagen pack and anything my parents did.

"Actually," Alastair said, "I pity you. You don't seem to have any more ambition than to be sidekick to this bitch."

It took every drop of willpower not to scratch his eyes out with my nails. He was trying to get to me. I couldn't let him. That was what he wanted. If I attacked him, he would have an excuse to shift and tear me apart. He was unlikely to be the only black wolf here tonight.

"Jake, I think we need to *vet* the guest list better for next year," I said coldly. The truth was, I made sure he was invited so I could keep an eye on him. Alastair Dagen was not the kind of man you turned your back on. Ever. If I could kill him without provoking the Onyx Ridge pack, I would do it and get it over with. Although, then the pack would just choose a replacement and I would have to start all over again with some other asshole. It would be easier to annihilate them, which I would do if I could. Some of the black wolves were actually useful, and paranormalkind in general didn't look too kindly on genocide. The fact the black wolves had tried so hard to annihilate the white twenty years ago wouldn't excuse me from doing the opposite now.

Even I had to follow some laws, though they chafed.

Alastair gave me a smug look, like he was certain I wouldn't be calling the shots this time next year.

In spite of myself, I got a shiver down my spine. I didn't know where or when, yet, but he would make a move against me. It was as inevitable as the sun rising tomorrow. His failure was just as inevitable.

"We should take our seats," Alastair said as though I was keeping him from his. "This should be interesting." He gave me a last look like he was peeling my dress off my body, then my skin under that. He turned and walked away leaving me feeling naked and dirty.

"I'm starting to think I should have taken you up on the challenge of wearing shorts and a T-shirt," I whispered to Jake.

"Don't let him get to you." He led me over to our chairs and we sat, one of his hands on one of mine. It was more than a possessive gesture. It was an offer of comfort in spite of me managing to hide how rattled I was from everyone but Jake.

"That's what he wants."

"He wants a lot more than that," I said softly. "He'd like nothing more than to see me on my knees."

"Want me to kill him for you?" One of Jake's eyebrows twitched, the only visible sign of his amusement. He was as good at containing his emotions as I was. Curious how he never attracted nicknames like Ice Bitch. What would they call him anyway? Ice Dog sounded like a rapper. He would probably enjoy that nickname. Maybe Ice Hole. No, he would like that too.

"I'd love that," I said. "I wish we could."

Just as I said that, the house lights went down, and the stage was illuminated. The men and women who attended the auction in the hope of buying a virgin to deflower fell quiet.

The auctioneer led out the line of eleven 'special guests,' as Jake called them. Eleven virgins who, for whatever reason, were so desperate for money, the only thing they had left to sell was themselves.

I vividly recalled stepping out on that stage nine years ago. I was barely eighteen, the minimum age allowed here. Other auctions allowed for younger virgins, but Crimson, or Black Gold as it was known back then, kept itself to a higher standard. When I bought the place, I kept that standard. I might be a killer, but I didn't sell children.

The stage then was older than the one in its place today, worn, shabby. The whole building was tired and falling into disarray. It was just another property belonging to the Onyx Ridge pack in general and the Dagen family in particular. One they paid little attention and even less money, to. It was me who saw the potential in this place.

The moment I stepped out onto the stage in just my underwear, I decided if I made enough money from selling myself, I would buy the place. Make it something special.

I recalled the feeling of fear and vulnerability. I saw it on the faces of the virgins on the stage now. They had no idea who would bid on them, who would win and what they would do with them afterwards. The money would change their lives, but would it be worth it?

"The nephew is the last one," Jake whispered, his mouth right next to my ear. "Guy with dark blond hair. Cooper Wheeler."

I hadn't really looked, but I looked now. Only through sheer strength of will did I keep my jaw from dropping.

You know when someone describes a guy as lickable? Well, I wanted to lick my way down this guy's entire fucking body. His abs must feel like solid rock. I didn't know which I wanted to touch him with more, my fingers or my tongue. Probably both.

Even with boxers on, his cock was obviously huge. He turned around slowly when the auctioneer told him to. Of course he had the most perfect, smackable ass I ever saw. His hair was tousled, like he'd just pulled off his shirt. A piercing in his left eyebrow caught the overhead lights for a moment.

My core throbbed. I was definitely going to need to change my panties.

And that was before he looked at me with his hazel eyes and smiled.

Holy.

Fucking.

Gods.

"You're staring," Jake said.

I blinked. "What? Oh." Alastair Dagen could have burnt the whole place down and I wouldn't have noticed. "That guy is Silas Wheeler's nephew?" He definitely didn't get his looks from his uncle.

I tried to remind the inner, panting orgasm-maker that was connected to my suddenly very hungry pussy, that Cooper was little more than a kid. Eight or nine years younger than me. The age gap was about the same as it was between Jake and I, but Cooper was probably innocent. And I certainly wasn't. He certainly fucking wouldn't be when I was done with him.

"Should I write a blank cheque right now?" Jake asked teasingly.

I realised I hadn't looked away from Cooper. Worse than that, I actually smiled back at him. Yeah, apparently the ice queen cracks for a pretty face and hot body.

"I mean, someone has to help him out of debt." Was I actually blushing? *Fucking hells*, I told myself. *Pull yourself together, woman.* I was unable to look at a trinket and walk away without buying it, and this guy was more than a trinket. He was a tasty-ass snack straight from the oven.

I swallowed hard.

I just wanted to help the kid. We *had* killed his uncle. And if Silas was in trouble with the Onyx Ridge pack, then this was the best way to get Cooper out of the hands of an asshole like Alistair Dagen.

At least, that's what I told myself.

"Your wish is my command," Jake said softly. "Any others up there you want?"

There were others up there? Oh yeah, ten of them. I forgot they existed for a few moments there. They all paled in comparison to Cooper.

"No, you?" I asked. Most of the virgins were girls. All of them were pretty, with perfect, lush bodies and soft curves. If Jake wanted to take one of them home, I would support that. I would hate her and want to scratch her eyes out, but I would do nothing to stop him. Just as he would support me if I desperately wanted to lick Cooper from head to foot.

Jake shook his head. "None of them look like my type. I prefer a woman with fire. Who doesn't mind burning the world down around her."

"That sounds dangerous," I said lightly.

"It is," he agreed. "I'm a masochist. But I also want you to be happy."

"I want that for you too," I said.

"I know you do." He squeezed my hand lightly. "I'm willing to wait until you realise we both want the same thing. In the meantime, let me buy you a present." When the time came to bid for Cooper's virginity, Jake raised his hand.

CHAPTER
FOUR

Cooper stared around my apartment with wide eyes. He was dressed now, in worn blue jeans and a black T-shirt that moulded to his body. Somehow he looked sexier than when he only wore boxers.

"This is where you live?" he asked. He looked like he didn't quite believe he was here.

I didn't quite believe it myself.

Jake questioned the wisdom of bringing Cooper up here in the first place, but he and I had some talking to do.

"Not exactly," I said. "I crash here sometimes. Jake too. There's a couple of spare bedrooms. It comes in useful." I sat down on the couch and crossed my legs, letting the split in my dress fall open to show most of my thigh.

"Right." Cooper gawked at the view outside the window for a while longer, then sat down on the couch near me. He glanced at my exposed leg and swallowed hard.

Jake flopped into a chair opposite us. His tie hung loose around his neck. The first few buttons on his shirt were undone, showing a glimpse of his chest. To anyone else, he might seem relaxed, unwound after a long night of schmoozing. I knew he would shift and rip Cooper's throat out in a heartbeat if he thought it was necessary. Hopefully it wouldn't come to that.

A jar of red cherries he'd snagged from the bar hung loosely from his fingers. Smartass.

"So—" Cooper said awkwardly.

"There's a few things you should know," I started. I nodded towards Jake. He was better at this shit than I was.

Before Jake could speak, Cooper said, "You killed my uncle."

Things went to a whole new level of awkward.

Jake cleared his throat and shrugged one shoulder. "Yep."

"Okay." Cooper nodded, his brow creased slightly. "If you hadn't, the Dagens would have. I told him he was gonna get in too much shit someday. He wouldn't listen. I even told him he should come to you for help."

He looked regretful. "They threatened him, I guess."

"That sounds like Dagen," I said. And me. Threats were a part of the job. "And now you have enough money to pay Dagen off. I don't expect anything in return."

No, that wasn't exactly true. I didn't expect him to fuck me just because we won the auction. When it came to sex, I was all about consent. I would call on him for a favour in return for us helping him out of the shit, but he didn't need to know that yet.

"I think I have a few hundred thousand left after I pay them off." Cooper smiled slowly. "Was that, like, some sort of record? What you paid, I mean."

Jake chuckled.

"It was high, but the record is higher," I said gently.

"Oh." Cooper's face fell. "What is the record?"

I took a few beats before I responded. "It's one point six million. Held by me."

Silence fell for a moment before Cooper broke it. "Oh," he said again. His eyebrows shot up. "You..."

"Sold my virginity for one point six million dollars, yes," I said. "One point two is a lot higher than most." I don't know who else was bidding, but I suspected they were bidding on behalf of Alistair Dagen. The moment anyone was aware of Jake's bidding, they would have wanted to push up the price, just to piss me off. Whatever, that amount of money was spare change.

"Okay," Cooper said. He looked from me to Jake and back again. "You two are... Together?"

I glanced at Jake as his expression tightened slightly. I would have missed it if I wasn't watching.

I looked back at Cooper. "No, not exactly," I said. "Just once, before we worked together." Before I drew that line.

Jake unscrewed the lid of the jar, pulled out a cherry and popped it in his mouth. "Best one point six million I ever spent."

That clearly took Cooper by surprise. "You bought... You paid... I..."

"It was a long time ago," I said quickly. I would never stop being grateful to Jake for making that winning bid. It was Alistair Dagen's father he bid against. If Dagen won, the night I lost my virginity would have been the last night I lived. I knew that with absolute certainty. What better way to finalise the conquest of the Ivory Claw Pack than the rape and murder of the daughter of the last Alphas on the tenth anniversary of their death? Even if I survived that night, they would have married me off to Alistair or someone equally horrible.

"Do you want to run your uncle's garage?" Jake asked bluntly. "Ivory owns it now, but maybe you could make some kind of arrangement."

Cooper shook his head. "Gods no. You're welcome to the place. I don't want any part of it. I would rather work for you."

Now I was the one taken by surprise. "For us? You know what we do, right?"

Cooper looked like he was ready to jump up and down in his

seat. "I know you don't take shit from anyone. I know no one dares to cross you. You're also smoking hot."

Jake tossed a cherry up in the air and caught it in his mouth. "Thank you." He chewed and wiggled his eyebrows.

Cooper grinned. "I mean, you are too, but I meant her." He nodded towards me.

"Of course you did," Jake said around his mouthful. "You're right, she is."

The smell of testosterone in the room was next level. It was sweeter than a drug.

"I would kill for you," Cooper told me softly.

His tone gave me a delicious chill down my spine. Call it an asset or a flaw, but us white wolves loved to kill. He was a white wolf too, I could smell it on him the moment I saw him. Nothing was more sensual. If I could bottle it and sell it like perfume, I'd be more ridiculously rich than I already was.

"I'm sure we can find an opening somewhere," I said. "I could always use more bodyguards when Jake goes all nursemaid on me."

Jake snorted. "I'll bet you can find an opening for him." He was teasing, but there was an edge of envy in his voice. He knew I wanted to fuck Cooper like an itch I needed to scratch. It was different from my feelings for Jake. More carnal.

Cooper actually blushed, bless him and his hot little fucking ass. He was too adorable for his own good. And probably mine.

"You really want to work with the people that killed your uncle?" I asked. "If it was me, I would want revenge."

Cooper shrugged. "Like I said, he had it coming. I... Kinda wish I'd been there to see it."

Fuck, there was a darkness in this guy. It turned me on so hard I wanted to come just listening to the sound of his voice.

"It was pretty awesome," Jake remarked."He ejaculated his blood all over Ivory."

"That was Jake's fault," I said immediately.

"Don't pretend like you hated it," Jake said. To Cooper he said, "If she wasn't a wolf, she would be a vampire. She has a thing for hot blood."

"I do not," I protested. "I just like how it feels and smells. And tastes. Besides, there's no such thing as vampires."

Jake gave Cooper a knowing nod.

Cooper grinned.

Boys.

It could be a good thing if they got along with each other. I had a feeling Cooper might make himself indispensable.

Jake stretched and put the empty jar down on the table. "I'm going to get some sleep. You kids have a good time."

I smiled and nodded. "Good night."

He gave Cooper a warning look which clearly said, 'If you fuck with her, you'll fuck with me,' then disappeared into the spare room he preferred.

I found myself gazing into Cooper's pretty, hazel eyes. "You have enough money now to make a good start in life. A legal one. Isn't that why you took part in the auction?"

"I wanted the money to pay off my uncle's debts and to put myself through university." Cooper glanced in the direction Jake went. He suddenly looked nervous, but excited at the same time.

Yeah, so was I.

"Oh? What are you studying?" I managed to keep my voice even.

"Visual arts," Jake called out from the spare room. Obviously he wanted to let Cooper know he was still listening, and that he'd been thoroughly vetted by us. Jake would have done an extensive background check before he even mentioned the auction to me.

"You're an artist?" I asked. "Jake has a PhD in eavesdropping."

"Just call me Doctor Claw," Jake said.

Cooper and I both laughed.

"I like to paint and draw," Cooper said. "Traditionally and digitally. I wanted to get into graphic design."

"Past tense?" I asked. "You don't anymore?"

Cooper took a full minute to respond. "I think there's a bigger world out there. More to life than staring at a screen or canvas. I can still do all that as a hobby."

I nodded slowly, then rose and moved to look out the window. "This life is not an easy choice to make. It's not an easy one to live. It looks like fun in the movies and on TV, but the reality is a lot more... Sometimes boring. Sometimes bloody. Do you really want to spend the rest of your life looking over your shoulder? Because you will. You won't even notice you're doing it. You'll find yourself lying to everyone you ever knew. Before you know it, the only friends you have are people you work with. They are the only ones who know what we do. They're the only ones who don't care."

Cooper stepped up behind me and put his hands lightly on my shoulders. "You make that sound more and more appealing."

His touch made it harder to think.

"I know I paid for your virginity, but I don't expect you to give it to me," I said, my voice huskier than I intended. "I don't want anything you're not prepared to give willingly."

"I want to give it to you," he said softly. He leaned in and kissed the side of my neck.

Just that light touch made my knees turn to jelly. I tilted my head to the side to give him better access.

He must have taken that as encouragement, because he kissed his way from my neck, down the top of my shoulders. He peeled one side of my dress off my shoulder, then the other. It slid down my body and pooled on the floor at my feet.

I stepped out of it, and turned to face him, wearing only white, lace panties.

He gulped. "Holy shit. You're gorgeous."

I slid my hands up the front of his shirt. I was right about his abs being as hard as a rock. I ran my fingertips up every defined muscle, pushing his shirt up as I went. When it reached the top of his chest, I pulled it out far enough to push it over his head and onto the floor.

"You're the gorgeous one." I leaned forward to run the tip of my tongue over his taut chest. "How are you possibly a virgin?" Honestly, I didn't give a shit if it was false advertising. He was just so incredibly fuckable.

"I was saving myself for you," he said smoothly.

I snorted. "Word of advice. Don't try to bullshit a bullshitter." The flattery was nice, but there must be a real reason.

"I was busy studying and working out," he admitted. "And most of the girls I know were... I don't know. Girls. I was always more into *women*."

"That's better," I said approvingly. "Never lie to me and I will never lie to you. We save that for people who try to fuck with us."

"Us." He grinned. "I like the sound of that. Does that mean I'm in?"

"Oh, you're in." I put my hands around his neck and pulled his face down to kiss him.

His hands went to my breasts. Lightly at first. Then with more confidence. He rubbed his wide palms against my nipples. "I never imagined anyone could feel so good."

Fireworks went off the moment our lips met. Flashes, wheels, cascades, the works.

Okay, maybe the cascade was in my panties.

"I want you," I said between kisses.

"I want you too," he replied.

I broke off the kiss, took his hand and led him towards my bedroom. I glanced at the door to the spare room. It was ajar. No doubt Jake was listening, still on duty against the chance Cooper might attack me. The security outside the door would be listening for the same thing.

I wasn't oblivious to the possibility, but I intended to enjoy the rest of the night. I could take care of myself anyway. Someone in my position would be stupid not to learn how, in person form as well as wolf.

I pushed Cooper down on my bed on his back and straddled his thighs. I undid the button on his jeans and slid the zipper down slowly. He lifted his hips and let me slide down jeans and boxers until his erection was free.

Just as I guessed during the auction, his cock was big. Enough for a good handful. Or mouthful.

I shimmied down until my shoulder was on his thigh, then lightly ran the tip of my tongue from his balls to the bead of precum on the end of his dick.

He moaned and his hips twitched. "Wow. That feels so..."

I smiled. "It's just the beginning." I licked him thoroughly, all the way around his length like Jake had with my vibrator. Cooper was quivering, and his cock rock hard by the time I took him into my mouth. At first, my lips barely touched him. I teased him with my tongue for a few moments before I began to suck.

"Holy fuck," he breathed. "I'm not gonna last long if you keep doing that."

I lifted my mouth off him to say, "Then don't. We have all night." A guy like him might be addictive. I lowered my mouth and went back to sucking while I slid my fingers up his legs and started to trace circles around his balls.

He groaned and started to pant through his nose. His hips moved, thrusting his cock harder and faster into my mouth.

"Ivory..." Whatever he was trying to say was cut off by him coming. He let off a half grunt, half shout and thrust furiously, before he stilled and ground up into me. "Gods, gods, holy fuck."

The only thing better than blood was the feel, smell and taste of hot cum. When it flooded into my mouth, I drank it like it was nectar, sucking until I got the last drop. Only when he sagged did I finally let him go.

"Wow. I thought I knew the meaning of mind blowing." He stared at me with wide eyes full of admiration and awe.

I smiled and crept up his body, stopping every few moments to lick here, run my fingers there. "You ain't seen nothing yet."

"I have a feeling you're right." His cock was already starting to twitch back to life.

I straddled his thighs again and thoroughly indulged my need to lick his abs and chest. "You realise you're absolutely, insanely gorgeous, right?" I said between licks. "I think you belong with us, because being this hot is probably illegal anyway."

He chuckled. "I was going to say the same thing to you." Without warning, he rolled us over so he lay on top of me. "My turn."

He gave the same careful attention I had given him to my breasts. In spite of me trying to put them in his path every couple of minutes, he left my nipples until last. When his tongue finally grazed across my aroused-as-fuck peaks, I let out a half moan, half pant.

"You taste delicious." He clamped his lips around my nipple and started to suck.

I had absolutely no words by now. All I could do was push my chest forward, pressing my breasts into his face.

His hands slipped out between my legs.

Eagerly, I opened them for him. I grabbed his fingers and guided them to my clit. I heard him swallow, then he tentatively ran his fingers over and around my nub and folds.

I let out a little whimper.

He froze. "I'm sorry did I..."

"Oh, gods, Cooper," I breathlessly. "Don't stop. That's perfect. You're perfect."

He sighed with relief and went back to doing what he was

doing so well. He rubbed my clit and slipped a finger inside me. "Wow. You're so wet. That is so fucking hot." He sounded like he just discovered potatoes were edible if you cook them. I mean, that was one hell of a discovery. So, apparently, was this.

"That's because I want you so fucking bad," I said. I was on the edge of coming. How I held out this long, I don't know. I slid my hand down and ran it over his cock. He was already half hard again before I touched him, but he was fully erect a moment or two later.

"Can I—" He traced a finger around the entrance to my pussy.

"I'm going to scream if you don't," I said. I wanted all of him inside me and I wanted it now.

He pulled his hand away and knelt between my legs.

I put my hand between us and guided his cock to my pussy.

When I took my hand away, he locked his eyes on mine and pressed the tip of his cock into me. His eyes widened.

I pressed my hands onto his tight little ass, lightly dug in my fingernails and pushed him down encouragingly.

Slowly, as though he wanted to record every moment of this in his memory, he slid down slowly, deeper and deeper until he was finally all the way inside me.

"Holy fucking hells," he said softly. "I thought your mouth was amazing. But this..."

I guessed he liked my pussy.

Taking his time, he started to slide in and out of me, making every moment last.

"You feel so good," I said. Whoever said size doesn't matter didn't have a cock like Cooper's deep inside them. The more he thrust, the closer I got to my own orgasm.

Supporting most of his weight on his hands and arms, he thrust harder, a little faster each time.

I moaned. "I'm going to come."

"I want to hear you," he said. "I want to hear you come."

I had briefly forgotten this was his first time. That he had probably never made a woman come before. I couldn't have stopped the cry that slipped out between my lips if I'd wanted to. But I didn't. I wanted to scream for him, to make this memorable.

"Coop." The shortened version of his name was all I could get out before I came, moaning and bucking so his cock rubbed my G spot and my clit, alternating as he thrust. My back arched and I all but screamed as I came, the orgasm slamming into me like a thunderous wall of pleasure.

"Ivory." He thrust hard, deep, frantic. His cry when he came again was no less intense than mine. His breath came in ragged gasps. "Fuck... Yeah... Fuck."

Finally, he sagged and rolled so he lay beside me while we both caught our breath.

"That was," pant, "absolutely," pant, "incredible."

I smiled over at him. "You are everything I hoped you would be. And more. Are you sure that was your first time?"

He grinned. "It was. But not the last." He leaned forward to claim my mouth with his.

CHAPTER
FIVE

I had to give it to the guy, he was a quick learner. And energetic. Before the fourth, or was it fifth, round, I almost begged him to stop so I could sleep. Somehow, he got me going again anyway. I finally fell asleep a couple of hours before dawn.

I woke to the late summer Sydney sun pouring through the window. I was tired and my body ached gloriously. Cooper was still asleep, his mouth open slightly.

"Morning." Jake stuck his head through the door. He looked rested. He must have slept with earplugs in and his smart watch on vibrate in case he was needed. "I've ordered breakfast from Scarlett's. It should be here soon."

I stretched, too sleepy to do more than mentally acknowledge that the covers were down to my stomach. It was nothing Jake hadn't seen before. "You're the best."

Money could buy a lot of things, but it couldn't buy the ability to cook. Neither of us had bothered to learn beyond making coffee and toast. When you own several restaurants, and have a private chef on call, it's a skill you don't need.

"Yeah, I know," he said distractedly. His eyes were on my breasts. And on the guy sleeping beside me. "Did you have a good night?"

I couldn't contain a smile. "I've had worse."

Cooper stirred. He opened his eyes and seemed confused for a moment, until he remembered where he was. "Hey." He sat up and ran a hand over his head. "Last night was amazing." He looked like he couldn't quite believe it happened.

"It sounded like it." Jake pushed the door open and stepped inside. So much for wearing earplugs.

He held a handful of papers and a pen toward Cooper. "I have a bunch of shit for you to fill out. Bank details, assuming you want to be paid. Tax details. And our offer for your uncle's garage. You just need to sign that and I'll lodge it with the relevant authorities."

Jake handed that to Cooper first.

Cooper signed it without even glancing at it, then handed it back to Jake.

"Huh." Jake folded the paper in two. "We should have offered less."

Cooper sat back against the pillows. "I told you, I don't care about the place."

"You should," I told him. "The property is worth over a million dollars." It must be later than I thought, if Jake already had someone assess the value of the garage.

Cooper looked surprised but unfazed. "I'm just happy to get something for it."

He really should be more careful, but I understood. Sometimes you just needed to move on with your life.

Says the woman who bought, and lives in, the home where her parents were murdered. In spite of the memory of coming home from school as an eight-year-old to find their blood splattered all over the walls, I had a connection to the place. That and I had to keep it out of the hands of the Onyx Ridge pack. It was the principle of the thing. Of course, I had the whole place gutted and completely remodelled before I moved in. Clinging to memories is one thing. Living inside my own personal PTSD is another.

"You can fill out the rest of the forms later," I said. "I'm going to have a shower, then we can work out what your role in the organisation will be."

Okay, I admit it, I pushed the covers off myself and walked naked to the bathroom in part to punish Jake for being all business this early in the morning. Especially after the night I had. I knew he did it to remind me not to get caught up in Cooper's pretty face and smoking hot body. I didn't need the reminder. Hadn't I proven to him yet that I knew how to put business before pleasure? If I didn't, I would have fucked his face a thousand times and not regretted any of them.

Both sets of eyes followed me until I closed the door. I listened for a moment, but it didn't sound like they were going to kill each other, so I stepped into the shower and washed myself of dried sweat and cum.

By the time I was clean and dry, my hair back in a ponytail, light make-up on my face and dressed in a knee length pencil skirt and a white silk blouse, breakfast had just arrived.

The guys sat at the table near the kitchen, in front of the wide window. Judging by his damp hair, Cooper had a shower in one of the other bathrooms.

"Jake said you wouldn't mind if I had a scrub," Cooper said.

I slipped into a chair. "Did he offer to wash your back?" I snagged one of the cups of coffee and peeled back the lid. It smelled divine.

"Of course I did," Jake said. "What sort of host would I be if I didn't?" He grinned and pushed a bowl of fruit salad, oats and yoghurt towards me.

I made a face. "I was hoping for pancakes."

"I know you were," Jake said. "I'm here to make sure you don't put that shit in your body, like you asked me to."

"This from the guy who had a whole jar of sugary cherries last night." I rolled my eyes at him.

"At least they're fruit," he pointed out.

"Just barely." I sipped my coffee. At least he didn't complain about me drinking that.

Cooper looked from one of us to the other. "Are you two always like this?"

"Smoking hot and as funny as fuck?" Jake asked. "Yes. Yes we are."

I snorted. "Jake likes to think he is my father."

"No," Jake corrected. "I like to think I'm your daddy. There's a significant difference." He wiggled his brows at me.

Cooper grinned. "You guys are awesome. I thought you might be all scary and shit, and you are," he added quickly, "but you're also really cool."

"Yeah. I am pretty cool for an old dude," Jake agreed.

"You're not that old," I told him. I tried not to think about the age difference between Cooper and Jake. There I was, just about bang in the middle. Okay, now I was thinking about being in the middle of them, the meat in a hot-guy sandwich. Sometimes it was hard to remember why I didn't sleep with Jake.

"No, I just feel like it sometimes." Jake looked towards Cooper. "Be careful. Hanging around with Ivory might cause you to age before your time. Before you know it, your teenage years will be over." He snapped his fingers.

"I turn twenty soon," Cooper said.

"It's started already." Jake grinned.

I picked up a slice of banana and threw it at him. It hit him in the side of his head, then fell into his lap.

He looked down at it. "I should insist you come over here and eat that."

Did he have any idea how much I wished I could?

He picked up the slice, threw it up in the air and caught it in his mouth. He grinned at his own prowess.

Cooper clapped.

"Don't encourage him," I said. "Sometimes I think he should have joined the circus."

"Sometimes I'm pretty sure I *did* join the circus," Jake said.

I stuck my middle finger up at him.

He grinned, but he looked like he would happily take my finger and suck on it for a while.

"So... Can I ask what the story is between the Onyx Ridge pack and Ivory Claw?" Cooper asked tentatively.

That brought down the atmosphere.

I sighed. "Many, many years of bad blood. My parents ran the dominant pack in the city. And my father's parents before them. The Dagens gathered enough power to move against them. They slaughtered my parents and a lot of other white wolves. They took over the territory. They ran it until about seven years ago, when I took it back."

"You were young when that happened?" Cooper asked softly.

"I was eight." I looked down at the table. "They liked to think they had morals, or some shit like that, so they didn't kill the children. They just sent us off to live with various associates of the Dagen family. I was raised here in Sydney by Helen Dagen, Alastair's aunt. It was her job to brainwash me into thinking my role in life was as the omega of their pack."

I looked back up and smiled savagely. "She was one of the first people I had killed."

"Taking out that hag was a pleasure." Jake had a self-satisfied smirk on his face.

"What about you?" Cooper asked him. "What were you doing? You wouldn't have been a kid, I'm guessing."

"I was doing what any smart wolf would do," Jake replied.

"What most of us were doing. Biding our time and waiting for the right chance, and the right person to fight back against Dagen. The moment I saw Ivory, I knew she was the person we were waiting for. She was so full of anger and hate. The stupidest thing Barnaby Dagen did was not kill her. He didn't see the rage inside her. He was so sure he won, he didn't even think to look."

"He was so sure we were all broken," I said. "If he won me at that auction, he might have been right. Everyone was happy to join me when I started to move against Dagen, but no one dared to start it before me."

"No one else had the guts," Jake said. "That includes me. If Dagen knew you would grow up to be a banana throwing pancake lover, he would have been shaking in his shoes."

I laughed. "That does sound terrifying, doesn't it?"

Cooper was staring at me with open admiration. "For a long time, I've heard about you and how badass you are, but you're next level. I can't believe I got to fuck you. Anytime you want to do it again, I'm here for it."

I believed him. The truth was, he was as easy to like as he was hot. If I was honest with myself, I would admit I could fall head over heels for a guy like him. The gods knew that would complicate my life even further. Not to mention my relationship with Jake.

In spite of not wanting to cross the line, I did love him. I loved him from the moment he won my auction, when he looked at Dagen with a smug expression on his handsome face. Dagen was a vengeful bastard, but even then the financial cracks were starting to show. Given time, his empire would have probably imploded without me lifting a finger. I just helped it along a bit.

Jake bidding against Dagen in the first place showed the world he had balls after all. That the Ivory Claw pack was not as beaten down as people thought. Stepping up could have gotten him killed. Instead, he helped me to get a whole lot of other people killed.

Jake sighed. "Welcome to my world, kid. You work for her now. The only time your cock will get near her, will be in your dreams."

"Is that what happened to you two?" Cooper asked. "Because you obviously have the hots for each other. I can smell it on both of you. Hells, it would be obvious to a human."

One of Jake's eyebrows twitched. "Do you always say the first thing that comes out of your mouth?"

"Yeah," Cooper admitted. "It gets me into trouble occasionally. But I'm not wrong."

"Sometimes it's not as simple as wanting to do something," I said softly. "You have to think about the consequences of doing it." The bad as well as the good.

"But you admit you want to fuck me?" Jake cocked his head and looked smug.

So. Fucking. Much.

I cocked my head at him. "Did I ever say I didn't?"

"Hell yeah." Jake grinned. He and Cooper shared a high-five.

Men.

I rolled my eyes at them. "Has it ever occurred to you that this, right here, is why I won't sleep with you? Because you need to grow the fuck up?"

They exchanged amused looks.

Jake shook his head. "Naw. You like my boyish enthusiasm."

He wasn't wrong. But that didn't make any of this simpler or easier.

"Sex complicates things," I said.

"I dunno, it seemed pretty simple to me," Cooper said. "I wanted you. You wanted me."

"If the next words out of your mouth are, 'wham bam, thank you ma'am,' you're fired," I said dryly.

Cooper grinned. "I don't know what that means, but I am grateful for last night. And I promise I can do whatever work you give me to do and focus on that, whether we're sleeping together or not."

"Maybe I'm the one who can't focus," I suggested.

"Ohhh, now I get it." Jake slapped a hand to his forehead. "All this time I thought you were worried I couldn't do my job. But it's you who are distracted by my devastating good looks."

I drummed my fingernails on the table. "Exactly. If you had a head like a potato, there would be no problem." I held back a laugh.

"So you would rather fuck someone that looks like a potato than fuck me?" Jake pouted.

I pretended to think about that for a moment. "They would have to have some a-peeling characteristics, but maybe."

Both guys laughed.

It felt good to sit around the table and chat like... Like friends. For a while at least, I could forget about the world, the Dagens and all that shit. We could almost be normal people. Almost.

"For the record," I said slowly, "I want to fuck both of you. I just don't want any of us to end up dead because of it. Is that so terrible?" It made sense to me.

"Sometimes life is too short to be sensible." Cooper sounded like an old man.

"That's fucking deep, kid," Jake said. He jerked his head side-ways, towards Cooper. "He's right though. You spent ten years of your life living with a Dagen. You could have married one and had mutant puppies. Instead, you offered yourself up for auction and took back what was ours. You spent nearly a decade taking chances with almost everything. Everything but your heart."

"That's fucking deep, old man." Cooper smiled.

"Isn't it though?" Jake said. To me he said, "I get it. We walked through the fire together. You think if we had a relationship outside friendship and work, and it ended, we would end."

"Wouldn't it?" I asked. "Just think, you could go on social media and complain about your psychotic ex. Isn't that what people do?"

"Have you ever seen me on social media?" Jake asked. Then softly he added, "You and I wouldn't end."

"You don't know that," I said. I noticed he didn't deny I was psychotic.

"Yes I do," he said firmly. "We are a team. Now and forever. Even if you wanted to get rid of me, you couldn't."

"I could have you killed," I pointed out. They wouldn't like it, but my men would do it if I asked them to.

"But you wouldn't," he said with certainty. "We've been through too much together to end that way." He gave me a long, intense stare.

"See?" Cooper said. "The sexual tension in here is through the roof. You two should just fuck and get it over with. But also me too. I don't mind sharing."

"The kid is wise," Jake said. "That sounds like a plan to me."

"I'm glad you two have it all worked out." I gave them both a dark look. "Maybe I should step outside and leave you both to it." Yeah okay, when I thought about that for a second, it was hot as fuck.

"Not without you," Cooper said. "But I wouldn't say no to a threesome."

Before I could respond to that, we were interrupted by a knock on the door.

"Saved by the bell," I said under my breath. I nodded for Jake to open the door.

"Morning boss, sorry to interrupt," Kyle said. He looked anxious.

"Actually, your timing is perfect," I said. "Is there a problem?"

"I'm not sure," he admitted. "I took those artefacts to Rachel, like you asked. She just got back to me about them. Something is really screwy."

CHAPTER
SIX

"Screwy in what way?" I looked down at the box that sat open on Rachel's desk. Jake stood beside me. Cooper gawked at the magic shop. Most of it was fake magic, designed to amuse humans. She kept the real stuff behind a magic wall. It all made me want to twitch. At the best of times, magic gave me the creeps. Screwy magic most of all.

Rachel brushed a strand of dark hair back over her ear. "Screwy in that most of them don't have any in them." She picked up a bright white stone that was shaped like a donut, and held it in the palm of her hand.

"This is just a rock. I sell the same kind of thing here. A witch can put a protection spell in it, or whatever." She shrugged. "Nothing very powerful."

I knew that, because I wouldn't let her sell them otherwise. Protection spells were harmless unless they protected someone I was trying to dispense with. Since they only protected against magic, they weren't much use against big teeth anyway.

"Is there any chance it had magic in it but it was used up?" Jake said.

"Almost certainly," she agreed. "There's a residue of magic in it. I can't tell what kind. The point is, like this, it's worthless. Not something the black market would bother with." She put the stone back and picked up another. "Same with this one. Except this one," she held up between her thumb and forefinger. "This is a bonding stone. Or it would be if it wasn't empty."

"Bonding stone." Jake took the stone from her hand and bounced it up and down on his palm a couple of times. "Two people touch it, and when their cum is combined, they form an... Empathic connection?" He gave me a speculative glance.

"That's what it's for," Rachel said. "Empty, it's just a rock."

"Could you fill it?" Jake asked.

"No," I said firmly. Even if I wanted to form a psychic bond with him, I would never fuck with magic like that. There was no telling what it might do to us in the long run. It might drive us insane, or turn us into assholes.

"I can't anyway," Rachel said. "I don't have that kind of magic. Very few witches do." She took back the stone and replaced it in the box.

She picked up a pair of silver tweezers and pulled out another. "This one does have magic in it. Specifically, it's a magic dampening stone. The kind used to stop witches from doing magic. That's why I won't touch it with my bare hands. The weird thing is, they're usually put into bracelets. Just by itself, a witch could just drop it if they wanted to, and the effect would be gone."

"I'm sensing a pattern here," Jake said. "Silas Wheeler might have just been selling these to a witch to be filled, or have a bracelet made."

"Or Dagen is trying to send us a message," I said. "The white stone can't be a coincidence. The rest of it..." I shook my head. "Couldn't he just send a letter, or a text, like a normal person?"

Cooper must have heard his uncle's name mentioned, because

he appeared at my shoulder. "Did you send his father any cryptic messages before you went after the Onyx Ridge Pack?"

"Not unless you call dead bodies cryptic," I said. There was nothing subtle about the slaughter we inflicted on the black wolves. We splattered their blood the way they splattered ours.

"White stone, bond, dampening," Jake mused. "What about the other three?"

"The black one shaped like a doughnut has some residual power in it," Rachel said. "It feels similar to the white one, but I still can't tell what it is. And that," she pointed, "is a siphon stone. Also empty." She shuddered.

"Used to suck out a witch's magic," Cooper said, his eyes wide.

"Even empty, that's worth more than the rest of them put together," Jake said.

"And the last two aren't magical at all," I said softly. "That's a bloodstone. And that's a black diamond." I knew my precious gems. "Black diamonds represent death. He is trying to tell us he is more powerful than we are. That he will siphon off all our work into his bank accounts and that the Onyx Ridge pack will bring about our death with lots of blood."

"What about the other two?" Cooper asked. "Bonding and dampening?"

"Nothing good," Jake said. "He knew we were going to put Silas down. He made sure this was waiting for us. How did he know?" He looked accusingly at Cooper.

Cooper raised his hands to either side and stepped back. "I've no idea. It was nothing to do with me, I swear. Silas probably didn't know either. He was just a go-between."

"Between Dagen and who?" Jake asked. "If we hadn't grabbed these, who would have?"

"It was always going to be us," I said softly. "Either he told Silas to leave them on his desk until we turned up, or one of our people is working for Dagen."

"It's not me," Cooper said. "I never even saw the box until today."

"For the record, it's not me," Rachel said. "Break-ins in the area have been way down since you guys took over. It's saved me thousands in replacement costs and repairs. I am a big fan." She smiled at me but it held a tinge of anxiety. Like she wasn't sure if I believed her or not.

I nodded. I had no reason to think the witch was in cahoots with Dagen. Our dealings had always been beneficial to both of us, and she was paid well each time.

"We know it isn't Ivory or me," Jake said. "That only leaves a couple thousand other people as possibilities." His tone was light but his face was worried. If Dagen was behind this, it might be the start of something bigger. And probably annoying.

I rubbed my forehead with my fingertips. I didn't need him doing shit.

"They might only be stones," Cooper said. "Just because it seems like they meant something doesn't mean they do. Black diamonds are worth a lot. The rest have some use."

"Except the bloodstone," I pointed out. "That's probably worth about three dollars. Why put that in there unless it has some meaning?" I looked around, but none of them had any more answers than I did.

"I could shove it down his throat for you," Jake offered.

"Fuck," Cooper said. "I was going to say the same thing."

Jake grinned. "Rock, paper, scissors for the privilege?"

I rolled my eyes at them both. "No one is going to shove it down his throat. You wouldn't get close enough anyway. If we could, I would happily do it myself."

Both guys looked disappointed.

I glanced at Rachel and shrugged. Men, what could you do?

She grinned in response.

I tapped my fingers on my thigh. "Alistair Dagen wouldn't

have handled these himself. He would have had someone do it for him. Coop, any idea who might have done that?"

He thought for a moment. "People came and went all the time. I didn't pay much attention to them when I was there. Which wasn't often."

"But you knew he was dealing with Dagen," Jake pointed out.

"Only because he told me. We argued about it." Cooper scratched his cheek. "I'm not sure if he dealt directly with them. There might have been a go-between."

"If Dagen knew we were working through Silas' garage, then he would want to keep his hands clean," I said. "He wants us to know he is involved, but doesn't want us to be able to prove it. If we make any kind of move against him, he could claim it was unprovoked."

"I'd like to know how many fucking pies he also has his fingers in," Jake said. He looked furious, like if we missed anything, he would blame himself.

"Let's find that out," I said. "Do a full check on any of the small side businesses. These are the pies he'll stick his fingers in first." After a moment I added, "And Crimson. He was there last night. The gods only knew what he might have gotten up to. Or tried to."

Jake nodded. "I'll get on it. But subtly. If he knows we're looking, he might act sooner."

"I have no doubt he will know," I said. "He sent us a warning. He wants us on edge." He certainly got that.

"Can we send him a warning back?" Cooper asked.

"We could send him your uncle's head?" Jake said lightly. "That's always a fun gift."

"Nothing says subtle like a decapitated head in a box," I said sarcastically.

"Why does it have to be subtle?" Cooper asked. "I've only seen this guy from a distance and I want to punch him in the face."

"He does have that effect on people," I agreed. "But it would have to be subtle because we can't be seen to provoke them. If Dagen wants a war, then that's what he'll get, but we won't be the ones to start it. Not officially." Unofficially, all bets were already fucking off, as far as I was concerned.

I picked up the black diamond, half expecting it to explode in my face or some shit like that. Instead, it just sparkled, reflecting the light. It wasn't worth much more than a few thousand dollars, but it certainly was pretty. "Maybe I should get this made into a ring. Or a necklace." I could wear it in front of Dagen and piss him off. That would be fun.

"I know a guy," Cooper said. "Will you let me have him make it into something for you?"

"Don't have it made into a motherfucking engagement ring," Jake growled.

Cooper looked surprised. "I wasn't even thinking that." His mouth curled up in a sly smile. "Until now."

I snorted. "We met yesterday."

"When you know, you know." Cooper grinned but I suspected it was mostly for Jake's benefit. "Fine, no engagement ring. But I have something in mind." He slipped the diamond into his pocket.

"What do we do with the rest of the stones?" Jake asked.

I looked towards Rachel. "Can you sell them for us?"

"Probably," she agreed. "I also know a guy. But—even the siphon stone?"

"Only a witch can use it on another witch, can't they?" I asked. "If it's no threat to any wolves, then I don't care."

If witches wanted to fuck with each other, that was their business, as long as they stayed out of my way.

"Okay." If that bothered Rachel, she didn't show it. She would get a nice cut of the proceeds anyway.

"Ivory, you should put the bloodstone in your house," Jake said.

When I looked at him questioningly, he said, "Humans think they have the ability to cleanse toxins out of your body."

I gave him a flat stare. "The more you say things like that, the more I want a really big slice of cake."

Cooper chuckled.

"I'm just looking out for you," Jake said sulkily.

"I appreciate that," I assured him. "Why don't you take it, you eat more crap than I'm allowed to."

He shrugged, but slipped the stone into his pocket. It would probably turn up somewhere at my place or at Crimson sooner or later.

Rachel closed the box and took it over to a safe in the corner.

"We are all going to have to watch ourselves," I said quietly. "Watch our backs. It might start with something small like this, but at some point he's going to come after us. It could get ugly." I should probably keep Cooper away from me until all of this blew over. It *would* blow over, I was certain of that. There was no way I was going to let Dagen win. By the time this was done, he'd wish he hadn't even looked my way. He should have dug himself a hole and crawled inside. The way they tried to make me do.

"I just remembered something," Cooper said.

His tone immediately had my attention, and my concern.

"What is it?" I asked. And why did I suddenly have a sense of dread in the pit of my stomach?

"Remember when I said I told my uncle to ask you for help?" When I waved at him to continue, Cooper said, "According to him, he had it under control."

"He was lying," Jake said simply.

Cooper shook his head. "You knew him. He was a terrible liar. He couldn't lie his way out of Swiss cheese."

"He's right," I said. "That was why we were working with him to start with. He was an unscrupulous little worm, but we always knew when he was full of shit."

"That was most of the time," Jake said.

"Exactly." I nodded. "He was never able to hide anything from us. Not for long anyway. So when he said he thought he was in control, he must have meant it. Or thought he did."

"How the fuck though?" Jake asked. "Was he high at the time or—"

"I don't think so," Cooper said, his brow furrowed in thought. "Not that time anyway. He just seemed really sure he was all over it."

"He must've had help from someone." I tapped my fingers on my thigh.

"Dagen?" Jake asked.

"No," Cooper said after a moment. "He was more scared of... I mean just as scared of him as he was of you."

I raised my eyebrows at the suggestion that Dagen could be scarier than me. Rude.

"Someone else then," Jake said. "Who? Did he mention someone?"

Cooper scrunched up his face in the most adorable way, obviously thinking furiously. "I feel like he mentioned someone, but the name won't come to mind."

"Was he trying to sell the garage?" Jake asked. "That would have solved all his problems. Well, all his financial problems. It wouldn't change the fact he fucked up so badly with us."

Cooper shook his head. "I don't think so. My uncle wasn't the smartest wrench in the toolbox, but he was proud. I think he was hoping if he kept paddling, the tide would turn his way at some point. There was never a chance of that though, was there? Not while Dagen was trying to use him to get to you. I mean, us."

"Not unless there was a mystery person helping him," I said. "Can you find out who it is? Your uncle might've kept something at his house. A phone number, anything?"

"I can try," Cooper agreed. He wandered off to play around with Rachel's plastic wands.

"What are you thinking?" Jake asked.

"I'm wondering if there is someone else out there," I said slowly. "Someone who is working with or against Dagen. With or against us. The last thing we need is a war on two fronts."

He searched my face carefully. "You're thinking Silas was working with Zeta, or the Witch's Council, or someone like that?"

The Witch's Council was barely a blip on my radar, but Zeta was a huge, powerful organisation with connections to several major world governments. They mostly stayed out of my way because I paid the right people, but if they wanted to cause trouble for me, they certainly had the resources to cause a lot of it.

"I hope not," I said. "I have no doubt I can take down Zeta if I have to, but it would be a lot of work and headache."

Jake raised his eyebrows at me.

Yeah, okay, it was a hells of a claim to make, and frankly one I hoped I never had to back up. It would probably cost me more than I wanted to pay to do it. Especially in stress.

"There is another possibility," I said, partly to change the subject. "The grey wolves have been neutral for a long time. If anyone was going to help Silas from getting stuck between us and the Dagens, it would be them."

"They usually stay out of shit like that," Jake pointed out. "Unless they've decided to take sides."

"I'm fine with that, as long as they take ours." I watched fondly as Cooper swished a plastic wand around in the air like he was in a movie.

"And if they don't?" Jake asked.

I sighed. "Then we're going to have to have a long conversation with their Alphas. They'll think twice about fucking with us." As long as it was only speculation, and not the start of a whole another shit fight. I didn't want to take on the black wolves while the grey wolves were nipping at my tail.

"You want me to talk to them?" Jake asked.

I tapped my hand on my thigh. "That might be a good idea, yes. Let's nip that in the bud before it bears fruit. You have a blank cheque to deal with whatever comes up." That didn't always mean money. It meant I trusted him to do whatever he had to do, offer whatever he had to offer, threaten whatever he had to threaten, to get the grey wolves to stay out of our way.

"Blank cheques are my favourite," he said. "Don't worry, by the time I'm done, they'll slink back into the shadows."

"I hope so," I said. "I need to get back to Crimson. I have a meeting with someone."

Jake frowned. "Anything I need to worry about?"

"I'm not sure," I admitted. "I'll fill you in afterward."

He hated it when I wasn't forthcoming with information, but he knew better than to ask. He would know when I was ready to tell him.

"All right, boss, I look forward to it. Come on kid, time to go. Stop playing with your wand." Jake grinned.

Cooper laughed, put down the wand and trotted back over to us like a puppy. "You're just jealous because my wand is bigger than yours."

I shook my head and followed them out while they bantered about cock size.

Men.

At least they sounded relaxed. Me, I was on edge.

CHAPTER
SEVEN

The man who sat across from me was attractive in a rugged sort of way. His brown hair was cut close to his scalp. The hair on his square chin was longer, but neatly trimmed. Brown eyes, almost the same colour as mine, watched me with cautious interest. He rubbed a scar which spanned the bridge of his nose, between his thumb and forefinger.

"This is an interesting place to meet." His voice was deep, almost raspy.

I sat back and toyed with the glass of apple juice in my hand. "Most people seem to like it." He requested the meeting. I chose the third floor of Crimson, because people were either uncomfortable or distracted here.

I sipped my juice and looked away from a nearby couch, where one man was trying to inhale the cock of another. Both seemed to be thoroughly enjoying themselves. Good, that was what the place was for.

He shrugged. "I'm more a doer than a watcher. I mean, if you're interested, I'm all for it." His voice was deep, husky.

I ignored his suggestion and the way my pulse raced a little faster. "You wanted to meet me. What do you want?"

"You know who I am?" he asked. He leaned forward to pour himself a glass of juice from the jug on the table.

"I know *what* you are," I replied. That should have been enough for me to say no to him stepping foot in Crimson. My curiosity got the better of me.

"And yet, you still agreed to see me. I'm surprised your alpha allowed it." He toasted me with his glass, then took a gulp.

He was so obviously after a reaction, I didn't give him one, except to say, "The Alpha doesn't get to decide who I meet with. What's your name?"

"You can call me Hutton," he replied.

"Hutton what?" I asked.

"Just Hutton," he said simply.

"If you can't even give me that much..." I started to stand.

He exhaled in frustration. "Wait, *please*. Aaron. Aaron Hutton."

I sat back down. "Your parents were—"

"Felicity and Ray Hutton. They were murdered by Dagen, just like yours." In a moment his face turned from congenial to pent-up rage and back again.

"And yet, you decided to work for Dagen," I said coldly. I had no sympathy for people like him. He wasn't the only white wolf to make that choice. I didn't understand it. I wasn't sure I wanted to.

"I was twelve years old when that asshole murdered my parents." Hutton's tone matched my own. "Me and a couple of other boys were sent to live with Gus Dagen. You've heard of him?"

"Of course I have." I barely contained a shudder. "The Butcher of Onyx Ridge. Even among wolves, he was known for his cruelty. My people fought over who was going to put him down." I don't know who actually did it, or how, except that he got what was coming to him. Or so Jake said. I had no reason not to believe him.

"Yeah. Well, he liked to practice," Hutton said bitterly. "But his favourite thing was watching us practice on each other. Once you get in a certain level over your head, it's hard as fuck to get out again. He had us all convinced we had no choice. When the Uprising took place, I took the hint and got the fuck out of there. Went underground. I figured if Dagen saw me, I was dead. And if anyone from Ivory Claw saw me, I was just as dead. Once labelled a traitor, always a traitor." He shrugged.

"The Uprising?" I asked. "I like that. And you're right, you would have been dead. Everyone back then was very... Pissed off. They tore apart one white wolf who worked for Dagen. I don't think I would have been able to stop them from tearing apart another." Would I have tried? That was a question for back then. There was a whole other set of questions for the present.

"Why now?" I asked. "Any time in the last nine years, you could have stepped forward. But you chose today. Why?"

"I asked myself the same question. Part of me is thinking I should have just stayed hidden. But..." He rubbed the scar on his nose again. "I've heard rumblings. Dagen is trying to get support. Think whatever you want about me and stuff I did in the past, but I'm fucked if I'm gonna sit by and let the black wolves take control again. They won't make the same mistake. They won't let the children live. If they come after the Ivory Claw pack, they'll kill us all this time."

His fingers were white around his glass. I was surprised it didn't shatter in his hand.

"What are you proposing to do about it?" I asked. Clearly he was done with hiding from the world. I could relate to that. There was only a certain amount of time a person could sit by and do nothing before it drove them crazy.

"I want to join you," he said. "Whatever needs to be done, I'll do it. I have a shit load to atone for, and I know it ain't gonna be easy. My people are gonna hate me, but no more than I hate myself."

Just when I thought I couldn't hate the Dagen family more, I did. Hutton was only a few years older than me, but he'd suffered worse than I had. I was treated like a piece of rubbish, but I was never made to kill my own kind. He was right about one thing, it *wouldn't* be easy. The question was, did I need that kind of division in my organisation right now?

If Jake knew I was meeting with Hutton, he would be pissed. That was too bad, I didn't answer to him. Still, some things went beyond little white lies. Meeting a guy like Hutton was one of them, especially somewhere as public as this. I was in no illusion Jake wouldn't know by the end of the day. I would tell him if someone else didn't.

"I'll think about it," I said. "What will you do if the answer is no?"

He gave me a measured look. "You want to know if I'll go back and work for Dagen?"

"Will you?" He might decide Dagen would be the winner of this battle. This war. Only an idiot sided with the loser.

"Fuck that." His blunt response made me smile. "I won't rest until every last Dagen is in some part of the seven hells, even if I have to go there with them."

"So you're reckless?" I asked. "Reckless will get you killed. It also gets other people killed." I got where I was by being ruthless, not stupid.

He put his glass down on the table. "No, I'm not reckless. I am twenty years of anger looking for a direction to go. I haven't had that. Until now. With or without you, I will bring Dagen down. I just thought you might want in on it." He gave me a knowing smile, like he suspected I wouldn't turn down a challenge.

I hadn't yet.

I smiled back. "That's cute that you think I need an invitation.

Or that I couldn't stop you with a flick of my wrist.

"Why stop me?" he asked. "I want what you want."

I regarded him for a moment. "You want death and destruction at any cost. If you start killing anyone in the Dagen pack, people are going to point the finger back at me, whether we are involved or not. They'll retaliate against me if they can't find you."

"You don't seem like the kind of woman who is scared of a little retaliation. Or much of anything else." His eyes lingered on my chest for a moment before he looked back in my eyes.

"I'm not," I replied coolly. "I also don't want to give Dagen the excuse to attack us."

"It's cute that you think he needs an excuse," Hutton said. The guy was getting more cocky by the moment.

"Did he send you?" I asked.

Hutton's face turned a fascinating shade of pink. He rubbed hard at his scar with the tip of his finger.

"No. He fucking did not. If I was anywhere near Alastair Dagen, one of us would be dead. Or both. Is that what you want? Do I have to bring his head to you on a silver platter to prove whose side I'm on?"

That sounded pretty fucking perfect to me. As if to punctuate Hutton's question, the woman on the couch near us came loudly. I turned my head to watch. She straddled one guy, while another was frantically thrusting at her rear hole.

"I think she likes the idea," I remarked.

"She certainly likes something," he agreed. "Those are some life goals right there." He gave me a look that was half suggestive, but laced with the tension of our conversation. He was clearly the kind of guy who took shit seriously, even when he wanted to joke around or flirt.

"For her, or for you?" I cocked my head at him and raised an eyebrow.

"Both," he agreed. "For one thing, she has two friends. I only have one." His eyes lingered on me.

I sipped my water. "We're friends now?"

"Friends. Allies. Whatever you want to call it. Hells, I'll even settle for fuck buddies."

I wasn't sure if the obvious erection in front of his pants was because of me, or where we were. Maybe both. This part of Crimson had that effect on people. That was one of the reasons I liked it so much. If you could stay cool and focused in a room full of people fucking, then there was hope for you.

"You know how to flatter a girl, don't you?" I said dryly.

"Honestly," he said, "I don't have a fucking clue. Dagen women are toxic. Ivory Claw women don't want to know me. I would freak the shit out of human women. Witches scare the shit out of me. Demons too."

"That doesn't leave much," I remarked.

"Yeah." He shrugged. "That's the consequences of doing bad shit, I suppose. It's lonely at the bottom." He hesitated for a moment before he added, "It's probably not that different for you. I bet you scare the crap out of every man you meet."

"Are you scared?" I asked.

"Hells yeah," he admitted. "Of course I am. Everyone here looks like they're having a good time, but I know I could be dead before I took two steps if you wanted."

"I'm sure you could make it at least *three* steps," I said.

"I'll aim for four if I have to," he said. "Even a guy like me has to have ambition."

I snorted. "You seem to have lots of that. You really think you could bring me the head of Alistair Dagen on a platter?"

"Not without help," he admitted. "That's why I'm here."

"You said you heard rumblings," I said slowly. "What did you hear and where did you hear it from?" Just like with Cooper, I wouldn't rule out the idea that Dagen sent him. Just because Helen Dagen's brainwashing didn't work on me didn't mean Gus

Dagen hadn't done a number on Hutton. He obviously had, since Hutton allied himself with them, at least for a time.

"One of the guys who were sent to the Butcher with me, he's still on the inside," Hutton admitted. "He's pretty fucked up. I've been trying to get him out for the longest time. They broke him. Close enough anyway. I kept a line open between us. He didn't say much, just that something was up. He thought Dagen was planning some shit. He got scared and didn't tell me anything else. He could get eviscerated for just that much if they find out."

I would have liked a lot more information, but I suspected that was all I was going to get. He couldn't tell me what he didn't know.

"You said you'd do anything," I said. "If I asked you to go back to Dagen, would you?"

I wasn't prepared for the look of absolute dread on his face. I knew that exact feeling. It took me back to when I saw Barnaby Dagen walk through the door before the virgin auction. I was in the darkness, offstage, but I saw his strut, the determined set of his jaw. Even from a distance I felt his cold fury. He had a plan for me, but I derailed it by taking part. I wouldn't marry the person of his choice and be a dutiful little beaten down omega. I defied him and he would take it out on every centimetre of my body.

The memory made my stomach turn.

"No more than you would, I'm guessing," he said softly.

I shook my head to clear it. "The past doesn't matter. The only thing that does is what we do today."

"Keep telling yourself that," he said. "Someday you might even believe it. But you know as well as I do, that the past is what shapes us. It's why people hate me, and why they're scared of you. The past is everything."

"Only if we let it be," I said firmly. He was right though. My life up until this point shaped every part of me. Whether I put it aside or not, it was still there in the back of my mind.

He sat back. "Some of us don't have a choice. And the answer is no. If I go anywhere near Dagen, it will only be to kill him. That doesn't mean I still can't be useful."

I was starting to realise that rubbing his scar was something he did when he was nervous or anxious. The skin on that part of his nose must be very smooth by now. Part of me wanted to find out. It was hard not to be drawn to someone who had the same broken, fucked up start in life. Jake had kept himself out of it. Cooper was too young to have lived any of it. Ben's childhood was a different kind of fucked up. Hutton and I would bear the scars of it forever.

"What can you do?" I asked. The two men who were pounding into the woman near us were getting louder and louder. One or both of them would come soon. The sight and sound of them was arousing, I have to admit. Not for the first time, I was glad I was a woman and didn't have a hard cock to show the world.

"You must have some skills."

"I'm good with my tongue," Hutton said. Apparently I wasn't as good at keeping my thoughts to myself as I thought I was.

I rolled my eyes. "Skills we can use against Dagen."

"Right." He gave me a rueful smile."I can fight. With guns and knives, hand-to-hand. With my teeth. With my claws. I'm proficient in a couple of different martial arts. And I can bake cupcakes."

"Cupcakes?" I echoed. "You should have led with that." Jake was really *not* going to like this guy. "Can you send Dagen a dozen chocolate ones?" Shame he wouldn't be dumb enough to eat them. A girl could dream, right?

"With laxatives in them," Hutton said wistfully.

"Or better yet, fast acting poison. Is there anything undetectable that he might eat?" I wasn't quite ready to let go of this idea yet.

"I don't think we'd get close enough to give him any." Hutton sighed.

I decided against telling him Alistair Dagen was in this very building the previous night. Although, if he got sick or died from anything he ate while at Crimson, it wouldn't be hard to trace the trail back to us.

"So I'm in?" Hutton asked.

"Because you have skills with baked goods?" I asked. "It's going to take more than that."

"You have to check with your alpha first?" Hutton asked. He raised an eyebrow at me in challenge.

"Word of advice," I said coolly, "stop suggesting I answer to anyone, even as a joke. That shit got old a long time ago. I don't just give a job to anyone who walks in off the street." Or ones I bid on. "If I did, I would be overstaffed."

He leaned in towards me. "The difference between me and them is that you *need* me. If you want to stop Dagen from doing whatever he plans, I can help. I *will* help."

"Whether I like it or not?" I asked. My tone was bordering on dangerous, but his proximity and the threesome in the corner of my eye was distracting and heady.

He locked his gaze on mine and his breath brushed over my cheek. "You would definitely like it."

Shit, he must be catching the same vibe. I don't know how I had any lust left after the marathon session with Cooper, but apparently I did. I reminded myself of who he was and what people like him did. He killed members of our pack for our enemy. However muddy the reasons for doing that, it still happened.

"You think so, do you?" I said.

He licked his lips. "Without a doubt. I—"

"What the fuck?"

The first sign I had that Jake was here was the man himself charging toward us. His face looked like thunder.

"What the *shit* is he doing here?" Jake snarled.

CHAPTER

EIGHT

Hutton jerked away. "I—"

Jake looked like he was about to shift and rip Hutton's throat out. Instead, he leaped towards him. His momentum knocked the table in front of me. Two glasses and the jug went flying.

Before I could move, I found myself covered in a couple of litres of ice cold apple juice.

The front of my white silk blouse was absolutely saturated. Juice dripped from my face, from my arms, from my hair.

Jake froze, his hands out to either side. "Oh. Shit." He stepped towards me. "Ivory... I'm so sorry."

I could only manage one word. *"Fuck."*

He reached for me to—I don't even know what. He was useful, but he wasn't a motherfucking towel.

I sidestepped him. "What the hells?" I growled under my breath.

"He's a traitor," Jake said. He turned to Hutton. "Get the fuck out." He waved towards the door.

Hutton took a step away.

"He's here at my request," I said coldly. "We are not done talking yet. I need to get clean. Don't kill each other."

"I make no guarantees," Jake said. "You can wait for us in the ground floor bar, asshole. I don't trust you running around up here. Before you have any thoughts, security is everywhere." He waved Ben over from the door and gestured for him to escort Hutton out.

Hutton shrugged. "I have no plans to try anything."

"You better fucking not," Jake snarled. "I should kill you myself and get it over with, but that would ruin the mood in here. Ivory hates it when people do that." He was angry, but he obviously hadn't missed the fact the juice made my blouse practically transparent. His erection pressed at the front of his pants.

I glared at him, then stomped past him towards the elevator. Men and their stupid need to out-dick each other. Did he really think I didn't know what I was doing?

Maybe I should kill them both and get it over with.

I stepped into the elevator and pressed the button to close the door before Jake could get inside. Recognising that might be childish and he might change his mind and actually kill Hutton, I pressed the other button to open the door again. I crossed my arms over my chest and stepped back to let Jake join me in the elevator car.

Neither of us said a word all the way up. Or when we stepped into the apartment. Not even when I saw Cooper sitting on the couch, a book in his hand.

"Jake can explain," I said before he could ask. "Maybe you can wash my back." I slipped into the bathroom before anyone could say another word.

I shed my clothes and stepped into the shower. Closing my eyes, I leaned forward into the hot, steamy water to rinse the sticky juice off my face.

The shower door opened and closed. Strong hands gently massaged my shoulders.

I dropped my head and savoured the feeling. "Mmmm, that feels good."

"Yes, you do."

My head snapped back up. Heart thundering, I turned around and blinked water out of my eyes.

"Jake..."

He was naked, muscles slick with water, cock already hard.

I couldn't deny how freaking hot he was. "You shouldn't be in—"

His blue eyes were even more intense than usual, dark with desire. "I'm done with excuses." He gripped my upper arms, pressed me against the side of the shower and slammed his mouth against mine.

I kissed him back at first, hungrily, but forced myself to break away. It took me a moment to catch my breath. "We agreed—"

"*You* agreed," he corrected. "I never agreed that we shouldn't touch each other. I never wanted to keep my distance. I *never* agreed to be platonic." He rubbed his thumbs over my wet, bare skin, tracing circles lightly. "I've waited long enough. I'm not waiting any more." He pressed his body to mine and kissed me again.

"I want you. I know you want me." He kissed down my cheek, down my neck.

My defences were gradually evaporating, washed down the plughole. "Shouldn't you be keeping an eye on our guest downstairs?"

He paused for a moment. "Ben can handle it." He went back to kissing my neck while his hands wandered down my sides.

"Jake..." My voice wavered.

"Please don't tell me to stop." His voice was muffled by my throat. "I'm not sure I can."

I knew there was no way in hells he would ever force himself on me. He knew I knew that. He might make me sticky, but he'd never hurt me.

I placed my fingers on his chest and pushed him back hard enough to dislodge his mouth. "If this changes everything..."

He placed his hands on either side of my face. "It won't. I promise. We're just giving each other what we know we want and need." Water poured down on us both. His eyes bore into mine, searching like he was looking for my soul.

I wasn't sure he would find one.

I swallowed hard. The last piece of resistance crumbled like a sand castle at high tide. *Gods, please let this be the only thing that falls apart.* If I lost him because of this, I would never forgive myself.

"Please... *don't* stop," I said softly.

His mouth crashed into mine. His tongue pushed its way between my lips, demanding entry, tasting my teeth, my tongue. Without words, he was telling me to let go. Let him be in control.

I melted against him.

He kissed his way down my cheek, down my chest. When he reached my nipples, he licked and sucked them mercilessly. Until all I could do was pant from the pleasure he sent smashing into my core.

Just when I thought I might go wild from that, he dropped to his knees. He firmly pushed my legs apart and dove in, face first. His tongue massaged my clit, licked over my folds like he was starving for a meal.

I pressed my palms against the tiles behind me to keep myself upright, and dropped my head back. Water gushed down over me. Body jets teased my nipples. I had them placed at exactly that height for a reason. Another one was positioned right behind where Jake's head currently was. Why not have fun in the shower?

My breath came in ragged pants.

Gods, I had imagined this for so long. Too long. I remembered my words to Hutton, about letting the past define us. I had done exactly that. And let fear guide me. Ironic that I could take on a pack of black wolves, but I was scared of a man who loved me, whom I loved in return.

"Jake," I moaned softly. "I'm going to come." I teetered right on the edge of the precipice, but my orgasm was still building like a dam trying to breach its walls.

He drew his face back and smiled up at me. "Not yet you're not. Not till I say so. I am the alpha here."

At any other time, that would have pissed me off. Here, it turned me on.

I laughed from deep in the back of my throat. "Do I call you daddy?" I teased.

He chuckled. "Beautiful El, you can call me whatever you like. Just say it loud. And not until I say so."

"Asshole," I grumbled playfully.

"That's me." He went back to eating my pussy.

I watched him while he did it. My eyes drank in his muscular body, deliciously covered in ink. That much of it wouldn't suit some guys, but it looked perfect on him. Sexy as fuck. My own skin, in contrast, was as pale as my hair. Flawless apart from a freckle here and there. The tattoo on my back and a small one on my wrist were all I wanted.

One of his hands gripped my thigh, the other crept around to grab my ass. Between them both, he held me firmly.

I inched closer and closer. The rebellious part of me wanted to come, whether he said I could or not. I wouldn't be me if I didn't at least think it.

The rest of me wanted, needed, to do what he said, to let him take control.

"I'm close," I said. I lightly rolled my hips, seeking more and more.

He pulled his face away. "Not yet."

Without his touch I drew back from the edge. I groaned. "Please. I need to come."

He grinned and wiped water off his face with one hand. "I think I like it when you beg. I might have to get you to do it more often."

I snorted. "Don't push it, buddy."

He chuckled and pressed his face back between my legs.

I moaned. *"Please."*

He rubbed his hand over my ass, and dipped it down between my legs. The tip of his finger grazed over my rear hole.

My knees quivered.

Encouraged, he pressed the tip of his finger inside me, while his tongue teased the entrance to my pussy.

"Mmmm," I groaned. "That feels so good."

He pressed his finger in further and thrust it in and out in rhythm with his tongue.

"Oh gods." I closed my eyes and savoured the sensations coursing through my body, making my pulse spike. "I can't not... I have to..."

"Not yet." His words were muffled but firm.

I growled, deep in the back of my throat.

He chuckled and pulled his face away long enough to say, "I can stop."

"Don't you dare." I glared at him with narrowed eyes but a smile tugging at the corners of my mouth. "Fucking clit tease."

He wiggled his eyebrows and went on doing what he was doing so well. He drove me closer to the edge and held me there, drew me back, then drove me forward again.

"I think you've been obedient long enough," he said between licks and flicks of his thumb over my clit. "Come for me."

Almost immediately, I came, panting and moaning as warm water and hot pleasure washed down over my body. I was lost in a whirlpool, a torrent, a flood that carried me away until every nerve ending in every part of me was singing.

Just as I hit the peak of my orgasm, Jake rose, turned me around and bent me over so the palms of my hands were pressed against the tiled seat to the side of the shower.

"Keep your hands there," he ordered. He gripped my hips and slid his cock deep into my pussy.

Instead of coming down, I came again at the feeling of him inside me. Harder and faster the second time, until I couldn't remember my name or where I was. I didn't care. I was lost in the most delicious place. I never wanted to leave.

Jake muttered something like, "Should have been more assertive sooner," and started to thrust slowly.

Maybe he should have, but I might have pushed him away anyway. Recent events made me realise life was too fucking short to deny stuff you shouldn't. That didn't matter now. What mattered was right here, in the present.

"You feel incredible," he whispered. "I had forgotten just how incredible. It's been too fucking long." He punctuated each word with a thrust.

All I could do in response was to say, "Mmmm," and wriggle my ass a little.

He smacked my ass cheek. "Sassy little minx."

"I'm not a cat," I retorted.

"No, but you have one hells of a pussy," he said.

I should have seen that one coming a kilometre away.

I closed my eyes and rocked my hips back and forth in rhythm with him. "And you're not a rooster."

He chuckled. "Just think how long you've been missing out on one hells of a cock."

I could have reminded him that I hadn't been short on cock over the last nine years, but that didn't seem like the classy thing to do. Instead, I said, "Anything worth having is worth waiting for." He knew the truth of that.

"Yes, you are," he agreed. "One million percent worth it."

For the longest time he kept a slow, leisurely pace, while I supported my way to the front of my hands and enjoyed the feeling of being with him. I try to remember why I denied us both this, but right now I couldn't. It all made sense at the time, if not now.

Gradually, his thrusts got faster. He slid his hands up my stomach and cupped my breasts. He palmed my already hard nipples.

"El, you drive me fucking wild, woman," he said breathlessly. "Absolutely feral."

"Just the way I like you," I said. "Wild and vicious."

He pinched my nipples hard enough to make me gasp in surprise. "Vicious like that?"

"Mmmm, yeah, like that." He wasn't the first partner to get rough, but it was the first time he got rough with me. I liked it.

He slapped my ass harder this time. Then again and again until it stung.

"Who is the boss?" he asked. "When I fuck you, who is in charge?"

"I am the boss," I replied, "except when you fuck me." Then it was up for debate, but I was happy to let him lead this time. Wait. This time? Was I really ready to accept that the line between us was gone now? That was a question for later.

"I won't forget it if you don't." He slapped my ass again, then gripped my hips. "I'm going to come inside you."

My whole body quivered. "Yes, please." Each thrust drove me closer to coming again.

"Say that again, louder," he insisted. "Tell me what you want me to do."

I turned my head to look over my shoulder. "I want you to

come inside me, please. *Please*." On the last word, I came again and so did he.

The whole world disappeared in a haze of frantic thrusting, panting, heat and pleasure.

I was pretty sure I screamed his name loud enough for all of Sydney to hear. I didn't care. Let them hear. Let them know I finally gave in to my long standing desire to fuck Jake. He deserved to hear it after being patient for so long. I deserved it too, because keeping him at arm's length was the right thing to do.

He grunted my name over and over. "El, Elodie, Elodie..." Then he slumped forward, his hands still gripping my hips.

Slowly and reluctantly, he slid out of me and helped me to straighten back up. His eyes searched mine. I knew he didn't want to ask, but he needed to know the answer.

"Any regrets?"

I could have said I did and shattered his heart into a thousand pieces. Instead, I decided to be honest.

I shook my head, my wet hair swinging and spraying droplets this way and that. "None. I know you think it's unfair that I pushed you away for so long—"

He pressed two wet fingers against my lips. "I understand why you did it. It was the right thing. At the time. We had to focus on..." He waved a hand around us. "All of this. Not just for us, but for the generations who will carry on the pack after us."

"That is legitimately the wisest fucking thing anyone has ever said in this shower." I smiled. "Probably in any shower, anywhere, ever."

He chuckled. "I can be wise when I want to." His expression turned serious again. "Can you promise me something?"

"That depends what it is," I said. I didn't want to make any promises I couldn't keep.

He looked me directly in the eyes and said, "Can you promise not to push me away again? I don't want this to be a one time thing. I want to be with you. Even if that means sharing you with guys like Cooper and Ben. I mean, at this point I think we would have to chase Cooper away with a stick, or have him killed. And he's, you know, a nice kid. But you and I, we've taken a step forward. I don't want to take a step back again." He cocked his head at me and gave me his best puppy dog eyes.

"I—" I considered how to respond. "I don't want to push you away again. But if I feel like it's putting either of us into the shit, I will have no choice. If we can still work together and not fuck this up, then... We can see how it goes." That was all I could give him right now.

He nodded slowly. "Fair enough. I know we can do this. I know I can. You're the most incredible fucking woman I've ever met. The second I laid eyes on you, I knew I would never get over you. If Dagen won that auction, I would have had no choice but to tear him to pieces to keep him from touching you."

"And that's the most romantic thing anyone has ever said in this shower," I said. What can I say? I'm a sucker for guys who want to spread the blood of my enemies across the nearest wall. I would do the same for them too. Strange how I already added Cooper to that. Had we only met the night before? It was hard not to be protective of him, as well as attracted to and turned on by him. The guy was both hot and adorable. Like Jake.

"I will try to remember to make daily, romantic death threats against people for you," Jake said with a smile. "Especially if doing that turns you on."

"It really does," I agreed.

He sighed and his smile faded. "I guess we better deal with the asshole downstairs."

I put a hand on his arm. "Not without me. Do you have any idea what he's been through?"

Jake shook his head. "No, but I know what he did. Him and

guys like him. They used to tail Dagen Senior like pack of fucking puppies."

"That's why you recognised him on sight?" I asked.

"Yeah." He placed his hands lightly on either side of my face. "I don't want a guy like that anywhere near you."

"I can take care of myself," I said.

"I know you can, but guys like him are trouble. I saw the way he was looking at you. If you give him an in, he'll take it. Worst case scenario, he'll betray you to Dagen. Best case scenario I'll end up sharing you with him."

"Is that what this is about?" I asked, only half teasing.

Jake kissed my mouth hard in response."I will always have a part of you no other guy will. You could have twenty lovers and no one could ever take that away from us."

"Twenty?" I mused. "That sounds like a lot to juggle, but I guess I could—"

"Not literally," he growled playfully. He leaned in to nip my ear.

"I don't think I could deal with that much testosterone," I said. "You can be there when I talk to Hutton, but you will back the fuck off until I decide what to do with him."

"Yes, boss," Jake replied reluctantly. "But after we're done there, I'm taking you to bed and I'm going to fuck you all night long."

NINE

"Stay close," I said to Cooper. I was clean and dry and dressed, but on edge.

"I'm happy to," Cooper said.

Jake looked surprised. It was usually him telling bodyguards to stay close to me. The fact I did it let him know how off-balance I felt. Or maybe that I actually listened to his warnings about Hutton.

"I could get Kyle and—" Jake started.

"No need," I said quickly. "Three of us will be enough to keep me safe." I hoped.

"Thank you for trusting me," Cooper said. "I was right, wasn't I?"

Jake gave him a funny look. "About what?"

"That you too needed to fuck it out," Cooper said. "You did, didn't you? I mean, unless Ivory was alone and..."

"We did," I assured him. "Yes, you were right." I patted his chest and let my hand linger there for a moment. Not even all those orgasms could take the edge off how lickable he was.

"So..." Cooper looked awkward. He obviously had something

to ask, but didn't know how to ask it. If he was going to hang around with us, he was going to have to learn to dive right in.

"So?" I arched an eyebrow at him.

"So if you and Jake are a thing..." he started tentatively.

Apparently Jake had abandoned all patience today. He said, "Ivory and I are a thing. I think she wants to be a thing with you too. That's fine with me, as long as she is happy and you don't screw with her. Or... screw with her, but don't screw her *over*."

"Oh." Cooper nodded. "That's fine with me. If that's what Ivory wants."

Did I? My romantic relationships tended to last a week or two. What was I thinking, trying to start up a relationship with not one guy but two? Especially now. I was probably thinking that life was too short and I might as well go for it.

"As long as we can all get along, let's see where this leads," I said. That was about as much commitment as I could give right now. Judging by the looks on their faces, it was enough. For now. I would worry later if they wanted me to choose between them.

In spite of telling Jake I didn't need any more security, Kyle and Layla followed us from the apartment door down to the first floor.

The moment the elevator doors slid open, I knew some shit was going down. Between the angry shouts and the stink of animosity, the mood was obviously ugly.

No prizes for guessing the reason for the mood.

At first no one noticed us entering the bar. I wrinkled my nose at the smell of stale beer and wine. Sometimes I wished I could get drunk, it looked like fun. But the smell...

"He's a traitorous motherfucker," someone shouted. "Get a rope and we'll string up the prick."

"String him up on what?" someone else asked. "Just cut his throat and be done with it."

"Naw, that'll just make a mess and get us all kicked out." At least someone kept their head.

A ripple passed through the crowd as people started to notice I was there. They moved aside like the tide parting. Some of them looked nervous now, others curious. They all knew who I was, what they didn't know was how I would react.

I stepped through the crowd to see a circle of people, all paranormal, standing around Hutton. The wolf shifter looked more resigned than scared.

Did he really think I would let him be killed here in my building? Without my order? Two people would die then, Hutton and whoever killed him. I didn't tolerate that shit on my property. Go and kill people somewhere else, don't do it here.

I glanced at Jake. He looked like he would be happy if someone had taken care of his problem before we got here. Too bad. On the other hand, it did serve to illustrate my point. If Hutton died while we were fucking, that was exactly the kind of thing I was trying to prevent by keeping Jake at arm's length.

Lucky for everyone involved that Hutton was still alive. For now.

Hutton looked very glad to see me. "I waited, like you asked," he said loud enough for everyone to hear. "Your customers aren't very hospitable."

"Not to traitorous assholes like you," a tall man growled. "Your kind aren't welcome here."

I narrowed my eyes at him. Like a typical coward, he looked away quickly.

"Let's grab a seat," I said. I waved toward a table to the side of the room.

I took a step before Hutton came running at me.

I barely had time to react, to put up my hands defensively, before he flew past me and tackled someone behind me.

I whirled around.

Hutton was wrestling on the carpeted floor with a man who held a long blade in his hand. Hutton had him pinned down but the man was fighting hard. His teeth were gritted and his eyes were on me.

"Fuck," Jake swore. "Get that knife off him. Bring up the lights. Lock the doors. See if anyone else is armed." He put an arm around me protectively and hustled me over to the bar. To a place where no one could stand behind, or jump out at us. Or at me.

My heart hammered in my chest. What the absolute fuck?

Hutton was still wrestling the would-be assassin for the knife. It was clear the man had already realised he was dead, he might as well try to finish what he came here for first. He tried to slash at Hutton's face, but only managed a slice across one cheek before Hutton grabbed his wrist and slammed it against the floor.

Cooper stepped on the attacker's arm and pressed down hard with his shoe.

The attacker snarled, but Hutton forced his hand open and snatched the knife. Before he could throw it, Ben was beside him. He took it from him and tucked the blade away on his hip.

Between the three of them, they hauled the assassin to his feet.

"How the fuck did he get that in here?" Jake growled. "Security must have been too busy watching over the traitor to do their jobs properly." He narrowed angry eyes at Ben.

Ben looked as rattled as I'd ever seen him. That is, calm except the furrowing of his brow and the lines around his eyes. If anything happened to me, he would blame himself. Jake would blame him too, even though he was supposed to watch Hutton, not the people coming and going.

I wanted to give him a reassuring smile, but I was shaken. I expected someone to come after me, but not like that. This was direct, even for Dagen. It was crude.

Blood trickled down Hutton's face from the slice on his cheek.

If it wasn't for him... A witch could heal a knife wound unless it went straight through my heart. I could have been dead right now.

"Ivory?" Jake asked softly.

His voice brought me out of myself. Here I was, the big bad wolf, the head of Ivory Claw, the... wolf mother, if you like, and I was rattled by some random asshole with a knife.

I nodded and forced my icy composure back into place. I set my gaze on the would-be assassin.

"I would ask who hired you, but it's pretty fucking obvious." My voice was pure ice. "Dagen sent you to your death."

The attacker bared his teeth. "Fuck you, bitch."

I gave him a dangerous smile. "It was going to be a quick death. Now, not so much." For calling me a bitch, I would let the guys take all the time they wanted. I inhaled the smell of fear and black wolf. The first was intoxicating. The second was nauseating.

Jake placed his hand on my lower back. "This could have been a setup." I didn't need to follow his gaze to know he looked directly at Hutton. "Convenient that he just *happened* to be there."

"I had no idea this was going to happen," Hutton argued.

"I've seen this guy before." Cooper nodded toward Hutton. "At my uncle's garage."

Hutton pressed his lips together in a firm line. "I was trying to help Silas get away from Dagen. All he had to do—"

"Save it," Jake snapped. "We don't have time for your shit right now. Take that asshole downstairs. Let's get some answers out of him." He turned to me and his expression softened. "Wanna come and join in some torture?"

I smiled. "You say the most romantic things. But I want to speak to Hutton."

"Not without me there," he insisted.

"You can come," I said. "Or you can join in the torture." I raked a fingernail slowly down the back of his hand until his breath hitched.

"You're going to make me choose between you and torturing this asshole?" His expression was pained.

I raised my eyebrows at him.

He sighed. "Fine. He probably doesn't know shit anyway." He nodded to Ben. "Get him out of here."

Ben nodded and he, Cooper and a couple of other security guys hauled the attacker away.

The crowd muttered, but most of them went back to their drinks. The lights went back down to the normal, dim level and the doors were unlocked.

I stepped towards Hutton and looked appraisingly at his cheek. "There should be a witch around here if you want that healed." Personally, I thought it would leave an awesome scar.

He shook his head and dabbed at his cheek with his fingertips. "It's nothing."

"If you're expecting gratitude, forget it," Jake snapped.

Hutton returned his gaze unflinchingly. "I'm not expecting anything. I saw the guy and acted, that's all."

"Were you working with him?" Jake asked. He obviously wasn't going to give Hutton a millimetre.

"We can talk about this somewhere else," I said. I nodded towards the office at the back of the bar. It was for the use of the manager and senior staff at Crimson, but I liked to commandeer it from time to time.

Jake was obviously not happy, but he nodded. At least I hadn't suggested going up to my apartment. I would fight him every step of the way if I did that, and this was too public a place for an argument.

We stepped into the office and I made myself comfortable sitting on the desk. That left the guys to stand, their eyes on each other like they were sizing each other up. Sometimes I wondered how humans didn't realise wolf shifters lived amongst them. These two had it written on every centimetre of their body, from their posture to their narrowed eyes.

Jake closed the door. "Answer the question," he demanded. "Did Dagen send you?"

"No," Hutton said firmly. "I haven't seen Alistair Dagen for nine years. I haven't been in communication with any of them. No one was happier when Barnaby and Gus Dagen were dead than I was."

"That's debatable," I said dryly. "I don't think even Alistair misses his father very much." Yeah, cry me a fucking river of blood. The bad apple didn't fall far from the tree, but I gathered there wasn't much love lost between father and son.

"No one does," Hutton said. "Killing him was a community service."

"You're welcome," Jake said. "Now, what do you want? You better give us a fucking good reason not to take you downstairs with the other asshole. I would enjoy hearing you scream."

"You usually enjoy screaming no matter who it is," I pointed out.

"Yeah, but I'd enjoy it more if it's this asshole," Jake said. "After all the things he and his friends did."

"Were fucking *made* to do," Hutton said forcefully. "You have no idea what it was like. Guys like you were sitting around, all high and mighty, ready to take credit for every move against Dagen. Meanwhile, you did absolutely fucking nothing. If anyone should be ashamed of themselves—"

Jake growled and took a step toward Hutton.

"All right," I said before this turned into a full-blown fistfight. "Those were dark days. No one came out of it unscathed."

Hutton snorted and gave Jake the side eye.

"Can I kill this motherfucker now?" Jake asked. He crossed his arms over his chest and gave Hutton a death stare.

Was it wrong that I found this whole situation really hot? The smell of testosterone, the body language, it was like a drug.

"Are you fucking kidding?" Hutton snapped. "You realise I saved her life, right?" He waved a hand towards me.

"Which I'm grateful for," I started.

"If you hadn't stepped in, someone else would have," Jake said coldly.

"Who? You?" Hutton laughed bitterly. "You were too busy being a smug bastard to see the threat. By the time you had, it would have been too late."

"Jake doesn't have eyes in the back of his head—" I tried to say.

"I would have seen it before he touched her," Jake growled. "If not me, then one of the members of our security detail."

"Yeah, they might," Hutton said. "But you would have taken all the credit. Guys like you—"

Whatever he was about to say was interrupted by Jake driving his fist into his face. He staggered back against the wall, blood streaming onto his shirt.

"If that gets onto the carpet, I'm going to be pissed off, Jake Blakesley," I growled.

Jake shook his hand and winced. "Be pissed off at *him*. He provoked *me*."

"You're both as bad as each other," I said scathingly. I hopped off the desk, grabbed a pile of tissues out of the box and pressed them to Hutton's nose. "I'm no doctor, but that looks broken to me. Now you *are* going to need to see a witch to heal it." I dabbed gently.

"My fist is fine," Jake said. He shook it and winced.

"If you're looking for sympathy for something you did to yourself, you've come to the wrong place," I said over my shoulder. "I said I wanted to talk, and that's what I meant."

I lowered the tissues to get a look at Hutton's nose, and of course the blood dripped from them straight onto my blouse. I sighed. At least it wasn't more juice.

"Jake, go and get a witch to fix this," I said.

"I'm not leaving you alone with him," Jake said.

I turned around and gave him a dark look. "There is a bar full of people right outside the door. Leave it open if you have to."

"I'm not gonna hurt you," Hutton said.

"I think he's more worried you're going to fuck me," I said.

Hutton looked surprised, but then he smiled although it obviously hurt. "I mean, happy to oblige."

I held up my arm to stop Jake from lunging at him again.

He grunted in frustration. "Ivory has better taste than that anyway."

"Not if she's screwing you," Hutton said. He glanced at me. "No offence. He just seems like kind of a dickhead."

"Jake has his moments." I looked back at him and smiled fondly.

"I have lots of moments," Jake said. "I'll get that witch. If anyone is willing to help this asshole. Don't blame me if they don't." He stalked out the door and left it open behind him.

"He's right about that," Hutton said. "They might be happy to let me suffer."

"They might," I agreed. "But I won't. They'll do as they're told. It's not as though I'm giving them a choice." As much as I hated messing with witches and magic, they had their uses once in a while. One or two of them owed me favours, which would come in useful when the time came.

"You said you were trying to help Silas Wheeler," I said.

Hutton shrugged one shoulder. "He was an old friend. From before. He was one of the guys sent to live with the Butcher. Every time anyone looked at him the wrong way, he would cry or piss his pants. Gus got tired of him and sent him away. He must have had a use for him, or he would have just had him killed. We kept in contact. He tried to get out, but Dagen is like quicksand. You get one foot out and..." He shrugged. "They grab hold of the other foot and pull you back in. I told him I was going to come to you, plead my case. I said if you would listen to me, I would put a good word in for him."

He shook his head. "Silas didn't buy it. He said he had it sorted out. He wouldn't tell me why or how, but he said he had a plan."

I nodded slowly. "It sounds like Dagen might have cancelled his debt in return for something. The gods only know what. Or if he carried it out before he died." Either way, if he was working with Dagen, he deserved what he got even more than I thought.

Hutton nodded towards my chest. "Sorry about the blood."

I looked down and grimaced. "I'm starting to get used to it." I might have to start sending Jake the bill for the dry-cleaning. Lately, every time he was around, I got messy. Sometimes good messy. Sometimes not.

Hutton gave me a funny look, but nodded. "I meant what I said. I'm not going to hurt you."

"I'm not that easy to hurt," I said. "But thank you for stopping me from having a knife in my back. That would really have spoilt my day." Not to mention my blouse.

"I believe you," he said. "The Queenmaker seems to think you're made of glass."

I blinked at him. "Is that what they're calling him now? Queenmaker?" I laughed. "That would go straight to Jake's head."

"He doesn't need an ego boost," Hutton said dryly.

"True that," I said. There was nothing wrong with having a healthy ego. I looked up at Hutton and wondered what the hells I was going to do with him, and how I could stop him and Jake from killing each other.

Jake hurried back into the office. "The witch is going to have to wait. We have a bigger problem."

"How the fuck did this happen?" I demanded. "And when?"

Jake shrugged. "Today, as far as I can tell."

I turned and stalked across the office to the window, then back again. "Eighteen months. I've been trying to buy the Lair for eighteen months and that little worm goes and sells it to Dagen?"

The Lair was another nightclub, close to Crimson. While Crimson was all about pleasure, the Lair was all about violence. Fights were hosted there nightly. It was one of the last properties in the area I didn't own. I'd already offered well above what the place was worth. I had done everything short of killing the owner and taking it. Now I wished I had.

I rubbed a hand over my hair. "He doesn't even want the place, does he? This is just him making a move against me. Into our territory." He was like a dog pissing on a blade of grass, just because he could.

"We could blow the place up," Jake offered. "Or burn it down."

"If I thought he would care, I would," I said. "That's what he would expect us to do." I paced back and forth again.

"Sometimes it's fun to do what's expected." Jake grinned.

"Just think how many innocent people you could kill," Hutton said scathingly. He had followed us up to the office because Jake didn't trust him to stay downstairs unattended. I wasn't sure how long this was going to go on for. I either needed to hire the man or send him away. Jake didn't seem to like either option.

Jake rolled his eyes. "We wouldn't blow it up while there was anyone in there. That wouldn't be very nice."

"And you're all about being nice, you?" Hutton asked ironically.

"As a matter of fact, yes, I am," Jake said. "I'm a motherfucking saint."

I laughed. "And I'm a virgin surrounded by three wise men."

Cooper raised his hand. "I'm wise."

Jake pointed at him. "Yeah, he's wise."

"That makes one," I said. Cooper and Ben hadn't been able to get any information out of the attacker. Cooper still seemed excited after telling me about how the man screamed, and how Ben let him cut his throat. A good time was had by all.

"Figures you'd be a virgin with these two clowns around," Hutton said. He and Cooper didn't seem to have a problem with each other. They had sized each other up, exchanged nods and got on with their lives. "Want me to fix that?" He grinned.

I stopped pacing and put a hand on Jake's arm before he could pick up a sharp implement and use it on Hutton. "Are there any other properties on the market in the area right now? Has Dagen bought any others?"

"I'm looking into it," Jake said. "It could be he's been buying things quietly for a while. But the Lair, that was definitely to get our attention."

"It worked," I said sourly. I leaned against the desk and rubbed my face. "I'm guessing the knife attack was a distraction from this. He probably hoped it would succeed, but this is his real gambit."

"Oh," Cooper said suddenly. He pulled his phone out of his pocket. "I got a text from a guy offering to buy the garage." He swiped across the screen until he found what he was looking for, then showed me.

Jake looked over my shoulder. "It's half again what we offered. You should take it. That's a good price."

I turned my head to glare at him. "Have you already forgotten who the buyer is?"

Hutton snorted.

Jake glared at him. "No, I haven't forgotten. But if he keeps buying, Dagen could bankrupt himself. That would be sweet."

I shook my head. "He's not going to make the same mistake his father did." If it was that easy, I would offer him Crimson, sit back and watch the house of cards collapse. No, there was something else going on here.

"I wouldn't sell the place to him," Cooper said. "He'd probably tear it down and make it into an apartment building."

"We might do that," I said.

"Yeah." Cooper shrugged. "But if you did, at least it would be tasteful. I could do some art for it." He seemed excited by the idea.

"That can go on the 'maybe' pile," I said. An expensive investment like that would require time and planning, and a lot of thought. It wasn't a bad idea though.

"So I should send a text back, saying no?" Cooper asked.

"No, just delete it," Jake said. "Don't give him the satisfaction of responding. That's what bullies want."

"I know." Cooper nodded. "I went to high school." He looked so sad I walked over and put my arms around him.

"Who would bully you?" I asked. "You're so sweet."

"If I give you a list, can you have them killed for me?" he asked. I wasn't sure if he was joking or not. I didn't think he knew.

That wasn't exactly how things worked though. I needed to have a better reason than that. I mean, if they beat him up...

"Make a list and I'll have Jake look into them," I told him. "Maybe you can kill one or two."

Cooper grinned. "I will, thank you."

I kissed his cheek and turned to see Hutton watching us.

"See, there's the difference between you and Dagen," he drawled. "He would have just said yes."

"I like to be fair," I said. "Killing indiscriminately is too easy, and pisses off too many people." There was a fine line between having people scared of us, and pushing them into trying to overthrow us.

Before I could say another word, my phone rang. It wasn't my private line, it was the one I use for business. I recognised the number immediately.

I grimaced and pressed the button to answer. "Alistair Blackheart," I said with mock sweetness.

He chuckled. "Is that the best you can do, Ice Bitch?"

I snorted and rolled my eyes. "Is that the best *you* can do?" He was obviously trying to get a rise out of me, but it wasn't going to work. Not today.

"I'll leave the insults to you, Elodie" he said smoothly. "I was just ringing up to see what you thought of my gift."

Calling me names was one thing, using my real name made me want to grind my teeth.

"What is he saying?" Jake mouthed.

I pressed the button to put Dagen on speaker phone. "You shouldn't have," I said. "It must have been expensive." I wasn't sure if he was referring to the artefacts, the Lair or the would-be assassin. All of that would have cost.

"I like to think of it as an investment," he said. "In a brighter future. One where black wolves rule, like they should."

Jake choked back a laugh.

"Isn't that a cheerful thought?" I said sarcastically. Ugh, talk about dystopia.

"I thought so." Dagen sounded smug.

"What do you really want?" I asked.

"What do any of us want?" he asked. "I want what's mine."

"Considering your family stole what you had from my family, that doesn't leave much," I remarked.

"You like to think you've won." His voice was lower, sinister. He would have intimidated a lot of people, but not me. "Neither of us started this war, but I intend to end it."

"I accept your unconditional surrender," I said sweetly. I tried to ignore Jake and Cooper giving each other a silent high-five. "Will you be retiring somewhere sunny?" A girl could hope, right?

Dagen laughed. "When I'm finished with you, you will be giving me your unconditional surrender. And your lapdog. I know he's listening."

"Hello, asshole," Jake said cheerfully. "You really should take Ivory up on her offer. It would be a lot less hassle."

"But a lot less fun," Dagen said. "Blood stains white fur so nicely, don't you think? Not to mention white hair."

Jake bared his teeth. "I prefer the way it shines off black fur, personally."

"You would know," Dagen said. "You've seen it often enough."

"That's where you're wrong," Jake said lightly. "I haven't seen it *nearly* often enough. Care to volunteer as tribute?"

"No, but I look forward to watching you die," Dagen said. "It's a bucket list thing. You know how it is."

"Right back at you," Jake said. "Nothing would give me more satisfaction."

"Hmmm, sounds as though Ivory needs to brush up on her bedroom skills." Dagen sounded impressed with himself coming up with that insult.

Cooper stood up straighter. He looked like he was going to say something in my defence.

Jake waved him back down.

"Don't give him the satisfaction," Hutton said softly.

Cooper looked like he wanted to argue, but he slumped back down and crossed his arms.

"It's not my bedroom skills you need to worry about," I said. "It's the fact I have experience in stomping the Dagen pack back down in its place. I'm happy to do it again if you push me to it. Just remember who broke the peace if you decide to do it. The blood will be on your hands."

"I will be happy to have Ivory Claw blood on my hands," he said. "Let it rain blood."

"Did you miss your last therapy session?" I asked. "You sound a bit unhinged." He sounded dogmatic, no pun intended.

"You didn't answer my question," he said. "I know you got the artefacts. Thank you for the money, by the way. I know you bought the boy so I could get paid. And because you were panting over him like a bitch in heat."

Okay, so the last part was accurate. Could I help it if Cooper was smoking hot?

I laughed. "Jealous? Did you want him for yourself?"

Cooper made a gagging face.

"I don't need to buy fucks," Dagen said. "They come to me."

"Isn't it nice to see that some people still give to charity?" Jake said.

I put a hand over my mouth to stifle a laugh. I could all but feel Dagen fuming at the other end of the line.

"I'm going to have to have a long think," Dagen said. "About which one of you will die first. One of you will watch the other, that's a given. Don't worry, I'll make it nice and slow. And painful."

"You must be a lot of fun at parties," Jake said dryly.

"I prefer funerals," Dagen said.

"We're happy to invite you to yours." Jake grinned. He was having way too much fun with this. "How about... This Saturday? Does that work for you?"

"I think you can die second, lapdog," Dagen said. "I would get a kick out of watching you see Ivory die."

"So, did you actually want anything, Alistair?" I asked coldly. "Or did you call to threaten us?"

"Actually I figured by now you would have heard that I bought the Lair. I just called to rub it in your face. And to see if the assassin I sent was successful. Obviously he wasn't. It seems to be a dying art these days."

I snorted at his pun. "Aren't you relieved he didn't kill me? Then you would miss out on watching me die."

"That would be a shame," he agreed. "But at least you would be out of my way."

"Sorry to disappoint you," I said. "Actually, sorry, not sorry. It wasn't even a good try. He didn't get close to me." Thanks to Hutton.

"No, but by the time you heard about the sale of the Lair, it was too late. The assassin was little more than a distraction. I didn't expect him to succeed."

"Be careful," Jake said. "All that thinking could be bad for your brain. You're not used to it."

Dagen clicked his tongue. "That was a pathetic attempt at an insult."

"That's the effect talking to you has on me," Jake said. "I feel like I have to dumb everything down."

"No," Dagen said slowly. "That's your usual level of intelligence. Did you ever wonder why my father had no use for you?"

Jake's eyes flashed dangerously. "Your father was smarter than you will ever be, which isn't saying much. He knew I would never work for him. Shame he wasn't smart enough to see a threat right in front of his face. He missed it with me and he missed it with Ivory. Then again, when it came to her, he was probably thinking with his cock. Is that why he wanted her to marry you? So he could keep her close?"

I made a disgusted face. The only thing worse than sharing a bed with one Dagen would be sharing it with two.

"He might have made a mistake, but I won't be making the same one. By the time I'm finished, there will be no way back for any white wolf." Dagen sounded certain. Not enough to worry me, but enough to know he was going to be a pain in the ass.

"You make a good threat," I said icily, "but it's going to take more than buying a nightclub and sending an inept attacker with a knife to ruffle my fur. Or some random artefacts."

He and I both knew they weren't random, but I was hoping to annoy him so that he explained the point of all of them.

"Random artefacts," he echoed. "I thought you were smarter than that. I guess I gave you too much credit."

"Maybe," I agreed. "Why don't you explain it to me?"

"Oh, I will. In time you'll understand the full meaning. And by then it will be far too late." He hung up the phone.

"That was ominous," Jake remarked. He looked unconcerned. "I always thought he should be an actor. He likes to be dramatic."

"I think he's been reading too many comic books." I put the phone down. "He's more melodramatic than dramatic."

"Can I ask something?" Cooper asked.

"Can we stop you?" Jake teased.

"I mean, I guess so." Cooper shrugged. "Have the black wolves and the white wolves ever tried to, like, make a peace treaty or something?"

I sat down on the top of the desk and crossed my legs at my knees. "My parents did. So I've been told. The black wolves responded by killing them. They never have played nice with others."

"Would you try now?" Cooper asked. "Just to save the hassle later?"

I considered the question. It was certainly a reasonable one, and something I didn't dismiss out of hand.

"If I thought he was amenable, I might," I said finally. "We have an uneasy truce right now. All he has to do is nothing and it can stay as it is. If he insists on provoking us, then all bets are off. Whatever blood is spilled after that, is on him." I cocked my head at Cooper. "I got the impression you were looking forward to spilling some blood?"

"I am," he agreed enthusiastically. "But I can do that if we don't go to war with him, can't I?"

"It sounds like you think we kill people every day," Jake remarked.

Cooper stammered. "I... I mean, not *every* day."

"Every day since you met us," I said. "But that's not normal. We don't just go around killing people for shits and giggles. In fact, Jake can go a whole month without killing someone. Maybe two months."

"It was three months one time," Jake said.

Cooper looked like he wasn't sure if we were joking or not.

"You have more restraint than Dagen," Hutton said. He toyed idly with his scar. "Some of them liked to hunt down humans just for fun. Sometimes they would kill them straight away. If there were women, they would..." He looked down at the floor. "Keep them alive a bit longer."

I didn't need him to draw me a picture to know what he was talking about. "Did you ever do that?" If he had, I would hand him over to Jake to do whatever he wanted with him. Some things were beyond forgiveness.

Hutton's head jerked up. "Rape a woman? Gods no. They didn't take us along for those hunts, they just bragged about them afterwards. Made me sick."

Plenty of paranormal people didn't think highly of humans. It wouldn't surprise me if white wolves had hunted in the same way. Not now, unless they wanted to have their balls cut off and shoved down their throats.

I caught Jake looking at Hutton with a thoughtful expression on his face.

"What are you thinking?" I asked softly.

"Lots of things," he said. "The first is that we should go down to the Lair in the morning and have a chat with the soon-to-be former owner. Find out what Dagen offered him that made him cave. Whatever it was, we would have given him more. It must have been something really good to risk pissing us off."

I nodded. "Agreed. Although they probably bonded over the fact that they're both slimy as fuck."

Jake snapped his fingers. "I should have realised something was missing. It's our slime factor. We should have raised that."

"Personally, I prefer not to lower myself by raising something like that," I said. "If I have to be slimy, I'd rather not own the Lair. What was the second thing?"

"What we're gonna do with him." Jake nodded towards Hutton. "In case you hadn't noticed, I don't trust him."

"That has not gone unnoticed," I said. "But we could use somebody with inside knowledge of Dagen's operations."

"It's not recent knowledge," Jake pointed out.

"If it's not recent, then maybe he should be given the benefit of the doubt," I pointed out. Okay, I wasn't that naïve. Normally it took me years to trust someone. I made an exception once before, and he was standing right in front of me. Cooper seemed to be another exception, although I wasn't at the same level of trust with him as I was with Jake. Maybe I was just a good judge of people.

"I'm willing to do whatever it takes to prove myself," Hutton said.

"Which is exactly what you would say if you were trying to infiltrate our organisation," Jake said. "You should go. If we decide to give you a chance, we'll know where to find you."

Hutton nodded. He obviously knew that was the best he was going to get right now. With a heavy sigh, he slipped out the door.

"There's one more thing I'm thinking," Jake said. He cupped my cheek. "I made you a promise and I intend to keep it. All. Night. Long."

ELEVEN

"Is it me, or is this place more rundown than the last time we were here?" Jake asked.

Jake lived up to every second of his promise. It was like he had nine years of pent-up sexual tension to release, or something.

Yeah, okay, I knew he had other lovers, even a girlfriend or two, but like me, they never lasted long. In his case, it didn't surprise me. He never made any attempt to hide how he felt about me. No girl likes to compete with another woman for a guy's attention, unless they have that kind of relationship. I might have agreed to share him with someone else, but he was always so focused on me, he never gave anyone a chance, not really.

Besides, I'm a hard act to follow.

"It's about the same," I said. "It *is* called the Lair. It wouldn't look right if it was fancy." I had planned to spend a shit load of money on it, and change the name. Something in keeping with Crimson, and my restaurant Scarlett. What? I like the colour red, okay?

The bouncers on the front door were hairy. I mean, *really*

hairy. They looked like gorillas, with a little extra dose of human hands and face. Demons, obviously. Demons came in every form, from ones who look like giant spiders, to those who would pass as regular humans. A lot were part shifter, or part witch.

"Good afternoon," one greeted warmly. He gave me a smile like we were old friends. No doubt, he could beat the shit out of someone if he needed to.

"Good afternoon." I nodded coolly. I tried not to wince at the fact it was afternoon. Since Jake decided to take his promise literally, we didn't get to sleep until dawn. By the time I woke again, it was nearly eleven. I was usually up by ten. Half-past ten at the latest. In my line of work, late nights were standard, but I liked to get some sleep while it was dark.

The other bouncer looked nervous. "Is the boss expecting you?"

"The old boss, or the new boss?" Jake asked smoothly.

The bouncer looked like he didn't know how to answer that.

The first bouncer slapped him on the chest with the back of his hand. "The new one hasn't taken possession yet, remember? The boss has to clear out his office and all that shit." He sighed dramatically. "I so wish you'd bought the place. It would be so much better under you."

The second bouncer slapped the first back. "If you still want to have a job, don't say shit like that." His eyes shifted back and forth and he lowered his voice, "Bernie is right, though. I remember the days under Dagen. They weren't nice to demons like us. I dunno, maybe it's time for a new job." He hung his head.

"Vernon," Bernie said. "Are you really thinking of leaving? I can't imagine working here without you."

I exchanged glances with Jake.

He shrugged. "We could always use good door staff at Crimson."

Both demons' eyes widened.

"That would be amazing," Bernie said. "I've always wanted to work there. It looks so... Fancy. Especially compared to this dump."

Vernon nodded vigourously. "Shit, yeah. I'm in." He looked like he was ready to leave right now.

"You should finish your shifts first," Jake said. "And put in your notice."

"And make a list of whoever else wants to jump ship," I said. Dagen might have the Lair, but that didn't mean I couldn't steal his staff. It would be a minor annoyance to him, but I would take it. Any chance to piss him off.

Jake grinned. "Even if there is no room at Crimson, we'll find somewhere."

Bernie looked like he was ready to pee his pants with excitement. "Yes, boss. I know there's quite a few who aren't sure about sticking around."

"Good." I nodded. "So, Haigwood is cleaning out his office?"

"I would expect so, boss," Bernie agreed. "I think he is as eager to get out of here as we are."

Jake snorted.

I knew what he was thinking. He didn't need to say that Haigwood could have put the place behind him a year and a half ago.

I stepped past the bouncers and into the Lair.

The place was dark and stank of sweat and stale alcohol. Two forms sparred in the ring off to one side of the room. I had done enough self defence in the past to tell neither was enthusiastic about being there. The blows they exchanged were half-hearted at best.

On the other side of the room was a long bar. A woman around my age with hair an interesting shade of blue was talking to a man in a leather jacket who sat on a stool.

There were no other customers.

"Looks like business has gone downhill," Jake remarked. Even in the afternoon, there should be people here drinking and talking.

"Nothing puts people off like the words 'under new management,'" I remarked. "Especially when it's not us." I had my reasons for wanting the Lair, but I hadn't realised until now that I wasn't the only one who wanted me to buy the place. Or at least, anyone but Dagen.

"I'm not sure if we should be offended or not," Jake said lightly. "Shouldn't we be the most notorious ones in town?"

I responded with a brief laugh. "There's a fine line between being notorious and being a motherfucker. Alastair crossed that line a long time ago."

We walked down the corridor that led to the offices and staff area.

Sure enough, Haigwood was busy packing all of his belongings into cardboard boxes.

If I didn't know he was a demon, I wouldn't be able to tell by looking. He could pass for a normal human. One in a nicely fitting, expensive looking suit, with a stressed expression on his face.

I stood in the doorway and watched until he finally noticed me. When he did, he looked like he was going to jump out of his skin.

"Ivory. I... Didn't expect you... To drop by," he stammered.

I pressed a hand against the door frame and tapped my fingernail on the wood. "You didn't? Why is that? Perhaps you were hoping to be gone before I heard you sold the place?"

I saw from his expression that he was hoping for exactly that. Sucks to be him.

"Well." He shrugged. "I thought you might be, somewhat... Not happy. But..."

Jake crossed his arms over his chest. "Why did you do it, Haigwood? Didn't we offer you enough money? Did Dagen threaten your family?"

I looked at Jake sideways. "We did that, didn't we?"

He nodded. "Of course. Maybe we didn't go far enough."

I clicked my tongue. "That would be disappointing. You might need to step up your game."

Jake frowned. "I thought my threatening game was on point. Haigwood, where did I go wrong? Help a guy out."

Haigwood licked his lips. "Your threats were just right. Except I don't think you believed me when I said I hate my sister."

"You weren't convincing enough," Jake said. "But I meant what I said about your aunt."

"Oh I know," Haigwood said quickly. "It wasn't about the threats."

"What was it about?" I asked.

Haigwood gulped. "I owed his family a favour. They loaned me the money so I could buy this place. And they took care of some things for me. I thought they forgot about it but they didn't."

"People like that never forget," I said. I should know, I am 'people like that'. "Did it occur to you to come to me? I could have bought this place and helped you to disappear."

"He said he would find me wherever I went. And that I would still owe him a big favour. Selling him the Lair, it seemed like the best way out."

Haigwood reminded me of a snail. Slimy, and if there was any kind of disturbance, he would hide in his shell. In this case, though, I actually understood where he was coming from. I didn't like it, but I understood it. Owing someone a favour could come back and bite you on the ass, hard. That was why I made sure I never owed anyone anything, except Jake. I owed him everything in a way I could never repay.

I grimaced. "At least tell me he paid above our last offer."

Haigwood smiled slowly. "Quite a bit above, actually. He seemed very eager."

Jake chuckled. "I hope the place goes right down the toilet. That would teach him."

I smiled. If Dagen's finances imploded before Alistair did anything, that would be okay with me.

"We could turn the garage into an underground fight club," I mused. "A little competition never hurt anyone." And if it did, then it was too fucking bad.

"We could call it Ruby," Jake said. "Or Garnet."

"Or Merlot," Haigwood chimed in.

"Or just Red," I said.

"Everyone gets what they want," Haigwood said.

"Not really," I said coolly. "I didn't want to bother with having to renovate. Well, not completely."

Haigwood sighed and stopped packing. "Are you going to kill me?"

"That's a good question," Jake said. He looked at me. "Are we going to kill him?"

I thought about that for a while before I made up my mind. Then I pretended to think for a while longer. Just to make Haigwood sweat.

"You pissed me off," I told him. "Killing you might make people who keep me waiting think twice about doing that."

Haigwood looked like he was trying to figure out which way to run. Whichever way he went, it wouldn't be fast enough.

"However," I said slowly, "I'm going to let you live, because I'm in a good mood."

Haigwood looked disbelieving before he broke into a smile. "Thank you. Thank you so much. I really like not being dead. I'll finish packing and then you'll never see me again."

"I know we won't," I said. I gave him a last nod, then turned and walked down the corridor.

"Two days?" Jake asked quietly. He knew me too well.

"Make it three," I said. "Let him think he is safe. Take

Cooper with you. He seems to enjoy killing almost as much as you do." I almost felt sorry for Haigwood, but he brought this on himself.

"Especially a worm like Haigwood," Jake agreed. "The world will be a better place without people like him. And his sister could use the money."

"Make sure she gets it," I said. "And let her know that we didn't take it and why. You never know when her returning the favour might come in useful."

"Consider it done." Jake nodded.

"Have you come to wallow in your loss?" Alistair Dagen asked as we stepped back into the bar area.

"I thought I smelled something bad." Jake waved a hand in front of his face. "I thought it was just the rundown shithole we're standing in, but now I know better."

"A shithole you wanted to buy recently," Dagen pointed out. He looked me up and down like he was trying to appraise the value of a prized dog.

I tried to ignore the sudden tightness in the front of his pants. The idea of being touched by him was sickening.

Jake wiped a hand across his brow. "Thank the gods we dodged that bullet."

"God. I like the sound of that." Dagen looked smug. "You're welcome."

I snorted. "Don't flatter yourself." Ugh, he was a repulsive motherfucker.

"Oh, I don't know," Jake said. "If he was a god, it would explain why so much of the world is shit."

"You have a point," I said with a nod toward him. "Think of all the things we could blame him for.

"Here's an idea for you," Dagen said. "Maybe you should open a comedy club. You two could be the headline act."

"Only if you come and be the clown," Jake quipped.

"Wouldn't that be a circus?" I asked. I hated clowns as it was. Dagen in the role would be nightmare material.

Jake shrugged. "Close enough."

"If I was the clown, I'd be the kind who rides the dog for everyone to see." Dagen gave me a look that clearly interpreted his meaning. Not that it was particularly subtle. It made my skin crawl.

"I'm pretty sure that would be a performing monkey," Jake said. "You're not smart enough to be one of those."

Dagen's expression turned cold. "You still haven't told me what you're doing in my club."

"We were just thanking Haigwood," I said. In spite of my discomfort, the words came out as icy as always. "The price he got for this place will push up property values in the area. And since I own most of it, it seems like I'm the one to benefit the most."

In spite of what Jake said, Alistair Dagen wasn't stupid. He would have known buying the Lair would have that effect. Either that was part of his plan or something he couldn't prevent from happening.

"Seems like you owe me then, doesn't it?" he asked.

Only a punch in the dick, I thought.

I smiled sweetly. "Like hells. I don't know what you want with a dump like this anyway. Since when were you into nightclubs?" The garage was more his speed. Used-car yards. Malls. Apartment blocks.

He shrugged. "I thought I would diversify my portfolio. I wouldn't want to put all my eggs into one basket, would I now? My father made that mistake, I don't need to repeat it."

"He made a lot of mistakes," I agreed. Like ejaculating into Alistair's mother.

"Like leaving you alive and unbroken," Dagen said. "He was always a sucker for a pretty face." He narrowed his eyes at me.

"You think I'm pretty?" Jake asked. "Thanks, I'm touched."

"Tell me something." Dagen turned his gaze to Jake. "You had the money, the resources and the contacts. Why did you not take on my father yourself? Why do nothing for so many years, then hide behind her skirts?"

Jake stiffened visibly. "I wasn't doing *nothing*, I was biding my time. Waiting for someone the pack would follow. That's Ivory, if only because she has a much better ass than I do."

"Yes, she does," Dagen agreed. "But that doesn't make someone a good alpha."

"That's true," Jake admitted. "She has other qualities."

"I'm sure she does." Dagen eyed my chest.

I was starting to reconsider the wisdom of not killing him. Maybe the hassle it would cause would be worth it not to have him looking at me like I was a piece of meat.

"We should go. We have business to attend to," I said as if I thought he was just lazing around.

"Leaving so soon?" Dagen asked. "But I haven't had the fun of kicking you out yet. Or having you killed."

"That wouldn't be very hospitable," Jake said. "We didn't kill you when you were in Crimson the other night."

Maybe we should have.

"That's why I'm letting you leave," Dagen said. There was more to it, I saw it in his shifty eyes. He was up to something, and whatever it was, it wasn't good.

"How kind of you," I said sarcastically.

"Yes it is," he agreed. He leaned in and whispered in my ear. "This time. Next time, things will be very different." His hot breath brushed my neck.

I suppressed a shudder.

He leaned back and I saw in his eyes that he was aware of his effect on me. I wanted to wipe the smug expression of his face with my fingernails. I might have tried if I didn't think he would enjoy it.

"What makes you think there will be a next time?" I asked. My ice queen façade was firmly back in place. "I can't see any reason why I would step foot back in here. Can you, Jake?"

"Nope," he agreed. "Not one." He looked like he was ready to punch Alistair in the face. Either he heard what the man said to me, or he could tell it was a threat.

Dagen clicked his tongue. "Don't be so literal. It doesn't have to be here. It could be," he spread his hands, "anywhere." He gave me a long look. It didn't take a genius to tell what he was thinking. In his mind he had me naked and on my knees. Or bent over something.

In my mind, he was lying in a pool of his own blood. I liked mine better.

I gave him an ice cold look, turned and started toward the door.

"He's a piece of work, isn't he?" Jake said once we were back outside.

"He's a piece of *shit*," I said. "I wish I knew what he was up to."

"Personally, I think he's all talk," Jake said. "He wants to rattle us. Don't give him the satisfaction."

I exhaled out my nose. "The only thing I want to give him is a one-way ticket to the seven hells. Remind me again why we don't kill him."

"Because if it's not him, it will be someone else from the Onyx Ridge pack," Jake said. "Some of them are worse."

Right now I was having a hard time picturing anything worse. "If he pushes my patience any further, I might have to change my mind. Have someone keep an eye on him. I want to know what he's doing before he even knows it."

"Someone like Hutton?" Jake asked. "He wants a chance to prove himself."

Hutton wouldn't like it, but I nodded. "Do it." Whatever it took to get one up on Alistair Dagen.

TWELVE

I was right, Hutton didn't like it. At first I thought he would give us a flat no. That he would walk out the door and disappear again. Hide like he had for nearly a decade.

"If I look like I'm going back, then everyone will hate my guts," he said finally. "They'll assume he," he nodded towards Jake, "is right that I'm a traitor."

"I *am* right," Jake said coldly. "That's exactly what you are. If you want a chance to convince us you can be more than that, here it is. Take it or fuck off. Better yet, Cooper over there is looking for an excuse to tear your heart out with his claws. Right, Cooper?"

Cooper cocked his head at Hutton and spoke like he was explaining why he had a favourite flavour of ice cream. "Not *specifically* your heart. Your head or throat would work too. I mean, not just yours either. People who aren't on our side in general. Y'know? It's nothing personal."

In spite of his words, I had a feeling he didn't really want to kill Hutton. The two shared the same brotherly vibe Cooper and Jake shared. He'd still do it if I asked.

"You really enjoyed killing that assassin, didn't you?" Jake asked him.

Cooper grinned. "Watching him die made me feel powerful. It was a rush. Almost as good as sex." He turned his smile on me.

Thank the gods his only sexual experience was better than killing someone. I still had it. That was gratifying to know. Better than murder. I should get that on a t-shirt.

"You're a bloodthirsty little prick," Jake said approvingly. "We have that in common."

"That and other things," Cooper said. His eyes were still on me.

"Anyway," I said. I turned to Hutton. "If you can help us, I will make it absolutely clear to everyone whose side you're on. The same will happen if I see any sign that you're planning on betraying us. You'll have more to worry about than Cooper."

Hutton nodded. "It seems like I don't have a choice."

"You don't," I agreed. "You said you would do anything. This is what we need you to do."

"Dagen is going to take some convincing that I want to work with him again," Hutton said.

"We've already put the word out there that Ivory thinks you're a traitor," Jake said. "It won't take long for it to reach him. Once he knows we rejected you, the Onyx Ridge Pack might try to contact you. The enemy of my enemy and all that."

Hutton bared his teeth at Jake. "So you already put my head on the chopping block. It's a fucking miracle I wasn't murdered on the way here."

Jake shrugged. "That was a risk I was willing to take."

"You really don't like him, do you?" Cooper asked.

"I can't think of a reason why I should," Jake said. "He's a lowlife."

"I like him," Cooper said. "Maybe you should give him a chance."

"Maybe you shouldn't be so fucking naïve, kid," Jake snarled. "You have no idea what it was like back then. You don't want to know."

"But I—" Cooper started.

"Enough," I snapped. "We have enough shit going on without fighting amongst ourselves. The past is in the past, leave it the fuck there. Focus on the present and future. That's all that matters right now. Got it?" I looked around at all three guys.

Jake's jaw was set firm, but he nodded. "Yeah, boss. We'll play nice." As if he wasn't the one doing the provoking.

"I always play nice," Cooper said.

"This is all sorts of fucked up," Hutton said with a grunt. "Fine, I'll be your spy. Chances are, Dagen will take one look at me and have me killed. They won't forget I turned my back on them. I'm starting to think I should have stayed lost."

"No shit," Jake said. "But you didn't. Now you have to be a grown-up about the choice you made."

Hutton looked at me. "How do you put up with this asshole?" He jerked a thumb towards Jake.

"I'm starting to wonder how I put up with any of you." I watched out the office window as a small boat sailed past. It looked like a nice day on the harbour. Sometimes I wondered what it would be like to have a simple life.

Then I remembered, I would probably be bored.

"At least I'm nice," Cooper said. "You're not gonna kick me out, are you?" He actually looked worried.

"Not today," I said. "But I make no promises if you start to behave like those two."

Cooper puffed out his chest and looked smug. "I won't."

"When you're as old as us you will," Jake said. "This lifestyle leaves people bitter, twisted and fucked up. All the good things."

Hutton nodded. "None of those things are good, but the asshole is right. Pack wars leave scars."

"Are you still here?" Jake asked. "Fuck off and spy."

Hutton gave me a look like he really couldn't believe I associated with Jake, much less fucked him.

The pair were like a couple of dogs fighting over a bone. I wasn't sure I liked that analogy much. I preferred to be licked and sucked rather than chewed.

"Ben will have a phone for you," I said. "The number to contact me is programmed into it. If you get into trouble, I will do what I can. That might be nothing."

He nodded. "Understood. I can handle myself." He pointed a finger at Jake, who had opened his mouth to make some sort of smart ass comment. "I'm not talking about my cock."

"Right." Jake drew the word out. "If you say so."

Hutton leaned over so he was almost nose to nose with Jake. "Not only do I say so, asshole, I'm going to be so useful to Ivory, the only one handling my cock when this is over will be her."

I raised my eyebrows at him. His absolute certainty sent butterflies fluttering through my stomach. Apparently I liked when guys got all alpha and possessive. If he proved himself, *when* he proved himself, I might just see if sex with him was better than killing. I had a feeling it would be, but the bar was pretty high.

Jake put a hand on his chest and pushed him back. "Never gonna happen, *asshole.*"

"That's up to her," Hutton said. "Not you." He shot me a panty-melting smile and stalked out of the office.

"You know, he calls me asshole more than Dagen does," Jake mused.

"Dagen probably says it where you can't hear," Cooper pointed out. "I mean, you wouldn't know, would you?"

Jake shrugged. "That's true, I guess. What sort of motherfucker talks about people behind their back?"

"Isn't that what we're doing right now?" Cooper asked.

"Yeah, but it's us. And he's him." Jake pulled a lollipop out of his pocket, took off the wrapper and stuck it in his mouth. "He deserves to be talked about."

"What the hells?" I asked him.

"Oh, sorry." He got up, walked over to a desk and opened a drawer. He pulled out an apple and tossed it to me. "I'd offer you a lollipop, but they're terrible for your teeth."

I was tempted to hurl the apple at his head, but I was hungry, so I bit into it instead. "One of these days, Jake Blakesley..."

"No one looks after you like I do," he said.

"I don't need looking after," I said darkly. "And if I want a lollipop, I'll fucking eat one."

"Do you?" he asked.

"Do I what?" I frowned at him.

"Want a lollipop," he said reasonably.

"No," I said. "But you're missing the point. I'm a grown woman, I can eat whatever I want." I knew as well as he did, that left my own devices I would probably eat whatever junk food came to hand. Still, he needed to stop treating me like I was a baby.

I finished the apple and tossed the core into the bin. "I'm going down to the gym. I need to work off some steam."

"I'll come with you," Cooper said.

"Fine." I finished scowling at Jake and turned a dazzling smile on Cooper. "If you can keep up, that is." He was obviously fit. I would be the one trying to keep up with him, but it didn't hurt to give him a challenge. Or a tease at least.

He grinned. "I can keep up. Are you coming, Jake?"

"Another time," Jake said distractedly. "I have a few things I need to deal with." He shook his head when I gave him a questioning look. "Nothing to worry about. Just tying up some loose ends and shit."

I nodded. "Okay." If he was anyone else, I would stick around until he told me what was going on. Since it was Jake, I trusted him to do what he thought needed to be done. He was probably just figuring out the best time and place to dispense of Haigwood. Those were details I didn't care to hear about. I just wanted to know when it was done.

Cooper followed me down to the gym in the basement and waited while I got changed into shorts and a t-shirt. I pulled my hair into a ponytail and tied it back with a hair tie.

"You look so cute," Cooper said when I stepped out of the changing area. He looked pretty cute himself, in shorts and a singlet. Okay, cute wasn't the right word for him. Hot as fuck comes to mind. His body was insane.

Part of me wanted to skip the workout and jump his bones. I'm sure he wouldn't have minded, but I really did need the exercise. More than just needing it, I wanted it. I liked the feeling of sweat trickling down my body after a good, hard workout session. It helped ease my stress and get my head back in the game.

Then I would jump his bones.

I sighed dramatically. "Cute? I'm a professional criminal. Head of one of the biggest criminal organisations in the country. And I get called cute." I pouted playfully.

Cooper gave me his best puppy dog eyes. "Awww, sorry." He put his arms around me and buried his face in my neck. "You're a badass, sexy, smoking hot, smart, beautiful woman."

"That's better," I said. I slid my hands around to his muscular back. Gods, was there anywhere on this guy that wasn't muscle?

"But you're also cute," he added. He tried to dodge out of the way, but I still managed to sock him on the chest.

"You're a brat," I said. "Lucky for you, you're a hot brat."

"Really?" He grinned slowly. "You think I'm hot?"

I wasn't sure if he was fishing for compliments, or really wasn't confident about his body. Fair enough, I wasn't confident at his age either. Great, now I felt old. I was only seven years older. That was barely anything. I did have a lot of life experience weighing me down though. So would he, if he stuck around me. I should push him away, but that ship sailed already. I might scare him off someday, but he was in, like it or not, for now.

"You're definitely hot," I said firmly. "I'm not in the habit of spending over a million dollars to get a guy's attention."

"I thought you just wanted to get me out of a sticky situation," he said.

"That too," I agreed. I wrapped my arms around his neck and pulled him down so I could kiss him. "I also wanted to get you *into* a sticky situation."

He chuckled against my mouth. "I didn't mind a bit." While he kissed me, he ran his hands down my body and cupped my ass cheeks. He pulled me closer to him, then reached down to hook his hands under my thighs. With what seemed like no effort at all, he picked me up until my legs were wrapped around his waist.

I already felt his erection through his shorts and mine. "We're supposed to be exercising."

"Sex is exercise," he said between kisses. He carried me a few steps to the wall and pressed my back to it. "It's good for burning calories."

I wanted to laugh and remind him Jake hardly let me eat any calories, but I didn't want to talk about that right now. I didn't want to talk about anything. Especially when he slid his hands up my shirt and cupped my breasts.

"We should really do a workout first," I said between increasingly frantic kisses.

"After." He tugged my shirt off over my head and dropped it on the ground. "I need you right now." He ground his erection into me and groaned. "Need you so bad."

After a couple of tries, he unhooked my bra and worked it

down my arms. He held me firmly in place while I let go to slide the straps down over my hands.

"God, you are so beautiful," he said breathlessly. He pushed me up a little higher so he could wrap his mouth around my nipple and suck.

I pulled up the back of his shirt and pulled it over his head. He held me in place with one hand, then the other while he pulled it off. It joined my clothes on the floor.

"Are you even real?" I asked as I traced circles around his chest with my fingertips. "You feel real, but you look far too incredible." I had seen a lot of hot guys in my day, including Jake, but Cooper was... in some sort of league of his own. Or something.

He made all rational thoughts leave my brain and go straight to my hungry pussy. In the back of my mind, I knew how dangerous that was. He made me more off guard than I should be. I should be looking out for threats to my life, but instead I was too busy thinking about getting his cock into me as soon as possible.

He chuckled. "I was going to," he licked my other nipple, "say the same about you. My cock has never been so hard, and I'm nineteen—nearly twenty."

Reminding me how young he was made me feel like a predator. But I was a criminal and a wolf, so predator came with the territory. At least he wasn't underage.

He lowered me to my feet just long enough to yank off my shorts and panties. I helped him out of his just as quickly.

He picked me up again and held me there with one hand while with his other, he positioned his cock outside the entrance to my pussy. He teased me for a while, brushing against my clit, then rubbing more firmly until I was panting and wet.

I groaned. "Please. I need you inside me."

"Soon." He was almost as breathless with need. "You're going to wait until I'm ready."

Gods, that was hot. I liked that he wanted to take control. As long as it didn't spill over into our work life.

I rubbed against him and tried to push my pussy onto his cock. I only had so much patience at the best of times.

"Not yet," he scolded. "And don't come either. Not till I tell you to."

"You suck," I said playfully. "You need it as much as I do."

"More," he said. "I laid awake all night listening to you and Jake. I got myself off once or twice, but it's not as good as this."

Okay, so the idea of him listening and touching himself made me melt a little further.

"We should all play together some time," I said. Oh yeah, I would *happily* be the meat in a Jake and Cooper sandwich. Bring it on.

"Yes please," he said. He slid his cock over my clit. His tip was already slick with precum.

"Coop Wheeler, if you don't fuck me..." I growled.

"What will you do?" he asked teasingly. He let go of his cock and grabbed both of my wrists in one hand. He raised them above my head and pinned them to the wall. He locked his gaze on mine.

I saw no sign in there of a naïve young man. Instead, he was confident, dominant. Determined that I would play by his rules. This was different from Jake's possessive, alpha dominance. This was a young wolf asserting himself.

It was sexy as fuck.

"I'll wait until you're ready to fuck me," I said. I wasn't meek, not for a moment. It was not a battle of wills, because I would have won that. It was a compromise. I would let him have this moment, in return for many others.

"Hells yeah," he said. He drove himself into me, hard. So hard I almost screamed and came on the spot.

I saw a flicker of hesitation on his face, concerned that he'd hurt me. In the next second, it was gone. He pounded relentlessly, hard, fast and firm.

Pinned as I was to the wall, all I could do was match his rhythm as best I could. I rolled my hips and adjusted so he could slam in deeper.

"Ivory," he said breathlessly. "You are... Everything."

"Hells yeah, I am," I agreed breathlessly. "Don't you forget it."

"I will never forget it," he said firmly. "I could never forget you." He gritted his teeth and ground his balls against the entrance to my pussy. "Fuck yeah."

He paused for a moment to slam his lips into mine. His kiss was as furious as his thrusts. His tongue pushed deep into my mouth, almost to the back of my throat.

I sucked on it like it was his cock.

"Mmmm." He simultaneously thrust into my mouth and my pussy.

It made me lightheaded and more aroused than ever.

He broke off the kiss long enough to say, "Come for me."

I couldn't have waited a second longer anyway. I came so fiercely it was almost painful. Wonderful, beautiful pain that filled every part of me and made my pulse spike better than any adrenaline rush.

He followed me half a second later. His grunts and groans filled the gym better than any exercise class. His hand tightened around my wrists, and he pressed me more firmly against the wall. He drove in with harder strokes like his life depended on it.

He let out a deep, guttural growl from the back of his throat. If he was in wolf form, he probably would have howled.

I cried out with him. My breath came in hard pants that got softer and softer as I came down from my high.

"Oh. My. Gods," he said. "Sex is way better than I ever imagined. Or maybe it's just you."

I laughed softly. "It's definitely just me," I joked.

He kissed me lightly. "That sounds accurate. Because you're pretty fucking epic. Now, we should do a workout."

I made a face. I had forgotten about that. "I guess we should." A lot of my frustration at dealing with Dagen was gone, but there was still some left in the back of my mind. Probably more than just a workout was going to eradicate, but it was a start.

THIRTEEN

"Good workout?" Jake asked as I stepped back into the office, Cooper at my heels. He peered at us over the rim of his reading glasses. It was clear from his expression he knew more than a workout went on. Or at least he suspected.

"Have you got a camera down there?" I slipped into a chair behind my computer and raised my eyebrows at him.

He grinned. "We have cameras everywhere. For security purposes, of course."

I snorted. "Of course." I had no intention, or need, to apologise for anything he saw when he was spying on me.

Cooper smiled and settled into a chair. "I'd like to see the footage if you recorded it."

"As it happens, I did," Jake said. "We can watch it later with some popcorn."

I opened my laptop and logged on. "What else have you been doing? Anything useful?" I rolled my eyes at him, but he just grinned back.

"Just running background checks on the Lair's staff. Most of them are demons, but a couple are witches. Some are actually human. One or two are shifters."

I nodded and tapped at my keyboard. "I can't help thinking Dagen buying the Lair didn't happen in isolation. He also made an offer on the garage." I nodded towards Cooper. "We always keep a close eye on anything that comes up for sale, whether we want to buy it or not, but I feel like we missed something."

I brought up files on the real estate listings and sales for the last two to three years.

"We would have noticed a pattern," Jake said.

"Only if it was obvious," I said. "He bought the Lair under Black Wolf Holdings. He wanted us to notice that." Anything I bought legally was purchased under White Wolf, unless it was shady. That stuff was under Ivory Claw, or one of my smaller companies.

"I'll help you look." Cooper pulled a chair over closer. Close enough that our shoulders touched. "What are we looking for, exactly?"

"I'm not sure," I admitted. "Something so subtle it was easily missed."

Cooper peered at the screen. "Is Dagen's name really Dagen?"

"Yes, why?" I asked.

"Well, your real name isn't Ivory? Is it?" Cooper asked. "And your last name isn't Claw."

I smiled. "Are you sure about that?"

He blinked a couple of times. "I'm pretty sure."

"It's not," I assured him. "But as far as I know Dagen is his name. Although, Asshole suits him better."

Cooper grinned. His smile faded and he pointed at the screen. "Someone named Tony Jones bought a hairdressing salon down the street. He also bought a computer repair shop. No one is going to look twice at a bunch of technology coming in and out. Have you had a problem with hackers?"

Jake's head jerked up. He looked outraged. "We have professional hackers on the payroll to prevent other hackers from hacking us."

"Say that three times fast." Cooper chuckled.

I laughed softly. "His point is, they won't get in here. That doesn't mean they haven't tried." I looked over to Jake.

He nodded. "I'll look into it." He seemed certain he wouldn't find anything. It was his job to know if they had, as much as it was mine.

"Has this Tony Jones bought anything else?" I said, half under my breath.

"I don't know, but don't you think Tony Jones is a good name for a gangster?" Cooper said. He seemed to like the idea.

"It's not as good as mine," I said distractedly. I was checking out every name on the list now.

"Can I ask you a question?" Cooper asked.

"Yeah, what?" I said.

"What is your real name?" he asked.

I hesitated. I glanced over at Jake, who shrugged. I had gone by Ivory for so long, I only thought about my birth name when Jake or Asshole called me that. It wasn't so much a secret as just... not me anymore. And it was an intimate thing between Jake and I.

"Hey look, here's another one," Cooper said before I could respond to his question. "Two and a half years ago, Tony Jones bought a newspaper stand. All the better to spy on us with?"

"Well spotted," I agreed.

"Should we go and talk to this Tony Jones guy?" Cooper asked. He looked like he was ready to jump up and down in this chair.

"Settle down, Murder Puppy," Jake said. "Let me see what I can find on this guy first."

Cooper sat back. "There might be more."

We kept on looking, but the only other people who appeared to have bought more than one property was us.

"Why a hairdressing salon?" I said finally.

"It looks harmless?" Cooper suggested.

"Like you," I teased.

He grinned. "Exactly." He leaned in to plant a lingering kiss on my mouth. "On the outside, I look like a nice guy. On the inside I'm—"

"A murder puppy," I finished for him.

"Is that my nickname?" He didn't seem bothered by that. "Ivory and the Murder Puppy. I like the sound of that. What is Jake's nickname?"

"The only people who give me nicknames are my enemies," Jake said without looking up from his screen.

"They're your enemies because they give you nicknames, or only your enemies give them to you?" Cooper asked teasingly.

"Both," Jake said. "Would it surprise you to learn this Tony Jones doesn't seem to exist?"

"I'm shocked," I said sarcastically. "How many other people who bought real estate in the area in the last few years also didn't exist?"

"Apart from us?" Jake quirked an eyebrow at me. "I'm guessing the number is higher than zero. I'll look into it."

I nodded. "Go back as far as you can. We don't know how long this has been going on." We should have suspected it, but the uneasy peace seemed to have kept Dagen in his box for the most part. My father used to say 'complacency is your enemy.' He was right about that. He was a very good example of where complacency got you. In his case, it was with his brains spread across the wall.

"If Tony Jones doesn't exist, then can we go and talk to him?" Cooper asked.

"I feel like that sentence shouldn't make any sense," I said. "I think it would be a good idea to go and take a personal look at his establishments."

"I wish he owned a bakery, or a donut shop." Jake stretched his arms over his head. "I could use some sugar right now."

"You'll have to settle for a trim," I told him dryly. Now that he mentioned sugar, I would kill for one of those custard and apple filled pastry things. Jake couldn't even object to it, since apples were a fruit. At this point, if he objected, he might get a pie to the face, courtesy of my hand. Knowing him, he'd wipe it off and eat it. Also knowing him, he would prefer to cream pie my pussy than have me cream pie his face.

"Newspaper stands usually sell snack food," Cooper said helpfully.

"Let's go there first," Jake said quickly. He opened the drawer beside him.

"If you're about to pull out an apple and give it to me, I'm gonna stuff it up your ass," I growled.

He closed the drawer again.

"If I had a drawer, I would keep jelly beans in there for you," Cooper said. "Do you like the black ones?"

I grimaced. "No. Yuck. I like the red ones and the white ones. And the purple ones. But if you did that, Jake would eat them all."

"Only to save you from all that sugar," Jake protested. "Not all heroes wear capes."

"Some of them are going to wear their face on the back of their heads if they don't back the fuck off," I said with mock sweetness.

"I'd like to see that." Cooper grinned.

Jake narrowed his eyes at him. "Who the fuck's side are you on, Murder Puppy?"

"Hers," Cooper said without missing a beat. "I'm sorry but you've seen her ass."

"Many times," Jake agreed. "I never get tired of seeing it. But mine is pretty impressive too, don't you think?"

"Of course," Cooper agreed. "But if yours is a ten, hers is a fifteen. I'm sorry, that's just the way I see it. Besides, she's the boss."

"Exactly," I said. "Always take the boss's side, regardless of the awesomeness of their ass."

"But an awesome ass doesn't hurt," Jake said.

"No it doesn't," I agreed. "Right then, let's go to this newsstand. I have a sudden need to satisfy my craving for jellybeans. And maybe get a magazine."

Did they even sell those at newsstands anymore? So much was digital these days, newsstands probably sold more snacks and bus tickets than papers.

"We should take Ben along with us too," Jake said. "With Dagen sniffing around, I'd rather be safe than conspicuous."

I considered that for a moment. I would rather be both. Nothing says 'look at me.' like walking down the street with three hot guys.

"Can you ever be inconspicuous?" Cooper asked. He watched me as I stood. "I don't know about anyone else, but I can't take my eyes off you when you walk into a room."

The feeling was entirely mutual.

"You're right, she can't," Jake said. "But that's the image she's spent years building. When she walks into a room, people pay attention. It's great until she wants to sneak around."

"Maybe I should wear a wig," I said dryly. "No one would recognise me as a redhead."

"I still would," Jake said. "I would recognise you anywhere. You could change everything about you and you would still have the presence to make people notice you. So maybe you should sit this one out. Let the pup sniff around."

I considered it for a moment. Finally, I shook my head. "No. I want Asshole to know we're sniffing around. Let him know we're onto his bullshit. Besides, the mysterious Tony Jones might not have anything to do with Dagen. He might be a regular, old human criminal. Or a front for someone else. If anyone else is trying to muscle in on my territory, they better know we're coming for them."

"And then they'll have their face on the other side of their head?" Cooper asked hopefully.

"Exactly," I agreed. I didn't know how I would do that, but it sounded like fun.

I led the way to the door and nodded for Ben to follow us. He looked at me and the other guys with a brief, but intense look. I could almost see him wondering where this left us and our occasional hookups. Truthfully, I didn't know. We'd known each other as long as Jake and I. Jake actually hired him to guard me after the auction. There was little about me he didn't know. And the man knew what to do with his tongue.

The question was, how complicated did I really need my life to be? That was yet another question for later. In the meantime, I offered him a smile. He responded with a faint one back, and a nod. He was never anything but professional when other people were around.

I rode the elevator down to the bottom of the building with a car full of testosterone. The smell was delicious. For a solid minute, I considered pressing the stop button and seeing how many orgasms I could have before someone tried to get us out. If we weren't on business, I might have. Besides, Jake and Cooper agreed to share, but Ben was a whole other conversation. One I wasn't ready for yet.

The newsstand was only two blocks down the street, so we walked. Jake took his place beside me, his hand on my back, while the other two guys walked in front and behind. We absolutely didn't go unnoticed. In fact, several people, men and women, stopped to gape at Cooper. And he said *I* wasn't conspicuous. Even with clothes on, he was a walking bag of sex. A human boner. A wet dream. A... You get it.

The gods knew Jake was just as hot, but in a dangerous, coiled aggression kind of way. No one would ever mistake him for someone who was harmless.

Ben—he looked like a bodyguard, with his dark trousers and vigilant, intense gaze. If there was something out of place, he'd notice it.

If the woman who worked at the newsstand was spying on us for Dagen, I would eat my left Louboutin. She looked younger than Cooper and smelled of pure human. And anxiety.

"Can... Can I help you?" she asked. "I'm sorry, this is only my second day. The guy who was here quit suddenly. I'm still trying to figure everything out."

I exchanged glances with Jake. No, that didn't sound suspicious at all.

"That's unfortunate," I told her. "I quite liked," I frowned, "what was his name?"

"Jason," the woman said. "Apparently he had some family stuff to deal with."

I nodded. "Jason. Of course. Well, I hope everything is okay with him. In the meantime, do you have any jelly beans?" I saw them the moment I walked up, but it didn't hurt to let her serve me. If I was nice, she would remember me, and she might come in useful someday. Or Dagen was using her and she would end up floating in the harbour in a day or two. Either way, I wasn't going to lose any sleep over it.

She pointed me to them and then moved over to serve another customer.

I grabbed a packet or two and ignored the look Jake gave me. "If you want some, you better buy your own," I told him.

He grabbed a couple but frowned around at the stand. "I have a feeling we need to get the fuck out of here."

His words and tone made the hair on the back of my neck stand up. Whatever vibe he caught, I caught it too now.

"Yeah," Ben said softly. He frowned, like he couldn't put his finger on what was up. If he was on edge, then so was I.

I nodded and placed the jelly beans on the counter in the centre of the stand. Jake added another two packets and three packets of corn chips. When I raised my eyebrows at him, he added three packets of salt and vinegar chips to the pile.

"Are you going to let me eat some of that?" I asked.

He leaned in to whisper in my ear. "I'm going to eat all the jelly beans and make my cum so sweet you won't be able to stop drinking it."

"The hells you are," I said. I was absolutely eating some of it. And his cum. I paid for everything and picked up my jellybeans and a bag of each of the chips. "Besides, it's tasty enough as it is." I gave him a smile, but I doubted anyone who was paying attention would miss the edge in my expression. I wanted to get away from here as quickly as possible.

"Come on, Pup," Jake said to Cooper. "We're stocked up on crap food for a while." He spoke lightly, but I knew that expression on his face. Every nerve in his body was on alert. He didn't know what he was looking for, but he knew he was looking for something. Call it wolf instincts, or too many years of having to watch our backs, but he sensed something. He appeared as unnerved as Ben.

"What is that?" Cooper asked after we took a few steps away. "There's a weird smell in the air."

Jake swung his head around to stare at Cooper, then sniffed. "Fuck, you're right. The hells is it?"

I sniffed and shook my head. "It smells like rotting fruit." I turned my head. "And it seems to be coming from—"

I looked directly at the newsstand as it was blasted to smithereens.

FOURTEEN

All three of the guys shoved me to the ground and threw themselves around me to shield me from the blast. They were lucky they didn't slam me face first into the ground. Getting injured in the explosion would be the least of their troubles if I broke my nose.

Instead, I ended up on my knees, my head down over them, arms over my face.

The explosion went on for what seemed like days. In reality, it was only a matter of seconds. Terrifying seconds in which I was almost sure I was about to die. I was going to end up in chunks like my parents had. No one would ever know it was me, because I made sure to have anything that would identify me erased from any databases anywhere in the world.

The worst part was, I didn't get to eat my jelly beans first. Yeah, okay, weird things cross your mind when you're sure you're going to die.

I slowly became aware the world had fallen still. My ears were ringing. It filtered out the sound of screaming and then the sound of sirens approaching the area.

"Ivory?" I realised Jake had said my name several times already. "Ivory? El?"

Gradually, I worked my way out of my state of shock. I blinked a few times and shook my head.

"I'm okay." I let him help me to my feet and looked around.

Where the newsstand was, only now a smouldering mess of metal and the remains of the woman who worked there were left. Several people lay close by, dead or badly injured.

"Shit," Cooper said softly. He had a gash on his cheek from where something hit him, but he otherwise looked okay.

Ben staggered to his feet with Jake's help and rubbed the back of his head. His hand came away red with blood, but he waved Jake off. "It's just a graze." He must have tried to shield all of us. He was incredibly lucky he wasn't killed as well. Was it wrong that I found that incredibly hot?

"Should we get out of here?" Cooper asked.

The sirens were getting closer.

"Can you walk?" Jake asked me.

"Yeah. I'm fine." I practically had a brick wall of guys between me and the blast. I was pissed off, but not hurt. I would have been even more pissed off if any of us died.

Jake grabbed my hand and led me away at a slow walk, while people came running from the buildings around us.

"That was too fucking close," Jake growled. "If the mother-fucker wants a war, then he's going to fucking get one."

"Lucky we didn't go for a haircut," I said.

Jake snorted his agreement.

"This is all kinds of fucked up," Cooper said. He looked a little dazed. He stopped and looked back at the carnage.

I dropped back slightly to talk to Ben. "Do you need to see a paramedic?"

He shook his head slowly. "No. I'm fine, boss. Thanks. I'll have a headache later, but no harm done otherwise." The back of his hair was matted with blood, but if he said he was okay, I had no choice but to believe him.

"That was badass," I said softly. I reached for his hand—the one not covered in blood, and gave it a squeeze.

He squeezed back and offered me a faint smile. "I try to be a badass as often as I can. I like that you noticed." The look he gave me went beyond professional. I suspected my return gaze did as well. If he died, I'd be more than pissed. It's funny how you don't really see what's in front of you until it's almost gone. Hells, why not complicate life a bit more? Our time on this planet was too short not to take risks.

"I always notice," I assured him. I realised I was still holding his hand and let it go. I caught Jake's glance, but he looked unworried. He was used to there being something between Ben and I. He might have assumed it would go further some day. As long as I didn't lock him out again, he was okay with it.

I turned my attention to Cooper, who was still glassy eyed. "Are you all right?"

He blinked. "Yeah, I guess. Just... This death thing doesn't seem like so much fun when it's almost you."

I snorted softly. "No. It really isn't. I would have to suggest he knows we're onto him now." Dagen must have realised we would go looking in the database once we heard about him buying the Lair. That, or someone told him we were coming.

"This is bullshit," Jake growled.

"It is," I agreed. "But at least we got out alive."

"Thank the gods for that but..." He waved a hand back toward the mangled newsstand. "We were supposed to do that. We're supposed to blow up *his* shit. He's not supposed to blow up his own shit to kill us. Who does that? It's fucked up."

I stopped and looked up at him. "You're pissed because he blew up his own property, and you missed out on doing it?"

He looked like he was struggling to deny it. "A little bit," he admitted. "But mostly it's because he could have killed us. He could have killed *you*."

"Pfft, I'm not that easy to kill," I said lightly. "He's tried twice now in two days and I'm still standing."

"It's the first bit I'm worried about." Jake ran a hand over his head. "He's tried to kill you. He's not going to go to all this effort and then just give up because he didn't succeed the first two times. He'll keep coming until he succeeds. Or we get to him first."

"At least he stopped me from eating those jelly beans," I pointed out.

Jake looked like he didn't know if he should be angry, or laugh in response to that. "I would prefer you to eat crap food than get blown up." He exhaled hard out his nose like an angry, fire breathing dragon. It was kinda sexy, seeing him like this. Furious, but alive. Especially the alive part. I'm fucked up, but I'm not that fucked up.

"Does that mean you're going to lay off on what I eat?" I asked.

"Nope," he said lightly, but immediately. "You might need to outrun him someday. Eating jelly beans would make it that much harder to do."

"Spoilsport," I teased.

"I still have mine." Cooper's hand trembled, but he held out a bag of jelly beans and one of chips.

"Shit gets blown up, but you hold on to the food?" Jake asked, disbelieving.

Cooper shrugged. "I guess I had them in my fist." They were both somewhat crushed, but more or less intact. "I'm not hungry anymore." He held them out to me, but Jake grabbed them first and dropped them in a bin as we walked past.

"We need a proper meal after this," he said firmly. "All of us. Maybe steak."

"I could eat steak," I agreed. Like Cooper, I wasn't actually hungry either.

"Me too," Ben agreed. He touched his head again, but the blood seemed to have dried already. That was fortunate. I would have insisted he see a witch otherwise. I might anyway. We couldn't risk losing him just because of the way he felt about them.

"I guess I could try one," Cooper agreed.

"Good." Jake patted him on the shoulder. "Besides, Ivory is going to need another shower and change of clothes."

I looked at myself and grimaced. My nice white blouse was now streaked with dirt and the gods knew what else. My skirt had a tear in it from where I'd fallen to my knees. My hair was probably a mess. On the up side, my shoes looked undamaged.

That was a win.

They wouldn't stay that way very long if I saw Alistair Dagen in the next five minutes. I would probably stab my heels into his skull. Why not? My blouse was already messy, it might as well have blood and brains on it too.

"I feel like I spend half my life in this shower these days," I said. "And the other half ordering new clothes."

"What part about that are you objecting to?" Jake asked.

"Neither of them," I replied. "I was just saying, that's all."

"The shower seems like a good place for you." He gave me a steady look. "You might be safer in there."

"And a lot more naked," Cooper said. Apparently he recovered from his shock. There was nothing like talking about, or thinking about sex to make someone recover quickly. Especially a guy. Okay, and especially me. And all the other women in those delicious groups on social media. And...

Okay, it's pretty universal.

Ben smiled, but he didn't disagree.

"You guys are not going to put me in a box for the rest of my life to keep me safe," I said firmly.

"Actually, I was going to stay in the shower with you," Jake said. "To keep me safe. You'll protect me, right?" He wiggled his brows.

"Me too," Cooper said. He frowned briefly, then added, "What is El short for?" He looked from me to Jake and back again. "I heard him call you that."

The side of my mouth drew back. "It's short for Elodie. That's the name I was born with."

He smiled. "That's pretty." After a moment, he added, "Can I keep calling you Ivory? It sounds so badass."

I smiled back at him. "Please do. Especially in front of other people." I gave Jake a meaningful glance.

He shrugged. "I didn't think anyone was listening. And I was worried about you. And you were going to tell him sooner or later. And Ben already knows."

"I guess so," I agreed.

"I feel like I just got membership into some exclusive club," Cooper said. He looked awed.

Sometimes he was so fucking cute I couldn't believe it.

I laughed softly. "You got that the moment I won your auction. And let me fuck you." The connection I had with the guy was so damn strong it was almost scary. Especially since we'd known each other for a handful of days. The bond I had with Jake grew over time, and was irreplaceable, but this was no less real. And Ben... That was something I needed to think about later. And then there was Hutton.

All of this thinking about guys and relationships was starting to make my body throb with heat. Nothing would ever be simple again, would it?

"We should hurry," Jake said. "I don't know about you three, but I'm not in the mood to answer questions from the cops."

I wasn't worried about the police. They either worked for me or wouldn't believe me if I told them about Dagen. Either way, talking to them would be a waste of time.

"See if you can slip them some evidence or something," I said. "I doubt they'll figure it out before he tries something else." People like him and me were too good at covering their tracks. It was what we did. Sometimes I felt sorry for the cops assigned to cases like this. Many of them were decent, hard-working people. Many were paranormal like us. They knew they would never get to the bottom of this, no matter how hard they tried. And the innocent people caught up in it... That blood was on Dagen's hands.

"I'm guessing the guy who quit two days ago wasn't a coincidence," Cooper said. "I mean, that would be the mother of all coincidences. Right?"

"Coincidences are usually as real as Santa," Jake said dryly. "He's probably disappeared off the face of the planet. Either voluntarily or not so much."

"We can try to track him down when the dust settles," I said. The people in the shops and offices nearby should at least have some idea what he looked like. They wouldn't be much help right now though, not with police and ambulances crawling around the area.

"Would it be a good idea to check if the hairdresser or the computer place had a sudden change in staff?" Cooper asked.

"Absolutely it would," I agreed. "If I was the type to gamble, I would bet on it." I wasn't a gambler though. Everything I did was careful and deliberate. Okay, most things. I could be spontaneous from time to time. It helped to keep people on their toes.

"Do you want me to go and ask?" Cooper asked.

"No," Jake replied. "They know who you are by now. We'll send someone they don't know. But not yet. That's the first thing they'll be expecting us to do."

"So they'd probably have someone waiting for us," Cooper said. "Unless this Dagen asshole likes blowing shit up."

"Generally speaking, blowing up your own businesses is bad *for* business," Jake said. "I don't think he would make a habit of it."

"Right," Cooper said slowly. "They probably figured the newsstand would be the most likely place we would turn up. For all the reasons why we went there first. And destroying that causes minimal damage to everyone and everything. I mean, what's a handful of dead humans?"

"That's about right," I agreed. Dagen wouldn't give a crap about collateral damage. Whatever it took to get to us. To get to me.

I hurried my steps as we approached Crimson. Partly because I felt exposed after the explosion. And partly because I looked like shit. The guys might get away with looking rough and dirty, but with me, it wouldn't go unnoticed. All right, lately it was becoming a more regular occurrence to see me with blood or juice, or whatever all over me. I didn't want it to become a habit.

"So when Jake said we were supposed to blow up Dagen's shit," Cooper said slowly. "A few dead humans happen then too?"

"You got a problem with that?" Jake asked.

A frown flashed across Cooper's forehead. "No. I was just wondering, that's all."

"We try to avoid unnecessary carnage," I said. "I'm not a fan of bombs, arson, shooting rampages, forcing trains off the tracks, bringing down aeroplanes, stuff like that. I prefer the personal touch of having people killed face-to-face. Or by an assassin if I have to."

"Can you send one of those after Dagen?" Cooper asked. "I mean, he tried."

"If you can call that guy an assassin." Jake curled his lip. "He was about as stealthy as..." He thought for a moment. "Throwing an elephant off a rooftop."

Cooper and I both laughed.

Then Cooper asked, "We don't do that, right?"

Jake stared at him in disbelief for a moment, then started laughing so hard tears rolled down his cheeks. "Do we... Throw elephants... Off..." He slapped his thigh.

His laughter was infectious. I smiled and patted Cooper on the shoulder as we headed through the private door and into Crimson.

"Jake laughs now, but he hasn't seen my to-do list," I joked. "The next item on it is throwing a giant animal off the roof."

"Only if it's a big, black wolf," Jake said between laughs. "Or even a small one."

I snapped my fingers. "I should have invited Alistair Dagen up to the helipad the other night." Not that he would be stupid enough to go up there with me. That would be far too easy.

"There's a helipad?" Cooper asked. "Can I see?" He looked like a little boy eager to open Christmas presents early.

"After I get clean," I said firmly.

He looked disappointed for a moment but then said, "So, can we send an assassin after Dagen?"

Jake gave him the side eye. "Are you volunteering?"

Cooper's mouth opened and shut a couple of times.

I decided to put him out of his misery. "Being an assassin takes years of training. Usually they have to learn to be stealthy and careful. Sneak in, sneak out. If you want to do the training, I can sponsor you, but I hope Dagen is long dead before you finish it."

Cooper gaped at me. "Me? An assassin? That would be fucking awesome." If he looked like a boy at Christmas before, now he looked like several Christmases, half a dozen Easters and a fistful of wet dreams.

"Wouldn't hurt to have a few more on the payroll," Jake said. "I have a feeling you'll be good at it, Murder Puppy. Just imagine, you get to kill bad guys for a living."

Cooper grinned.

That, right there, is a very good reason why he would make one hells of an assassin. No one would see a guy who looked like him coming, until it was far too late.

"Then you could come home and draw a picture of your victims," Jake said cheerfully.

I shook my head at him. "That is some fucked up shit right there. Also, no, don't do that because that's evidence."

Cooper looked slightly disappointed, but he nodded. "Yeah, okay I won't do that."

"And in answer to your question," I said, "I haven't ruled out sending an assassin after Dagen. Right now though, it would be obvious who sent it. He might be trying to provoke a war, but we aren't there yet."

Jake looked like he wanted to argue, but I gave him a firm look.

"He has his toe on the line, but he hasn't crossed it. None of us died, and he hasn't blown up anything we own. Until he does, then we just keep doing what we're doing, and be careful."

"Fine," Jake said. "But if he sticks his toenail over, I'm going to chop it off. And his toe. And then the rest of him."

"Get in line," I told him.

Jake looked thoughtful. "I'm a wolf, I don't really do 'getting in line.' How about we do it as a pack?"

"Works for me," I agreed.

The elevator doors slid open to the tenth floor. Ben stepped out first, eyes cautious, vigilant.

I waited until he signalled that it was safe. It should be, it wasn't that easy for anyone but us to get up here, but we know what complacency can do. Right?

"Stay out here," Jake told him. "No one goes up or down without my say-so. I'll arrange for a witch to look at your head."

Before Ben could do more than nod and look slightly irritated, Jake ushered the rest of us into my apartment.

"I'm going to have a shower." I unbuttoned my blouse and let it slip down my arms and onto the floor.

"I have a better idea." Jake grabbed my hand and drew me to him. "How about I get you messier before you get clean?" He pressed his mouth to mine in a demanding kiss.

I felt the hooks of my bra release, but it took me a moment to realise it was Cooper who did it. He pulled my bra down off my arms and slid his arms around me from behind. He ran his hands up my belly slowly, then started to knead my breasts.

I leaned back against him, taking Jake with me.

"I think she likes the idea," Cooper said.

Jake pulled his head back and gave me a smouldering look with his dark eyes. "Good, because neither of us was asking."

Holy fuck

That sent a shiver up desire down to my core.

Cooper leaned around to kiss the side of my neck. "Nope, we're not. We're wolves. We take what we want."

That was one way to ruin a perfectly good pair of panties.

While Cooper started taking off my skirt, Jake ran his tongue around my lips and down my cheek to my neck.

I groaned softly. My body ached, but they kept their touches light except when they both grabbed the top of my panties and ripped them. They ended up with about half each.

Jake pressed his erection to the front of my leg, and Cooper into the back. It was all I could do not to beg one of them to stick a cock *somewhere*.

"Your bedroom, *now*," Jake ordered.

I had no words. All I could do was nod and do as he said. Both guys stripped on the way, leaving a trail of clothes on the floor. By the time they manoeuvred me onto the top of the covers, they were both naked.

Gods burn my soul, I wanted them both so badly. They couldn't be more different from each other, but they were both as sexy as hells.

Jake traced around my lips with the tip of his finger. "Open for me." He lay beside me, so close all I could see was his flat stomach and rock hard cock.

I opened my mouth and let him slide his cock inside my mouth.

"You can take more than that," he said. He pushed himself all the way to the back of my throat.

I tried not to gag, but he put a hand on the back of my head to keep me from pulling away. I was used to being in control. Used to taking a guy in as deep as I wanted. This was different. Letting go was difficult, but I wanted to. Needed to.

He pulled halfway out and pushed in just as deep. "Good girl."

I raised my eyebrows at him, but he only smirked in response.

Cooper hooked my legs over his shoulders and settled his face down between my thighs. There was nothing stealthy about the way his tongue went to work on me. He lapped at my folds and my clit like he'd been doing it for years. His hands slid under my hips to firmly grip my ass.

With him working my pussy, and Jake fucking my throat, I was on the verge of coming in only a minute or two. I sucked hard and bucked gently in rhythm.

"Don't let her come," Jake said to Cooper. "*We* decide when that happens."

Cooper made a sound of agreement and pulled his face back.

I made a sound of *dis*agreement, like a growl in the back of my throat. The noise was cut off by Jake ramming his cock harder into my mouth. I did gag this time, but then he slid out of me and patted my head like I was a dog.

"Roll her over," Jake said. To me, he said, "Straddle him." He reached into the draw beside my bed and pulled out some lube. Trust him to know where I kept it.

Cooper lay on his back. He gripped my hips and lowered me slowly onto his cock. "Mmm, hells yeah. Have I mentioned lately that your pussy is amazing?"

"Not lately, no," I said. "Your cock is pretty amazing too." I rolled my hips and rubbed my clit as I rode him. I closed my eyes and breathed hard out my nose.

Jake knelt behind me and bent me forward. He reached around and lightly gripped my throat. "No coming until we say so. Understood?"

I murmured to let him know I understood.

Apparently that wasn't enough. He tightened his grip slightly. "Say it."

"I understand," I said between already ragged breaths.

"Good." He let go of my throat and unscrewed the cap of the lube. He squeezed out a finger full and rubbed it all over my rear hole. He tossed the tube aside and positioned his cock outside my entrance. Slowly and gently, he eased himself inside.

"Don't tense," he said.

I swallowed hard and nodded. I was trying not to, but the feeling of two cocks inside me at the same time made me feel so full I thought I might burst. In the best way possible.

He gradually pushed himself deeper, giving me time to adjust each time. Finally, he slid all the way in and started to thrust slowly. He put his hands on my hips and guided me to keep rising and falling while he stayed inside me.

"Holy gods," Cooper whispered. "I can feel you both."

Of course, there wasn't much more than skin and muscle between my ass and my pussy. They must be bumping tips with each thrust.

Holy.

Fucking.

Hotness.

I couldn't decide what turned me on more, this, or if they touched each other directly. I decided to call it a tie and closed my eyes to enjoy every feeling, every sensation they sent through me.

After a moment or two, the three of us had a rhythm going like we practised this every day. Maybe we should.

Desire rose like a relentless tide, bearing down on me and threatening to wash me away.

"I need to come, please," I said. Gods, I was begging. Only two people in the world would ever make me beg, and they were both fucking my holes right now.

"Not yet," Jake said.

Cooper smiled up at me. "Yes, we're not ready for you to come yet." He was obviously enjoying this very much.

Hells, so was I.

I groaned with the effort of keeping an orgasm at bay. With Jake pounding at me from behind, and Cooper slamming into me from below, it took every drop of self-control I had. And a bunch I didn't know I had.

"Please." The word slipped from between my lips before I knew it. If they didn't let me come soon I was going to cry or burst. Or something. Shit was gonna get messy.

"Should we let her?" Cooper asked. Apparently he was a nicer guy than Jake. "Or we could make her last a bit longer." Or he wasn't.

Jake chuckled. "A little bit longer."

"Assholes," I told them.

As if that was somehow an invitation, they both ground into me harder than before. Faster. Deeper. I wanted to scream.

"Okay," Jake said after another minute or two. "You can come now."

I came oh, so, fucking hard I saw stars that were probably

from another universe, or some shit. I didn't care. I rode the wave to the peak and screamed my throat raw as my blood thundered through my body.

Both guys came at almost the same time, a few seconds after me. The whole world became a chorus of grunts, groans and panting. Sweat, cum and racing pulses.

The high was so delicious, it took time to come down from. That was fine with me. I could have stayed lost in it for days. Weeks. Forever.

We sagged down onto the bed together and panted, spent and messy in the most perfect way imaginable.

FIFTEEN

Ben stuck his head into the bar manager's office on the first floor. "Boss, there's a couple of cops here to talk to you." The expression on his face clearly said what he thought of that. If it was up to him, he wouldn't let them in. Truthfully, that would have been my preference too, but it was easier to deal with them and their suspicions than to brush them off and have them sniff around later.

I nodded. "Show them in." I wished they would call ahead so I could wear something more... distracting, but a deep red, silk blouse with a plunging neckline, and a black skirt with a slit halfway up my thigh, would have to do. Yeah, sometimes I wear colours other than white, and this outfit would make most guys' eyes pop out.

The male cop who stepped inside was evidence of this, but of course his partner was a woman. She had that 'I am not going to be so easy to impress' expression on her face. So many people looked like that when they first met me. Like the rest of them, she would learn.

"I am Detective Ian Gilbert, and this is Detective Fiona Singh."

He was at least in his fifties, with salt-and-pepper hair and faded blue eyes. To his credit, he tried to keep his eyes on my face. Every so often, they would want to down to my cleavage and linger there for a few moments.

"We'd like to ask you some questions," Singh said. Her gaze was firmly fixed on my face, eyes narrowed like she thought she knew what I was up to.

She didn't have a fucking clue.

"Of course." I rose and shook both of their hands, but took just a *little* bit longer with Gilbert.

His cheeks flushed.

"Please, take a seat." I sat and waved toward the chairs on the other side of the desk. "Whatever you need, I'll help as much as I can." And if I couldn't, I could always help them to the bottom of the harbour.

"You were a witness to an explosion." Singh crossed her arms over her chest.

I kept my expression icy calm. No wonder they struggled to solve cases. That was three fucking days ago. If I could, I would laugh.

Instead, I sighed. "I was near the newspaper stand when it blew up. It was terrible. I've never seen anything like it." Not on *that* day. I've witnessed plenty of carnage in my time. This one barely rated a mention.

"Why have you not come forward to give us a statement?" Singh asked.

I feigned ignorance. "Oh. Was I supposed to?" And say what, exactly? The stand was collateral damage in a pack war? They wouldn't buy it, even though it was true.

"You want to help us find out who did it, don't you?" Gilbert asked. He was obviously trying to appeal to my sense of justice, but he wasn't going to achieve it by talking to me like I was a kid.

I gaped at him. "You mean it wasn't an accident?" Like hells it was. I put a hand over my mouth. "How awful. Why would anyone do that?"

Because Alistair Dagen was a motherfucking piece of shit, that's why.

"That's what we'd like to find out," Singh said. "We're trying to get to the bottom of it. That's why we need statements from everyone involved."

"Involved?" My eyes widened. "You don't think I have something to do with it?" I looked toward Gilbert as though pleading with him to believe me.

"No," Gilbert said quickly, his hand outstretched toward me. "But we need to find out who was. You want to help with that? Right?"

I wanted to stab him in the eyeball with a fork if he kept being so condescending.

"Of course I do," I said honestly. "All those poor people. They deserve the truth. Their families must be beside themselves wondering what happened. And why." I thought back to the hours, days after my parents were murdered. I thought I knew the answer to those questions, but the more time passed, the more I realised the situation was much more complex. It was about so much more than just my parents. Power struggles were rarely about individuals. People like me just got caught up in them.

"Did you see anyone acting suspicious in the area?" Gilbert asked.

I thought for a moment. "No, not that I can think of. I mean, no more shady than usual. This is Sydney, after all."

Gilbert chuckled. "Yeah, it is."

Singh gave him a dark look. She gave me the impression she didn't like him very much. Tough shit, that was her problem.

She looked back at me. "Why did you not stay in the area until the police arrived? Or render assistance to those who were injured?"

"Honestly?" I sighed. "I panicked. The newspaper stand exploded and I was knocked off my feet. People were crying. Other people looked dead. It was scary. I didn't think I was badly hurt enough to need an ambulance, so I thought I should get out of the way." I turned my best puppy dog eyes on Gilbert. "You just said it wasn't an accident. What if it happened again? The safest place to be was away from there."

Gilbert nodded his understanding.

I should get an acting award for this shit.

Singh was not so easy to convince. "So you ran?"

"Staggered," I replied. "My ears were ringing and my balance wasn't quite right."

I sat back in my chair and decided to level with her. "The fact you're here would suggest that people were able to identify me on sight. That would be because I am what the media would refer to as a rich nightclub owner. Whenever anything goes down, we're the first to have fingers pointed at us."

I sat forward and propped my elbows on the desk. "Everything we do here at Crimson is legal and transparent. We pay taxes, we pay our staff above minimum wage. Our hygiene standards are above minimum requirements. If there is even a sniff of drugs, the customer is not allowed in, or is kicked out. You will have records of the police being contacted on those occasions." Only because it helped us to look like we were above board. And because I hated drugs. Keep that shit out of my properties if you like being alive and with functioning knees.

Singh nodded that that was indeed true. Obviously she looked into my background before she came.

I went on. "The very fact that Crimson is all about sex means people are happy to assume the worst about me and those who work with me. That doesn't mean I went around blowing up any newspaper stands. In fact, I only went there to buy a bag of jelly beans." I spread my hands.

"Some would suggest that fleeing the scene of the crime would imply guilt," Singh said. She really wasn't letting up, was she? What a pain in the ass.

"Others would suggest that somebody who is as easily identifiable as I am would be pretty fucking stupid to blow up a newspaper stand with myself standing really close to it," I said. "I don't have a death wish."

"Do you have any enemies?" Singh asked.

I held back a snort. Did I ever?

"There's a long list," I said. "It starts with any number of conservative politicians and ends with people whose partners prefer to be here than at home." I frowned. "You think this was aimed at me?"

"Do you?" Singh asked.

"I think I ducked down the street to get a bag of jelly beans and got caught up in some shit that happened to go down when I was there," I said. "Why blow that up if they were after me? It's not like I go down there every day. They might have been after someone else in the area. Or whoever owned the place." I shrugged. "Not to tell you how to do your job or anything." I smiled sweetly and not at all sincerely.

Gilbert smiled back, but Singh grunted.

"If anything else like this happens, contact us," she said. "Having to track you down took time and resources we can't afford to waste."

Yeah, she probably asked someone on the street.

"I'm sorry," I said. "I didn't mean to cause any inconvenience. I really didn't hear anything or see anything out of place." That was sincere, I really hadn't. The most suspicious things I saw were Jake, Cooper, Ben and me. Luckily for us, being ridiculously attractive wasn't a crime.

Gilbert nodded and stood. "If you think of anything, please contact me. Us." He cleared his throat.

Singh rolled her eyes and then tried to look like she hadn't. She had a lot of work to do if she ever wanted to become an actor.

Just for shits and giggles, I rose and leaned forward to shake Gilbert's hand again, giving him a nice eyeful of cleavage.

He stared and gulped, then managed to shake my hand. "Thank you for your time." His voice was an octave or two higher than before.

"You're welcome," I said smoothly. I took back my hand and offered it to Singh.

She gazed at it and turned and walked out the door. Gilbert looked apologetic, then followed, just as Jake stepped inside.

He closed the door behind him. "It's always a good day when you get a visit from the po-po."

I sank back into my chair and snorted. "Waste of fucking time." I told him about the conversation. "Can you believe they actually thought I would try to blow myself up?"

Jake chuckled and shook his head. He pulled a lollipop out of his pocket, then apparently thought twice and put it back.

"Did you enlighten them?"

"What would be the point?" I asked. "Gilbert was only here to get his cock sucked. Or because Singh made him come. She was only here to further her career. You know the type. She sniffs around until she finds something on me, just so she can collect the accolade for bringing me down." She wasn't the first. She would be the last. They were an annoyance, but little more than that. She would disappear if she became a problem. Gilbert could be bribed or blackmailed. I would prefer to deal with two of him than one of her any day.

"Do you want her dead?" Jake asked lightly.

I rubbed my forehead. A headache was starting to threaten my temples. "No. If she disappears now it will be too obvious. Even an—"

My head jerked up. "Shit. Have someone keep an eye on her.

This is exactly the kind of crap Dagen will be looking out for. She dies, it gets pinned on me. I don't need that kind of bullshit right now." Or ever.

Jake nodded then rose and came around behind me. He placed his hands on my shoulders and started to massage them.

"You know they would never make it stick."

"I know, but I don't need the publicity. It's bad for business." And I didn't want to be locked away in a cell for any length of time.

I closed my eyes and enjoyed the feeling of his hands smoothing out my knotted muscles.

"Maybe it would be easier to kill her on our terms," Jake said. "We can make it look like an accident. Dagen will make it look like the murder it really is."

"I'm not sure if you're saying that because it's a good point, or just because you would like to kill someone," I said.

He chuckled. "A bit of both? If she is going to create trouble for you, then it will be a pleasure. And if Alistair Dagen is going to use her to create even more trouble, then even better."

"Unless this is exactly what he wants us to do," I said. "In which case he'll make sure someone sees the accident. Fuck." My headache was getting worse.

"He's getting very good at getting into your head," Jake said. "You should start charging him rent."

"Oh, I am," I replied. "It accumulates every time I think about him. As it stands, his great-great grandchildren will inherit the debt." I grimaced at the idea of him reproducing. I didn't doubt he had, but he was smart enough to keep that information from me.

The door opened and closed. I opened my eyes long enough to see Cooper enter and flop down in a chair.

"I saw the cops outside just now." His ridiculously gorgeous face creased in a frown. "They asked about my uncle. I told them he was out of the country for work, but I don't think they bought it."

"Fucking hells," I muttered. "You better make her and Gilbert have a nasty accident. And figure out who at the station is letting them sniff around. I pay them well enough, I shouldn't have to deal with this."

"My guess is an anonymous tip," Jake said. "I'll talk to our people down there, but you know how it is. Sometimes they have to pretend to look into us."

"It didn't seem like pretend to me," Cooper said. He squirmed in his seat.

"You weren't even there," I pointed out. "Don't worry, we'll deal with it. I've already created a paper trail that will lead straight to Dagen. Our purchase of the garage was totally legal. Dagen's dealing with Silas was not. At least, that's what it will show."

Cooper grinned. "Just when I think you couldn't get more awesome, you get more awesomer."

Jake stopped kneading my shoulders for a moment. "Is that a word?"

"I dunno." Cooper shrugged. "It is now."

"It fits me," I said. "But don't get too excited, you haven't seen how much paperwork you have to fill out to start assassin training."

Cooper's expression dropped. "Really? That much?"

I let him stew for a moment, then smiled. "No. Of course not. What self-respecting assassin would leave evidence like that around for people to find?"

Cooper's grin was back. "Great, because I hate filling out forms. It makes me stabby."

"What doesn't make you stabby, Murder Pup?" Jake asked.

"Ivory," Cooper replied. He looked sly before adding, "Unless you're talking about stabbing my cock into her pussy. Then I'm definitely stabby. A lot."

"You and me both, Pup," Jake said. "You and me both." He kissed the top of my head.

"She does have that effect on people, doesn't she?" Cooper sighed and gave me a look that made my heart do a flip in my chest like a gymnast.

I adored both guys in different ways but to the same extent. I had known Jake for practically a lifetime, and Cooper for the blink of an eye, but I couldn't imagine my life without either one of them. I couldn't even bring myself to think the L-word, I was so scared of what would happen if I did.

Love made you vulnerable. It was a distraction, potentially a dangerous one. It could get you hurt. But fuck, I felt what I felt.

"Don't you two have a former nightclub owner to dispense with?" I asked.

"Haigwood," Jake said. "Yes we do." He turned my face to kiss my mouth, then drew back and gave me a look almost identical to Cooper's.

He straightened up. "Come on, Pup." He started toward the door.

Cooper rose, leaned over the desk, put his hands on my upper arms and pulled me to my feet. He drew me closer, kissed my mouth firmly, then let me go.

"Coming." He flashed me a panty melting smile and started after Jake.

"I think I'm going to go home for a while," I said. "I need a break from this place. And some more clothes."

Jake hesitated halfway out the door and frowned. "I could come with you—"

I waved him out. "I'll be fine. I'll just duck over there and come back. I'll take Ben with me. Maybe give him a blow job while we're there," I said teasingly.

Jake groaned. "Lucky him."

Neither guy had a hint of annoyance or anything on their faces other than envy for Ben.

"Go do your jobs," I scolded. "I'll see you both later."

Cooper blew me a kiss. "Later."

Jake pulled out the lollipop, took off the wrapper and grinned at me before he shoved it into his mouth.

I shook my head at him. "Go." Before I changed my mind and kept them here to fuck their brains out. Or took the lollipop and ate it myself.

"Okay, okay, we're going," Jake said. He turned to winked at me, then closed the door behind him.

CHAPTER
SIXTEEN

"Did you know Jake gives me shit because all my cars have manual transmission?" I asked. I stopped my little white Cobra at the lights and glanced over at Ben. He didn't look any worse for wear having survived the explosion. He looked more worried about surviving my driving. I would show him I was a good driver.

He chuckled. "He might have mentioned it a time or two. I know for a fact at least two of his are also manuals."

"The ones he keeps as collectors items." I nodded. "But the rest are automatic." He preferred to drive an oversized truck or SUV. I liked classic, dainty cars and I hated the idea of them sitting in a garage gathering dust.

"According to him," I continued, "I just like to keep my hand on the stick." I smiled over at Ben who chuckled again.

"There's nothing wrong with that," he said. "Plenty of people say they make better cars."

"Exactly," I said. "I knew you'd be on my side."

"Every time," Ben agreed. "Boss." He added after a moment.

"If you disagreed with me, would you say so?" I asked.

"No, boss," he said. A smile tugged at the corners of his mouth. He had ways of letting me know what he was thinking without coming out and saying so. And we both knew it. He'd been working with me long enough.

"What would you do if I asked you to do something you didn't want to do?" I asked.

"I would do it anyway," he said. "Are you planning on doing that?"

"Not planning on it, no. But the night is young." Not really. It was edging eleven p.m. by now. That was early for us though, I supposed.

"I look forward to anything you might ask me to do," he said smoothly, and with more than a little hint of husky desire.

"Are you flirting with me?" I asked. When the light turned green, I put the Cobra into gear and floored it.

Ben jerked back against the seat. "Do you want me to flirt with you?"

"I don't know. I'll have to think about that one. I'll let you know." I wound around a delivery truck and headed toward William Street. That would take us east toward Point Piper. No road in Sydney got you anywhere quickly these days, but this was the fastest way home. On a good day, that was. On a bad day, I wished I took the helicopter home.

"Okay. You know where to find me." I caught a quick flash of his grin in a street light before we headed into heavier traffic.

I glanced up into the rear view mirror. "That black SUV has been following us almost since we left Crimson."

"Yeah. I've been watching it in the side mirror." Ben twisted around to look out the back. "They could be going the same way."

Another SUV, also black, pulled out of a side street right in front of us. It sped up a little, then dropped back so both SUVs were equal distance from us.

"What about that one?" I asked. I wasn't worried. Not yet.

Plenty of people drove cars like that, and even more drove erratically. The guy in front of us wouldn't be the first driver to pull out in front of another car and then slow right down.

"Coincidences are like unicorns," Ben said. "They might look good on paper, but they don't actually exist."

"And that's how I know you've been hanging around with me for too long," I said. "You're getting cynical."

"To be fair, I've been cynical for a long time. Growing up around witches will do that to you." He kept glancing back behind us, then ahead again. "I think we need to get off this road."

"I think you're right," I agreed. If the two SUVs were just driven by random Sydneysiders, then we would lose them. If not, then we would know they were there for us.

"Hold on." The SUV in front of us slowed down as the light turned orange, but I swerved and wove around him. We shot through the lights just as it turned red.

With apparently no regard for anyone else in the road, both SUVs followed us. They certainly drove like they were evil.

"Okay. That answers that question." Unfortunately, neither one hit another car on the way through. Worse luck.

"Shit, look out," Ben called out as a third SUV pulled out of the street in front of us.

I managed to break hard enough to avoid running into the back of it, but like the last one it sat right in front of us. One of the others pulled up beside us, leaving the last one to follow.

"I'm a wolf, not a cat, but I know boxes have four sides," I remarked. I peered through the windscreen.

"Up ahead," Ben said. "There are two cars before it."

"I see it," I said. I had two options, let us get boxed in or swerve into oncoming traffic.

I took the third option. I braked hard and swerved into a side street, narrowly missing a white delivery van.

"There's at least four of them," I reasoned. "We're either going to have to fight, or we're going to have to run."

"Got it, boss," Ben said. How the fuck did he sound so calm? "Let me out here, I'll lead them away. Assholes won't be able to tell one white wolf from another in the dark." Somehow, he had managed to strip off, but leave his seatbelt on. Those were some skills right there. He unclipped his seatbelt now and let it slide back into place.

"I hope you're right," I said. It wouldn't take them long to realise the wolf they were chasing was bigger than the one they were actually after.

My heart pounded like a drum. I pulled the Cobra up on the side of the road and opened the door beside me.

Ben, already in wolf form, bounded across my lap and shot out the door.

I ducked down. With any luck they would think there was only one of us in the car.

Two of the SUVs wove around the Cobra and followed the white wolf up the street.

The other two stopped behind and in front of the Cobra.

I grabbed up my phone and hit a button on the screen. After a moment or two, Jake's voice came through the speaker.

"Hey." He sounded calm, but he knew this number. Not just that it was me, but that this was one I would only use during an emergency.

"Jake." I tried to keep my voice from wavering. "I need you to do something for me."

He obviously caught the tone in my voice. "El? What's wrong? Where are you?"

"Everything is under control," I lied. "But I need you to do something for me. I need you to call in a favour."

Four forms got out of the SUV in front of me. I looked in the rear view mirror and saw another four.

Fuck.

I quickly told him what I needed him to do.

"Okay, but tell me where you are. What the fuck is going on?" He sounded frantic.

The forms got closer. Not surprisingly, they were all men in black suits. Dagen's men.

I swallowed. "Just... Do what I asked. *Please.*"

"El," he said insistently.

"Jake. I love you." I sucked in a deep breath.

"Elodie, I love you too." He sounded confused.

"Bye," I told him.

"No. Wait. Elodie. *Elodie!*" My name tore out of his throat like something between a shout and a sob.

I ended the call and tossed the phone onto the floor of the car. I took off my watch and threw it down on top of it.

I flicked off my seatbelt. There wasn't time to strip, or to even give a shit about ruining another set of clothes.

I half closed my eyes and shifted into my magnificent white wolf form. Silk and cotton tore to shreds. Buttons popped loose and went flying. I shook the fabric loose and bounded out of the car.

Dagen's men had already started to strip and shift before I bolted past them and headed in the opposite direction from the way Ben went.

I was smaller than the black wolves, which made me more agile, but they were faster. And there were eight of them.

I ducked between parked cars and looked for somewhere, anywhere I could fit that they couldn't follow. Anything to give me even a minute or two head start on them.

I stuck to the shadows, but being white, I had the distinct disadvantage of standing out, even at night.

In wolf form, the smells of the city were stronger, more pungent. Fumes from cars, rubbish and the stink of black wolf.

They would smell me too.

I slowed down to squeeze under a broken fence. I shook and slinked across a used car lot. None of the cars parked in there would have keys in, even if I did have time to check. Worse luck. Another car would be handy right about now. Especially since the black wolves were squeezing under the gate, one by one.

They glided after me like shadows of night.

If I could hide my scent, I would slink under a car and wait them out. I couldn't. If I did that now, they would pin me down.

How the fuck was I going to get them off my tail?

I bolted towards the road and along the sidewalk. It was way too open here. Fuck.

I loped along the ground as fast as I could push myself. And then a little bit more. I didn't need to look over my shoulder to know they were gaining on me. I could hear them and smell them. They made no attempt to hide their presence. They didn't need to. They knew they had me outnumbered.

I just had to outsmart them.

No pressure.

I headed up the steps to an overpass which stretched across the road. It stank of urine and fresh paint. The local council had recently tried to cover graffiti, by the look of it. And by the look of the new graffiti, they weren't successful for long.

I bolted across the overpass and down the stairs on the other side.

When I was sure the black wolves were following me, I darted across the road to the first set of stairs and headed back the way we all came. With any luck, my scent would be masked by theirs.

They followed me back across the road and narrowly avoided being hit by a passing car.

Crap, that would have helped to thin the pack a little bit.

A glance over my shoulder showed me they weren't fooled by my little trick. If anything, they were closer now. Too close for me to risk squeezing under another gate. I could practically feel their breath on my hindquarters.

Hoping I was heading the right way, I bolted down the street and around the corner. I managed a burst of speed to put some distance between me and my pursuers.

I ran across another road and ducked behind a row of bushes and into an alleyway. I sprinted through there and out the other side. If I calculated correctly I should be one street over from where I was trying to go.

I followed the sidewalk and almost skidded around a bend.

If I could just get far enough ahead...

I bolted past the traffic lights Ben and I stopped at. It seemed like days ago now. It couldn't have been more than twenty minutes.

I flew across the road and into the side street, my heart in my throat. Usually I loved to run in wolf form, but this was bullshit. There was nothing fun about this. Not at all.

My heart rose when I saw my car still parked by the side of the road. It sank again when I saw it was surrounded by several black shadows.

Fuck.

My hesitation was all it took. One of the wolves behind me leapt. He grabbed onto my hind leg with his teeth.

I yelped and scrambled to get away, but his jaw locked down tighter. I felt a snap and crunch of bone.

Shining blood stained my fur.

Instinctively, I kicked for everything I had, but another black wolf grabbed onto another of my legs. Lighter than the first, but firm enough to keep me in place.

Yet another wolf jumped at me and pushed me off my feet. He wrapped his jaws around my throat. His teeth pressed lightly. Not hard enough to do damage, but hard enough for me to get the message.

I took it. I did what any sensible wolf would do. I lay completely still. I hated myself for doing it, but my choices were that or have my throat ripped out. I didn't want Dagen to get the better of me, but I didn't have a death wish.

I closed my eyes and tried to ignore the searing pain in my leg. There was no way in fuck wasn't broken.

I waited. Why wasn't I dead yet?

I got the answer to that a minute or two later, when yet another dark SUV pulled up. To the surprise of no one, Alistair Dagen stepped out. His shoes made a clicking sound as he walked across the road. He had something in his hand but I couldn't tell what it was until he got closer.

He crouched down beside me. The look of triumph on his face was almost too much to bear.

Motherfucker.

"Shift back," he snapped.

I stared back at him, sending thoughts of him dying suddenly. Maybe wishing for a comet to drop out of the sky onto his head.

At a signal from Dagen, the jaws around my throat tightened.

I swallowed. It was harder to do that. Harder to breathe. The adrenaline from the chase gradually seeped away. Despair threatened to replace it.

No, I told myself. *Just because I'm pinned to the road right now, doesn't mean I'm beaten. No way.*

I huffed out my snout and shifted back into person form.

The wolf's jaws were barely off my neck when Dagen snapped something else onto there. A collar?

He leaned down to speak in my ear. "I've always wanted a pet dog. My parents wouldn't let me have one. Just so you know, that collar will prevent you from shifting. Don't try to take it off, it will hurt like hells. Or better yet, try." He patted my bare ass.

I bared my teeth at him.

He ignored me and stood. "Get the bitch into the back of the car."

A couple of his guys had already shifted back into person form. They grabbed me and pulled me to my feet. With my leg mangled as it was, I couldn't have done it by myself anyway.

"Don't call me bitch," I hissed.

With a snap of his wrist, he gave me a stinging backhand across my cheek.

If it wasn't for the guys holding me up, I would have fallen from the blow and the blaze of pain that blossomed across my face.

"Fuck you," I growled.

He struck me again, harder this time. Hard enough that I felt a crack across my cheekbone. I tried, but I couldn't keep from crying out in pain.

"You will learn, bitch," he snarled. "Get her into the fucking car."

They had to half carry me most of the way there, I couldn't support any weight on my leg, and my head spun.

It wasn't until we got almost all the way there, that I finally saw Ben lying on the ground near the tyres. He had a collar around his neck like the one I had and was clearly badly injured, but alive. He looked up at me with regret in his eyes, but I smiled. Nothing he did would have changed any of this. At least he hadn't gotten himself killed.

They pushed me into the back of the car, then picked up Ben and pushed him in after me. He groaned with obvious pain.

The car door closed behind us and the lock audibly clicked into place.

"This is fucked," he whispered.

"Yeah," I agreed. "But we're alive. We need to focus on staying that way, no matter what happens." My leg and face both throbbed with agony, but I clung to the fact they hadn't killed us yet. That meant there was hope. And while there was hope, I was going to find a fucking way out of this.

The engine started and the car pulled away from the side of the road.

I closed my eyes and prayed to any god who would listen that Jake did what I told him to.

If he didn't, I was screwed.

CRIMSON

RUTHLESS CLAWS BOOK 2

PROLOGUE

JAKE

"*Fuck*."

Cooper and I stopped around the corner and left my SUV by the side of the road, engine thrumming.

I wanted, needed, to run. My heart thundered. Fear and adrenaline coursed through my body. Too much.

Reluctantly, I put up a trembling hand to keep Cooper at a slow, careful walk. This was exactly when running in blindly could get us killed.

If there was a chance Ivory was still alive...

No. She *had* to be alive. I wouldn't accept anything else. She was infuriating as hells at times, but the woman was my whole fucking world. If she was dead, I might as well be too.

I sniffed the air. The scent of her lingered, white wolf and lavender perfume. It was faint. She was long gone. Along with a whole fucking pack of black wolves.

Her white Cobra was parked by the side of the road, the door open.

"What—" Cooper started.

"Shhh." I sniffed around again. There was no one here. A

human or two somewhere nearby, but not Ivory or her body-guard, Ben, and not Alastair Dagen.

A smear of mostly dried blood was on the road a few metres from her car. Hers. Another smear lay a few metres away. Ben's.

It wasn't enough to indicate that either of them were dead. They were alive when they were taken from here.

I couldn't smell petrol or any sort of accelerant. I also couldn't rule out a bomb rigged to blow if I touched her car. I stepped close enough to peer inside. Her phone and watch lay on the floor, faintly illuminated by the nearby streetlight.

"Her mother's watch," I said softly. I teased her for not wearing a smartwatch, but she preferred the older technology. And the connection with her mother. "She would want us to get it, but not at the risk of our own lives."

"I'll get it," Cooper said.

I raised my eyebrows at him. When he didn't even flinch, I stood back, hands raised.

"Go for it, Pup." I shouldn't let him take the chance. Ivory would be pissed when she found out. She'd be equally pissed if there was no bomb and I let her watch get stolen.

He moved closer to the car. "How did you know where to find it anyway?"

"I put a tracker on all of her cars," I said unapologetically. "For just this kind of situation."

"Does she know?" He reached in tentatively.

"I don't know," I said. "Probably. It was always hard to fool her."

Cooper nodded. He snatched up the watch, and her phone for good measure, then leapt back.

The car didn't explode.

"How do we find her?" he asked. I didn't need to look at his face to know he was as scared as I was. His voice was laced with it and he smelled of worry and fear. A great combination in an enemy, but not so much in a friend. And one of the guys I shared Ivory with. I knew, at some point, Ben would join us in that too. I thanked the gods he was with her. If anyone could protect her until I rescued her, it was him.

"We do what she asked us to do," I said finally.

"But—" He frowned at me.

"We know who took her," I snapped. "The only chance we have of figuring out where, is to do what she asked." I thought for a moment. "How do you feel about driving a Cobra? She won't want it left here."

"Depends. You think it would explode if I turn the engine on?" He looked at it doubtfully.

"Only one way to find out." I grinned and waved my hand toward the driver's seat.

Cooper frowned but climbed in and closed the door behind him. He turned the key over. The engine purred to life.

I nodded, satisfied. "Follow me back to Crimson. Then we need to get to work."

CHAPTER
ONE

IVORY

I don't know which hurt more, my leg or my face. It might be a tie.

I dropped my head and watched blood drip out of the teeth marks on my calf and pool on the floor of the car. Whatever, it wasn't my fucking car. Sure, it was my blood, but chances were, I wouldn't need it much longer.

I glanced over to Ben. He had a similar injury to one of his legs, and claw marks on his chest and back. He was clearly in as much pain as I was. Like me, he was a stubborn prick and was trying not to show it. Neither of us wanted to give Dagen the satisfaction of hearing us scream.

"Where do you think we're going?" he asked, his voice low.

I shook my head and winced at the searing agony that small movement caused.

"I don't know," I managed to say. I didn't know why we were still alive, much less where the asshole was taking us.

Dagen's words, 'You'll learn, bitch,' suggested he intended to keep me alive for a while longer. How much longer was anyone's

179

guess. Given I had no desire to learn anything from Alistair Dagen, he'd probably kill me out of frustration.

My best hope right now was that Jake was doing what I asked him to do. He knew the organisation as well as I did. Better. He'd keep it running. Nothing was stopping Ivory Claw from wiping out the Onyx Ridge Pack now they had moved against me directly, personally. Jake and Cooper would have a field day doing just that. Jake waited nearly two decades for this. My only regret was that I'd miss all the fun.

Ben would, too, come to that. He enjoyed a good killing as much as the next wolf.

"I'm sorry," he said softly. "I should have—"

I would have frowned at him, but my face hurt too badly from where Asshole hit me. Twice. For that alone, I should rip his head off. I would, if I got the chance.

"For what?"

"Letting them touch you." He grimaced toward Dagen, who sat in the front passenger seat.

I waved a couple of fingers in dismissal. "There were sixteen of them and only two of us. If anything, it's my fault for not traveling with an ostentatious-as-shit entourage." I said that last bit loud enough for Asshole to hear me.

He didn't respond.

I lowered my voice again. "The only thing you could have done was kill me. If you did that, you'd have to make sure they killed you right after. Otherwise Jake would hunt down your ass and make your final days a living misery."

Ben managed a pained half-smile. "Yeah, he would, but I would never kill you. Unless you ordered me to. And..." he gestured toward the collar around his neck. Identical to mine, it was to stop us from shifting into wolf form, "this makes it harder."

That was the point, of course. I was sitting in the back of a black SUV, completely naked, but the inability to shift made me feel barer than the lack of clothes. My inner wolf was my better half. Stronger, faster, deadlier.

Without her, I was nothing more than Ivory, head of the biggest criminal organisation in New South Wales. Okay, that was a lot, but I still needed my wolf to be whole.

"For the record, I wouldn't order you to kill me," I told him. No matter how bad things got, I always managed to find a way out. I would do it this time too.

"That's good." His gaze flicked toward Dagen. He looked like he had something else to say, but shook his head slightly. He looked back at me with meaning in his eyes.

Maybe I should have been taken by surprise, but I wasn't. He was one of my most trusted bodyguards. We'd worked closely together for years. That spilled over into the bedroom a time or two. I may never trust anyone the way I trusted Jake, but Ben was in my top three. Cooper rounded that out, although we'd only known each other a short time. In my line of work, trust was everything.

I reached over and laced my fingers through his. Hopefully Dagen would only assume we were two prisoners consoling each other. A sniff of anything more and he'd use that to his advantage.

"There's a private airfield up this way," Ben said a few minutes later.

I peered through the window. He was right. A road sign read 'private property' but a hangar and a short airstrip appeared as we drove out from behind a series of industrial buildings.

A jet stood outside the hangar. Several cars and people occupied a small carpark.

"Fuck," I said under my breath. I assumed Asshole would take us somewhere in Sydney. That was a big enough haystack to find two needles in. Out of Sydney could mean anywhere in Australia, or even another country.

Hells, he might be planning to make us skydive once we were over the harbour—without a parachute.

Ben's hand tightened on mine.

I turned back toward him questioningly. "Don't like flying?"

He curled his lip, but didn't take his eyes off the window. "Don't like witches."

I didn't know which one of the people standing waiting was a witch, but if he said one of them was, I believed him. His hatred of them was well known. He was orphaned young and raised by witches who had little love for shifters. I didn't blame him for his bitterness. After Dagen's father murdered my parents, I was raised by his aunt. Helen Dagen was as nasty a piece of work as her brother. Having her killed was a pleasure.

"Trust Alistair to be working with witches," I said. I already knew that about him. He was the one who left the set of magic-filled stones at Silas Wheeler's garage.

Ben turned toward me and frowned. "I guess we know what the meaning of the dampening stone was."

Dampening stones stopped a witch from using magic. In this case, it was a message to say he'd found a way to stop us from shifting.

I remembered the last stone and shuddered. Bonding stone. If that was infused with magic, then touched me and one of Dagen's men, or Dagen himself, spilled their cum inside me, it would form an empathic bond between us. The idea of that kind of link with him was even more sickening than the idea of him touching me in the first place.

Judging by the fierce expression on Ben's face, he was thinking the same thing. And was determined not to let it happen.

I appreciated the sentiment and knew he'd die for me, but I preferred not to think too much about it. I would deal with it if and when the time came.

The SUV pulled up near the plane. People swarmed around it,

mostly men in black suits. A woman in blue jeans and a cat t-shirt strode along behind them like she owned the airfield. The witch, I assumed.

Ben looked like he desperately wanted to shift and tear her head off, literally.

"Someone you know?" I asked softly. I unwound my hand from his before anyone saw.

"Yeah. Irina." He didn't elaborate. I didn't ask him to. There would be time for that later.

"Get them," Dagen ordered. He opened his own door and moved away from the SUV.

"Gods forbid he got his hands dirty," I said sarcastically.

"Can you stand?" Ben's brow corrugated with concern.

"Not without help," I admitted. "I think I'm about to get some."

One of Asshole's men opened the door and leaned in to grab me. I let him pull me up and out. I almost fell, but another goon moved to the other side of me and slipped an arm under mine.

I looked at him sharply, wanting to tell him to fuck off, but I would have face planted on the ground without help. Being naked in front of about thirty men who loathed me because of what I had done, or who I was, or both, was bad enough. As a shifter, being naked didn't bother me as much as it might bother others, but vulnerability—that bothered me a lot.

Alistair Dagen looked down his long nose at me. I thought he was going to make some triumphant announcement, or gesture that would make all his goons clap, or something inane like that.

Instead, he waved at the witch. "Heal them. I don't want blood in my plane. But leave the bruises on the bitch's face." Of course he was the kind of prick who liked to leave marks.

I rolled my eyes at him, even though it hurt like fuck.

The witch, her expression haughty and unimpressed, stepped

toward me. Mercifully, she crouched and started to knit the bone in my leg back together.

Unfortunately that too hurt like fuck and I couldn't keep from crying out in agony.

Dagen smiled.

If not for the goon's tight grip on my arms, I might have lunged at him the moment my leg was fixed.

Instead, I stood and endured in silence while Irina healed my broken cheekbone. Her expression gave away nothing of her thoughts. Not even slightly. If I was carved of ice, she was made of rock. No, brick. Brick walls could be torn down and left in ruins. She deserved that for working with Asshole.

By the time she stepped toward Ben, all my pain was gone. Another henchman handed me clothes to put on. Track pants and a t-shirt, both too big, but still, clothes.

Ben glared at Irina in disgust when she stepped toward him. He looked like he'd prefer to be in pain than have her touch him.

Now I could frown again, I did just that, sternly.

He gritted his teeth and stood his ground while she healed him of his scratches and scrapes.

The expression of absolute disdain on her face while she did it suggested she remembered him too. For some reason, that bothered me.

Jealousy is an irrational emotion, so I decided on protectiveness instead. Under the circumstances, it made a lot of sense anyway. We were all each other had right now. Us, and what dignity we had left.

I dressed quickly. If I wore pyjamas, they might look like this. Loose and comfortable. I felt around inside a pocket and found a hair tie. They were someone else's clothes then. Irina's perhaps? Whatever, clothes were clothes.

I pulled my hair up and fastened it back out of the way. In the window of the SUV, I caught a glimpse of my reflection. I looked less like big, bad Ivory and more like Elodie, the woman I spent the last nine years putting behind me. My birth name; Jake was the only one who called me that. With the exception of Alistair Dagen, when he was trying to be an even bigger asshole than usual.

I could have been this woman I saw in the glass, had life not turned out differently. Suburban wife and mother— Oh fuck, who was I kidding, that would never have been me. I was always destined to shake things up, to make waves. It was in my nature.

In that vein, I smiled sweetly and said, "No shoes?"

"You're only getting clothes so you don't mess up my plane," Dagen said, his voice a low snarl. "I don't want you to cream the leather."

The suggestion I might be turned on by him in any way was both laughable and disgusting. At another time I'd make a comment about Ben being hot enough to do that for me, or even one of his goons. I didn't want to draw any further attention to Ben. Nor did I want to give anyone else any ideas.

Instead, I just made a gagging sound and stayed still while two goons reattached themselves to my arms.

I caught sight of Ben, who was now dressed and looking better for having been healed. He wore a tight fitting black t-shirt which was drawn firmly over his muscular chest, and light grey track pants.

If Asshole chose that outfit to distract me, he almost succeeded. I didn't choose bodyguards for their looks—in fact, Jake vetted most of them—but there was a reason I had a past history with the guy that went beyond trust and into lust. Dark hair, brown eyes and only a smattering of tattoos here and there, he was the definition of tall, dark and smokin' hot.

And yeah, those track pants clearly gave away the other reason for the attraction. He had a cock like a racehorse, but without the excessive speed.

"Get them on the plane," Dagen snapped. "And find Jake Blakesley. Take him to our destination." He frowned at me, then at Ben, as if we were somehow to blame for Jake not being here.

Then I understood. He assumed Jake would be in the Cobra with me. That was a logical assumption. We were usually together, or not far from each other. If he took us both, it would effectively cut the head off the organisation. Of course, there were others who could step up to take our place, but all of that would take time and planning. And maybe some bloodshed.

Thank the gods Jake and I weren't together tonight. He would have battened down all the proverbial hatches by now, and been on high alert for anything suspicious. Not that he wasn't always cautious, but he wouldn't be caught unawares, like I was.

I could kick myself for that, but fuck it. A girl should be able to drive around her own city without getting attacked by a rival. Or anyone else for that matter.

The goons pushed me toward the plane. I considered resisting. Even without shifting, I had the self defence skills to take on two of them. It was the twenty or so others which were the problem. Add to that the fact Dagen was all too happy to break my bones. There was no guarantee he'd keep telling his pet witch to heal them.

Head high, I climbed the steps and into the plane. They shoved me into a seat at the front, and arrayed themselves beside and around me.

More goons shoved Ben up the steps and toward the back of the plane. We exchanged a quick look before he trudged past, looking pissed off, but resigned.

I knew it was too much to ask that we be allowed to sit together, but to make it worse, Dagen slipped into the seat directly behind me. As if the stink wasn't bad enough. Shame to ruin a perfectly good plane with the smell of black wolf.

Fortunately, it was offset by the scent of two white wolves.

Make that three. I forced my expression to remain neutral when Hutton stepped inside the plane. I hadn't seen him outside, so either he just arrived, or he was behind the tinted windows of a car.

His nostrils flared, but he didn't even glance my way. He kept going past and headed to the rear of the aircraft.

I barely gave him more than a flick of my eyes before my gaze slid away. I knew Jake didn't trust him, but we'd sent him to work for Dagen to find out what he was up to. That was still his job, as far as I was concerned. If he wasn't on our side, I'd find out soon enough. If he was, then he could report back to Jake, whether or not I made it out of here in one piece. Hopefully he was smarter than to try to rescue me, or anything stupid like that. All that would do was blow his cover and get him killed.

I might be *the* Ivory but this whole thing was bigger than me. People's lives depended on Ivory Claw. Their livelihoods too. I hadn't spent years building it up only for my own benefit. I mean, that didn't hurt, but that wasn't my sole motivation.

The moment the plane door closed, I felt like they'd cut off my air supply. It was immediately harder to breathe. More difficult still when every breath brought the smell of testosterone, black leather and jet fuel. A heady combination under other circumstances. The scent of filthy rich men and their minions.

In this case, a filthy rich man whose parents killed mine. Whose parents I killed in retaliation. A man who wanted everything I had, and was apparently done waiting to make a grab for it.

He leaned forward and his breath grazed my neck. I cursed myself for putting my hair up and leaving my throat exposed.

"Sit back and enjoy the ride," he said, his voice low and menacing. "The fun and games are just beginning." He brushed the back of his hand over the bruises on my cheek.

"Shouldn't you be buckled up?" I asked. "I'd hate it if we hit turbulence and you got hurt. On second thought, don't buckle up." I twisted around just far enough to give him a sweet, sarcastic smile.

He turned his hand and wound it around my neck. He squeezed, pressing his fingers into my skin.

I responded with a stare of pure ice. If he thought he'd scare me with a threat of strangulation, he'd have to think again. I wasn't afraid of much, and certainly not of dying. It would be inconvenient, but not the fear it was for most people. I'd seen so much of it, I was desensitised by now.

He squeezed tighter, obviously annoyed at my lack of reaction, but he hadn't done all of this just to kill me in a fit of irritation. He waited until my vision started to blur, then released and pushed me away.

"Ice Bitch, I'm going to have fun with you." His smile was chilling.

"I can't wait." I sat back around, checked my seatbelt and thought up ways I was going to make him pay for this. I made a mental list I could check off later, one by one. By the time I was done, he'd wish he never took his first breath.

The engine turned over and the plane started to taxi toward the runway.

CHAPTER
TWO

I didn't realise until the plane lifted off that I hoped we'd go south. I knew people there, in several locations. People Jake would contact first.

My heart sank as the plane rose and headed north.

I recalled that Dagen had properties on the north coast. Hells, so did I, for that matter. Mostly rental properties with perfectly ordinary people living in them. They didn't much care who owned them, as long as they had a place to live, and the rent didn't go up too often.

Whatever, they weren't people who could help me.

"Nice view, isn't it?" Dagen asked.

Without thinking, I glanced out the window.

Fucker.

He made sure we passed right over the top of Crimson on the way. From here, it just looked like a tall building with a helipad on top. Not much different to a dozen other buildings in the area. I half expected it to explode after we flew past, but it didn't.

I knew very well that dear, old Asshole wanted to own the

place. Blowing it up would be dumb, even for him. Still, I wouldn't put it past him, just to see the look on my face.

"It's okay." I squinted, but of course Jake didn't appear on the helipad with a bazooka, or even a dragon, to knock the plane out of the sky. He and Cooper were down there somewhere, worrying. I could feel it.

Or maybe I was projecting my own emotions. I was as worried about them as I was about myself. Maybe more so. Not because they couldn't take care of themselves, and each other, but because Dagen was a motherfucker who held a grudge against them both as well as me. Jake more than Cooper, but anyone involved with me was automatically Dagen's enemy. Anyone involved with him was mine. Anyone but Hutton, until I knew for sure where he stood.

We reached cruising altitude out over the ocean and the goon beside me unbuckled his seatbelt.

I kept mine on. There was still time for the guys to send a dragon shifter after us. Maybe a phoenix. We had both on the payroll. Failing that, lighting might appear out of a perfectly clear sky and strike us.

None of that happened. Dagen's men moved around the plane, talking in low voices and giving me open glances. Some of them looked uneasy, but most looked triumphant, like outnumbering Ben and I and sticking us on a plane somehow meant they won.

The one or two who dared to catch my eye got an icy gaze in return. They all blinked first, then turned away.

That's right, bastards, I thought. *I'm not beaten yet. Even after my heart stops, my legacy will fight on. And my guys.*

I itched to look back and check on Ben, but forced myself to keep my eyes forward. My senses were open to the smells around me: anxiety, fear, indifference. Smug-as-fuck, that was Dagen. I didn't get any indication that anyone planned anything. Rather, I felt like everyone was waiting, anticipating whatever Asshole had planned for Ben and me. Or me, at least. I wasn't sure Ben registered on their radars. Good. I would do what I could to be sure it stayed that way.

"It won't be long now," Alistair said in my ear.

Fuck, I hadn't noticed him leaning forward again, but there he was, his breath on my neck again.

"Has it ever been long?" I asked sweetly. "You seem like the sort of man who has to overcompensate in other areas. This plane, for example." I gestured around me. It was actually smaller than my jet, but I couldn't resist taking a dig at the size of his cock.

He chuckled. "It's long enough and thick enough to break you in two, bitch."

"Don't call me bitch," I said over my shoulder. I braced myself for him to strike me, or try to choke me again. Something.

He chuckled again. "I give you full points for trying to pretend you haven't lost. Or maybe you aren't ready to accept it. But you will. Everything you have is mine now. Or will be soon." He slid his fingers along the side of my neck.

I shivered involuntarily. If I didn't know vampires weren't real, I'd start to wonder about him. He was creepy, liked black suits and seemed to be obsessed with my neck. Was there a word for that? I knew it wasn't neck-rophilia, but the thought made the sides of my mouth twitch.

"Dream on," I told him. "Nothing of mine will ever be yours. Jake will make sure of that."

Dagen snorted and let his fingertips rest against the pulse point at my throat. "There's nothing your lapdog can do now. In a couple of days, he'll be dead. Along with that boytoy of yours. Wheeler's nephew. He's as good as dead. I have no use for him."

I pretended to yawn. I really wanted to jerk away from his touch, but I wouldn't give him the satisfaction of knowing he creeped me out.

"Do we get a meal on this flight?" I asked. "Or a movie? The service on board sucks."

"How about I shove my cock down your throat?" he said. "That should fill you up."

"I said meal, not a tiny bag of nuts," I retorted. I was gagging at the idea of his cock anywhere near my mouth. And bracing myself for him to hit me. For some reason, even nice guys didn't like it when you said their dick was small.

His fingers dug into my skin, just above the collar. "You think you're so, fucking clever, don't you? You will regret every single word that comes out of your mouth." He slid his fingers around, worked them under the back of the collar and yanked it back so hard I gagged as it dug into my throat.

"You're my pet, bitch. You will learn to behave," he hissed. "I am your master now. Get used to being on your knees."

I struggled to breathe, much less think up a good comeback to that. I leaned back to take some of the pressure off, but he tugged harder.

My vision started to blur. My head swam. I reached up and tried to hook my fingers around the collar, to pull it away from my throat. I struggled to draw a breath, even half a breath.

He shoved me away and the pressure was gone.

I coughed and sucked in a few, frantic breaths before I managed to regain my composure.

"You see, bitch?" He gloated like the fucking prick he was. "It's so easy to take everything from you. I can do it with one hand."

"I'm sure your hand gets a workout," I said between coughs.

"Thinking of things I'm going to do with you, it did," he agreed. "But now I have your mouth, I can give it a rest."

"If you put any body part near my mouth, I'll bite it off," I said evenly. I rubbed my throat and winced. The skin already felt bruised. "I need to pee," I said after a moment. "Please tell me this toy of yours has a toilet."

I glanced back between the gap in the seats as Asshole nodded at one of his henchmen.

"Leave the door open and watch her."

"You're not going to watch me yourself?" I asked. That seemed like something he'd get off on.

He ignored me.

Spoilsport.

The goon beside me reached for my seatbelt and unclicked it before pulling me to my feet and ushering me to the rear of the plane.

I didn't dare to glance at Ben as I walked past, but I saw he was alive. For now. I managed a tight half smile that he may or may not have seen, and shuffled past.

Hutton sat on the other side, a couple of rows back. He didn't look my way either.

The toilet was nothing to write home about, but moving around the plane gave me the chance for a good look. Slightly smaller than mine, it was fitted out to carry people, not be luxurious. It had no couches, no room in the back for a bed, no bar. None of the fun things.

"I won't tell if you turn your back," I said to the henchman.

He seemed unimpressed. "Hurry up, or I'll help you. I'm sure the boss won't mind."

I was almost certain the boss *would* mind. Dagen seemed like the kind of prick who didn't share his toys until they were broken and chewed. Unless he got something out of it.

I rolled my eyes and did what I needed to do as quickly as I could, glad the t-shirt was long enough to fall almost to my knees. If the goon thought he'd see anything, he'd be mistaken. Still, the lack of privacy was discomfiting, bordering on humiliating. Which was the point. They were trying to get to me. They'd have to try harder than that.

I stepped out of the tiny cubicle—without stealing anything, or ripping off the toilet seat, how amazing is that—to the murmur of hushed, concerned voices and the sound of a soft alarm from the direction of the cockpit.

I laughed softly. "That would be about bloody right. I get dragged aboard Dagen's fucking jet and then it crashes into the ocean. This is the most Mondayish Thursday I've had in a long time."

"It's Wednesday," the goon said.

"That figures." I shrugged. "Wednesdays are often disappointing. I was born on one."

"Quiet," the goon snapped.

I decided he looked like an Eric. He had a long face and a chin like a slide. His nose was also long and his eyes too close together.

He grabbed my arm and shoved me back toward my seat.

The beeping increased. I was no expert, but it sounded like a fuel warning. Or someone put their seat back too far and bumped someone else's knees. People on planes were so inconsiderate.

I added Eric to the list when he shoved me faster.

"Hurry up, bitch," he growled. He must have been taking etiquette lessons from Alistair.

"Don't call me bitch," I growled back.

Eric's face turned pink. I was almost certain he'd hit me if he had permission to.

"Bitch is appropriate," he said instead. "You murdered my parents and grandparents. If the boss let me, I'd open the door and throw you out."

I rolled my eyes. "Take it up with the boss. His family started the killing."

"You kept it going," Eric pointed out. "You could have just done as you were all told. Stayed out of the way. We could all have lived our lives."

"I have two words for you," I told him. I frowned. "Wait, is brainwashing one word or two? Whatever. What the Dagens did was little better than genocide. We weren't going to take that lying down."

Eric shoved me back toward my seat.

I half fell over both of them before I managed to scramble back and grab both sides of my seatbelt.

Dagen wasn't in his seat, he must be in the cockpit. How appropriate.

Eric looked down on me with eyes laced with barely contained fury. I had no doubt in my mind that if we weren't on a plane full of people, and if he wouldn't get in major trouble for it, he would take out his frustrations on me. Whether that would be with his fists or his cock, I don't know. Maybe both.

I clicked my seatbelt and tried not to appear rattled. It was easy enough to think Alistair Dagen was the enemy here, and he was. But I was also surrounded by men who hated me as deeply as I hated them. Men who were bigger and stronger than I was, especially if they worked together.

Eric flopped down beside me and placed his hands in his lap, over his dick.

Yeah, I figured that might be his weapon of choice.

I gave him a long look. "You'd regret it."

He shrugged one shoulder. "Maybe. Maybe not. Might be worth it at the time."

"Yeah, but for how long after that? Until your boss cuts your throat? Where is that going to get you? Just dead, that's where."

He shrugged. "Dead, but vindicated."

"Right, then." I couldn't even claim it was the first time I talked to a man so casually about my own potential rape. If it wasn't for Jake, that would have been my fate years ago.

I was acutely aware he wasn't here right now.

"So, is the plane going to crash?" I looked between the seats in front of me, but the cockpit door was closed.

"I don't know," he admitted. "If I'm going to die anyway..."

I actually laughed. "Dude, if you can do it before we hit the water, then I'm not your problem."

He smirked.

Before he could speak, the plane shuddered.

"This wasn't how I imagined dying." I sighed. "What's your name?"

He glanced over at me. "Huh?"

"If we're going to die together, I figured I should know your name." I winced when the plane shuddered again. "Is it Eric?"

"What? No. It's Toby. Tobias." He looked back over his shoulder at something.

"What is it?" I asked. "Dragon? Phoenix? Pterodactyl?"

"I dunno, I can't see," he said. His head snapped back toward me. "Did you do something?"

The question took me by surprise, but then I laughed. "Yes, absolutely. I'm sitting inside the plane, while trying to make it crash so I die too."

Thankfully he had at least a basic understanding of sarcasm.

"If you're going to die, you'll want to take as many of us with you as you can," he said.

I smiled. "Well, yes. A queen needs servants in the afterlife." I rolled my eyes. "Whatever is going on, it's not me. Your boss probably skimped on the cost of maintenance. Or he has other enemies, apart from me. I mean, not everyone looks favourably on the days of Dagen rule over the state."

After a moment, I added, "Tobias, are you in on an assassination attempt? I'd think better of you if you were."

"Fuck off," he snarled. "I'm loyal. The only person I'd assassinate is you."

"That's very touching." I looked back through the plane. I couldn't see Hutton, but I met Ben's eyes. Electricity zapped between us. If I was going to die, I'd rather be in his arms than here with Toby.

I wanted to get up and stagger through the plane to him. I would find Hutton, and the three white wolves could huddle together and wait it out.

But if we didn't crash, we would have shown all our cards. *I* would have. Revealed that I had feelings for Ben, and that Hutton sort of worked for me. I couldn't rule out the possibility that this was some kind of twisted trick.

When the fuck did I get so cynical? Oh yeah, when I came home from school to a home decorated with my parent's blood.

Wonderful. I would die alone because I was suspicious of everyone's motives. Yeah, well, it kept me alive for this long.

"So, Toby Tobias. Does this plane have parachutes? No? Oxygen masks? Airbags?"

"Barfbags." He nodded to the pocket in the seat in front of him.

"For the record, Dagen being a tightass is going to kill us all." The plane shuddered harder this time. It dropped for a good two seconds. My stomach flew up into my throat.

"Too late for a fuck?" Toby asked. He almost smiled. Almost.

"Good to see you have a sense of humour," I said dryly. "I think we have time for me to blow you a kiss."

He sighed. "Can you blow my cock? Even if I don't finish, I could die kinda happy."

"You can shift and suck it yourself," I pointed out.

"No wonder we all hate you," he said. But I had a feeling he didn't hate me anymore. Funny how seeing a monster as a real person makes them seem like less of a monster.

I laughed softly. "Nothing worse than a woman who won't put out," I said sarcastically.

I groaned as the plane dropped again. I might need that barfbag yet.

"For what it's worth," I said slowly, "I know how you feel.

We're people who got caught up in shit. Then we kept on with the shit. I was hoping it would end with me."

"It still might," he said from behind clenched teeth.

"Dagen and I die, it won't end this," I said. "If anything, it'll make it worse." At least he'd be dead. That was a plus.

So would I, that was a minus.

"Nothing will end this while both sides are left," Toby said.

That was an oversimplification, but he might not be wrong.

"Yeah, but I couldn't bring myself to kill all of you." I glanced over at him. "My bad, I guess."

It might not be a mistake I made again, assuming I got out of this alive. Shame, he was tolerable, if you can get past the whole temptation-to-rape me thing. That was a big hurdle.

"Yeah, your bad." He smiled at me, but his eyes betrayed his terror. He signed up to die for Dagen, if he had to, but not like this.

"I hope you can float," I told him.

He sighed. "I can't even swim."

The plane dropped again.

"Well, fuck," I said softly.

"Yeah, well fuck. Dagen is a shitty boss anyway."

I laughed, low and husky. "You better hope to die if you're going to say that out loud." I wasn't going to give up until I was done. "Can you take this collar off me? I'd feel better if I could doggie paddle."

"It needs magic for that," Toby said. "I don't have any." Was that actual regret in his eyes?

"Figures." I closed my eyes when the plane shuddered and dropped. "Worst ride ever."

Toby snorted. "Yeah."

The alarm got louder as the plane headed downward.

THREE

I squeezed my eyes shut until I realised the plane levelled off. The alarm still sounded, but softer now. We banked steeply and headed in a north-westerly direction.

I leaned over and spoke softly in Toby's ear. "I won't tell anyone you said he was a shitty boss." I patted his arm for good measure. It didn't hurt to try to make allies, even amongst the enemy. Especially amongst the enemy.

"I...only said that because I thought I was going to die." Was he pissed off at me, himself or both?

"You will die if he knows you said that." I was guessing. Dagen was petty but was he that petty? If I had to guess, I would say yes, yes he was.

From the expression on Toby's face, I was right.

"He won't hear it from me," I said. "Promise." I made no guarantees about the people around us having overheard. That was his problem. I also wouldn't guarantee I wouldn't tell someone and have them tell Dagen. That would depend on how he treated me from now on. If he tried anything, I would make absolutely certain Dagen knew about it. I knew he knew that too.

Yes, I could also be petty.

"I presume we're not far from our destination." I peered out the window.

Toby grunted. He was back in full grumpy goon mode. I sensed I wouldn't get anything else out of him. That was fine. I didn't want to be his friend, and I didn't want to risk lowering my guard. He was the enemy. As if I could forget for a moment.

The alarm pinged as we passed low over a town on the north coast. Onyx Head, unless I missed my guess. Where else would black wolves hang out? It was one of those sleepy towns that got trendy and expensive with the injection of cash from people like Dagen. It was probably full of movie stars and drugs or some shit. Cooper would probably love it. Jake would tell them all to get fucked and go surfing. He was a pretty good surfer when he got the chance to get out in the water.

As for me, my skin burned just thinking about going out in the sun.

The alarm was still pinging as we headed towards a small runway. Not surprisingly, a fire truck waited beside it. Presumably that was just a precaution. They didn't actually think we were going to burst into flames on landing. Right?

The wheels hit the runway with barely a bounce, but we flew along so fast I thought we would take off at the other end. Of course, we didn't. The plane slowed and turned to taxi back along the runway and towards the small airport.

"Well, we survived that in one piece," I remarked under my breath. Was that a good thing though, or a terrible thing?

The plane came to a stop and the goons hurried to get the door open and the steps out. Dagen emerged from the cockpit looking slightly pale. He was the first one off the aircraft.

Like a rat deserting a sinking ship.

Toby unbuckled his seatbelt and nodded for me to do the same.

I was tempted to thank him sarcastically, but I decided not to screw with our uneasy peace. Instead, I unclicked and even stood without being asked, or dragged to my feet. That didn't stop Toby from grabbing my arm and pushing me to, and then out, the door.

I managed to look dignified when I stepped out in the breeze of what was now mid-morning.

"I hope you fire whoever is supposed to maintain that for you." I jerked my head back toward the plane and gave Asshole an insincere smile.

"I'll have them killed," he growled.

I couldn't even call him excessive, it's exactly what I would do. Anyone who risked my life like that forfeited theirs. Especially if they cut corners.

"Get the bitch to the car," he snapped. His mood was worse than before. Bad enough to put me on edge.

He watched me through narrowed eyes, clearly expecting me to remind him not to call me that.

I wasn't scared of him, but I wasn't stupid. I could tell he was hoping I'd give him an excuse to break my other cheekbone. Or just kill me outright.

"Come on." Toby shoved me over to one of the waiting cars. Not a black SUV, to my surprise. Rather, it was an ordinary, black sedan.

No four wheel driving for us today. Shame, that might have been fun.

Toby opened the door and let me climb in without help.

Before he could follow me inside, Dagen snapped, "Not you. I can see on your face she got to you already." He nodded to another of his men. "Terminate him. You two, stay close to her."

Toby looked shocked, but they dragged him away before I could react, or respond.

Dagen was more astute than I gave him credit for. And a *really* shitty boss.

I sat back and watched out the tinted windows while the henchmen took Ben to another car.

Hutton followed the goons who were dragging a white faced Toby to yet another car. I wasn't sure if I should curse his name or not. I didn't want Toby dead because of me, but he was still one of Dagen's men, more or less. If Hutton exposed himself in some attempt to save Toby...

I ducked my head. There was nothing I could do or say that would change anything now. For all I knew, Hutton would be the one to kill him. I hated not being certain which side the man was on. Just because he made it clear he wanted to fuck me didn't mean he wasn't ready to strangle me.

I had that effect on some people. I have no idea why.

Much to my joy, Dagen climbed into the front passenger seat of the car and we pulled away from the airport.

This whole exercise must be costing him a fortune. Between the men, the cars and the plane, I'd conservatively guess half a million dollars. I'm not saying I'm not worth it, but I would have done it on a much more conservative budget. Or just killed him and not bothered with all the bullshit at all. Lucky for me, his approach was different to mine.

We slipped out of the carpark and onto the coastal highway. Traffic was light at this time of morning. Lucky, because a parade of dark coloured cars would get noticed in a place like this. They might think I'm a movie star, or a rock star. I mean, I *am* a rock star, but I can't sing for shit. Ask Jake, he says I howl. So does he, if we're honest.

Fuck, I already missed him so much it hurt. Cooper too. I should be having breakfast right now and arguing with Jake because I want to eat some sugary crap, when all he lets me eat is healthy stuff. Why do I let him tell me what to eat? It's just a part of who we are. Like an old married couple. If I really wanted to eat cake for breakfast, I would do it. I didn't really want it, but I liked to pretend I did.

Okay, sometimes I did actually want cake. The point was, it was like a running joke between us that most people wouldn't understand.

I forced my head back up. I had to pay attention to where we were going. I had to keep an eye out for a chance to get the hells out of this situation. If I ran, I needed to know which way to head.

We turned up a private road with the bush heavy on either side. Bush a person could get lost in, if they could cover their scent.

We slowed and passed through a heavy gate. The fence disappeared into the brush on either side, but it was tall and solid. Not insurmountable. I hoped.

I glanced back to see the gate swing shut behind the last car.

When I turned back, Dagen twisted around his seat, watching me, his eyes triumphant.

I flipped him off. I wasn't beaten yet.

He turned back as we drove out of the brush and past a wide expanse of lawn. In the middle of that was a predictably huge house, with a multi-car garage attached to the side.

The driver slid the car into a space near the middle and killed the engine.

"Home, sweet home," Dagen said lightly.

It must be a recent purchase, because I didn't recall his parents owning anything like this. If they did, I would have taken it and used it. It looked like a nice little bolt hole.

"Get the bitch out of the car," he ordered. "Bring her out to the lawn."

Once again, goons gripped my arms and led me out of the garage and into the sun.

I blinked and squinted against the glare. It was bright out from behind tinted windows, but it was pretty here. And quiet. I reassessed my thoughts about this being a nice place to stay. The lack of city noise would drive me crazy in a day or two.

The goons led me across the grass to a small shed.

"Guest accommodation?" I guessed.

They didn't say anything, they just walked me inside.

Dagen followed a moment later. "I have something for you, pet."

"No thanks," I said immediately. Unless it was my freedom, I wanted nothing from him.

His men walked Ben in and my heart stopped. For a long moment, I thought his present would be to kill Ben. I definitely didn't want that, if that was his idea of a gift.

"Shackle him over there," Dagen ordered. He nodded toward one of several sets of restraints attached to the wall. Either he planned this for a while, or this was just a regular day in the life of the sadistic asshole. My bet was on both.

"And you," Dagen said to me, "can bathe first. I don't like dirty pets in my house."

For the first time, I noticed a bath in the corner of the building. It was full of water that looked clear, but cold.

"I prefer showers," I said.

"Strip her," Dagen said softly.

Oh yeah, he was absolutely living out some kind of dark fantasy right here.

"I can take my own clothes off," I said coldly.

Either they didn't hear or they didn't give a shit. While two men held my arms, another tore the t-shirt off my body, ripping the fabric in two. He tossed the shirt aside and slid his hands into the sides of my track pants, against my skin, before pushing those down to my feet.

The assholes on my arms jerked me forward, forcing me to step out of the pants.

I didn't need to look to see the erections. The smell of arousal filled the room like stale heat.

I caught Ben's expression. He pulled against the shackles, obviously ready to rip off some heads.

I shook mine. There was no point in him getting killed, not over this.

"Get in the bath." Dagen's voice was rough. He made no attempt to hide the tent in his pants.

I contained a shudder and stepped into the icy water. My skin pebbled before I even sank down to my ass. It was fucking cold, but it provided some illusion that I was covered.

"There's soap and shampoo." Dagen crossed his arms over his chest and watched.

I followed his gaze and snorted. Dog shampoo. The man was a fucking hypocrite. As if he wasn't also a wolf.

"I prefer people shampoo," I said.

"Use that, or I'll wash you myself," he snapped.

Ugh, hard pass. I picked up the shampoo and poured some onto my hand. It smelled nice at least, like vanilla. It probably kept away fleas too. Bonus.

"This would be more fun if I had a squeaky toy to play with," I remarked. I placed a hand on my head and let the shampoo trickle down before I started to lather.

"You'll have a bone to play with soon enough," he said.

By now, at least a dozen of his men stood inside the shed, watching me wash myself in a bath meant for a pet dog.

I tried to pretend I didn't care. That I didn't care who saw when my breasts rose above the water as I lay back to rinse. I tried not to think about what every man dressed in a black suit would do to me, given the chance.

A sliver of fear and humiliation crept under my skin and took hold. I had worked hard for so many years to make sure I was never treated like this again. I surrounded myself with people who respected me, feared me.

Here, I felt stripped back, beyond just my clothes. Vulnerable. Worse still when I recalled how little it took for him to bring me down to this.

Toughen up, I told myself. *You've gone through worse. You'll get through this.*

I soaped and rinsed quickly, then climbed out of the water before anyone could 'help' me.

I shivered, not just with cold. I stood in front of so many men, dripping like a wet dog.

"Here." Dagen grabbed a towel from a nearby shelf—clean by the look of it—and stepped almost close enough to hand it to me.

I would have to move toward him to take it. The expression on his face sent chills down my spine and froze me to the spot.

"Well?" he demanded.

I wanted the relative, false safety of the towel wrapped around myself, but I couldn't bring myself to move. Everything in me was screaming at me not to get any closer to him.

Ben sensed it too. In my peripheral vision, I saw him strain against the shackles.

Dagen lowered his hand and took the handful of steps to me.

Unable to stop myself, I took a couple back.

He smiled. If you can call lips turning up on the sides, combined with a sneer, a smile.

He gave the faintest of nods and I was surrounded by three henchmen. Assholes. *Henchholes.* Two took my arms, another stood behind me.

"I tried to be hospitable," Dagen said slowly.

Without meaning to, I snorted. If this was hospitable, I hated to see how he treated people he really didn't like.

Dagen's body stiffened and his mouth twisted into a slanted scowl. He snarled. *"Enough of this shit."*

He backhanded me across the same cheek he left bruises on a few hours earlier.

The blow was so hard, I was knocked back a step. Searing pain bloomed in my cheek.

Later, I wouldn't remember if I fell, or was pushed by his henchholes. Either way, I landed heavily on my knees on the hard floor. I tried to stagger back to my feet, but all three of them held me in place. One on each shoulder, the other with his hands on the sides of my neck. His fingertips brushed my throat.

I forced myself to breathe. Panic rose inside me. Blind fear that made thinking hard, like it used to when I was a kid. An orphan. My heart raced so hard it might stop from the effort. Panic threatened to swamp me, drag me down into the darkest places I thought I left behind, in the past.

I held back anything more than a wince of pain, and the sob of fear that threatened to escape my lips. I kept my eyes on the ground for a good couple of minutes.

It was okay. I was okay. I was alive.

Whatever happened now, I could deal with. I told myself all of that and more, but I wasn't sure I believed it, deep down.

When I looked back up, Dagen stood in front of me. The look he gave me sent the coldest shivers through my spine. I had absolutely no doubt in my mind what he intended.

I swallowed and shook my head. "No," I whispered. Every centimetre of me trembled.

He unzipped his pants to expose his erection.

Shit.

No.

No.

Nope.

I shook my head vigorously, and writhed and struggled with everything I had.

In the back of my mind, I acknowledged Ben's shouts of outrage and despair. He was as powerless to help me as I was.

Three men held my head still while Dagen shoved his cock between my lips. He rammed it all the way to the back of my throat until I gagged.

"Take it all, bitch," he growled.

I wanted to bite, but he slammed into me again and again. All I could do was keep breathing and not literally choke on his cock.

I fought against the hands that held me, but their grip was tight. I thought I knew how it felt to be vulnerable. Until now. This was the first time in my entire life I felt totally, absolutely, utterly powerless. I wanted to crawl back into the bath. I wanted to stand in front of them dripping wet and naked. I could take all the humiliation they had to give. Anything but *this*.

"Fuck, yes," Asshole muttered. "That shut the bitch up."

The other assholes, the ones holding me so their coward of a boss could rape my mouth, actually laughed. *Shitheads.*

Tears poured down my cheeks. As they dripped off my chin, a tiny part of me hardened, like a callous over my heart. I would survive this. I would make every last one of them pay. They would live to regret having touched me and then they would die.

His pounding slowed, his breathing became more ragged.

I gagged. *Gods, no.*

A moment later, he shuddered, rammed his cock as far down my throat as he could and came.

Hot cum squirted into my mouth. I wanted to spit, to throw up. Die. Something.

Anything.

"Come on, bitch," he grunted.

I tried not to. I shook my head, but they held me fast. His cock was still deep. I had no choice but to give in to reflex and swallow. The taste was sour, like lemon juice dosed with salt. I immediately wanted to throw it back up onto his feet. Or onto the bastards that held me down. They were a bunch of fucking cowards, all of them. Four men against one woman who was smaller than any of them.

"There we go, that wasn't so hard, was it?" he asked. "Good girl." He actually patted my head before he slid out of me and left me gasping on the floor.

I managed to spit a couple of times, but my mouth was already dry.

"I'd call her first lesson a success. Bring her inside." He zipped up his pants like nothing happened, and walked away.

I was dragged to my feet and hauled toward the main house. Ben was unshackled and pulled along behind me. I knew I didn't imagine the streaks of tears on his cheeks too, the fury in his eyes. He would tear them to shreds the second he got the chance.

Hold on to that anger, I thought. *You're going to need it.*

Gods, I could use a mint right about now. Or better yet, tooth-paste and a stiff toothbrush. Even better than that, Jake at the gates with an army.

Right now, I couldn't throw off the feeling help wasn't going to come, even from within myself.

FOUR

I thought they might take me back to the garage, or a dog kennel. I wouldn't have put it past Asshole, and right now I didn't care. I just wanted to curl up in a ball and try to pretend what just happened, hadn't. Maybe cry for a while before I think of ways to carve him up with a blunt, rusty tool of some kind.

I was led straight past the garage and into the main house, across expensive hardwood floors and up stairs covered in thick, plush carpet.

To my surprise, everything was tastefully decorated. I expected tacky wallpaper with giant flamingos on it. Or for every-thing to be black. I would bet a million dollars Alistair Dagen hadn't decorated the place himself. Everything from the finish-ings, to the placement of the furniture looked staged, like an expert arranged everything carefully.

Even the art on the walls looked impersonal, except for a few Dagen family photographs here and there. Not one of them showed a hint of a smile. In spite of him claiming he wanted revenge for their deaths, there didn't seem to have been much love lost between Alastair Dagen and his parents. Fair enough, they were all jerks.

"I was going to accommodate you in the bathhouse," Dagen said. "But I thought you might prefer some creature comforts. Consider it a taste of the way you could live if you behave yourself."

I didn't even roll my eyes. For one thing, it would hurt my face. For another, I refused to give him an excuse to touch me again. Instead, I forced my expression into one of icy serenity and kept it there like a steel facade. I was ashamed of myself for letting my mask crack. That couldn't happen again. He got off on getting to me and I couldn't give him the satisfaction.

I wouldn't.

One of the goons opened the door and stepped aside. Ben and I were pushed into a room which was nothing short of luxurious. It was the kind of space that would look right at home in my house. Well, almost. I wouldn't have chosen those gold doorknobs on what I assumed was the bathroom door. I also wouldn't have chosen quite that shade of grey for the carpet.

"You'll notice there are two bedrooms in your suite," Dagen said as though offering some kind of gift. "I thought you might appreciate your privacy. Unfortunately, you will have to share the bathroom. But there is hot water. I'm sure you'd like to wash the dirt off your *knees.*"

He sounded so fucking smug. I wanted to push him out the window.

Ben looked at Dagen, then at me. He swallowed and looked like he was barely able to contain himself. His hands were curled into fists.

I shook my head. As tempting as it was to let him take a swing at Dagen, there was no point risking him getting killed for it.

"In case you're wondering, the window doesn't open," Dagen said. "And of course there will be guards on the door. A meal will be brought to you in an hour. And yes, there are cameras and microphones all through the room. Just in case you decide to try to plot your escape. There's no way out."

If he didn't think I would take that as a challenge, he had another thought coming. But he knew that, I saw it on his face. His smug, hateful face.

He ignored Ben, but patted my cheek before he turned and left.

The door clicked shut behind him.

Ben exhaled loudly and reached out a hand toward me. "Ivory—"

I shook my head and held myself out of reach. "I'm okay," I lied. I turned away and hurried into the bathroom. I didn't want to see the pity on his face. I couldn't deal with that right now. Holding myself together was difficult enough.

I caught my reflection in the mirror. One side of my face was black and purple with bruises. In contrast, the other side was starkly white, even for me.

Barely containing a sob, I dropped to my chafed, sore knees beside the toilet and threw up everything in my stomach. It wasn't much. I tried not to think about what it actually was. I was just relieved to have it out of me.

At some point, Ben crouched beside me and held my hair off my face. He lightly rubbed my back with one hand. Somehow, he even managed to snag a towel and wrap it around me.

"This is bullshit," he said, mimicking my thoughts exactly. "You deserve better than this."

I spat a couple of times, then sat on the cold floor and exhaled. "Do I? I've done some pretty shitty things in my life. Maybe this is what I get for all of it."

One side of his mouth drew up. "You don't believe that," he said. "I don't."

"You sound like Jake," I said.

He managed a smile, albeit faint and watery. "Thank you."

I rolled my eyes, then winced. I was right, it did hurt. "Are you sure it's a compliment?"

"Absolutely," he agreed. "Jake is a legend. Almost as much as you are."

I tucked my legs close to myself. "I don't feel like much of a legend right now." I felt like a rag doll who got left behind by the side of the road in the rain.

"Do you want to have a shower?" He stood and turned on the water. "It's actually warm. And there's proper shampoo, and body wash." He picked up a bottle and took a sniff. "Okay, I was half expecting that to be full of piss, but it smells all right."

I grimaced. "Don't give him any ideas." I would absolutely not be surprised if he had them switched out in an hour or two.

"Sorry." Ben put the shampoo bottle back. "I had a peek in the wardrobe. There's even clothes in there for us. They look like they might fit, more or less. You, anyway. I had a feeling they planned for Jake to be here, not me."

"I think you might be right." I looked around for cameras. It seemed unlikely Dagen would miss the opportunity to watch me have a shower. I couldn't see one, but I knew they were there.

"Do you want to talk about it?" Ben asked softly. "What Dagen did... I mean..."

"Don't," I said. "Don't go there. Don't think about it. I don't want to. It's—" I shook my head. "It's in the past." Yeah, right. As if I wouldn't have nightmares about the way his cock grazed my teeth. About the way he felt. About the way he tasted.

My stomach heaved. I leaned over the toilet bowl and retched, but there was nothing left to throw up.

"Okay," he said gently. "It's forgotten." He sounded compliant, but I wasn't fooled. He wouldn't forget any more than I would. Worse, he would blame himself because he couldn't stop it, even though there was nothing he could do.

I gave him a long, firm look. "Remember, we have to do whatever it takes to survive. No matter what that is. We keep looking for a way out, a gap, a hole, *anything*. In the meantime, we survive. Understood?"

"Understood." He looked like he had more to say, but wasn't sure of the right words. He never was much of a talker. Instead, he gave me a look that spoke more volumes than the National Library. I knew he cared about me, but I didn't know how much until now.

He crouched back down. I managed to keep from flinching when he put a hand on the side of my face that wasn't a mess of bruises.

"It's my job to keep you safe," he said, his voice just above a whisper. "Right now, I'm failing spectacularly at that. I wouldn't blame you if you hate me."

Gods, as if I could ever hate him. He was a rock in the middle of a motherfucking hurricane. He always had been. He was the anchor I needed right now.

"We are outnumbered," I reminded him as gently as I could. "You're not failing at anything. You're keeping me sane." I leaned over and lightly kissed his cheek. Then I remembered the last two things that happened to my mouth, and grimaced.

"Ugh, sorry. I should brush my teeth next time." For an hour or two, until the inside of my mouth was sterile.

He smiled. "It's my job to suffer for you." He looked at me sideways, a hint of something more in his eyes. "What would Jake and Cooper think?"

"They just want me to be happy," I said. Jake knew I had a past with Ben. And he trusted the man. That was everything. As for Cooper, he adored Ben for letting him kill the man who tried to assassinate me. To me, that seemed like a very good reason to like someone.

"Funny." He cocked his head. "That's what I want too. Enjoy

214

your shower. Let me know if you want me to wash your back." He tried to smile, but his expression was as haunted as mine.

I supposed it wasn't easy to watch while being unable to stop what happened. That was the point, of course. It was all about power, and putting us in our place.

I nodded. "Yeah, thanks." What I wanted right now was a few minutes to myself. Although, if Dagen was going to watch, we should give him a show. On the other hand, I did my share of touching another person for a while.

I loved nothing better than a long shower, but this time, the one I took was quick. I washed everywhere, taking special care with my face and my knees. I rinsed my mouth several times. It would never get the taste out of my memory. On the day I died I would remember. My stomach turned again.

When I stepped out of the bathroom with a towel wrapped around my body and another round my hair, I smelled the evidence that Asshole actually followed through with his promise of food.

"Is that...bacon?" Maybe I misjudged his evil just a little bit.

"Yeah, but it's undercooked," Ben said.

Or maybe he was as evil as I thought.

Before I ate, I stepped into the wardrobe and rifled through the clothes. Most of it looked like things I would wear: dark skirts, white or red blouses, even heels. A shelf contained several different sizes of underwear. The fact he didn't know what size I wore was perversely satisfying. Clearly he hadn't broken into my house and gone through my underwear drawer. That was good to know. No, it was *really* good to know. It meant his creep factor was ninety-nine point nine percent, rather than one hundred percent. A small but significant difference.

It didn't make him any less of an asshole.

There was even a box of makeup tucked away in a corner. Rude. What made him think I wore makeup?

I opened the lids of a few of the pallets of eyeshadow, and tested the mascara. None of it was my preferred brand, but it would do.

By the time I stepped out of the wardrobe, I was looking and feeling myself again. For now.

"Did you leave me anything?" I asked.

Ben paused with his fork half way to his mouth. He glanced down at his plate, then back at me before he realised I was teasing.

"I left plenty," he said before he shoved his fork into his mouth. "I tasted a bit of everything. Just to make sure it was safe to eat."

I slipped into a chair. "That's good thinking. Unless you died."

"At least we wouldn't both be dead," he pointed out. He didn't seem the slightest bit concerned at the idea of eating poisoned food to save me. I guess that was the job he signed up for as my bodyguard.

Still, with this—whatever this seemed to be growing between us—I wasn't sure how I felt about him risking himself. Losing bodyguards was part of the job. Losing people I cared about...not so much. Under the circumstances, it might be safer not to care. As if I could switch that on and off like a tap.

I grabbed two slices of bread and put bacon, cheese and all the greens onto my sandwich. Jake would almost approve. I thought about taking off the bacon, but he wasn't here to see it. And, you know, I am actually an adult.

In theory.

In spite of the persistent turning in my stomach, I bit into my sandwich and ate. It would suck if I saw the opportunity to escape, but didn't have the energy to do it.

The moment the food hit my stomach, it wanted to bounce back out again. My hands trembled. I tried to force them to stop.

My heart raced, vision blurred. All I could see was his cock in front of my face.

It was suddenly incredibly difficult to breathe.

"Have they cut off the oxygen in here or something?" I tried to sound light, but failed. I wanted to run to the window and suck in a bunch of air. He said it wouldn't open, but I could break it. Maybe a chair through the glass...

"Ivory? Ivory. The air is fine. You just need to breathe." How did Ben sound so calm?

"Look at me," he insisted.

"Who is the boss here?" I managed to say. My heart pounded, but it slowed a tiny bit at the sound of his voice. I looked straight at him and breathed in and out through my nose.

He smiled. "Still you. It looks like bacon doesn't agree with you. I better eat yours." He pretended to reach for it.

At least, I assumed he was pretending, because he seemed relatively attached to his hands.

I slapped one of them lightly. "If you touch my bacon, you won't need to worry about whatever Dagen might do to you," I mock growled.

Instead of stealing my bacon, he put his hand on one of my hands. "Are you okay now? No one will think less of you if you freak out once in a while. I do it too." He looked like patience itself right now. Just like how I *should* look.

"I wouldn't be much of an ice queen if I melt at the first sign of trouble," I said. Okay, being on my knees on the floor, choking on the enemy's cock, was more than the 'first sign of trouble.' It was a traumatic event on par with finding my dead parents in pieces. But I was Ivory. I was carved of ice and pain. I didn't give in. Didn't back down. I lived my life on my terms and no one else's. I would not let Dagen take that away from me.

Not ever.

"You don't always have to be the ice queen," Ben said gently.

"You're so much more than that. You're the strongest, smartest woman I've ever met. I'll do whatever it takes to be sure you get out of here."

"You're going to make me blush," I said. It was nice to hear, but I was starting to think I wasn't worthy of any of the guys. Like Dagen's touch tainted me somehow. Or maybe I was just a shitty person to start with.

Ben chuckled and squeezed my hand. "I'm sure you've heard all of this before. And more. You deserve to be told every bit of it." With a grin he added, "Boss."

"You don't have to call me boss," I said. "Unless we're in front of Dagen." If the place was really full of cameras and microphones, then we might as well be in front of him now. We probably said far too much, but it was to late to take it back.

"Or I could come up with my own name for you," he mused. "Cooper calls you Ivory. Jake calls you by your birth name. Maybe I should call you something else."

"As long as it's not ice bitch." I grimaced.

"It wouldn't be 'bitch' anything," he said firmly. "I'll think of something. Maybe Queen of Bacon."

That actually made me laugh, albeit bitterly. "We should be careful. That bacon might not be made out of pig."

Ben pushed his to the side of the plate. "That might be what they do with people who betray Dagen. Or piss him off."

"It could be Toby." I made a face at it. "The guy I sat next to on the plane."

"It sounds like you were sitting next to someone friendlier than mine," Ben said. He poked the bacon with the tip of his finger. "The guy next to me wouldn't even say hello. I mean, whatever. I wasn't there to make friends."

"Are you sure?" I teased. "You might have a future as one of Dagen's goons." As if that would happen.

"Firstly, I have a job," Ben said slowly. "Secondly, nothing bad is going to happen to my boss anytime soon, so I won't need a new job. Third, I have a sense of humour. That seems to be lacking around here. And last, I prefer white shirts to black." A slow smile crept onto his face. "Especially on women. Particularly on you, with a bit of juice mixed in."

"You saw that?" I grimaced. Jake accidentally spilled juice all down the front of me a few days ago. I looked like something out of a wet T-shirt competition. I had to walk through Crimson looking like that too.

"Every bit." He grinned. "There wasn't a person in the whole place who wasn't looking at and appreciating you."

I cocked my head at him. "I'm starting to think that you're cheekier than I realised."

He thought about that for a moment. "No, I've always been like this. I've just been overshadowed by Jake for so long." His eyes widened. "Shit. I didn't mean I was enjoying any of this. I mean... Fuck."

He closed his eyes and shook his head. "If you feel like stabbing me with a fork right now, go ahead. I won't fight back."

I patted him on the arm. "I don't tend to do my own stabbing. I hire people to do that."

"You want me to stab myself with a fork?" he said. "Because I will. Boss."

I pretended to consider that. "Not today," I said finally. "I admit it has been hard to see you past Jake. And Cooper. I wish we'd done this under completely different circumstances, but here we are. It is what it is. And for the record, I prefer the spork as a weapon of choice." I managed a small smile. I liked Ben. I could see this blossoming into something more.

Ben looked surprised, but grinned. "A spork? Why one of those?"

I shrugged one shoulder. "Because it's unexpected. You would see a fork or knife coming. But a spork looks mostly harmless, until it isn't."

"Like you?" he suggested. "Beautiful and sweet on the outside, deadly as fuck on the inside."

"Exactly," I agreed. "I'm just like a spork. And you know what the best part about them is? After you stab someone with them, you can eat soup." I hoped Dagen was listening. He would probably assume we were talking in code. Nope, it was just silly conversation in the life of Ivory. Something to keep us both sane.

"So... I'm guessing I can't call you spork as a nickname?" Ben asked. He wiggled his brows.

"Oh, gods no." I made a face. "I really would use one on you then. Now, you've been here long enough to have assessed at least fifteen different escape routes, right?"

"Sixteen, if we can get enough grease off the bacon. I think we might have eaten too much of it for that." He looked down at the table and sighed. "I tried the windows when you were in the shower. They're double, maybe triple glazed. Not even a chair is going through those suckers. There's no other doors to the outside. No other internal doors. We could try to break through a wall, but they would probably hear us. The floor is solid. We could pull out a light fitting, but neither of us would fit into the hole. Judging by the distance to the ceiling, and the appearance of the house roof, there isn't much of a roof cavity anyway. Not enough room to crawl through."

He sucked in a frustrated breath through his nose. "The only way in or out is through the door we came in. Judging by the overkill we experienced on our way here, there's probably a small army outside. Our best bet is to wait until he moves us somewhere else and be alert for an opportunity."

I nodded. "That was very thorough. Remind me to give you a pay raise when we get out of here." This was the point where I usually joked about giving blow jobs. Instead I felt the edge of a panic attack again.

Fuck Dagen. I hadn't had a panic attack since I was a kid. I didn't want to start having them now. If I got anywhere near his cock, he would be lucky if I stabbed it with a spork.

I pushed the panic down and finished my sandwich.

It was only a matter of time before Dagen came for us again.

CHAPTER
FIVE

The door creaked open.

My first thought upon waking was to make sure the housekeeper oiled the hinges. My second was that I wasn't at home. Or at Crimson. I was at Dagen's country house, lying in a wide bed next to Ben.

I sat up and peered through the room.

With a snap, the lights turned on. I squinted against the sudden glare.

"Wakey wakey." Alistair Dagen's voice was chipper. Of course he was evil. Only an evil person would sound that cheerful before the sun even rose. Amiright?

Ben and I sat up. He placed his hands protectively on my shoulders.

"We're awake," I said. I wanted to tell him to fuck off, but decided on the non-confrontational approach of saying nothing more.

"Is that how you greet your host, bitch?" Dagen snarled. "Looks like you need another lesson. Fortunately, that's what I'm here for. Get up." He crossed his arms over his chest and watched.

If he expected us to be naked under the covers, he would be disappointed. Both of us had slept fully dressed except for shoes. I loved my heels, but not enough to sleep in them. Plus, they're not practical footwear for an escape.

I tried to keep my hands from trembling as I pushed the covers off. I waited for some sign of movement from Dagen. Some suggestion he might step towards me. Push me back on the bed. Get his goons to hold me down again while he forced himself on me. Anything.

He made no move. Instead, he waved in the direction of the door. "Take them downstairs."

No less than six of his men closed in around us. Hands gripped my upper arms like a crab's pincers; firm and painful.

We were marched downstairs like they were taking us to a funeral. Maybe they were. Ours.

I doubted it though. Dagen went to a lot of effort, why would he kill us now? I mean, it might make sense to his fucked up brain, but it didn't make sense to mine.

We were led across the hardwood floor and through a door at the back of the house. The only furniture in the room was a narrow bed and a couple of small chairs.

A row of restraints like those in the shed were attached to one wall. They took Ben to these and snapped the shackles around his wrists so he faced the room. A faint grimace was the only sign of his discomfort. He could either sit with his arms above his head, or crouch. There was no way for him to get truly comfortable.

That, I guessed, was the point.

"Get her over here," Dagen gestured towards the bed.

I shuddered and resisted, digging my bare feet into the floor. The henchholes dragged me over and pushed me down on my back. My ankles and wrists were snapped into restraints at the top and bottom of the narrow bed frame.

This wasn't fucking good.

The only thing I could do was pick up my head and look over towards Ben.

He looked furious. Either at Dagen or at himself. Knowing him, he was angry at both.

I gave him a forced half smile of reassurance, then lowered my head back down and looked up at the ceiling.

Icy calm, I remind myself. Whatever he has planned, I can get through this.

"Good. The doctor is here," Dagen said. He sounded more smug than ever.

What the fuck?

I picked my head back up and looked around. Sure enough, there was a man in what looked like a white surgical coat. He was pushing one of those trolleys they have in hospitals. The kind that contains surgical instruments.

The witch, what was her name? Irina was right behind him.

"What the hells?" I asked. Fuck not being provocative. What the hells screwy shit was Dagen doing?

The doctor moved around to the side of me and picked up a needle. He tapped the side of it with his finger, before he slid it into my arm. "It's okay," he said softly. "You won't feel a thing."

"What the fuck?" I demanded. "Dagen? What are you doing?"

Ben looked like he was ready to pull the restraints right out of the wall. His face was red. A vein throbbed in his forehead.

Dagen moved over to the other side of me. He brushed hair off my temple, then ran his knuckles down my cheek.

"I'm just being responsible," he said.

His words sent a shiver down my spine.

"What are you talking about?" I asked. I didn't think I fucking wanted to know. Panic started to rise again but this time I let it. It was a perfectly rational response to whatever the hells was going on.

"Oh, you know what they say." He leaned down to whisper in my ear. "Be sure to spay and neuter your pets."

Forget panic and chills. His words sent disbelief, then red-hot fear flooding through me.

I shook my head vigourously. "No. No you can't. Even you can't be that—" I couldn't think of a word that went beyond evil. Whatever it was, that was him.

Everything was a blur and I realised I was crying.

I turned my head to plead with the doctor. "You can't do this. *Please.*" I tried to fight against the restraints, but the needle must have contained anaesthetic. I could barely move, much less fight.

I even glanced at the witch. She was concentrating on something. Whatever it was, she wouldn't meet my eyes.

Of course not, she was as bad as they were.

My eyes got heavier. My whole body felt like jelly. All I could do was say, "Please," over and over until my voice got faint even to my own ears. I wasn't sure if I was speaking out loud anymore. It might have just been my brain unwilling to comprehend what was happening.

"There, that's better," Dagen said soothingly. "Maybe I should keep you like this. You're a lot more... Compliant."

I stared at him with wide eyes. If I could shoot daggers at him I would. Or sporks. Or anything.

"You can't do this," Ben growled. The anguish in his voice threatened to break another part of me.

Dagen chuckled. "Why? So you can get her pregnant? No. The Keelan line ends here. With her. There will be no next-generation hells bent on revenge. The cycle ends. Now. But don't worry," he added lightly. "You'll both be awake to see it."

I couldn't feel it, but I was vaguely aware of the doctor and a couple of Dagen's men taking off my clothes and putting them aside on a chair. All nicely folded. How fucking thoughtful of them. The doctor even put a sheet over me, up to my belly. And another over my breasts.

As if I gave a shit about modesty right now.

As if I didn't want to lose my shit when he pressed a scalpel to my abdomen.

As if tears didn't slide down my cheeks at the tugging sensation as he slid out parts of me and set them aside in a kidney dish.

As if I didn't weep softly when they took away my ability to have children.

In the back of my mind I admitted I would be a shit mother, and I never planned on having babies, but the choice should have been mine to make.

Mine. No one else's.

Instead, I was surrounded by the enemy, while the doctor, his face expressionless, violated me in the worst way I could ever have imagined.

Sick as fuck didn't even start to describe what this was. This was sicker than the very lowest of the seven hells. The hell reserved for the worst of the worst.

I squeezed my eyes shut and gave into the sense of nothingness the anaesthetic gave me. If I couldn't feel anything physically, then I would pretend I couldn't feel anything emotionally. I spent years mastering the art of not feeling anything. I had to shut it off when my parents died, so I could survive. When Helen Dagen tried to teach me I was worthless, I boxed up my feelings so I didn't give in to her. On the surface, it looked like I did. I was quiet, shy, even meek. I didn't put a toe out of line. I didn't give her an excuse to beat me. That didn't mean she didn't do it anyway, when she got angry at something or someone, but the excuse never came from me. I hated myself at the time, but I did what I had to do to survive. I would do that now. I would feel nothing. I would be a block of ice. A whole fucking iceberg.

"There," Dagen said finally. "All done. That wasn't so bad, was it?"

I didn't give him the satisfaction of opening my eyes, or even twitching. I gave him nothing. Nothing at all.

While the doctor dabbed at my abdomen, Dagen whispered in my ear, "This is your second lesson, but not the last. This is just the beginning. When I am done with you, you will be broken. You will beg to hand over everything you own to me. There will be no bloody uprising, not this time. Just a melted bitch who will be grateful I let her be on her knees in front of me. Everything you have, your properties, your money, your power, your influence and your body, will be mine. Do you understand, bitch?"

I opened my eyes and looked into his filthy, repulsive face. "Don't. Call. Me. Bitch," I said coldly. I would freeze all of the hells over myself before any of that happened.

"I can see you're in denial," he said lightly. "Would you really prefer to see every white wolf in the state lying dead?"

Well, no, I wouldn't fucking prefer that. But I was also not going to let him break me. I would get out of here and make him regret ever having taken a breath.

I turned my face away from him. There was nothing he had to say that I wanted to hear.

"Get to work," he ordered. He walked away to speak to the doctor, leaving me to my thoughts until the witch stepped closer. He said something about healing me and felt a tingle of magic on my abdomen.

Evidently I wasn't going to be allowed the long recovery period from the operation. Whatever. I didn't particularly want to be vulnerable for weeks anyway.

My wrists and ankles were removed from the restraints and the sheets slid off my body.

"Get up and get dressed," Dagen ordered.

One of his men brought my clothes over and put them on the

227

bed beside me. He didn't even try to hide the fact he was staring at my breasts as I struggled to sit up. I curled my lip at him, but he moved away without even a hint of embarrassment.

Silently, I added him to the list of people who would regret their behaviour towards me. Him and all the other men who watched me hop off the bed and dress.

All of them but Ben. His eyes were on my face. They were full of concern and anger. He clearly wanted to rip off a few heads as much as I did. He was supposed to keep me safe, but they stole that away from him and left him to crouch helplessly against the wall.

I would definitely let him kill a few black wolves before we were done. As many as he liked. I suspected that number might be high. Good. They deserved it. Every last one of them.

They fucked with the wrong people. They chose the wrong side. I would fuck back so hard, they would beg to be killed.

I buttoned up my blouse and tried not to look over at the kidney dish which sat on top of the surgical trolley. Truthfully, I couldn't tell by looking, what the doctor took. Enough, I guessed. I wasn't going to ask. The specifics didn't matter, it wasn't like they could put it back in now anyway.

"That looks tasty, wouldn't you say?" Dagen said lightly.

"You're a twisted son of an omega aren't you?" I asked. That was pretty much the lowest thing a wolf could be.

The comment obviously pissed him off, but he laughed. "It's good to see the doctor didn't take your sense of humour. I look forward to breaking that, too."

I might be poking the hornet's nest, but I said, "You can take my freedom, but you can never take my sense of humour. Especially around a joke like you."

Thanks to the anaesthetic, I barely felt the slap across my face. I staggered a couple of steps back before I was caught by Ben, who had just been released from his restraints.

"You are a slower learner, than I gave you credit for," Dagen said derisively. "Fortunately, I like a challenge. The more they fight, the more fun they are to break. Take them back to their room."

I took a step towards the door.

"Wait." Dagen waved at two of his men. "Shift."

Without hesitation, they stripped off and shifted. Their black wolf form might have been impressive except for the whole being-a-pack-of-assholes thing.

Ben's hands tightened on my arms, but Dagen picked up the bowl and sniffed the contents. He turned to flash me a smile, then scooped out what was inside and tossed a bit to each of the wolves.

They snatched it up and swallowed it down without bothering to chew.

I turned and retched.

"I thought you would have thicker skin, Elodie," Dagen said.

I looked back and met his gaze unwaveringly. "My biggest regret in life to date is not having you killed when you were younger, Alistair," I said coldly. "That's not a mistake I'll make again."

He laughed. "How cute you pretend you have any power left. You can make all the threats you want, but you can't do anything to me. On the other hand..." He waved the bowl at me. "I can do whatever I want to you. Get some rest. You're going to need it." He turned away, only to turn back a moment later. "And practice breathing through your nose. You're going to need that too." He smiled like he got a participation trophy and strode out of the room.

"He is a motherfucking piece of shit," I growled. I started to take a step in the direction he'd gone, but I was so wobbly on my feet I almost fell. Ben caught me and swept me up into his arms. Under any other circumstances, I would have growled at him for picking me up like I was a helpless child. The only good reason for carrying me anywhere was to take me to bed and fuck my brains out. Otherwise, I could walk, even on wobbly legs.

Today though, I didn't think my legs would hold me, and better he carry me than one of asshole's motherfuckers. Still, I hated the feeling that I was this vulnerable.

I was Ivory, the big bad she wolf, but right now I felt like little more than a tepid puddle of water than an ice queen. I wasn't even the kind people slip on and break their necks. I was the kind they wiped up with a towel with barely a second thought.

"I've got her," Ben said firmly. "I'm not going to argue, or try anything. She needs to rest."

I hoped he *would* try anything if an opportunity arose, but that was going to be a lot harder when he was carrying me. But I was selfish and didn't insist he put me down. The warmth of his body and the anticipation of revenge were the only things keeping me going right now. I couldn't decide which one was more compelling than the other. They might be equal.

With what felt like no effort at all, Ben carried me up the stairs and back into the pretty cell where we'd spent the night.

Someone had left a fresh tray of food on the table, but I had no appetite. The smell of it made my stomach turn. At least I knew I wouldn't be eating anything from myself. Yeah, okay I recognised how sick that thought was. But I wouldn't have put it past Dagen to try that. I didn't think there was anything he wouldn't do to fuck with me.

The door closed and locked behind us and we were alone. For now.

Ben lowered me down to the bed and sat beside me. "I won't ask if you're okay. Not even you would be okay after that, and you are the most badass woman I've ever met."

"You need to get out more," I said dryly.

He laughed softly. "I'm working on it, believe me. Sooner or later he and his assholes are going to make a mistake. When they do, we'll be out of here." After a moment he added, "Of course, their first mistake was messing with you to begin with."

It sounded like he had more faith in me than I had in myself.

I couldn't help it. I started to cry. Just softly, and with tears that rolled down my cheeks so slowly they were cold before they dripped off my chin, but crying nonetheless.

Ben put his arms around me and drew me to him, so my face was pressed against his chest. He rubbed my back and whispered words I couldn't make out. The tone was soothing.

My body shook with silent sobs for a good five to ten minutes before I started to wear myself out. I lay against him for a good while longer.

"I wish you were somewhere away from here and safe," I said. "But, selfishly, I'm glad I'm not alone."

He kissed the top of my head. "I wish we were both somewhere else, but I'm glad I'm here for you. We will get out of here. I promise. Whatever it takes."

Whatever it takes. His words echoed through my mind. That was what worried me.

What might it take?

CHAPTER
SIX

We were left alone for three days. Someone delivered food three times a day, always much more than we could eat.

I didn't have much of an appetite. I ate because I had to. And because Ben gave me long, worried looks if I didn't. I was pretty sure he was trying to channel Jake, except he didn't say a word when for dinner I ate a slice of cake left over from the lunch tray. It wasn't very good cake, and by the time I ate it, it was stale.

Whatever, it was sugar.

Ben and I took turns pacing across the room. Partly for exercise, and partly just to burn off our frustrations at being locked inside. I never thought I would wish for a treadmill, but after two days, I would have liked to run.

"I know this is all part of his plan, but it's pissing me off." I stomped across the room and back again. "I can be patient if I know what I'm waiting for. Although, whatever we're waiting for is bound to be shit."

"Probably," Ben agreed. He sat back on the couch, long legs crossed at the knees. Even when he was pacing, the man looked calm. Of course, it was his job to keep his cool at all times. Hells, it was my job too, but a thousand scenarios ran through my head while Dagen kept us waiting. Most of them involved my blood, his cock or both. Nothing I wanted to think about. So of course, it was all I could think about.

I focused on Jake and Cooper and what they were doing right now. I knew they were still alive, or Dagen would have come in here to brag. I also knew he hadn't found them, or he would have dragged Jake in front of me, or vice versa. While they were still out there, there was some hope. At least hope that my organisation would survive long after I did, out of the hands of Dagen and the Onyx Ridge pack.

I barely managed to contain a startle as the door swung open.

Dagen himself strode into the room, several of his asshole minions following on his tail.

"Are you enjoying the accommodation?" He gave me one of his best slimy-as-fuck smiles.

I responded with an eye roll and said, "Fuck off." Maybe I was poking the beehive again, but it was getting harder and harder to think what he might do that was worse than what he already did.

He raised one eyebrow at me. "That's why I'm here."

I forced myself to stand my ground, when I really wanted to take several steps back. Into last week. Maybe the week before. That would give me time to avoid this happening.

Ben rose and moved to stand behind me, his hands on my shoulders.

In some ways that made it easier, and in some it made it harder. His support meant the world to me, but he wasn't going to be able to stop Dagen from doing whatever he wanted.

Dagen put a hand in his pocket and pulled out a stone suspended on a leather cord.

My eyes widened involuntarily.

Fuck.

"I see you know what this is," Dagen said. "I have to admit, it wasn't easy to find a bonding stone with bonding magic in it. Even with money and resources, they are rare. But you know what it's like. If you want something badly enough, you can get it." He raised the stone up in front of his face and smiled at me past it.

"It's pretty, isn't it?"

I shrugged as if I didn't care. "It looks like a rock to me."

"Appearances can be deceiving." He stepped closer to me.

I swallowed and started to tremble. Ben's hands tightened on my shoulders.

"You have a choice to make," Dagen said slowly. "I'm going to put this around your neck. You know what that means." Before I could say anything," he added, "You'll form a bond with the next man who fucks you. Specifically, ejaculates into you."

I eyed the stone. "No shit. I choose to *not* have that happen."

He chuckled. "That isn't your choice. You get to choose to fuck your bodyguard."

Ben twitched.

I looked at him over my shoulder. "So you can beat the shit out of him and I could feel everything he's going through?" What the hells kind of choice was that?

"I can take it," Ben said firmly.

I half turned to face him. "And you would feel everything he does to me." Asking anyone to share my fucked up mind and emotions was a lot. Too much.

I turned back to Dagen. "What's the other choice?"

The smile he gave me sent a shiver down my spine. "I fuck you. You'll have all the fun of seeing yourself through my eyes. And I'll have the fun of feeling you break."

"She chooses me," Ben said. "Whatever you do to me will be better than you touching her."

Dagen smirked at him. Of course he knew what the choice would be. "Looks like the bodyguard's feelings go deeper than just a working relationship. Isn't that sweet? You have an hour. If a bond isn't formed by then, it's my turn." He slipped the cord around my neck and made sure the bonding stone touched my skin.

"It doesn't matter if you take it off now. It's touched you. The magic is under your skin, where it will stay for a couple of hours."

Ben's grip on my shoulders was almost painful. I thought he might change his mind once he remembered magic was involved. Was that another one of Dagen's tricks, or just an unlucky coincidence?

"Get to it then," Dagen said. He crossed his arms over his chest.

"What, no privacy?" Apparently there was too much to ask for.

"Pretend you're on the third floor at Crimson," Dagen said. "Performing in front of the crowds."

"Crimson is more tastefully decorated than this place," I said dryly. With a barely contained sigh, I turned to face Ben. He looked to be thinking.

"I'd like to make this as easy on you as possible," he said softly.

I appreciated the sentiment, but there were seven other men in the room. Nothing about this was going to be easy.

He leaned down to whisper in my ear. "For what it's worth, I want you. Very much." He caught my mouth in a tentative kiss that suggested he didn't mind being watched. Or preferred that to watching Dagen force himself on me again. Yeah, that was a no-brainer.

Truthfully, I didn't mind being watched. Even by Dagen, as fucked up as that was. Maybe we could teach him what sex looked like when two people cared about each other.

I let myself be caught up in the moment. It was just Ben and I. No one else was in the room with us. Our tongues danced. His hands slid up and down my sides. He led me over to the bed and lay me down before he lay over me, his body shielding mine from view.

He kissed my neck and around my throat. He kissed the top of my chest and I knew he wanted to lick and suck my nipples. Instead, he left my blouse and bra in place and kissed his way back up to my mouth. With one hand, he pulled my skirt up high enough to work his fingers underneath. His fingertips grazed the front of my panties.

My hands wandered down to caress his already half-erect cock through the fabric of his pants. I admit, I was impressed at his ability to be aroused when he had to be. I suspected Dagen assumed he wouldn't be able to perform. That would give him the excuse to step in. But, no, Ben was ready when I needed him. The man was a fucking hero.

Yeah, okay, part of me was terrified of what Dagen would use this bond for, but at least I could enjoy Ben's cock for a while. And very much appreciate the fact it wasn't Dagen's.

Ben tugged my panties down far enough for me to kick them off.

I unzipped his pants and pulled them down to free his erection. I was tempted to look at Dagen, to see if he was envious of the size of Ben's cock.

When Ben's hand slid across the seam of my pussy, I forgot all about Dagen again. All I could think about was having Ben inside me. I doubted an orgasm was in my immediate future, but I was wet enough for his cock.

I hitched my skirt up just enough to spread my knees and pull him into position.

His eyes firmly fixed on mine, Ben slowly slid into my body, bit by bit. Every couple of seconds, he would stop and let me adjust to his width, and make sure I was okay.

I was as okay as I could be, under the circumstances. His cock felt amazing and I wanted him to fuck me with it for hours. Anywhere but here.

I kept my eyes on his and gave him a tentative smile. "I'm all right," I said softly. "You feel amazing."

"You feel pretty incredible yourself," he said with a smile. "Is it wrong that I want to fuck you, no matter where we are?"

"When you're hot, you're hot," I said jokingly.

"You are definitely hot." He claimed my mouth again in a searing kiss. At the same time, his hips started to move, thrusting slowly, then with increasing speed.

In spite of my assumption, I got more and more aroused with every thrust into my slick core. I wanted him to tear off my clothes and taste every part of me. I wanted to do the same to him. I sent a little prayer to the gods that we could do that someday. For now, this needed to be quick, not thorough.

His strokes became gradually faster and faster, in time with the pounding of my heart and the racing of my blood.

I slid my hands up the back of his shirt, my nails grazing the skin of his back.

"Fuck, that feels good," he whispered. "Nothing is better than the claws of my she wolf. Except her pussy." He thrust faster. His breathing became as ragged as mine.

My claws dug into his skin as I came. There was no screaming, no moaning, just a soft panting and a wash of pleasure that swept me away until it too was gone.

Ben came a moment later, with a series of quick, hard strokes. He gave out a soft, long, low groan and ground his hips against me. He thrust a few more times before exhaling out his nose and sagging down beside me.

A moment later I became aware of his feelings. Relief, pleasure and a deeper sense of love than I expected.

He picked up his head and we blinked at each other for a while before he smiled. "This is... Different."

I snorted. "Welcome to my fucked up feelings."

"Not fucked up," he said firmly, but gently. "Intense, but beautiful. Just like the outside you."

I didn't even see Dagen coming until two of his assholes grabbed Ben's arms and pulled him away from me. Another one drove his fist into Ben's stomach.

I gasped, unable to contain the surprise of not only the assault, but the way I felt Ben's pain through the bond. Fuck, that asshole could hit hard.

Dagen nodded, satisfied. "Okay, let him go." He gave me a smarmy smile. "I had to be sure."

I tugged my skirt down. "You could have just asked."

"Would you have told me the truth?" he asked.

"Considering the choice was to be fucked by you, then yes, I would have," I said coldly. "The bonding stone did its shit." I pulled the cord from around my neck and tossed the stone to the floor. I got to my feet and straightened my clothes. My heart was racing like crazy. I had, of course, considered the possibility that having Ben bond me was an experiment. Dagen wanted to know for sure that it was possible before he bonded me.

I waited for him to make a move towards me, but he didn't. Instead, he scooped up the bonding stone and put it back in his pocket.

"Enjoy your bond. We'll put it to a little test later." He gave me a smile before he swept out of the room, followed by his goons.

"Any guesses as to exactly how many screws he has loose?" I waited until the door was locked before I turned back to Ben.

He stood leaning forward, his hands on his stomach, a grimace on his face. When he saw me looking, he straightened up and schooled his expression back to calm.

I wasn't fooled for a moment, but I let him keep his dignity. He deserved that and more.

"My guess is at least twenty-seven," I said.

Ben smiled and sat back down on the couch. "My guess would be thirty-two. With at least another three or four missing."

"At least," I agreed. "Are you okay?" I sat down beside him.

He put an arm around me to draw me closer. "I'm alone with the most beautiful woman in the world, with a bond to her no one else has, not even Jake. This should be pretty fucking perfect."

"That's a whole lot of irony for a Sunday," I said. I cocked my head. "It is Sunday, isn't it?"

Ben shrugged. "I have no idea. It feels like a Sunday."

"In that case, I dread to think what Monday might bring. You know whatever he has planned is going to be shitty. For some reason he didn't want to form a bond with me. Probably because I'm too amazing for him, and also I would know all his plans. Or have a better idea of them anyway. He said the magic wears off in a couple of hours, so he won't touch me until then. After that..."

"I hate magic," Ben said. "But if it keeps him away from you, then I hope it lasts for a long time. You know this bond will, don't you? As far as I know, it will last until one of us is dead."

"I would much rather be bonded to you for the rest of my life, than bonded to Dagen for even five minutes." The idea made my stomach twist. I didn't want him to touch me in the first place, but add a bond to that, it was pretty much worst nightmare material. Although, if there was anything I'd learnt from Dagen, it was that my idea of a worst nightmare wasn't as bad as anything he could think up.

"I would also prefer to be bonded to you than him," Ben said. "For a moment there I thought he was suggesting that. That he or one of his men..."

I looked at Ben in horror. "Gods, don't give him any ideas."The idea of being raped was bad enough. The thought of watching and feeling while someone raped Ben was enough to push my sanity down half a notch. I wasn't sure I could handle having that happen to someone I cared about. And I cared about Ben deeply.

More and more as the days went on. It wasn't just the forced proximity, or his calming presence. I saw sides to him I hadn't known were there before. And I liked it. And for some reason, he liked me in spite of the fact everything he was going through was because of me.

"It's not on my wish list," he said. He kissed my forehead. "I can think of a few other things to wish for."

"Freedom," I said. "Bacon that's cooked properly. Some decent cheese. The jellybeans we never got to eat."

"A big, juicy hamburger," he added to the list. "The kind with beetroot on it."

I wrinkled my nose. "Really? Beetroot?"

He shrugged one shoulder. "I like the way it stains my fingers. It looks like blood."

"Oh." I nodded. "That makes sense." I glanced towards the door. "How long do you think it will be this time? They might keep us waiting for another three days. Or four. Or a week."

"Hmmm. What could we do to pass the time for a week?" He wiggled his brows at me. Before I could say anything, he said, "Hear me out. I'll know exactly what you like, because I'll be able to feel it. What better way to see how this bond works?"

Men.

"Yes, I'm sure that's exactly why some witch invented bonding magic," I said sarcastically. "So they could fuck better."

"I know several witches who would have invented it for exactly that," Ben said. "They wouldn't have invented it for romantic reasons."

"I suppose it is a good way to use magic," I conceded. More than that, I wouldn't have to explain why he needed to keep his cock away from my mouth. That was something I was *not* ready for.

Just the thought of it made me start to tremble again. In a matter of moments, I was back on the edge of panic.

"Oh gods," Ben said. "I'm sorry I didn't mean to—fuck." He ran a hand over his head. "I shouldn't have—"

I shook my head. "It's not your fault." I leaned forward over my knees and tried to catch a breath. I tried to think about anything else, but the memory of his cock in my mouth crashed over me. I gagged like it was happening all over again.

I tried to suck in a breath, but it got caught in my throat and I squeaked instead.

Ben put his hands on my shoulders. "Breathe. Come on, my beautiful she wolf. Breathe. He's not here. It's just you and me. If I could take away your pain, I would do it. I would take all of it. Every drop. But you know what? We will not let him win. I'll kill him with my bare hands if that's the last thing I do. It will be worth it."

I managed to regain enough of my composure to say, "He deserves to die painfully and slowly. I don't know how, but I'm going to make that happen." I was sure of that as I was sure I was still Ivory, the big bad she wolf. He would pay dearly for everything he did.

SEVEN

It was four days, in the end. After I got over my panic attack, and had a very ordinary cheese sandwich for lunch, I took Ben back to bed to test his theory. As it turns out, he was right. The moment he discovered how much I like having my nipples sucked, he spent a good hour or two doing just that. With no one to watch us, and really nothing else to do, we spent a lot of time exploring each other's bodies and getting closer.

The whole time, I couldn't help but think our time together was coming to an end. I didn't know how or why, but I savoured every moment as if it was the last.

We were sitting on the couch talking about nothing in particular when the door finally opened again.

"Let's play a game," Dagen said as he stepped into the room.

I cocked my head at him, then looked around him. "I don't see anyone with a Monopoly board." Thank the gods for that, I hated Monopoly. Still, there were worse games to play. I had a feeling we were about to find that out.

Dagen laughed. "I've already won the Monopoly. Or I will, very soon."

"Really? I would have thought you're the kind of man who would tip the board over when you're losing." I rose to my feet.

"I might," he actually agreed. "But I'm winning. Take them downstairs to the lawn."

There was something about the words that sent a chill down my spine. I glanced over to Ben who sent thoughts of reassurance. At least one of us was confident.

We were taken back down to the grass near the shed.

Four more of his henchholes waited there for us.

And Hutton.

Judging by the bruises and blood on Hutton's sullen face, and the way two goons held his arms, Dagen decided he wasn't on his side. I guessed that meant he was on mine. The timing sucked, but the relief was real. In spite of Jake's misgivings, I liked the guy.

Hutton glanced at me like he didn't recognise me. His shoulder twitched like a tiny shrug. He must have been caught doing something he shouldn't have. That was the only sign I got that he knew I existed.

I returned his glance with one of indifference.

"Did you think I'd be fooled?" Dagen asked. "By a white wolf amongst my men?"

I turned my indifference on him. "He's a traitor to our kind. He might as well be a black wolf. Those guys Gus corrupted are beyond saving." Some didn't take it well when I took back my territory. They got used to being able to kill indiscriminately. One or two died defending black wolves. A few more were disposed of quietly. No one took pleasure in that. It wasn't too surprising Jake didn't trust Hutton. The past was murky at best.

"Then you won't miss him when he's dead," Dagen said lightly.

I matched his tone. "I guess not."

To Hutton's credit, his expression didn't change. I had no idea if he was pissed off, or understood I was pretending I didn't care for his sake. I got nothing from him at all. A total closed book. He could have taken lessons in being carved ice from me.

"As for your bodyguard," Dagen went on, "you're going to miss him a little bit more. Or his cock anyway. Don't worry, mine will console you. Now you can't get pregnant, you'll be a lot more fun."

Yeah, I figured that was the point of the surgery. Not just that I couldn't breed, but that he couldn't breed with me. That was a small blessing, I supposed. Carrying his whelp would be a whole other nightmare.

"No thank you," I said, my voice frozen steel. I somehow managed to keep myself from trembling. I forced the flashbacks into the rear of my brain. "I don't want your cock, and I don't want to play games. This bullshit has gone on long enough. You think you're going to break me, but you won't." He'd have to kill me first.

Dagen leaned in closer. "That's what they all say. Right before they break." He reached up and pinched my nipple through the fabric of my bra. Just when I thought he might let it go, he twisted it so hard I let out a tiny gasp of pain. "I've barely started."

In the corner of my eye, I saw Ben take a step towards us before a couple of Dagen's men grabbed him. I felt his anger. How much he wanted to rip Dagen to pieces.

I shook my head. He should be looking for a chance to get out of here. Get away. Run.

He sent back thoughts; he didn't want to leave without me.

If you get a chance, you have to go, that's an order. I couldn't tell him in words, but those were the feelings I sent to him. He wanted to resist, I felt that through the bond too, but I was firm.

Dagen let go of my nipple and pushed me away. "I know you want me, but you'll have to wait. Our game comes first."

I staggered back but managed to stay on my feet. It was getting harder and harder to keep my composure. More difficult still when some of Dagen's men started to undress. For a moment, I thought I was the toy in this game.

Then they shifted and cold dread formed in my stomach.

"I see you understand," Dagen said smoothly. "It's been a while since we've had a good old-fashioned hunt. I've been looking forward to it. It's entertaining and a good way to get rid of two white wolves. The rules are simple. Hutton and the body-guard will get a minute head start. In fact, I'm feeling generous. Make it two minutes. Then the black wolves will give chase. Whoever catches and kills them, wins. In fact," he smiled as though he was a game show host or something, "whoever kills them, can fuck the bitch after I do. With her lovers' blood all over them."

I wanted to call him a sick fuck, but it was something I probably would have thought up myself. Blood and fucking are a perfect combination. Blood and rape, however, were a different story.

Two henchholes held Ben, while the witch crossed the lawn and removed his collar with a snap.

I both saw and felt what he was thinking.

He could shift and go after Dagen.

You have your orders. Shift and get the fuck out of here. My expression was firm. If he stuck around, they would kill him. I was certain of that. This might be his only chance. He *had* to take it. Even if I never saw him again, I needed him to be safe. If he died, if either of them did...I might break after all.

Ben's expression was defiant. He hesitated, but I was insistent. He nodded reluctantly, then glanced at Hutton. Something passed between them. Something silent, but almost palpable.

I didn't know what it meant, but the two men had come to some kind of understanding.

Dagen glanced at his watch. "Your two minutes starts... Now."

Ben and Hutton shifted simultaneously, shredding their

clothes in the process. They bounded off towards the trees, headed in opposite directions. Two white, magnificent wolves.

Barely two minutes later, Dagen nodded towards his wolves. With barely a sound, they started off after Hutton and Ben. Half one way, half the other.

I thought about making a run for it, but several goons remained arrayed around me. Far enough to give me some space, but close enough to react if I moved. Dagen was excited enough without me provoking him further.

Another man leaned against the side of the shed, a cigarette hanging from the corner of his lips. Not a goon, if his outfit was anything to go by.

He pushed himself off the wall and walked toward me.

"How about we sneak off and get to the end bit of this?" he suggested. He gave me a wink to show he was joking. For some reason, I sensed he was harmless. No, harmless wasn't the word. Just... less likely to rape me. That didn't mean I lowered my guard. Not for a second.

"What would the boss think?" I nodded towards Dagen. He was watching the trees intently, obviously enjoying the idea of his men killing Ben and Hutton.

The guy shrugged one shoulder and ashed his cigarette on the grass. "He doesn't pull my strings. He just pays me to do a job once in a while."

I looked more closely. He wore a long, black leather jacket. His neat beard held a sprinkle of grey. His dark hair was pulled back, the top tied in a ponytail. I guessed he was around the same age as Jake.

"Lucifer Fisher," I said.

He gave me a half bow. "In the flesh. And you're Ivory."

I didn't need to confirm that he was right. Who else would I be? "What is an assassin doing here?" I presumed he hadn't come to kill me. Or take part in the hunt.

"Would you believe I came to the area to surf?" he asked.

"No," I said simply. My attention was half on the conversation and half on feeling Ben run. The bush was thick, and it was slow going. What slowed him down also slowed down his pursuers. I tried not to let my fear for him bleed out into the bond. Now would be a really bad time for him to be distracted.

"They said you were smart," the assassin said approvingly.

I cocked my head at him. "They said you were stealthy. But here you are, standing right in front of me."

"If I didn't want you to see me, you wouldn't," he said. "Being an assassin is a lonely job. Sometimes I like to have a conversation with someone who's not..." He nodded towards Dagen.

"An asshole psychopath?" I guessed.

He chuckled softly. "Something like that. Some of us aren't happy the Onyx Ridge pack's name is being sullied by an alpha who doesn't have all of our best interests at heart."

That surprised me. Not that he was thinking it, but that he would come out and say it with Dagen standing a few metres away. Not to mention his goons who were even closer.

"Those are brave words, Lucifer Fisher," I told him.

"Call me Luca," he said. "I'm not scared of Alistair Dagen. I'm much more scared of you." He gave me a lopsided smile and pulled out another cigarette. He offered me one before lighting his.

I shook my head to decline the offer. "Under most circumstances, I would suggest it's wise to be scared of me," I said. Anyone with any sense should be. I had a long memory and a lot of resources. "I seem to be slightly disadvantaged right now."

"A situation I'm sure you will remedy before too much longer," he assured me. He took a long draw on his cigarette. "Alistair's dislike of women means he tends to underestimate them."

This assassin seemed to have more faith in me than I had in myself. It was strangely gratifying.

"I'm starting to think you know something I don't," I said. "If the black wolves are planning a coup, you have my full support."

Luca looked amused at that. "If we were planning anything, would I tell you? At the end of the day, you're still the enemy."

I thought about that for a moment. "Sometimes we end up in bed with people we don't expect to end up in bed with. For mutual benefit."

He nodded and dropped his cigarette butt to the grass. He put it out with his heel. "So if any of us were planning anything, you would help if it was to your benefit?"

"I might be persuaded," I agreed. "Whoever replaced the current asshole would have to be an improvement. Would it be you?"

Now he looked surprised. "Me? Gods no." He laughed. "No black wolf in their right mind would follow me."

"Why not?" I asked. "They follow him. Surely he is the bottom of the barrel, not the top."

Luca shrugged and pulled out another cigarette. "He has a lot of support because of who his parents were." He looked at me like he was suggesting that was the reason people supported me.

"Sometimes parentage is a good reason *not* to follow someone," I said dryly. "No one could claim my parents were saints. My father had more mistresses than he had hair on his head. My mother was... Let's just say she wouldn't have won mother of the year." She was distant at best.

"And you've risen above all of that," Luca said.

Let's see, I had a few boyfriends, if you wanted to call them that. If I was still able to have children, I would be distant like my mother, busy, distracted. Maybe I was more like my parents than I'd like to admit.

I pushed down the panic that threatened to rise at the

memory of the surgery. I couldn't let that leak into the bond with Ben either.

He had run through a small stream and was currently lurking in some bushes near the fence line.

"I can't claim to be perfect," I said slowly. "But I wouldn't do the things Dagen does. Even if I had the equipment. If I had to choose between me and him, I would align with me."

"And how would the rest of the white wolves feel about working with black wolves?" Luca asked. "That is an old hate that runs deep."

"That's true," I admitted. "It wouldn't be easy." For all my talk about supporting a coup, it would be very difficult for me to put my own prejudice aside and work with them. It might be impossible for Jake. For Ben too. For him it would be like working with witches. Cooper was the only one too young to have lived through what the rest of us did. Lucky him.

"So," I said slowly. "Is there a plan?"

"Not that I know of," Luca said. "But like I said, if there was, I wouldn't tell you. No offence."

"None taken," I said. "Just think about what I said."

He pulled a lighter out of his pocket and lit his third cigarette. "How is your boy doing?"

It took me a moment to realise he knew about the bond. How? I was tempted to ask, but no doubt Dagen's goons liked to gossip.

"He's still alive," I said. He was no closer to finding a way out through the fence though. I hoped to the gods there was one. Obviously the point of this hunt, and the bond, was to have me feel the moment Dagen's men ripped Ben to pieces. It would be like killing me, but I would still be alive. If he wanted me to break, that would certainly expedite the process. It was a simple, but fucked up plan. Just the way Dagen liked it.

"Why aren't you taking part?" I asked. "I thought an assassin would enjoy killing."

Luca raised his eyebrows at me. "I prefer subtler methods. And I like a challenge. A handful of black wolves against two white ones... The odds aren't really in their favour."

That was true. If Ben couldn't find a way out through the fence, then he didn't stand much of a chance against his pursuers.

Same with Hutton, wherever he was. The baying of wolves sounded distant. He could have led them a long way from the house. What had passed between him and Ben? A plan to separate? To give themselves half a chance? Maybe they hoped to draw all of the black wolves after one of them, giving the other guy a free pass.

Who knows what men are thinking on any given day?

"Even if you got to fuck me afterwards?" I asked bluntly.

"Considering Alistair wasn't factoring consent into his gracious offer," Luca said ironically, "I'm not interested." He gave me a slow smile. "Do I look like the kind of guy who needs to force himself on a woman?"

I couldn't help but smile back. "You look like the kind of guy who would charm the pants off even a white wolf. Under different circumstances, of course."

He inclined his head. "Of course. You're not what I expected."

I snorted. "Neither are you. You're very articulate for a black wolf."

"And for a white wolf, you don't have your head up your ass," he said. "And you haven't threatened me yet."

"Would you like me to?" I asked sweetly. "I'm sure I could think of something."

He chuckled. "I'm sure you could. So could I. You are, after all, still surrounded by black wolves."

I sighed. "Don't remind me." They were closing in on Ben. I could feel his heart pounding. My sense that we were running out of time was stronger now. A sliver of fear crept up my spine. My gaze turned towards Dagen. He looked excited, like he knew the end was close. It was only a matter of time before he turned that excitement on me.

"Has anyone ever asked you to assassinate themselves?" I asked.

"Are you asking me to?" Luca asked. I couldn't tell what he thought of the suggestion.

I shrugged. "You know what's going to happen to me."

"I also know death is very permanent," he said. "Don't go asking for it until you're sure. And you have a way to be sure I get paid for it. After all, Alistair would be pissed off if I did it. It would have to be worth it."

"Sorry, I seem to be without my phone," I said. "Maybe I could borrow yours?" It was worth a try, right?

Before he could answer, the bush in front of us burst into flames.

EIGHT

ll hells broke loose. The baying of wolves turned to screams of pain and fear. The air was thick with it. That and smoke.

Through the bond I felt Ben's surprise, a flash of terror, then relief. He darted through a hole in the fence that hadn't been there a moment ago. It was hot. So hot he was worried it would catch his fur on fire. Then he was through and bounding out the other side.

The black wolves followed him through, right on his tail. But then they froze.

He was surrounded. By people and white wolves. Familiar faces. Hutton. Cooper.

Jake.

I wanted to sob, but I clung to my composure.

"Fuck," Dagen swore. His face was red with fury. He rounded on me. "What did you do, *bitch?*" Of course, he had no way to know what was going on beyond the fire that was quickly spreading through the trees. Unless he had a bond with one of the hunters. If so, I hoped he had an agonising, slow death. Just like the one Dagen deserved.

"What?" I asked innocently. "I've been standing here the whole time." I backed up a step, and hated myself for doing it, but his expression was pure murder. More than that, he looked like he was ready to tear me apart with his bare hands. And take his time doing it.

He saw my reaction and smiled.

Smiled.

He was a fucking bully who got off on scaring people who were less able to fight back.

"Get the bitch around to the back of the house. We need to evacuate." At least he had that much sense.

A tree about fifty metres away exploded. A heavy branch was thrown so far it smashed into the bathhouse. Everything inside that was flammable immediately caught fire.

That was the distraction I needed. I cursed the fucking collar that prevented me from shifting, and bolted as fast as I could across the grass and away from the house. I headed towards the driveway and hoped like hells it was wide enough to act as a firebreak.

Behind me, Dagen shouted. I glanced over my shoulder as a couple of goons started after me, but the rest followed Dagen towards the back of the house.

Coward.

He probably thought the fire would take care of me so he didn't have to. Or he was just thinking about saving his own ass, and that his men would deal with me.

The further I ran, the thicker the smoke became. It got into my lungs, made it harder and harder to breathe.

A sensible person would probably turn and run the other way. I could let Dagen's men grab me and get the hells away from the growing flames. I weighed up my options and decided that I would prefer to face the fire than the things Alistair Dagen would do to me. Maybe that made me a coward. Maybe it didn't.

These last couple of weeks had proved there were worse things than dying.

The smoke made my eyes water. I coughed and blinked away tears. The only consolation was that my pursuers were suffering as much as I was.

Through the bond, Ben sent thoughts of reassurance. He was close.

The men behind me were closer. Their shoes pounded on the gravel. They must be so sure they could catch me, they didn't even bother to shift. They might be right.

I threw out my hands to protect my face as a tree exploded a couple of metres away. Heat washed over me like a furnace. It was moments like this when I remembered I wasn't made of actual ice. I would melt the same as anyone else.

I sensed Ben's worry. He wanted to come to me. He was telling Jake and Cooper where I was. They were getting frantic.

I sent back thoughts that I was fine. They needed to stay where they were. That was an order. I added my relief that Ben was safe. If I didn't get out of this, at least he had. Hutton too.

Another tree exploded. I narrowly avoided being hit by a red-hot branch. I swerved at the last moment but slowed enough for one of Dagen's men to grab my arm.

"Are you crazy?" he hissed. "We need to get the fuck out of here."

"Go ahead," I said between coughs. "Tell your boss I'm dead." I would be if we stood here for much longer. So would the guy whose fingers dug into my skin.

"Come on." He tried to drag me back towards the house. His companion caught up with us and grabbed me by my other arm.

We were all coughing now.

"You two can get out of here alive if you shift," I pointed out. "I can't shift, all I'll do is slow you down."

I was right and they knew it. I saw it on their faces. "I can't run any faster. You saw me." I turned my face and wiped tears on my sleeve. "Save your own asses. Dying in a fucking fire is above your pay grade."

They exchanged glances. They might also kill me, then run, but that would waste valuable seconds. Both knew that too.

One nodded. "I hope you die painfully, bitch." He shifted and loped back towards the house. His companion followed half a second later.

"Right back at you," I told them. I waited for a tree to explode and take them out, but instead they safely disappeared from view.

Shame. I was getting really, really tired of being called bitch.

I staggered back down the driveway, but my thoughts were foggy. Smoke inhalation, I knew, was worse than the flames themselves.

The smoke was so thick now it was getting more and more difficult to tell the difference between driveway and brush. It was also getting harder to fight the urge to sit down. I could just give up, let the smoke take me, but fuck that. This was nowhere near the hardest thing I had ever done. I wasn't going to let it beat me. Not with the guys so bloody close.

"Ivory?" Jake's voice was the single sweetest sound I've ever heard, even though it was laced with fear.

I tried to shout back, but got caught up in a coughing fit.

"Ivory?" That was Cooper. "Where are you?"

Ben asked the same question, but through the bond. Gods, he felt so close.

My head was swimming now and my lungs were burning. I wanted to rip off the collar, shift and run the last—it couldn't be more than a handful of metres.

All I could do was let the tears stream down my cheeks and run blindly towards their voices, to where the bond took me.

I staggered past burning bushes and the twisted remains of the front gate. That was the surest sign I had that Jake had done exactly as I'd asked. I only knew of one person powerful enough to do that, and set the bush on fire.

"Ivory!" Jake shouted again. "She's over here."

I took a handful more steps before I fell into a strong, tattooed pair of arms.

"She needs a healer. Where is that witch? Paxton?" Jake shouted loud enough to make me wince. "Oh gods, sorry." He wiped the tears of my cheeks with his thumbs. "Elodie, I was so fucking—" He shook his head. "I thought..."

I spoke although my voice was hoarse and my throat burned like hells. "I'm okay." That was a flat out lie and we both knew it. "I will be."

"Ivory!" Cooper bounded towards me like a puppy. He threw his arms around me and gave me a squeeze. "Ben said you were okay, but I needed to see you. How did he know?"

I squeezed him back. "That's an answer for later." I felt Ben before I saw him, and reached to lace my fingers into his.

We shared a look. The kind people share when they've been through something together only they would understand.

"I'm glad you're okay," he said softly.

"You too," I said.

Jake and Cooper looked surprised at this new intimacy between us, but neither seemed like they would question it. They were just relieved to see me and Ben alive.

Truthfully, I was pretty fucking relieved myself.

"You should sit down," Jake gestured towards one of the waiting cars.

Hutton sat on the ground, his back leaning against a tyre, face pale. Judging by the amount of blood on his skin, the black wolves caught up to him. A man with dark hair and a blonde-headed woman crouched beside him.

"Hutton told us where you were," Jake said. "Gave us a bunch of useful information, before he was caught. If it wasn't for Harmony and Paxton, he wouldn't have made it."

On hearing their names, the pair turned and rose.

Ben stiffened.

Harmony was half witch, half demon. Presumably that was close enough to being a full witch for Ben's taste. Paxton Evans was a full witch, but if he saved Hutton, then he got a pass as far as I was concerned.

"She's breathed in a shit load of smoke," Jake said. He helped me to sit down beside Hutton.

"And I want this fucking collar off from around my neck," I said. I was tired of feeling like a pet dog.

"That should be easy enough," Paxton said. Judging by the look on his face, he clearly knew smoke and a magic collar weren't the only things wrong with me right now. They were the only things he could heal though.

He put a hand lightly on my arm. I felt the tingle of magic. Almost immediately, the burning in my lungs started to recede. With his other hand, he gripped the collar and it fell away from my neck. He glanced at it for a moment before handing it to Jake.

I nodded towards Harmony. She was pregnant when we first met and she was pregnant again now. I couldn't contain a pang of jealousy. It was going to take time to come to terms with what Dagen stole from me. I may never accept it, but I could try to be happy for her.

"I assume you started the fire?" I asked.

She smiled. "It wasn't exactly my intention. I was trying to blast the gate open. Sometimes my magic does what I want it to. Sometimes not." She sighed through her nose and lightly rested a hand on her belly. "This little one was trying to help too. She doesn't understand restraint yet."

"Like her mother," Paxton said teasingly.

Harmony gave him a fond look, which he returned. She looked a lot more content when I saw her last.

"I appreciate it either way," I said. "This makes us even." She came to me a year or so ago, wanting a siphon stone so she could get back the magic which was stolen from her. I managed to secure a stone, but gave it to her with the condition that she owed me a favour. I had no idea at the time what that favour would be, but I thanked past me for the insight. Having Jake call on her to fulfil her end of the bargain saved my ass today. And Ben's and Hutton's too.

Having powerful people owe you a favour was worth more than money. I would have to see if I could find a way to do something else for her. It wouldn't hurt to have her in my pocket again. Just in case.

I heard the thrum of a helicopter engine. For a minute or two, I forgot all about Dagen. Now, I watched his chopper rise above the burning treetops and head off in a southerly direction.

"I knew I should have bought the helicopter and equipped it with missiles," Jake said darkly.

"Fuck," I said softly. "I don't suppose you brought a dragon with you?"

"I would have, but no one asked," Paxton said. "There, that will stop you from dying of smoke inhalation. It's going to take longer to fix the internal damage. I presume you'd rather not do that here." Shit, he was blunt.

Everyone's eyes were on me. Jake looked like he was ready to climb the tree tops and bring down the chopper himself.

"*Internal damage?*" he asked.

"It's nothing that can be fixed," I said softly.

"I can't put anything back," Paxton agreed. "But whoever healed you didn't heal everything. There's scar tissue that's going to be a problem if it's not dealt with." He muttered something about unskilled witches.

258

"What are you talking about?" Jake asked. "Put things back? What the fuck?"

"Later," Paxton snapped. "In case you hadn't noticed, the fire is spreading. Unless you want to get burnt to a crisp, I suggest we get out of here."

Jake quickly nodded. "Everyone, get into the cars." He reached for my hand. He and Ben helped me to my feet. From there, it was a step or two into the back seat of the closest vehicle. Jake headed around to the driver's side door, and Ben slid in next to me. To my surprise, Harmony and Paxton helped Hutton into the other side before they hurried to another car.

"Hey," I said softly to Hutton. "Seems like we have you to thank for getting out just in time."

He shrugged. "I did what you sent me in there to do. I found enough information on Dagen to even shut Jake up."

"Don't count on it," Jake said. He waited until Cooper slipped into the passenger seat before he gunned the engine and followed the other cars out towards the highway. "But you led us to Ivory, and for that I will be eternally grateful."

"But you still don't trust me?" Hutton said.

"That depends what information you found," Jake said. "Let's just say the jury is still out."

Hutton grunted under his breath.

"Jake will come around," Cooper said confidently. "You did almost get eaten by wolves."

I should probably step in and say something, or tell them to shut up, but all I wanted to do right now was lean against Ben, close my eyes and pretend the last couple of weeks never happened. Paxton's blunt tone, although clearly not intended to be hurtful, cut me right down to the bone. Somehow it made everything seem so much more painfully real.

"I know it doesn't seem like it right now, but you're going to be okay," Ben whispered in my ear. "You're the strongest person I know."

"I'm not sure about that," I said. "If it wasn't for you being there with me, I probably would have unravelled."

"No you wouldn't," he said. "You're Ivory. You wouldn't have let Dagen win. You still won't. If I was him, I would be shaking in my shoes."

"There is no way you would ever be him," I said firmly.

He put an arm around me and pulled me to his chest.

Cooper twisted around in his seat. "So, are you two a thing too?"

Jake turned his head just enough to hear without taking his eyes off the road.

I glanced over my shoulder at Ben. "We'll see." Honestly, right now I could barely think straight, much less make any kind of promises. There was still the chance the closeness was only because of what we endured. Once we got back to our lives, we might go back to boss and bodyguard. That might be all Ben wanted.

All of this was a conversation for later.

"You and I could be a thing if you give me a chance." Hutton gave me a cheeky grin.

"Like I said, we'll see," I said. "Can a girl rest for a while first?"

"Of course, take all the time you need," he replied easily. "Just don't take too long."

I managed a weary smile, but that was the best I could do right now.

Apparently not quite ready to let the matter lie, Jake said, "I don't know about the Hutton thing, but I trust Ben almost as much as I trust myself. Now I think about it, I'm not sure what took you two so long. I'm pretty sure Ben has been hot for you since he met you."

Ben chuckled. "He's not wrong." He didn't elaborate.

Evidently he was willing to let the matter lie for a while. Or physical attraction was as far as it went, and this was his way of pulling back.

I looked out the window in silence and wondered what would have happened if I'd gone with Dagen. Could I somehow have stopped him from getting on that helicopter? Or better yet, thrown him off it? Or would he be taking all of his frustration out on me right now? It was probably just as well I would never know the answer to that. He would never have the opportunity again. If Jake had to handcuff me to him, he would never let me out of his sight again. That would chafe eventually, but I didn't want him out of my sight either. Any of the guys.

I cracked my eyes open. "What happened to Toby?" I asked Hutton.

"They were about to kill him when a guy in a leather jacket said he would deal with him," Hutton said. "He said he was part of the Onyx Ridge pack. Dagen's men seemed to know who he was. They handed him over."

I nodded. Luca Fisher, I presumed. That might mean there was hope for Toby yet. Or Luca had some agenda of his own. I had no doubt he did. Everyone had an agenda.

We reached the highway and headed south, a convoy of SUVs and other vehicles. Wolf shifters with black wolf blood on them, or their own blood. People like me, slightly charred and tainted with ash. But alive. The scratches and scrapes, bruises and dirt were nothing.

It was the internal shit that weighed heavily on my mind. I felt as though at some point, I was going to lose my shit completely. Unravel. Cry for a week or two. I didn't know when or where, I just knew it would happen.

I needed to hold it together as best I could in the meantime.

And make a plan.

Alistair Dagen would pay dearly for what he did to me.

NINE

"What is this place?" We pulled up behind Paxton's white SUV outside a building on a quiet suburban street.

"It's a house that belongs to a friend of a friend," Jake said. "I figured the three of you would appreciate a chance to clean up before we got back to the city."

Considering I was a mess and Ben and Hutton were wrapped in old blankets found in the back of the car, that was a fair guess. There was more than likely more to it than that though. Regrouping. Debriefing. A thorough health check.

"That's very thoughtful," Hutton said with a hint of sarcasm.

Jake looked at his reflection in the rearview mirror. "Unless you want to walk the rest of the way..."

"If you don't stop, you can *both* walk the rest of the way," I growled. I was getting tired of their bickering. It was helpful to exactly no one and it made my frayed nerves worse.

Both guys actually shut up, but they still shot daggers at each other with their eyes.

Ben gave me a squeeze and helped me out of the car, even

though I tried to wave off his help. Cooper was at my other elbow a moment later.

"If you guys are going to start to smother me..." I didn't know what I would do. I appreciated that they cared about me and wanted to look after me, but at this rate I would have to turn in my badass she wolf card and slink away with my tail between my legs. In spite of the last couple of weeks, I still wanted to believe I could take care of myself. I *could* take care of myself. I had done it since I was eight years old.

"We don't want to smother you," Cooper said. "We just love you. We were scared we would lose you. Well, I was. Jake said you would be okay. He said you wouldn't let a little thing like a kidnapping take you from us."

"That sounds like Jake." I gave Jake a look. I knew him better than that. He would have been just as worried as Cooper, if not more. He knew the shit Dagen was capable of. No doubt he was just trying to reassure Cooper.

"Did he let you kill anyone?" I asked.

Cooper sighed. "No. Not even Dagen's men. He left that to the other guys."

I patted his shoulder. "I'm sure there will be plenty of time for that later. There's lots of black wolves left in need of killing."

He brightened up. "Yeah, there are. I hope I can get in on it this time."

I exchanged glances with Ben. He looked amused, like he was listening to his kid brother talk about a playdate. I guessed he was, in a way. It did seem to be Cooper's idea of fun.

We walked up the front steps and entered the house after Jake unlocked the door.

"Nice place," Hutton said. "Cosy."

The whole house was smaller than the apartment at Crimson, but it would do.

"There's clothes in the wardrobe that should fit you all," Jake said. He waved vaguely towards one of the rooms.

"I'd like a word with Ivory," Paxton said. "In private." After a moment he added, "Harmony can be in attendance if you're worried I can't keep my hands to myself." He looked like he was on the verge of an eye roll. He was a doctor after all. Hopefully a better one than the asshole who worked for Dagen.

"I'm sure there's nothing you could talk to her about that we can't hear," Jake said.

"Doctor/patient confidentiality," Paxton said. "You four are not impartial." He waved me towards another room like he wouldn't take no for an answer.

All four of the guys looked like they were ready to punch the shit out of him.

It was Harmony who put up her hands to defuse the situation. "Paxton wouldn't ask if it wasn't important. I'll keep a close eye on him."

Jake seemed unsure as to if he should trust either of them, but they had helped get me away from Dagen. That gave them a metric shit ton of credibility as far as I was concerned.

I nodded at the guys to back down.

"I'll be fine," I said. "I can take care of myself." Frankly, it wouldn't hurt to be checked over by an actual doctor, not that butcher Dagen hired, or the witch, Irina.

We headed into the other room and Harmony closed the door softly behind us.

"I'll make this brief," Paxton said. "You were held prisoner by an asshole. That is not something you get over straightaway. You can ask Harmony. She knows all about it."

"Paxton kept me locked in a room for five months," she said lightly. "It really does fuck with your head. Well, it was Zeta, but he worked for them. Or *with* them. It's complicated."

Paxton shrugged. "I was trying to keep her safe."

I looked at them both in surprise. "If a man did that to me, I would cut off his balls."

Paxton responded to that with a wry smile. "What makes you think I have any balls left?"

I wasn't sure if he was joking or not, but Harmony grinned.

"So that's not yours then," I stated and waved at Harmony's belly.

She pressed her hands to her bump. "She's Jordan's. He's the guy who was with me when I asked for the siphon stone. He wanted to be here, but he is looking after our other baby. We're still in hiding from Zeta."

I nodded. "I appreciate you taking the chance to help me." Not that they had a choice.

"Yeah." Paxton nodded. "I wanted to finish the healing I started up north. And give you a chance to talk about what happened with someone who is not going to get emotional and start beating their chest."

I wanted to deny that the guys would do that, but he was right. If I wanted to talk about things, it would be better to do that with someone impartial.

He put a hand on my arm. I felt the tingle of magic again. "He broke a cheekbone? The witch didn't heal it properly either."

"Dagen told her to leave the bruises." I stood still, trying not to show how disconcerting his touch was.

"She left more than that."

I felt movement under the skin, then Paxton nodded.

"That's better. Leg too? Anywhere else? Apart from your abdomen? You know you'll never have children?"

I nodded and tried to ignore Harmony's look of sympathy. She was much sweeter than I was.

Before I could respond verbally, Paxton added, "Vaginal tearing?"

I winced at how blunt the question was.

Even Harmony looked surprised.

"No," I said. "He didn't touch me there. Not my ass either," I added before he could ask.

"Is there any chance he drugged you and did things you can't remember?" he asked. He lowered his hands and crossed his arms over his chest. "I know these questions are invasive, but they're important. You don't have to tell me, but tell someone. Get therapy. Whatever."

"Is that what you did?" I asked Harmony. I saw the fond looks she gave Paxton and wondered how the hells she ever forgave him. I mean, there's room in the world for all sorts of relationships, but if someone like Jake locked me up, I couldn't imagine forgiving him. I would probably let Cooper kill him. On the other hand, Jake would never do that.

I sighed. "No, I don't think he drugged me and did anything. Not unless he drugged Ben as well. It's not really his style though. He's a bully. He likes people to know what he's done. He likes an audience."

"Paxton," Harmony said softly. "Can you wait outside with the others?"

He hesitated for a moment, then nodded. "Take your time." He backed out the door and closed it behind him.

"I don't know about you, but I need to sit." Harmony lowered herself down to the bed in the middle of the room.

I took the hint and sat beside her. "Why don't you hate him?"

She glanced towards the door. "Paxton and I are complicated. Fucked up, absolutely. But we work. He understands me and I understand him. And yes, I have a very nice psychologist who helps me work through all this. And three other guys who help keep Paxton in check. Do you want to talk about what happened to you?"

I closed my eyes and sucked in a breath. "Not really. I'd like to just put it behind me. You're going to tell me I can't, aren't you?"

Harmony put a hand lightly on one of mine. "I'm going to tell you it's not that simple. You wouldn't have called in that favour if you had a choice. I've heard about this Dagen guy, he sounds like a nasty piece of work. And I know the kinds of things men do to have power over women. Taking away your ability to have children was as big a violation as forcing himself on you. Taking away your choice... It's evil."

"You're telling me," I said lightly. I didn't have any women friends, so this felt strange. Usually Jake and I just let each other rant and rave before we got back to work. It wasn't that he wasn't a good listener, but neither of us was very good at sharing deep feelings. Obviously, since it took us so long to get it together.

"He did... Other things?" Harmony asked gently. "You don't have to talk about it if you don't want to. Just know that if you do, I'm here for you." She gave me a funny look and then added, "The first time we met, I was terrified of you."

"If the next words out of your mouth are that you're not scared anymore, I'm going to be really pissed off," I said jokingly.

She laughed softly. "No, I'm still scared of you. But now I don't think you're going to have me killed."

"Not today," I agreed. "I think I'll save all of that for the black wolves."

"You're going to spill a lot of blood, aren't you?" she asked.

"A lot," I agreed. "I should have done it a long time ago. I was so busy trying not to provoke a war that I got myself caught up in a trap."

"Trying not to provoke a war is a good thing," she said. "Especially when you've got organisations like Zeta ready to step in and take advantage of any unrest."

"I should try to find a way to pit Zeta and Dagen against each other," I mused. "Let them kill each other off."

"Please do," Harmony said with surprising enthusiasm. "That would take care of both our problems."

"I'll see what I can do," I said. If I could pull that off, it would be one hells of a move. And Harmony would owe me favours until the end of time.

I looked down at my knees. My heart raced and sweat spun up on my palms. If I was ever going to share this with anyone, it would be now. I couldn't imagine telling the guys, or even talking about it with Ben. The memory was too bitter, too raw. It always would be.

"My mouth," I whispered. Tears trickled down my cheeks.

"Your— Oh." My words must have taken a moment to register. "I'm so sorry. I should have blasted his helicopter out of the sky. It was either that or heal your friend Hutton. Paxton needed my help..."

She looked so apologetic, I found myself squeezing her hand.

"You made the right choice," I said. I would have said the same thing if Dagen had crashed and burned, literally. The past was the past. There was no point living in it. That said though, I was glad Hutton didn't die.

"This Dagen asshole must be really scared of you," she said. "If not before, then he should be now. I would be, if I did something like that to you. He tried to take away your power, but it didn't work. You're still just as badass as ever."

I wiped the tears off my cheeks. "You're right. That was exactly what he was trying to do, and he failed. And I'm going to make him hurt really, really badly. I'm glad you didn't destroy his helicopter. It would have been over much too quickly. He deserves to have his toenails and fingernails pulled out one by one. Literally and figuratively. And maybe every hair on his body as well."

Harmony grinned. "He deserves all of that and more. He's gonna really wish he hadn't crossed you."

"He certainly will," I agreed. "So will all of the men who work for him." Starting with the ones who held me down. "Every last one of them." I nodded with absolute certainty. "Thank you. It really did help to talk about it. But if you tell anyone what I told you, including Paxton, I will have you killed."

I wasn't joking now. No one else needed to know what happened. I would think about it this one last time, then never again. At least in theory.

Harmony smiled gently. "I would never tell anyone. You have my word on that. But if you ever want to talk about it a bit more, or about anything else, I'm happy to listen. Any time. I'll give you my number. As long as you can assure me it will never end up in Zeta's hands."

"It won't," I assured her. She was smart enough not to threaten me if it did, but I couldn't imagine any circumstances where I would give anything to Zeta other than a side eye and maybe a middle finger.

I also wasn't naïve enough to think this made Harmony and I friends. She was sweeter than I would ever be. Tough, but kind. Her children would grow up surrounded by love. If I'd had any children, they would have grown up surrounded by violence and blood. There was nothing wrong with those two things, but it wasn't the best environment for a child.

"The guys are probably itching to talk to you," she said. "They clearly adore you. Jake was beside himself when he contacted us. He tried to pretend he wasn't, but it was obvious. I don't think he slept in the last two weeks."

"Probably not, knowing Jake," I said. Now I felt a little bit bad because I had spent a lot of the last few days under the covers, fucking Ben. Not everything about the last two weeks was bad. Most of it, but not all of it.

"And Cooper," Harmony said as she got to her feet. "I'd be surprised if he doesn't walk along behind you, kissing the ground as you go." She laughed. "He's like a besotted puppy. Jake even calls him pup."

I didn't explain that it was short for Murder Pup, Jake's nickname for Cooper. Given to him because of Cooper's apparent fascination with murder.

"Cooper is very sweet," I agreed. He was certainly going to make an interesting assassin someday.

I stepped out the door and into Jake's arms.

"Were you listening?" I asked accusingly.

"Of course not," he said. "I was waiting patiently for you." He squeezed me like he had no intention of ever, ever letting go. He looked exhausted but he smelt like home.

I pressed my head against his chest and exhaled softly. "I wasn't sure if I would ever see you again."

"Of course you would," he said. "You can't get rid of me that easily. I would follow you to the bottom of the seven hells if I had to."

"So would I," Cooper said. He looked like he hadn't slept for two weeks either. He stepped over and gave us both a hug.

"Me too." Ben joined us on the other side.

Hutton cleared his throat.

When I looked over at him, he shrugged. "Just give me a chance? I did almost die for you."

Jake sighed loudly.

"Hutton did help us a lot," Cooper said. "Even you said so, Jake. We wouldn't have found her if it wasn't for him."

"You would have found me," I said. But it would have been too late for Ben. Too late for Hutton. Too late to prevent me from being violated further. Maybe too late to prevent me from being broken.

"Hutton did lead us right to you," Jake said grudgingly. "But I still want to reserve judgement until I see the rest of the information. And make sure there's not a virus in the message you sent."

"If there is, I didn't put it there," Hutton said.

"I can ask Freddie to have a look for you," Harmony said. "He's a genius with computers. If there's anything funny in there, he'll find it."

It was Jake who nodded. "I've heard that about him. I'll have our people look at it, but it wouldn't hurt to have a second set of eyes."

Harmony nodded. "Of course, he'll be happy to help. And if you meant what you said about pitting Dagen against Zeta, we'll help with that too."

"Anything to bring down those assholes," Paxton agreed.

I would have to see what they could do to help. I wasn't going to let their agenda get in the way of mine. My target was Dagen and the Onyx Ridge pack. Zeta would be collateral damage at best. They didn't need to know that though. They just needed to do what I asked when I asked them to do it. And they would, I would make sure of that.

CHAPTER
TEN

"At least this place is still standing," I said as we pulled into the garage underneath Crimson. Jake pulled the SUV into the space beside my Cobra. "You drove her here?"

"I did," Cooper said. "Jake can't drive a manual."

Jake looked over his shoulder and scowled at Cooper. "I can drive one, I just let you drive that time because we had two cars and two of us." After a moment he admitted, "And if there was a bomb in the car, it would blow up Cooper, not me."

Cooper put a hand around his mouth and loudly whispered, "Jake can't drive a manual."

I knew very well Jake could, and this little display was just to cheer me up.

I managed a smile. "Maybe not, but it's always sensible to let someone else drive a car that might explode."

"That's usually my job," Ben said. "Thanks for taking one for the team, Coop."

Cooper grinned. "Any time." His smile faded into a frown. "I don't actually want to get blown up though."

"Me either," Ben said. "The risk is just part of the job. It's what

272

keeps it exciting." He gave me a faint smile and a nod. Exciting didn't accurately describe the last couple of weeks, but we got through it. More or less sane.

"I could use a bit of boredom for a while." I followed Ben out of the car and stepped over to inspect my Cobra. She didn't seem to be damaged, lucky for Cooper and Dagen. She was even parked inside the lines.

"These were still in there." Jake pulled out my phone and my mother's watch and handed them to me.

His fingers lingered on my palm and he locked his blue eyes on mine. "I thought about hiding that and getting you a smartwatch, but I figured you'd be pissed if I did."

I wasn't expecting the joke, so it took me a moment to realise what he was saying. When I did, I snorted and socked him lightly on the arm. "I like this watch. I took it off so it wouldn't get damaged when I shifted." I slipped it back onto my wrist and shoved my phone into the pocket of my skirt. There were probably a million messages on there. I would deal with those later.

"Thank you. I wasn't sure if I would see either of them again." Of course, they were just things. The watch and the Cobra had sentimental value, but at the end of the day they were replaceable. Like my phone.

Jake looked like he had something to say, probably plenty, but he took my hand and led me to the elevator. Cooper stayed close to me on the other side, and Hutton and Ben followed a couple of steps behind.

Through the bond, I felt Ben's tension rise slightly. That is to say, he was still the epitome of calm, but now he was on alert for any dangers. He was watching me and my every move, every step, looking for every possible risk on the way to the elevator. Inside the elevator. Inside the apartment as we stepped into the familiar space. Only once he'd walked around the apartment, looking carefully, did he relax slightly.

I wished I could relax. Being back here felt both familiar and strange. Like nothing had happened, but everything had happened at the same time.

I walked over to the window and stood looking out at the view. Ferries and other boats slid across the shining water of the harbour. A cruise ship was moored at Circular Quay. Tiny people moved about, either getting ready to board, or disembarking from some adventure.

Life went on. A lot of the people out there would know who I was, but just as some rich nightclub owner. Not one of them would give a shit what happened to me. Plenty of them would probably think I deserved it. That I should be brought down to earth. And those were just the humans who had no idea shifters actually existed. A lot of the shifters who weren't wolves, had reason to dislike me. Just because Ivory Claw took better care of the city, and the state as a whole, than Dagen, didn't mean I wasn't part devil in their eyes.

Truthfully, I didn't really give a crap what they thought about me, as long as they stayed out of my way. I wasn't in this for the popularity. Still, it would be nice to know that if people were forced to take sides, I could be sure they would take mine.

"Elodie," Jake said softly.

I watched his reflection step up behind me. Tentatively, he put his hands on my shoulders.

"I'm fine," I said before he could speak. "Glad to be home. I assume there's a list of things I need to catch up on. I'll look at it in the morning. Unless there's anything you think I should see now." The last thing I wanted to do was think about work, but just as life went on, so did business. I couldn't afford to lose money because I was wallowing in self-pity.

"No, there's nothing urgent." He nestled his face into my shoulder. His breath brushed over my neck. "We've been taking care of things at the same time as we were looking for you. I figured you would growl at me if I let everything slide." His tone was light but I knew him better than to be fooled by it. He was obviously worried about me.

"Growl if you're lucky," I said. "Bite your head off if I came back to a total mess."

"Which head?" he asked teasingly.

I immediately stiffened. My breath caught in the back of my throat. The idea of his cock, anyone's cock, anywhere near my mouth...

Ben tensed in response to my sudden discomfort. Knowing he knew exactly why didn't make it any easier. I had to remind myself he'd also been through an ordeal. He'd almost died. He needed time, just like I did.

I mentally waved him down and forced myself to take a breath. "Either of them," I said, my voice more terse than I intended.

"Elodie, I'm sorry, I didn't—" Jake gently turned me around to face him. "I wasn't trying to pressure you." He locked his blue eyes on my brown ones. His emotions were written right there on his face. Including the thought that he failed me by not keeping me safe. As if he could watch me every hour of every day. As if Dagen wouldn't have taken us both and made Jake watch...

I swallowed. "I know you weren't," I said. "We wouldn't be us if we didn't joke around a bit. Right?"

He gave a slight shrug of one muscular, tattooed shoulder. "There's joking, and then there's saying things which upset you. I didn't mean to do that."

I knew he wasn't sure what he'd said wrong. That was half the problem. I couldn't really know what would set me off, and I wasn't ready to go into detail about what happened. I might never be. Too many people already knew for my comfort.

"I'm just tired," I said. "I'm sure we all are. It was a long drive back. You know me, I'm tough as nails unless I'm tired."

"I do know you," he said softly. "I know you'll keep everything bottled up inside if you can, because you're sure you can deal with it all by yourself."

"Because I *can* deal with it by myself," I said. "I'm a big girl, Jake, in case you hadn't noticed. I don't need you to hold my hand or fuss over me."

"Those are two of the things I do the best," he said. He gave me a boyish smile that made my heart flip.

"Maybe you need a new set of skills then," I snapped. I regretted the words the moment I said them. I stepped away from him and ran my hand through my hair.

"I'm sorry, I just—"

"Need an apple?" he asked, teasing gently.

"You and your fucking health food," I said, my tone lighter now. "Right now, I could use a big plate of bacon." I glanced at Ben before I added, "Cooked properly."

Ben smiled and nodded.

Jake didn't look impressed at being left out of an in-joke, but he forced a smile. "If you want bacon, I can send the Pup to get you some."

I resisted the urge to remind him that if I wanted bacon, I could send Cooper for it myself.

Cooper hopped up from where he was sitting on the couch. "I can get us bacon. Maybe some eggs and toast. I know it's dinner-time but if that's what you want..."

I held back a sigh. Apparently he was going to fuss over me too. I appreciated the attention, but I wasn't made of glass. I wouldn't snap if they looked at me the wrong way.

I looked over at Hutton.

He shrugged. "I've never been very good at fussing over people. I'll leave that shit to these guys. If you want to know about the inner workings of the Onyx Ridge pack, I'm your dude. If you want me to go down on you, my tongue is all yours. I'll even go and get your bacon for you, but I guarantee I'll eat at least some of it on the way back. But fawning, just not my thing." He placed his hands behind his head and leaned against the back of the couch.

"Told you he was an asshole," Jake said. "Eating someone else's bacon is a new low." He pretended to glare at Hutton, but something had changed between them. It was more of a friendly rivalry than two men who hated each other.

Or maybe they were just being nice for my sake. Whatever. It was easier if they'd just got along anyway.

"I wasn't suggesting I eat your bacon, babe," Hutton said to me. "I'll happily eat Jake's."

"Is bacon a euphemism for genitals now?" Cooper asked.

Jake and Hutton both turned to stare at him. Ben started to laugh silently, but so hard he was soon doubled over, his palms pressed against his thighs.

Jake shook his head, but his momentary surprise and outrage soon turned to laughter as well. "It is now."

Hutton smirked. "If it is, then I retract what I said about Jake's." He looked at me. "But I'll definitely eat all of yours, babe."

I rolled my eyes at all of the guys. Was it possible for them to go more than five minutes without thinking about their dicks? Or my pussy?

I pulled out my phone. "I think I just order pizza." I looked at them all, challenging them to interpret that as some sort of innuendo.

"Hutton wants his with extra sausage," Jake said.

Yep, there it was. I should have seen that one coming.

"As long as it's not your sausage," Hutton retorted.

"I like mine spicy, like you," Cooper said to me. He gave me such an adoring look my heart almost melted on the spot. I didn't deserve anyone as fucking sweet as he was. He really was like a wolf pup at times. Naïve but also vicious. It didn't hurt that he was hot as hells and a quick learner in bed.

I pressed the buttons on the pizza restaurants app, and talked as I went. "Sausage for Hutton. Pepperoni for Cooper. Extra pineapple for Jake."

"Sick fuck," Hutton told Jake. The expression on his face was half grimace, half smile.

Jake shrugged. "It's healthier this way. Don't forget extra olives."

I added that to the order, plus meat lovers for me. I looked over to Ben, who had finally stopped laughing.

"Vegetarian with extra cheese, please, angel," he said.

I wasn't the only one who raised my eyebrows at the endearment. "I'm not sure I'm much of an angel," I said.

He smiled softly. "Yes you are. Very much so."

"One hundred percent accurate," Jake said firmly. "Right, Pup?"

"Right," Cooper agreed.

Even Hutton nodded.

"I can argue with one or two of you, but not all of you," I said. I pressed the button to complete the order and put my phone away. "I'll let you guys fight over who is going to go downstairs and meet the delivery person."

"Cooper and Ben can go," Jake said. "I'll keep an eye on you. You should be safe enough here."

"I'll keep an eye on you too, babe," Hutton said. "Can't trust a guy who has extra pineapple on his pizza."

"Can't trust a guy who keeps flirting with my woman," Jake retorted.

"It's up to her to decide whose woman she is, right babe?" Hutton said.

The testosterone in the room was off the charts. Usually, I liked it. Today it felt like a pressure on my chest.

"Just lay off each other," I snapped. "Or I'll kick you all out. After the pizza is delivered."

Both of them snapped their mouths shut so fast their teeth clicked. I wasn't sure if it was the threat of being kicked out, or the promise of missing out on pizza. Maybe both. Whatever, it got the desired result.

No one said being a wolf was easy. Especially when more than one of them wanted to be alpha. I needed to lay down the law more stringently, apparently. Jake got to play the role of alpha while we were in public, but I was the one in charge around here. They could argue amongst themselves about who was beta and who was omega, as long as they did what I told them to.

I sat down in one of the plush armchairs. Partly because I wanted to sit by myself and partly because the chair faced the rest of the room. I trusted all four of the guys with my life, but I couldn't sit with my back to them. I was going to be extra cautious for a while. A long while, probably.

No one would blame me for that. Frankly, fuck them if they did. I thought I was on guard before Dagen took me. I knew now that I wasn't on guard enough. I was distracted and let the asshole's mind games get to me. I had to be more focused than that. I had to be on my game every minute of every day.

Every second.

Jake knelt down in front of my chair, one hand on one arm, the other on his knee. "I didn't do enough to keep you safe, and I'm sorry for that. I expected Dagen to come after one of our businesses. I didn't think he would come after you personally. It's a ballsy move, especially for him."

"We should have anticipated every possibility," I said. "We took him by surprise by not being together. We should do that more often. Be apart. It wouldn't help the organisation if he takes us both out."

I sighed out my nose. "I was right, you know. About us being together. I thought we would be too distracted, and we were. It could have gotten one of us killed. Or both of us."

"El..." He looked like he was struggling to find the words to say. To deny the truth in what I was saying.

"I'm right and you know it," I said firmly.

"No, I don't know it," he said. "We weren't together because I was dealing with Haigwood, like I've dealt with a million things before. You drove yourself home like you've done at least as many times. Neither of us was any more or any less distracted than usual."

He closed his eyes for a moment and shook his head. "I remember what you said to me after you told me to contact Harmony. You told me you loved me. I know you, you don't say things like that unless you mean them."

"People say things when they're sure they're about to die," I said. Gods, my tone was colder than ice.

"Bullshit," he said. "I get it, you're freaked out. I don't know what Dagen did to you, but it obviously wasn't good. I wish you would confide in me, but if you feel like you can't..." He sucked in a breath. "Hells, Elodie, at least don't shut me out. We've been through too much together. You're my whole fucking universe." His voice was choked with emotion.

"I thought I lost you. Believe me when I tell you I just about ripped heaven and earth apart to find you. When I found your car parked by the side of the road and you not in it..." He swallowed audibly. "I could have ripped every black wolf in the state apart with my bare hands. I tortured a few for information. They're all dead now." He smiled fiercely. "They fucked with the wrong woman."

He turned one of my hands and laced his fingers into mine. "I think I've proved to you that I'll give you all the space you need. All the time. I'll do that again if I have to, for as long as it takes. Just, please don't keep me waiting for another eight years."

I bit my lip to keep from crying. I didn't need a bond to know how deeply he felt for me. I knew it since the day we met. I felt the same way.

But feeling vulnerable was worse than feeling lonely.

"Jake—"

He pressed a finger to my lips. "Don't tell me no. Don't say anything. There's plenty of time for that. Let's just enjoy our pizza and that you're home with us again. We don't need to worry about anything else right now. Okay?"

I nodded and took his hand gently to move it away from my face. "I give you no guarantee I won't change my mind, but I shouldn't make a decision on an empty stomach."

Only, I already had made a decision. At some point he would have to accept it. He wouldn't like it, but it was how things had to be.

CHAPTER
ELEVEN

"Oh, fucking hells." I looked down at the corner of pizza which had dropped off my slice and slid down the front of my blouse. It left a long red smear, like blood, all the way down the fabric.

Jake chuckled. "You can't even blame me for that. It's not my fault this time."

"You look even more tasty," Cooper said.

I flashed Cooper a smile and flipped Jake the finger before picking up the corner and popping it in my mouth.

"I'm stuffed." I was surprised Jake let me eat as much as I wanted to without saying a word. Because of that, I ate an extra two pieces I didn't need and might regret later. Whatever, I didn't regret it now. I would have to work out twice as long in the morning, but I would welcome that to being locked in a room.

"I'm going to turn in," I said.

In unison, the guys all stood, like they were going to follow me into my bedroom. When they realised what they'd all done, they all stopped and looked at each other.

"Rock, paper, scissors?" Cooper asked.

"Alone," I said firmly. "The four of you can sort out the other two bedrooms and the couches. I need some time to myself."

Before they could argue with me, I turned and headed into my room. I closed the door behind me but didn't bother to lock it. If anyone got past the security and four guys, than a lock couldn't keep them out.

I dropped my clothes on the floor on the way to have a quick shower and pull on sleep shorts and a singlet. I half expected to find at least one of the guys waiting for me on or under the covers, but the room was empty. The bed was cold.

I pulled the covers up over myself and tried to get comfortable.

Ben sent reassuring thoughts through the bond and I sent him back assurances that I was fine.

While his special dose of calm was soothing, the bond was disconcerting. Mostly, I didn't want him to know how I really felt. At best, he would worry about me. At worst, he would tell the other guys and they would start fussing over me all over again.

I should have asked Paxton and Harmony about the possibility of breaking the bond. Ben had a job to do, and this was another distraction that we didn't need.

I made a mental note to contact Harmony on the number she gave me and see if they could tell me how to break it. I couldn't imagine Ben wanted to be attached to me like this for the rest of his life. My mind was frenetic and chaotic. He didn't deserve to be inundated with that, constantly. He didn't mind now, but eventually he would. I was certain of it.

I lay awake for a long time, listening to the sounds of the guys' voices, and them settling down for the night.

Knowing Jake, he had a bedroom to himself. Cooper had all but moved into the third bedroom before I was taken. Hutton would probably sleep on the couch. Knowing Ben, he would stay awake all night watching over us all. The man was nothing if not diligent about doing his job.

I knew right now he thought of it as more than a job. I would have to remedy that. We formed a bond, aside from the magical one, because of our shared ordeal.

Now we were back, we had to return to being boss and bodyguard. Whether he liked it or not.

Whether *I* liked it or not. Letting myself get close to him was a mistake. I knew that now. We turned to each other because we were stuck in a horrible situation we weren't sure we would survive. I should have been tougher than that. I should have kept my distance. Easy to say when we were stuck in a room alone, but fucking him was unprofessional and stupid, and Dagen had taken full advantage of it.

In the back of my mind, I reminded myself that if we hadn't, I would have a bond with Dagen right now. And his slimy touch would have been all over my body.

I shuddered and pulled the covers tighter around me.

Here, alone in the dark, it was easy to let monsters crawl over, and under my skin. Memories I hid from when the guys were around found me here. Being held down. The surgery. The smell of blood before Dagen's wolves ate the parts of me he stole.

My stomach turned and the pizza threatened to come back up. I threw back the covers and staggered to the bathroom. I managed to hold back my hair and leaned over the toilet just before I lost every crumb of pizza, and then some.

I sank to my knees and waited until my stomach was completely empty before I rose and rinsed my mouth. I brushed my teeth and fled back to bed before any of the guys decided to check up on me.

Shit. I shouldn't have to worry about people caring about me. I was Ivory for gods' sake. People should be scared *of* me, not scared *for* me. And I certainly shouldn't feel like I needed to scurry around my own apartment above my own nightclub.

I pulled the covers back over myself and tried again to get comfortable. At least with my stomach purged, that was easier. I no longer felt bloated and stuffed. I just felt... Empty. Not just my stomach, but the rest of me as well.

Good. Empty was easier to deal with than vulnerable. Numb was a lot less painful. This was exactly the place I had retreated to after my parents' deaths. I built a wall of ice around me to shield myself from Helen Dagen and the rest of the Onyx Ridge pack. It got me through then, it would get me through now.

I closed my eyes and pushed everything away until it was at arm's length, or further. The memories. The monsters. The guys. Everything.

No more crying. No more letting things get to me. The last thought I had before I dropped off to sleep was that I needed to build a frozen steel wall around my heart.

The empty feeling persisted when I woke an hour or two later. I was disoriented, but glad to be pulled from the dream I was having.

In it, was a girl of about four or five years old. She had white hair. At first, I thought she was me.

She turned to me with her big blue eyes and said, "Mummy?" Her resemblance to Jake and me knocked the breath out of my lungs.

"I'm not your mummy," I told her. "I can't be your mummy. Not ever."

She blinked slowly. More slowly than someone would in the waking world. "But why? Where is Daddy?" She looked around. We were home. Not at Crimson, but at my harbourside mansion. Me and her and Jake. And Cooper. And Ben. And Hutton. All of us, together. And this kid. This kid who couldn't exist, no matter how much I wanted to dream her into existence.

"Daddy?" she shouted. "Something is wrong with Mummy. She doesn't know who I am."

"It's..." I stammered. "I'm just pretending. Of course I know who you are."

She popped a hip and planted her fist against it in a pose must have learned from me. "Then what's my name?"

"I—"

I woke to the sound of an alarm. I sat up and rubbed my eyes. What the fuck?

The door opened and the light snapped on. Jake stepped inside wearing only boxer shorts. He had a phone to his ear.

Even half asleep and confused, I had to acknowledge how fucking hot he was. His body was a ripped tapestry of tattoos. Every bit of him was decorated muscle. I wanted to ignore the alarm, drag him down and fuck his brains out.

The sensible part of me realised it would be stupid to ignore an alarm. I pushed off the covers and grabbed a dressing gown to wind around myself.

"What is it?" I asked.

He frowned. "Apparently the building's sensors have detected a gas leak. We need to get out of here, just in case they're right." He waved at me to hurry up.

I nodded. If there was a gas leak, it would only take a match, or a cigarette butt to take the whole building and us with it.

Hard pass on that, thank you.

"Let me guess, this has Alistair Dagen written all over it." He was probably pissed that we burnt down his country house. At least I assumed it burned down. The fire was looking fierce when we drove away. Whatever. That was firmly in the 'not my problem,' basket. This, on the other hand...

Jake followed me out into the sitting area just as Cooper appeared from his room. He rubbed his eyes and looked even more sleepy than I did. And just as painfully sexy as Jake. How was I supposed to keep my distance from these guys when they looked like they did? There should be a law or something.

Oh yeah, there probably was and they, being criminals like me, broke it.

Men.

Hutton either slept with his clothes on, or had dressed really quickly. Either way, he had everything on but his shoes. And you guessed it, he was no less sexy than Jake or Cooper.

Neither was Ben, who was the only one who was fully dressed, including his shoes. He was also the only one who actually looked awake and alert.

"We'll have to go down the stairs," Ben said. "The elevators go off-line during an emergency like this. Just in case."

"Right," Jake agreed. "We don't want anyone getting stuck in there."

I assumed all of that was for Cooper and Hutton's benefit, because I knew all of that. Sometimes they seem to forget that I actually had a clue about what goes on in my own organisation. That was another thing I was going to have to remedy.

I lifted my chin and marched past them all to the door leading down to the stairs. At times like this being on the tenth floor sucked. I couldn't even cheer myself up with the idea that I would burn off all the pizza I ate. That was long gone.

"I should go first," Ben said. "To make sure it's safe."

It took me a moment to realise he was right. It was, after all, his job. This was not a time to let pride get in the way.

I nodded. "You and Cooper go first. Jake and Hutton, you two follow me. Keep your eyes and ears open. If there is a gas leak, it could be dangerous. If there isn't, then some other shit is up." Something that probably involved a pack of black wolves and a whole lot of fuck nope.

We trotted down the stairs in virtual silence.

Ben's shoes had rubber soles, so they didn't make a sound as we moved. Of course they did, he wouldn't be much of a body-guard if he banged around as he went.

I kept my senses open and tried to keep my eyes from absorbing the sight of Cooper's bare back. Like the rest of him, it was rippling muscle. Absolutely ridiculously lickable muscle.

Shit, I had to stop thinking like this. It was not doing me or them any good. I reminded myself of my frozen steel wall. This was not a good time to be distracted.

"You okay, babe?" Hutton whispered. "You look pale."

I glanced back over my shoulder. "I'm fine. I could have used a few more hours of sleep, that's all." I realised he identified my growing panic before I did.

Judging by the way he glanced back at me, Ben did too. As ever, he was an island of calm in the middle of my chaos. He was focused on his job, but he allowed himself to take a moment to be concerned about me.

I gave him a look that reminded him once again that I could take care of myself. He gave me a minute nod and turned back towards the stairs in front of him.

"Couldn't we all?" Hutton said lightly.

I stopped mid-step. "Is he planning something? You would have a better idea of that than any of us."

"I wish I could say no," Hutton said. "But I remember some-thing like this happening before. It didn't end well. We should get the hells out of the building." Now he looked pale.

I nodded and resumed trotting, faster than before.

We reached the fifth floor without seeing anyone else. From there, the stairs got busy. Floors four and five housed the brothel.

Sex workers were ushering clients out the door and down the stairwell. Some of the clients were in an obvious hurry to save themselves, but others seemed more concerned with their reputa-tions. I recognised a couple of businessmen and local politicians. Being seen here would be damaging for them, to say the least.

Boo fucking hoo. They made that choice when they walked through the door. Curious how one or two who preached about 'family values' ended up here. They were hypocrites, but their money was as good as the next person's.

One of them noticed me and looked like he was ready to drop back behind me in the hope that any press who might be waiting outside would focus on me and not notice them.

They apparently changed their minds when Cooper and Ben ushered them forward. There was no way they would let anyone leave behind us. Or rather, they wanted to keep everyone in sight. It was never a good idea to turn your back on men like these, even though most of them were only human.

Only a couple of people stepped out of the doors at the third and second levels. By the time we reached the ground floor, the bar was empty.

I made a mental note to upgrade the evacuation procedures for the brothel. They should have been long gone before we got down there.

"You'd think the fear of dying would be greater than the fear of getting caught with your pants down," Jake remarked.

"When you build a house of cards on your reputation, then you have to be careful which way the wind blows," Hutton said.

"That's deep," Jake said. "Did you read that in a fortune cookie?"

"If you don't stop it, I'll have you both made into fortune cookies," I growled. "Hutton is right. Our clients rely on our discretion. That's why they come here and not somewhere else. And why they go out the side entrance while we go out the front." It would take us another minute, but it would keep our reputation intact.

That might be all Dagen planned, embarrass our clients into being too scared to come back. That would be bad for business.

Apparently the clients in question heard the words 'side

entrance,' because they started to move faster. They followed the employees to the small door which led to an alley behind Crimson. From there, they would have to make their own way away from the area.

We headed across the wide foyer, out the large front doors and onto the street. Only a handful of staff stood outside. Our customers had dispersed, no doubt in a hurry to get as far away from a potential explosion as they could.

"Would you really have them made into fortune cookies?" Cooper asked.

I thought he was serious until he broke into a grin. "Why? Do you want to kill them for me?" I kept my voice low, in case anyone was listening.

His eyes widened. The conflict going on in his brain was obvious and kind of adorable. He wanted to say he would if I asked him to, but he wouldn't want to kill Jake. And he probably wouldn't want to kill Hutton.

I put him out of his misery before he had to answer. "I wouldn't ask you to do that. Besides, I don't think either of them would make very tasty cookies. Burgers, maybe." In spite of my empty stomach, the idea of food made me feel sick again.

"Now I'm hungry for a burger," Cooper sighed sadly.

"How do you have room for more food?" Hutton asked him. "You ate half the pizza."

Cooper shrugged. "I'm a growing boy."

"You will be growing if you keep eating like that," Hutton agreed.

Cooper, being the mature almost-twenty year old he was, stuck his tongue out at Hutton. "Don't worry about me. I'll work it off. Right, Ivory?"

I didn't have the heart to correct him right now, so I turned my attention to Ben. He was scanning the area, his eagle eyes taking in everything.

"Is anything out of place?" I asked. "Apart from us."

"Yeah, something," he agreed. "I can't quite put my finger on it. I would suggest we're being watched, but there are security cameras everywhere. Chances are, some of them aren't ours. Or aren't in our control."

"He does like to watch," I said. If I knew which cameras he might be watching us from, I would flip him the finger.

"There's no smell of gas," Ben pointed out.

I nodded slowly. "I noticed that too. Why get us out here then?"

He scanned the buildings around us, and the sky. "And how?" he asked. When I looked at him questioningly, he added, "The building's sensors were triggered by something. Or someone. Either from inside the building or remotely."

"Right," I said slowly. I didn't like either prospect. Either someone at Crimson was working for Dagen, or he'd found a weakness in our security system.

"Or he got us out here so we can see that." Jake sounded furious.

I turned and followed his gaze. "Fuck."

My restaurant, Scarlett, was on fire.

TWELVE

"Mother fucking son of a dingo's balls," I swore. "Couldn't he have sent a text message?" As if that would have been *so* much better.

Wailing sirens headed towards us. They echoed through the streets for a good two to three minutes before the fire trucks swung around the corner and stopped outside the restaurant.

Jake still had his phone to his ear. "Yeah, well, get someone out here. If there is really a gas leak... Yeah, well, hurry up." He hung up the phone and scowled. "Fucking gas company. If they worked for us I would fire them all. By the time they get someone out here to check, the whole place could have gone up. If that happened it would take the whole fucking block with it."

By now we all knew the gas leak was a load of bullshit, but he was right to be pissed off. If Crimson was flammable, we would all be incinerated.

"Gas leaks seem to follow you."

I was so busy watching the flames pour out of the front windows of my restaurant, I didn't see Singh or Gilbert approach until Singh spoke.

"Or is it just disaster?"

Unfortunately, that was a fair question.

I sighed. I was genuinely frustrated at the situation and confused why they were both still alive. Out of the corner of my eye, I caught Jake's expression. Apparently he was wondering the same thing. Or maybe he was just realising he'd forgotten to have them killed because he was so busy looking for me. Either way, he might end up in a hamburger patty yet.

"Like I said the last time we met," I said wearily, "people like me become targets. In the case of the gas leak, it seems to be a fault in the sensors. Hopefully that's all it is. I apologise for the disruption."

Crimson wasn't the only place evacuated. The area contained other restaurants, clubs and hotels. I didn't *need* their support or goodwill, but it was easier than having everyone around pissed off at us. The hotels in particular sent a lot of customers our way.

"And the fire?" Singh said. "That is your restaurant, isn't it?"

"It is," I agreed. "Or it was anyway."

"So your restaurant catches fire on the same night that you may or may not have a gas leak in another one of your properties," Singh said slowly. "That sounds like an interesting coincidence to me."

I shrugged. "I guess that's your job to figure out if it was a coincidence or not. I'm not going to go around setting fire to my own restaurant, am I? It's not like I need the insurance money."

"You might have some other motive," she said. "You know anything about the disappearance of Jefferson Haigwood?" She was obviously trying to catch me off guard by the sudden change of topic. I was tired, but I wasn't going to be caught out that easily.

It was good to know some of the killings I ordered actually took place.

I cocked my head at them. "The owner of the Lair? I wasn't

aware he had disappeared." That was true, it wasn't a disappearance. On the other hand, I actually *had* disappeared and apparently that went unnoticed by these assholes. They had their priorities inside out.

"He has," Singh said. "Hasn't been seen for about two weeks. You don't know anything about that, though, I suppose?"

"Not a thing," I said. I hadn't asked Jake or Cooper for any details, so it wasn't a lie. Not exactly. "Are you trying to accuse me of something?"

"Not at all," Singh said lightly.

Bullshit.

"It just seems coincidental that Silas Wheeler went missing, then Jefferson Haigwood. You get caught up in an explosion, then an apparent gas leak and now a restaurant fire." She gave me a hard look.

"If you're going to continue this line of conversation, we should continue in the presence of my lawyers," I said coldly. She was obviously trying to get a reaction out of me. Mentioning lawyers *was* a reaction, but the words were out now and I couldn't take them back. "Shouldn't you be down at my restaurant investigating the fire?"

"That's not our department," Gilbert said.

I had forgotten he was there until he spoke. Now I turned my gaze on him, I saw him mentally peeling off my dressing gown. He probably assumed I was naked underneath. I wanted to mentally peel off his skin and feed the rest of him to the wolves. Yeah, we don't always throw bodies in the harbour.

"What is your department?" I asked. "Harassing citizens in the middle of the night? Maybe you two triggered off the sensors?" Stranger things had been known to happen.

Gilbert chuckled. "It's not the kind of harassing I'd like to do in the middle of the night."

Singh and I both gave him twin looks of disgust.

"I think it's time you both left," I said. "If you have something to say, come back in the morning." Or better yet, don't come back at all.

Singh actually had the grace to look apologetic. Only for Gilbert. I saw on her face she was still certain I was up to something.

"I'd like to speak to your employee first," she said. She nodded towards Cooper. "He looked nervous when I mentioned Haigwood."

Cooper gaped at her, but had the sense to keep his mouth shut. His eyes flicked to me, obviously seeking guidance.

"His uncle disappeared, then Haigwood. You think the two are connected," I pointed out. "What are the chances whoever is behind this will come after him? That would scare anyone."

Cooper's eyes widened as if that was an actual possibility.

"Perhaps he can tell us," Singh said. "We'd like to talk to you. Away from her." She jerked her head towards me.

Cooper gaped again. "I—I guess so." He glanced at me.

I nodded.

Singh clearly thought I was giving him permission to talk to them. She thought I was arrogant, because the police didn't need my permission to speak to someone, but here I was, giving it.

Only I wasn't.

I was giving him permission to kill them. I preferred he not do it alone, but that couldn't be helped. I should have made up some shit about Hutton being our lawyer, or something, but it was too late for that.

"I'd offer you my office, but it might not be safe in there," I said helpfully.

I might send them into the building before we got the all clear, but not Cooper.

Also, he was about to make a big mess. I didn't want to have to replace the flooring. Again. Not in there, anyway. In other parts of the club, it was a frequent occurrence. Especially the third floor. Cum stains could be so hard to get out of the carpet.

"We'll just step down this way," Singh said. She waved toward a spot in front of a lit window.

Cooper looked nervous, but excited.

Jake shook his head at him and smiled indulgently. Once the cops had moved away, he softly said, "Murder Pup. He really does get a kick out of that, doesn't he?"

"So do you," I pointed out. I could happily commit a bit of murder myself right now. "I want to see what's going on down at Scarlett." The firetrucks had been working there for quite some time and seemed to have the blaze under control. With any luck, it might not be as bad as I thought at first.

A girl could hope, right?

Jake nodded. "Ben, Hutton, go with her. I'll stay here and see if the gas company actually turns up."

He would also keep an eye on Cooper. The guy couldn't kill the cops in full view of everyone, so there might be a chance yet for someone to help him with the job. Better that than risking people hearing screams.

Things really started to get awkward then.

With the guys walking so close to me we almost touched, I headed down to Scarlett.

Two of the cleaners stood outside, both looking anxious. That anxiety rose when they saw me coming.

"Is everyone okay?" I asked.

"Yes, Ivory," one of them said. "It was only me and Leslie in there at the time." She cleared her throat. "I have no idea what happened. One minute I was cleaning the toilet, the next minute there was smoke everywhere."

Leslie nodded. "It didn't start in the kitchen. I was in there, cleaning the stove."

"Did you see anyone else around?" I asked. The police should be asking this. They probably would, later. Someone other than Singh and Gilbert. No doubt the fire department would also conduct an investigation to determine the cause of the fire.

Leslie shook her head. "No one. But..." She thought for a moment. "Now I think about it, I heard the back door open and close. I thought it was Jane, but then she came running from the bathroom area."

"So you got out through the front door?" I asked.

"Yeah," Jane said. "Just in time too. Something went woosh just after we stepped out." Her eyes were wide.

"I'm glad you got out," I said honestly. I had people whose job it was to die for me, these cleaners were not two of them. They were just staff on my payroll. People who didn't deserve to be dragged into Dagen's shit.

"Thank you, Ivory," Jane said. "Us too. Should we go or..."

I hesitated. "I think you should probably wait. Someone is going to turn up sooner or later with questions for you. Just answer honestly." Although both shifters, a tiger and a dingo, they would have little knowledge of the organisation they really worked for. It was unlikely they would say anything incriminating. Unfortunately, it was also unlikely they would say anything which would lead to Dagen being arrested or even blamed. Still, as long as it didn't lead to me, then it was what it was.

After a moment I added, "I'll find you both work at some other part of the organisation. Don't worry about that. And if you need some time off, take it. With full pay." It was the least I could do. They were almost burnt alive.

They both looked relieved at that.

"Thank you, Ivory," Jane said fervently. "I was freaking out. I can't afford to be off work."

I nodded to her. Okay, sometimes I forget there are people in the world like her. Lots of them. Most people weren't like me, with more money than they knew what to do with. Even growing up with Helen Dagen, I had everything I physically needed, and more.

That is to say, I always had a pair of shoes and a couple of changes of clothes. Helen was not what you would call generous, especially with me. She wasn't much nicer to her children, but she didn't raise a hand to any of *them*.

"And you won't be," I assured Jane. "You two do excellent work, I'd be crazy to let you get away."

Just as I finished speaking, another police car pulled up.

"Looks like the people who will want to talk to you." I stepped aside from the two cleaners and gave the police space to do their job. No doubt they would want to talk to me at some point as well, but Jane and Leslie were actual witnesses.

"Are you sure you trust them, babe?" Hutton said in my ear. "They could be working for him."

I would have to find a way to encourage him to stop calling me babe. "They've been working for me for years. It's possible they had something to do with it, but I think they're genuine."

"I agree," Ben said. "That was a nice thing you did."

"Giving them time off with pay?" I asked. "It seemed like the right thing to do." I looked up at him for a moment. "Is that what you need, too? Some time off to deal with all the things that happened to us?"

"No," he said quickly. "I'm fine. What about you? Will you take some time off?" He looked like he was giving me a challenge.

"Hells no," I said. "I don't have time to take time off. No more than I have already taken off."

"I wouldn't call that time off," he said gently. He looked like he was going to step towards me but stopped when I almost took a step back.

At least the bond was good for something. Reminding him that personal space was a thing. It was a thing neither of us had

had much of recently. I needed to make sure I got some from time to time.

"He's right, you know," Hutton said. "We should all take some time off. We've been through stuff."

I forgot he was behind enemy lines for longer than Ben and me. I hadn't had a chance to talk to him about it yet.

In the meantime, I asked, "Do you need time off?"

"Naw." He waved a hand in the air. "I'm good. I've had nothing but time off for the last few years. I am a man of action. I need to have things to do. I prefer those things don't include getting mauled to death by black wolves, or being exploded following a gas leak, but I'll take what I can get."

"That's good, because those things are pretty much a part of the job," I said. "Right, Ben?"

Ben gave a quick tilt of his head. "That is accurate, yes. It's a tough job, but someone has to do it."

"Yeah, I'm sure fucking the boss is a really tough job," Hutton said dryly.

The side of Ben's mouth twitched, but he didn't dignify that comment with a response. He must know I was pulling away from all the guys and wouldn't appreciate him talking to Hutton about what went on between us.

Everything in the past had to stay there. End of story.

The firefighters started to pack up their hoses and step out of the ruins of Scarlett.

With a sigh, I walked towards the woman who seemed to be in charge. "Is it gutted?" I asked.

She turned to me. "Are you the owner?" When I nodded, she said, "It's extensively damaged. We won't know the full extent until it's cold enough to go through and assess. I would think you're looking at a complete gut and rebuild of the interior. Fortunately, the fire didn't spread to the buildings on either side and the exterior seems to be intact. Again, we'll hold a full inspection in the morning. In the meantime, no one is allowed in or out. We'll put up tape. You know how people are though, they'll try to go in anyway."

She gave me a meaningful look as if she fully expected me to duck under the tape the moment they drove away.

Fuck that. I had a nasty enough dose of smoke inhalation yesterday, I didn't need one today. Or was it tomorrow already? Whatever.

"I won't be going in there," I assured her. "I let my staff know to stay out. Thank you. I'll be sure to send a few vouchers along to the station once we're back up and running. You can all have a night out on me." I really was being a fairy godmother tonight, wasn't I? I would have to be careful of that, people might start to think I was nice.

She nodded. "I don't think any of us would turn that down. If you excuse me, we should get going." She glanced at Ben and Hutton, then climbed back into the fire truck.

"See, that's another difference between you and Dagen," Hutton said. "He would have had them killed because they didn't put out the fire before it started."

I snorted. "Yeah, he would. That's the sort of asshole he is." That and so much more. So much, much more.

I ran a hand over my hair. No doubt I wouldn't be allowed to start the cleanup until after the fire investigation, and the insurance investigation. At this point, I just wanted to get started on the rebuild. Every day the restaurant was closed would cost me money. Just because I wasn't short of a dollar didn't mean I wanted to lose it. I didn't get rich by throwing it away.

I glanced over towards Crimson. Jake was pacing back and forth. Stalking, really. One man, by himself, dressed only in boxer shorts. A man I loved so much I would push him away along with the rest of them. For their own good.

"In the time it took the firefighters to arrive and put out the fire, the gas people still haven't arrived," Hutton observed.

I nodded. "I noticed that. Strange that a private company is less efficient than a government entity. It's usually the other way around."

"Maybe Dagen owns them," Ben said. "That would explain their inefficiency."

I snorted. "Yes, it would." I started back towards Crimson, keeping an eye out for Cooper or anything out of place. I had so many reasons to be on edge, I couldn't even figure out which it was right now. Maybe all of them all at once.

I reached Jake just as the gas company finally arrived.

"It's about fucking time," he snapped.

They gave him a look, but got out their equipment and headed into Crimson to check it out.

THIRTEEN

"Of course the place is clear," Jake said. "What did they fucking expect? They'll probably send us a bill for coming out."

"And we'll pay it," I said calmly. I sipped my water and leaned against the back of the couch. They gave us the all clear an hour ago. Only the five of us, the cleaners and a handful of sex workers came back in.

Cooper's hair was still damp from the shower he had to wash all the blood from his skin. He hadn't stopped smiling since he reappeared from wherever he took the cops.

Jake muttered something and went on pacing. He'd pulled on a pair of worn jeans over his boxer shorts, but the rest of him was bare.

I tried my hardest not to appreciate the view.

I looked over to Ben, who was stretched out on the other couch, sleeping lightly. His head lay at an uncomfortable angle that would probably hurt later. I didn't have the heart to move him, in case he woke. It was almost dawn and he had been up for twenty-four hours.

Hutton and Cooper sat in chairs opposite each other and watched Jake stalk back and forth across the room.

"The security cameras near Scarlett just *happened* to be broken last night," I said. "Asshole must have planned this in advance."

Jake stopped and looked over at me. He snapped his fingers. "You're right. Accessing Crimson's sensors remotely wasn't something he thought up at the last second. Or if it was, he wouldn't have been able to pull it off that quickly."

"So he might have had access for a while," I said slowly. I resisted the reflex to look around the room. There were no cameras in my apartment. Not that I knew of anyway. If Jake put them in without my knowledge...

"That's a cheerful thought," Hutton said dryly. He *did* glance around. "Any chance our private conversations were overheard?"

"No," Jake said firmly. "This place is clean unless he snuck someone in with a listening device or some shit." After a moment he added, "Which is unlikely, but possible. And a very good reason I should get Ivory out of here." He looked toward me. "I'll take you home for a few days. You could use a break."

"Do I get any say in this?" I gave him my best 'I am not amused' face.

"No," he replied lightly. "The whole building was evacuated and Scarlett is a burnt out ruin. The gods know what he'll pull next. He's trying to get to you." He hesitated for a moment. "He kept you both alive for a reason."

I closed my eyes and scrunched up my face. I didn't particularly want to talk about Dagen, but this was a conversation we needed to have.

"He wanted me to hand over everything to him. Just... Sign it over. He thought he would break me until I did what he wanted." I opened my eyes and exhaled out my nose. "I think that's what this was. He's trying to make me crack."

Jake looked disbelieving. "He just wanted you to sign all of

Ivory Claw's assets over to him? Did he have any idea that's impossible?"

"I thought it was best not to let him know," I said. "He would have gone after you even harder."

Cooper looked confused. "Why is it impossible?"

Jake looked over at him, then glanced at Hutton. His jaw twitched. "In order to make any big decisions, any documents have to have three signatures on them. Mine, Ivory's and a third-party we keep tightly under wraps for just this reason. She couldn't sign anything over if she wanted to. Neither could I." He ran a hand over his head. "It's probably just as well he didn't know that. He probably would have killed you and declared war on the rest of us."

I placed my empty water glass on the table in front of me. "Another very good reason for me not to tell him. But what he did is as good as declaring war on us. So as far as I'm concerned, game on."

"After you take a few days off," Jake said firmly. "You can get dressed, or I'll *take* you like that." It was obvious by the way he emphasised the word, that he had more on his mind than driving me to my house.

"Is this where you'll throw me over your shoulder and carry me all the way if I try to refuse?" The idea was both aggravating and kinda hot at the same time.

"Yep," Jake said. He crossed his arms and gave me a look that was so fucking sexy it was unfair. I wanted to melt right into the couch.

And I wanted to run away and never looked back. *For his own good*, I reminded myself. That was all.

I remembered the little girl in the dream. The only way he, or any of them, would be a father, was if they gave up on me and found other women. The idea hurt like a dagger to my heart, but it wasn't fair to them to wait around for me. Not when I knew I couldn't be with any of them.

"Fine. I'll get dressed." I stood and started towards my room.

"Need some help?" Cooper called out.

"No, I'm good." This time, I locked the door behind me. I knew without a shadow of a doubt at least one of them would follow me if I didn't.

I leaned against the door and sucked in a few shaky breaths.

Why was I more scared of my feelings than anything Dagen might do to me?

I could put it down to our growing war with the Onyx Ridge pack. Not only was I scared of being distracted, I was worried about getting so attached I couldn't deal with it if I lost any of them.

For the same reason, I needed to discourage their attachment to me. I had no plans to die anytime soon, but if I did, they needed to focus for the good of the organisation and every other white wolf in the state. The younger ones in particular.

I wanted them to grow up in a world where they didn't need to worry about shit like this.

I pressed my palms to the door and pushed myself off it.

With hurried steps, I walked to my wardrobe to get dressed and make myself a bit more presentable. It was almost dawn and I had an hour or two of sleep, but I didn't need to look like it.

Out of habit, I pulled a dress off a hanger. I paused and considered it for a moment. Low-cut in the front and the back, and with a long split in the thigh, it was exactly the kind of thing I liked to wear.

Today though, the idea of showing that much skin made me feel uncomfortable.

I chewed my lip for a moment.

This was exactly the kind of mind fuck Dagen got a kick out of.

Making me feel vulnerable. Making me feel like I should wear a turtleneck and a skirt that fell to my ankles.

"Fuck you," I whispered. I didn't wear dresses like this because I like to be looked at. I wore them because I liked the way I felt in them. I would not be made to feel ashamed of the way I looked or dressed. I wouldn't hide, because if I did, then he won.

I slipped into the dress and looked at my reflection in the long mirror that hung on the wall.

"Yep, you're still a smoke show," I told myself. In a shade of deep red, the dress clung to my curves, flattering me to perfection. It fell to just above my ankles, but the split showed most of my right leg.

I'm not going to say I didn't feel a moment of self-conscious-ness. I did. I almost considered taking the dress off and putting on a skirt and blouse. And buttoning the blouse all the way up to my throat. And maybe throwing one of those wearable blankets over the top of the outfit. That would hide me.

Unfortunately I didn't own a wearable blanket anyway, so the dress would have to do. I brushed my hair and pushed my feet into a pair of heels. To the casual observer, I was still Ivory, the big bad she wolf. The woman who held influence over almost every corner of the state.

If you looked more closely, you might see a hint of Elodie, the woman who was struggling to keep all of it together.

I made another mental note. This time it was to have Jake contact all of the members of the wolves' conclave. Consisting of the alphas of each state of Australia, it was an uneasy alliance at best. We rarely met. When we did, it was because of situations like this. When one group was trying to overthrow another.

White wolves held sway in Western Australia and Tasmania. Black wolves lead Victoria and South Australia. Of course, Queensland had to be different, so their alphas were grey wolves.

They tended to be neutral, so they would either stay out of it or try to mediate.

The Northern Territory, just to be really different, was led by a pack of dingoes.

The Western Australian and Tasmanian packs would send wolves if this turned into full-blown war.

South Australia wouldn't bother to return my messages. The dingoes would stay out of the way of all of us.

It was the Ironhide pack of Victoria I was the most interested in. They were led by Kian Quinn, with some help from his brothers, Tyler and Reed. Although as ruthless as the average black wolf, they tended to be more reasonable than the Onyx Ridge assholes. Kian might not help me directly, but he was proud of his reputation and that of black wolves in general. He may do nothing, but he might also send someone to assassinate Alistair Dagen.

If he could get a moment's break from trying to stop his brothers from seducing every woman in sight. Including me.

My taste didn't usually run to black wolves, but Reed Quinn could do some pretty amazing things with his tongue.

What? Even I had moments of weakness.

I grabbed my phone and unlocked the door. The moment I opened it, I wished I'd gone for the turtleneck and long skirt.

Four sets of eyes turned to drink in the sight of me. Blue, hazel and two sets of brown, they all had the same hungry look in them.

Hungry like the wolf.

Maybe I could go for one more round with all four of them, right here right now. Imagine the amount of orgasms I could have.

I swallowed and pushed away the thought as hard as I could.

Ben felt it, I saw it on his face. And then, of course, he was worried about me.

Fucking bond. The sooner I got the thing broken, the better. I would make that phone call when I got home to my place.

"Wow," Cooper said, open admiration on his face. "You look hot."

"Yeah, babe," Hutton said. "Fuck me upside down, you're gorgeous."

"I'm also the boss," I said coolly. "Something you all seem to have forgotten. Close your mouths."

Four sets of jaws snapped shut.

"Ben," I continued smoothly, "get some rest. You too, Hutton. Cooper, I'm sure Jake has assigned you duties? Good, make sure they're done. Are you coming, Jake?" Without waiting for a response, I swept towards the elevator.

I knew they were exchanging glances behind my back. Let them. They were my employees and I had overstepped with them. That changed as of now.

"Um, okay boss." Jake hurried after me. While I was getting ready he had taken some time to pull on a faded grey T-shirt. He might have even washed his face.

Sometimes I envied guys. Although there was nothing to stop me from wearing jeans and T-shirts and having my hair cut short. Nothing except I wouldn't feel like me. What can I say? Once a high strung, high maintenance girl, always a high strung, high maintenance girl.

"Are you okay, El?" he asked after the elevator doors slid shut.

"I'm about the same as the last hundred times people asked me that," I snapped.

I sighed and held up a hand before he could respond. "I'm fine. No, I'm not fine. I will be fine when Alistair Dagen is dead, and all of his shitty henchholes with him. Can you dig me a shallow grave for them? I'll dance on it."

"If you want a shallow grave for them, then a shallow grave is what you get," Jake said. "Just say the word. I'll organise the pack and we'll go after him tonight if you want."

"You know where he is?" I asked.

He sighed in frustration. "No, not as of this exact moment. If I had to guess, I would say he's not far away. He would want to keep an eye on the shit he is pulling. You know what they say about people always returning to the scene of the crime."

"Isn't that just on TV?" I asked. I had never gone back to any of the places where I killed people personally. But then again, the place where Helen Dagen's house once stood is now a women and children's crisis centre. The land was donated by an 'anonymous benefactor.' Every year, I send them funds to keep operating. It was a pet project of mine, so to speak, designed to help families stay together and away from abuse.

Jake shrugged. "I don't know. I've never gotten very far away from the scenes of mine."

"I suppose that's true." I watched him in the corner of my eye. "Maybe you should. You could take a break too, when all of this is over. Go to Tasmania for a holiday, or something."

He put a hand on my cheek and turned me to face him. "Don't."

I tried to keep from flinching. "Don't what?"

"Don't do that whole, 'go off and meet a nice girl' thing. We had that conversation before. You know I'm not going anywhere. I don't want anyone else."

"You know what he did to me," I said. I told him about the surgery during the drive. That was all though. I couldn't bring myself to mention what happened in the bathhouse. None of it.

"I can't have children. If you ever want—"

He cut me off with a loud laugh. "Me? A father? That's the funniest thing I've heard all month. No, really, it's been a shit month."

"You don't say," I said dryly.

He lightly pressed his forehead against mine. "If children were something you wanted, or if it happened, I would roll with it. If that was what it took to make you happy, then I would do it. But it's not something I want. Our world is crazy and you already have an heir to pass all of this down to. Assuming she has children."

Even when we were alone, I felt uncomfortable talking about her. As the last signee on any hand over documents, I tried to keep her existence a secret from everyone. I assumed Dagen had no idea I had a sister.

Well, half sister. Daughter of one of my father's lovers, we had different mothers. Different lives. We met in secret, for her safety, but she knew all about the organisation. She would only step in when my body and Jake's were both cold.

"She will. She is much more maternal than I am. Maybe you and her..."

He shook his head, making his skin roll lightly over mine. "Don't even go there. She's cute, but she's not you."

"But you admit she's cute." I pulled my face away from his and raised an eyebrow at him.

He looked up and around. "We probably shouldn't be talking about any of that in here."

"You're right," I said. "Your private life is your business."

"Elodie—" He exhaled in frustration. "I am never, ever going to give up on you. You can try to push me away but I'm not going."

"I'm damaged," I said, my voice tight. "You deserve better."

"No I don't," he said with a slow, self deprecating smile. "But the truth is, there is no better than you. As much as you don't want to believe it."

"Not for a minute," I agreed. Especially now. The truth is, I've always been damaged. For a long, long time. Sometimes it's an asset, because you can justify the horrible things you do by remembering the horrible things other people have done to you.

And sometimes, you just feel like shit.

"I know he did things to you," Jake said carefully. "I know you don't want to talk about it. But it doesn't change how I feel about you."

"It changes how I feel about myself," I admitted. "It made me realise I was right to avoid getting involved. It's the best thing for everyone."

"Don't you think I should have a say in what's best for me?" he asked.

"Of course," I agreed. "But I can't be part of that equation." No matter how much I desperately wanted him to hold me and kiss me right now. He was always so good at fighting off my monsters. Monsters except for Alistair Dagen. He was one I would have to take care of myself.

The elevator pinged and I stepped out on the ground floor. My phone beeped a moment later. I pulled it out and looked at the screen.

"Fucking hells."

CHAPTER

FOURTEEN

"Fucking peak hour traffic," Jake grumbled. He held down the horn for a few seconds. The sound made me wince. "That's a green light, dickhead."

He changed lanes in front of another car. When that driver honked his horn, Jake stuck his hand out the window and flipped him off.

"It's nice to see you don't give in to road rage," I said dryly. It was a welcome distraction, albeit a temporary one.

He snorted. "It's not road rage until I start ramming some motherfuckers. Which is going to happen really soon if these idiots don't get out of the way."

"Maybe you should get the car fitted with a bazooka. Then you could just blast them all off the road." I pushed my sunglasses back up my nose.

"Trust me, I've thought about it." He pressed the horn again. "Or having it fitted with legs that elevate the car so high I can just drive over them. Better yet, we should have brought the helicopter."

"Under the circumstances, I think it's just as well we didn't," I said. "We might not have anywhere to land when we get there."

"You're right," he admitted. "This is still bullshit."

"Yeah." I leaned my head against the back of the seat behind me, but kept my eyes open. Every time I saw a black SUV, my heart raced. If I saw two of them within a kilometre or so of each other, my palms broke out in a sweat.

Every time, they turned off into sidestreets, or driveways, but I watched closely until they were out of sight.

"Are you..." He cleared his throat. "Sorry."

"If the next words out of your mouth was going to be 'in the mood for vanilla ice cream,' then yes," I replied. "I'll settle for banana ice cream too. A big bowl of it."

"Yes, that's totally what I was going to say," he lied. "How did you guess?"

"If you know me as well as you say you do, then you know when I need ice cream," I said.

"I do know," he said. "That's why I keep those apples around. They should satisfy sugar cravings."

I shook my head and didn't deign to answer. We were almost at my street anyway.

We went through another light and around a corner. There we were confronted with a couple of firetrucks, a few police cars and an ambulance.

"Looks like a murder scene," Jake muttered.

I sighed. "I wish it was a murder scene." I undid my seatbelt and was out of the car half a second after it stopped moving. I waited for Jake to catch up before I slipped between the emergency vehicles and stood gaping at my house.

It was still there, small mercies for that. Unfortunately it was also leaning right over a massive sinkhole which had opened between the foundation and the boundary fence. How lucky my neighbours were that it just *happened* to stop on my property.

"Fuck," I said breathlessly. "I give him points for being original, but bloody hells. The whole house might as well be gone."

"Is this your house, Miss?" A young police officer addressed me. Or to be more specific, my chest. She was pretty, with dark hair and blue eyes. It would be a shame if I had to kill her for annoying me right now.

"Not for much longer, by the looks of it," I said.

She looked up at my face and blushed. "The firies said they called an engineer. They might be able to shore it up. It's possible they could save it." She looked uncertain about that. "At least they might be able to make it safe so you could go in and get your valuables. Luckily, it doesn't seem to be a danger to the other houses in the area."

"Well, that's some consolation," I said dryly.

Her eyes widened and she looked like she was about to stammer out an apology.

"It is definitely a consolation for her neighbours," Jake said quickly. "I'm sure they'll appreciate it." Apparently he had worked off his aggression on the road, because he was congenial now.

"Of course it is," I said from behind gritted teeth.

She gave him a grateful look, which lingered longer than it should have, before she turned and walked away.

I shook my head at her back.

"She's just doing her job," Jake said.

"Like the gas company last night?" I asked sweetly. I knew I pressed just the right button when he scowled.

"Useless bloody..." He muttered something under his breath.

I wandered over to the curb on the other side of the street and sat down.

The sinkhole was obviously made by magic from Dagen's witch. I made yet another mental note. Get a siphon stone and have someone take her magic before I killed her slowly.

I drew in my legs because the whole street didn't need to see my ass in a g string. I looked over at my teetering house and sighed.

I remembered the day so long ago when I came home from school to find blood all over the house. Four men, all black wolves, stood in the kitchen. Damp hair suggested they had all recently had showers. Coffee and plates of sandwiches suggested they'd been there for a while.

Waiting for me.

I stood with my schoolbag over one shoulder and waited calmly for them to kill me. To this day, I don't know why I didn't run. Perhaps on some level I knew they weren't going to kill me. Honestly, I don't know why they didn't. It would have saved the pack a lot of hassle and death. I guess by sparing the daughter of the alphas, they thought they wouldn't look quite so bad.

"She looks like fun," one of them said.

Another gave him a funny look. "She's a kid."

The first black wolf shrugged. "I meant for hunting, not fucking, but we have our orders. Come on, kid." He downed the last of his coffee and jerked his head towards the door.

I hesitated, then lowered my bag to the floor. Without a word, I followed them past the table where my parents' heads sat, and out to a waiting vehicle.

"A million dollars for your thoughts." Jake sat down next to me.

"I'm just thinking I should have strangled Alistair Dagen when I had the chance," I said.

"When did you get a chance?" he asked.

I shrugged. "I didn't. But I still could have found a way, or at least tried." Maybe if I'd pretended to break, or pretended I wanted to spread my legs for him, I might have had a chance to be alone with him.

It was silly to even think it. There was no way I would have been anything but alone with him and several of his goons. The moment my hands went anywhere near his neck, they would be all over me.

I suppressed a shudder.

"That looks bad," Cooper said as he sat down on the other side of me.

I turned slowly and gave him a long look. "What are you doing here?" That was before I noticed Hutton standing behind me, rather than resting like I told him to.

"You said I should do whatever Jake told me to do," Cooper said. "He said to stay close behind you. He did say I should try not to let you see me, but I figured—" He nodded towards the house.

"It seemed like you could use some company," Hutton said. "Ben is keeping an eye on things at Crimson. And taking a nap."

Before I could say anything in response, the house shuddered. Dirt from around the edge of the sinkhole dislodged and fell. Dirt and foundations.

Fuck.

"Everyone back!" someone shouted.

The ground rumbled. Several windows shattered under the pressure. Seams in the brickwork started to come apart. The whole building listed heavily.

I wanted to close my eyes, cover my ears and pretend it wasn't happening. I could have gotten up and walked away. Come back when it was over.

Instead I rose, crossed my arms over my chest and watched my house tear itself apart and slide into the sinkhole.

Someone put an arm around me. I didn't register who. I just leaned against him until there was nothing standing but a stubborn brick wall on the other end of the property.

"Well, shit," Hutton said. "That would have been cool if that wasn't your house."

"Yeah," I said absently. If anyone started with the 'at least no one was hurt,' bullshit, I was going to push them into the sinkhole myself.

My phone rang.

I put it to my ear, and barked, "What?"

I wasn't even slightly surprised to hear Alistair Dagen's voice on the other end of the line.

"I see you received my present," he said smoothly.

"Fuck you," I snarled.

"You seemed to enjoy doing just that," he said. "Shame you left so early. Think how much more fun you could have had."

I was tempted to throw my phone in the sinkhole.

"I hear your house burnt down," I said sweetly. "What a shame. It was so pretty out there."

Jake scowled when he realised who I was talking to. He mouthed that I should put the asshole on speaker phone, but I ignored him. Dagen was highly likely to say something I didn't want Jake to overhear.

"It was just one of many," Dagen said lightly. "No loss. Unlike your house. I understand your parents so tragically died there."

"You would know," I said. "Your parents killed them. But, like you, it's one of many properties I own. I could put two houses on this block and make a ton of money. I've been considering it, but you helped me make up my mind. Thank you so much." I wanted to pick up a brick and smash him in the face with it. Or better yet, in the balls.

The phone was silent for a moment. "I'm always happy to help out an old friend. Especially someone with such a warm, wet mouth."

I was ready for him to say something like that, but it still sent disgust snaking through my body and into my stomach. It reminded me I hadn't eaten since I threw up all that pizza. That was probably just as well. I might have vomited on the remains of my house.

Later, I would think of the perfect come back. Right now my brain was frazzled and blank.

All I said instead was, "We're not friends, asshole. In fact, why don't you come down to the harbour? There's a nice big hole right in front of me that I could throw you in. I'm sure no one will miss you."

"Maybe your hole wouldn't be so big if you weren't such a slut," he said.

Ouch. A burn and a slut shame rolled into one. This guy was pure class.

I laughed. "At least I don't have to pay for it." I was tempted to retort that at least I didn't have to have three men hold someone down for me, but the guys were right next to me.

"Perhaps, but I can father children," he said.

I could just picture the smug expression on his face.

He hit me right where he aimed, in the heart.

I managed another laugh. "Yes, you're one up on me. I can't father children. Funny though, because I'm pretty sure my cock is bigger than yours."

He chuckled. "Ah yes, my cock. I'm sure you dream about it at night. Do you remember how it felt when I squirted hot cum down your throat?"

I ended the call. I wanted to put the phone down on the ground and grind my heel into the screen. That would achieve nothing apart from breaking my phone. The hassle of replacing it outweighed the satisfaction I might get from destroying it.

I would get much more satisfaction from destroying Dagen.

My phone pinged with a text message. I almost ignored it.

I should have.

I glanced at the screen.

You look sexy in that red dress. Yeah, he actually ended the message with a full stop. What a monster.

"Motherfu—" I gripped my phone tight in my hand and

looked around. My heart pounded like thunder. My palms were almost sweaty enough to drip.

"El? What is it?" Jake grabbed my wrist and turned it far enough to read the screen.

"He's here somewhere," I said. "He's watching me. Us. We need to find him."

Jake started to look around too. "I don't see anyone but the emergency crews, and..."

The neighbours were trickling out of their homes. They cast anxious glances at the empty lot where my house once stood.

"In a window?" I squinted, but light reflected off every window I saw.

"Um, babe," Hutton said.

I turned to him. "What? You see him?"

He shook his head. "No." He pointed toward a security camera directly opposite my wrecked house. "I'd guess he's watching through that."

"Fucking creep." I stuck up both middle fingers to the camera.

My phone pinged again.

I look forward to breaking both of those. Right before I break you, bitch.

Yep, I should have ignored him, but I wrote, *Don't call me bitch,* and hit send.

He responded a moment later with a laughing face emoji and a dog. A second later he added an eggplant, a donut and a panting, hot face.

"Ewww." I thought about replying with a clown or devil face, but he might think I was referring to myself.

"You know you can block him, right?" Cooper said. He sounded like a teenager explaining new technology to someone who prefers older technology...

Oh. Well, anyway, I grimaced at him. "He'd only change numbers and contact me again. He's a slug." And frankly I could have done without the mentions of what he did to me. I knew he was trying to get to me, but shit, it was working. I should be tougher than this.

I *was* tougher than this.

The street was now buzzing with people, including TV cameras and roving journalists. They seemed to be hunting for witnesses to talk about my house sinking into the earth.

Newsflash, I didn't want to talk about it.

"Let's get out of here." I glanced at Jake.

He sighed, but nodded. "Hutton, Cooper, you guys stay here and deal with any questions. Tell them you don't know anything, but you're authorised to liaise with the owner to organise the clean up. We'll do whatever the engineers recommend."

"You trust me, huh?" Hutton looked smug.

"Fuck no, but it's not safe for Ivory. You can't do too much damage here." Jake gave him a sarcastic smile, then put a possessive hand on my back to guide me to the car.

"Are you going to tell me I should try to trust him?" he asked as he opened the passenger side door.

I gave him a look for apparently assuming I suddenly lost the ability to open a car door. "At this point, I'm not sure I trust myself."

"As long as you trust me." He actually waited until I was sitting in the car before he closed the door and walked around the other side.

"Yeah, I might," I told him as he slipped into his seat. Part of me wanted to tell him to find a quiet street so I could fuck him in the back seat. It was long enough to comfortably fit us both. Jake did like luxury in all of his cars.

Then I remembered I was trying to keep my distance. And this was Sydney. Quiet streets were like virgins—hard to find, and harder to fuck in. Yeah, okay, that sounded better in my head.

"You can always trust me," he said, his blue eyes intent on my face. "You know that, right? Whatever happens, whatever or whoever you do, I will always be right there, ready to catch you."

Fuck, he had so much love in his tone it broke my heart a little. How was I supposed to keep my distance from him when he adored me as much as I adored him? We had tied our lives together a long time ago. Some knots couldn't be undone, even if they strangled us both.

"I don't plan on falling," I said softly. Literally, figuratively or in love. I knew he understood my triple meaning. I also knew he didn't buy it any more than I did.

Frozen steel, I reminded myself. Even if I ripped out my own heart in the process.

I don't know, maybe I had no heart. If I did, surely I wouldn't turn my back on someone who looked at me the way he did. Maybe I was a coward. I had never let anyone in fully, since I was a kid. I trusted people, sure, and that was a huge deal, but lowering all of my walls... That was something else entirely.

I supposed I fit the nickname Ice Bitch. I acknowledged long ago I wasn't a nice person. I was okay with that. I was a killer surrounded by killers. I was cold, sarcastic, composed, distant.

But when I looked back at him, a hidden part of my heart begged to melt. To let him in. To let Ben, Cooper and Hutton in. I was a crappy person, but even crappy people needed to be loved.

Except Dagen. He could fuck himself. But me— Ivory was damaged, but Elodie needed to be held, comforted and protected from the big, bad world.

Which side of me would win? I had no idea, but it was going to be an epic boss fight.

FIFTEEN

"A lot of this is useful, if we can believe a word of it." Jake adjusted his reading glasses and pointed at the screen. He hated wearing them. The fact that he was showed how much material Hutton sent. He either had to wear them, or he'd have a massive headache later.

"Dagen did let him back into the fold pretty quickly," he added.

"I don't think he bought Hutton's loyalty to him for a second," I admitted. "Letting him have access to that information was a test. Hutton failed." Or passed, depending on the criteria. I knew I could trust him. I should have known Dagen wasn't dumb enough to be fooled.

"So it's probably useless." Jake snatched his glasses off his face and rubbed the bridge of his nose between his thumb and forefinger. "A red herring to feed back to us."

"It's a very extensive red herring if it is," I pointed out. "We can actually confirm quite a bit of that ourselves. Either Hutton was going to pass the test or he was going to be killed. It's possible Dagen thought he had nothing to lose." No, I didn't buy that either. Alistair Dagen was not stupid. This would be a lot easier if he was.

I stopped pacing and sat on the side of the desk. "Somewhere in there is some kind of trap. Something that looks harmless, but when we look into it—"

"It will blow up in our faces. Get us killed," Jake finished for me.

"Killed if we're lucky." I drummed my nails on the desktop. "It's probably best to stop looking at it. Knowing him, it'll be something which would spark our curiosity."

"It wasn't just the cat that curiosity killed," Jake said. "But now I feel like we have a puzzle to solve. See if we can find the deadly clue hidden in the files."

"If you need something to hunt, I could throw you a ball," I said dryly.

He chuckled. "Would you? It's been a while since I've had that much fun. Maybe we could get one of those big, inflatable ones and go to the beach."

"Are we still talking about balls, or something else inflatable?" I teased.

He grinned. "It's not exactly the kind of threesome I have in mind." He ran the tip of his finger over the back of my hand. The touch made me shiver.

"Jake—"

He rose from his chair and moved to stand in front of me. He placed his hands on the desktop to either side of me.

"Shhh." He brought his lips to mine in a whisper soft kiss. It was barely a brush.

Heat flooded right to my core.

He pulled away and looked me in the eyes, conveying a thousand emotions in one glance.

I felt like I lived a hundred lifetimes in that brief moment.

Then all of that disappeared when he slammed his mouth against mine.

Where the first kiss was soft and tender, this was fierce and possessive. The alpha wolf claiming what was his.

He snaked a hand around the back of my head. His tongue dipped into my mouth, testing, tasting, running over my lips.

His other hand slid up the outside of my thigh, under my dress. He cupped my ass and gave it a squeeze.

I broke off the kiss. "Jake..."

"Shhh," he said again. He slid his hand from the back of my head, down my arm and onto my other thigh. Slowly, he sank to his knees. He pushed my thighs apart and rubbed the back of his knuckle against the gusset of my panties.

I bit my lip to hold back a groan. I was already panting at his touch.

And he was merciless.

He grabbed the front of my panties and literally tore them away. He gripped my thighs with firm fingers and vigourously attacked my pussy with his tongue. He licked me all the way from my clit to my rear hole.

He tickled that a time or two before focusing all of his attention on my clit and entrance.

I didn't bother to hold back a second groan. "That feels so good." We shouldn't have been doing this, but gods, I couldn't stop.

"It tastes so good," he said, his voice muffled by a mouthful of pussy. "I want to feel you come on my face. But not yet."

If he kept doing what he was doing, I wouldn't be able to stop myself. And he did keep doing it. He dipped his tongue in and out of me, then stroked me from front to back, and back again.

I pressed my palms to the desktop for stability, and rocked lightly against his mouth. "Oh gods, I'm so close."

"Not yet," he said. He looked up at me and pulled back his mouth long enough to say, "Touch your breasts for me."

While he got busy with his mouth again, I unzipped my dress and slipped it down my shoulders. I unhooked my bra and placed it to one side on the desk. My nipples were already hard before I started to run the tips of my fingers around and over them.

"Good girl," he said.

For some reason, his words made me hotter than ever. "I need to come. Please."

His fingers gripped my thighs tighter. "Okay, Elodie. Come for me."

He licked me so hard it almost hurt, but I came hard, grinding my pussy against his mouth. The scratch of his stubble against my sensitive skin pushed me over the long, steep drop to blissful oblivion. My vision blurred. My mind knew nothing but pleasure.

I think I screamed his name, but all I knew was that my throat was raw afterwards.

I was only halfway down when he rose, and pulled me off the desk.

He grabbed a handful of fabric and jerked my dress the rest of the way off. With one hand, he turned me around and bent me over the top of the desk. With the other, he unzipped his jeans and pushed them down his hips.

I barely had any warning before he pounded his cock all the way inside me, from tip to balls.

I cried out in surprise. If I thought he would give me a moment to compose myself, or get used to the feeling of him inside me, I was wrong.

Just as his tongue was merciless, so was his cock. He pulled all the way out, then slammed back in, over and over. He was like an animal, asserting absolute control over his mate. Every bit of me was his and he would do whatever he wanted to me.

He slid a hand up my belly and cupped my breast. He gripped it hard enough to hurt, but at the same time it felt so good.

The moment his tongue touched my pussy, I had relinquished every bit of control to him. It was hot and it was liberating. Just like when he and Cooper had both taken control and fucked me, I wanted more. I wanted him to dominate me.

I leaned my elbows on the desk and dropped my head almost to the wood. I spread my legs a little further apart to let him go in deeper.

"That's it," he said. "Perfect. Gods, Elodie, you feel so good." He ran the heel of his hand up and down my taut nipple. "So fucking good." Without warning, he pulled out of me. He turned me around, put his hands on hips and placed me back on the desk.

"Lie back." He grabbed my feet, and placed them on the top of the desk, so I was lying with my knees spread as far apart as they could go. He took a moment to admire the view, before he grabbed my ankles to keep me in place and drove himself back into my body.

He slid a hand between us and rubbed my clit.

I closed my eyes.

"No," he said. "Look at me. Watch me while I fuck you."

Holy shit, that was hot.

I opened my eyes, but had to pick up my head to see as much of him as I could. I propped myself up on my elbows and watched his chiselled torso move as he thrust in and out of my slick heat.

"It's the best view in the world, isn't it?" he asked.

"Billion-dollar view," I agreed. I had to admit I attracted some pretty hot guys.

He smiled and massaged my clit firmly with his thumb. "Come again," he ordered. "I know you can."

"Mmmm, I'm sure I can," I agreed. Between his thumb and the friction of his cock sliding back and forth across the most sensitive part of my body, I was close again.

"Of course you can, you know why?" he asked. "Because I told you to. And because when I fuck you, I am in charge."

There was something about those words that turned me on so hard. I moaned.

"You like to hear that?" he asked. He paused his thrusting and rubbed me harder. He leaned forward and whispered, "I'm the boss. Come for me again."

I came all right. Like thunder, lightning, fireworks and vanilla ice cream all rolled into one. Every nerve in my body lit up in a rush of heat, blood and pleasure. I cried out as the warmth rushed over me, from my toes to the top of my head.

He started to thrust again. After maybe a dozen strokes, he came too, with a series of hard, animalistic grunts.

Finally he flopped forward, panting.

I lowered my legs so they hung off the side of the desk, and looked up at the ceiling.

Fuck.

Fuck. Fuck. Fuck.

I sat up so he slid out of me. I rubbed my forehead with my fingertips and exhaled. What was I thinking? Oh, right, I wasn't thinking.

"Jake..."

His head jerked up.

"I'm sorry. I should have— We shouldn't have done that," I said softly.

"Elodie—"

I swung my leg over and dropped to the floor. "I'm sorry. This was a mistake. I should have stopped it before it went this far."

The look on his face was like a stab to the heart. I guessed he assumed fucking meant we could move forward the way we were before Dagen took me. Or maybe he hoped it would convince me.

"Bullshit," he said after a moment of shocked silence. "Nothing about this was a mistake. I love you. I know you love me.

You say you only said it because you were scared but I don't buy it, El. You wanted this as much as I did. Not just this." He waved at the desk top. "*Us.*"

For the first time since we met, he looked like a lost boy. Like he was desperate to find the right words to fix this, but knew it was like putting a small bandage over a severed limb.

"Wanting something doesn't mean it's a good idea," I said coolly. I pushed all the walls I had lowered for the last hour or so back into place. "I don't want to lead you on. It's not fair to you."

He snorted and pulled his jeans back up. "I'm a big boy. I can decide for myself. I decided the moment I met you. I know for a fact you did too. I also know you feel the same way about the other guys. That's why you trusted them so quickly. It was because you knew there was something there. Something that binds you to them, the same way we are bound together. I know they feel the same way about you, even Hutton." He grimaced.

He put his hands on my shoulders and looked me in the eyes. "I know you've been through a lot—"

"Because I let my guard down," I said. "I can't do that again. Ever. Not with you and not with any of them. Not even with myself. It won't be the restaurant or my house next time. There is nothing he won't try to take from me to break me. How do you think I will feel if the next thing he takes is you? Or any of the guys? I can't..."

I swallowed down a knot of emotion. "I can't afford to be that vulnerable. The best, safest place for all of you is as far away from me as you can get. Let me deal with Dagen and—"

"If you think I am walking away from you *ever*, much less right now, you're out of your mind," he said. "Whether you like it or not, we are a team. We feel what we feel. We can't turn it off. I don't want to. I don't think this was a mistake. I will never, ever regret making love to you."

He dropped his hands and took a few steps away. He let out an exasperated sigh and turned back. "I wish I knew what I had to say or do to convince you."

I saw the sincerity in his eyes, heard it in his voice. If there was a single word or act he could say or do to convince me, he would say or do it.

I looked down at the floor, then back up again."There is nothing you can say or do. You know how stubborn I am."

"And you know how stubborn I am," he said. "I will die before I give up on you."

"You might die *because* you didn't give up on me," I told him.

He shrugged. "Then I die. But I would rather die by your side, fighting Dagen, or some other monster, than live without you."

He was nothing if not romantic.

I had no answer for him.

I crouched down to scoop up my dress off the floor. That was something I had always done. I hated to bend over, especially in front of other people. For some reason, it made me feel unbearably vulnerable. I frowned at the remains of my ruined panties. I held them up between my thumb and forefinger.

"Was that necessary?"

He grinned. "Absolutely. Yes. I'll buy you some new ones." Without missing a beat, he added, "I will tear those off as well."

He really wasn't going to give up, was he?

"At least I'm not covered in blood, juice or mud," I said. "For once." There might be a blade or two of grass on the back of my dress, but I decided not to look.

"I knew I should have come on your stomach," he said. "Next time."

It was just as well he hadn't. The idea of his cock even that close to my face made me want to shudder. I probably would have run away screaming. I had a panic attack...

Like I was starting to have right now...

His phone rang. I thought he was going to ignore it, but he glanced at the screen. "I should get that."

"Saved by the bell," I muttered.

I picked up my own phone and headed towards the apartment for a change of clothes. If either of the bodyguards standing outside the door were surprised to see me walk past naked, they gave no sign. Internally, I was a trembling mess, but this was another thing I refused to change just because I felt threatened by Dagen. What kind of shifter was modest anyway?

I padded silently past Ben, who was asleep on the couch. He stirred when I got close, which didn't surprise me. Between the bond and his vigilance, he probably knew I was there. Even in his sleep.

I threw on an old T-shirt and a pair of track pants. The kind of clothes I wore to work out in. I should go down to the gym and do that after I made this call.

I opened contacts and pressed on one of the names. It rang a couple of times before a male voice came on the line.

"Yes?" Paxton said. He must have recognised my number, because he asked, "Do you want to talk to Harmony?"

"No," I replied. "It's you I need to talk to." As briefly as I could, I explained the reason for my call.

"Yeah, that's something I can do. If you're sure."

"I'm very sure," I said. "It's the right thing to do. For everyone." I expected him to say something about not making decisions on behalf of other people, but he didn't.

Instead he said, "Is tomorrow okay?"

"It can wait until then," I said. I ended the call with all the usual niceties that neither of us were comfortable with.

"Anything wrong?" Jake asked.

I hadn't heard him come in, and I almost jumped out of my skin as a result. I turned around and tried not to look guilty. "Everything's fine. You? That call seemed important."

"You suggested I contact the conclave. That was Kian Quinn. He and his brothers will be up next week. The Tasmanian alphas have confirmed they are also coming. The grey wolves from Queensland left us on read." He shrugged. "I was thinking I should organise some extra 'entertainment' for Tyler and Reed Quinn, so they can let off steam when they get here." He rolled his eyes towards the ceiling. As if he wouldn't fuck me every chance he got.

Still, he had a point. The brothers did seem to be insatiable. Jake's attempt to keep them away from me was about as transparent as a brick wall.

"Do you think I can't handle them?" I asked.

"I know you can handle them," he said. "But didn't you just say you didn't want any distractions?"

Trust him to turn my words back on me like that. He was right though. Tensions between white and black wolves were strained enough without me fucking a pair of them. Truthfully though, I wasn't even tempted. Why would I want burgers when I had perfectly cooked bacon I was trying to resist?

For a moment I thought about a burger with bacon piled on top of it, but I was probably getting greedy. Although, giving control to four guys...

Gods, when did my vagina become so needy? And how the fuck was I actually supposed to resist four, hot guys?

CHAPTER

SIXTEEN

"Come in." I stepped aside from the small side door of Crimson to let Paxton, Harmony and Jordan come inside.

Jordan, another one of Harmony's boyfriends, had almost as many tattoos as Jake. Like Jake, he looked like the sort of guy who would hurt you if you looked at him the wrong way.

I was certain he would hurt anyone who lay a hand on Harmony. The looks they exchanged clearly showed they adored each other. I hadn't met her other two guys, both Jordan's brothers, but Jordan and Paxton couldn't be much different.

I guessed that kept her life interesting.

Jordan gave me a measured look. "Thanks for helping us when Harmony needed to get her magic back. Sorry I couldn't be there to help rescue you. Kayden, our son, is going through a phase. He's a powerful witch. When he's being difficult, it's best to have someone around who can use magic."

"We wouldn't want magic to go awry," I said dryly. Personally, I would be okay with it not existing at all. Although, it did come in handy for healing. It was certainly more efficient than human medicine.

"We really wouldn't," Paxton agreed. "Fortunately, Harmony's sister was available to take care of him today. What you need us to do will take a lot of magic. I'll need all the help I can get."

Harmony hadn't said a word since she walked through the door, but she offered me a reassuring smile.

Confiding in her the other day helped at the time, but now... Now it was disconcerting knowing she knew what happened to me. She wouldn't tell anyone, but still, she knew.

"This way." I led them over to the elevator. It was a squeeze with me, three of them and two of my bodyguards. I didn't trust Harmony and her men enough to leave security behind.

I wasn't naïve; three wolves stood little chance against three powerful witches, but it was better than taking them on alone.

"Nice view," Paxton said as he was ushered into my office on the tenth floor. "Who said crime doesn't pay?"

Harmony gave him a sharp look.

Jordan looked alarmed, but relaxed slightly when I smiled.

"The people who say that aren't doing it right," I said. "Fortunately, that's most people, or property prices in the area would be even higher than they are now."

I waved them towards the couches on the side of the room and pulled out my phone to send a text to Ben. I could have summoned him through the bond, but that was something neither of us should get used to.

He wasn't far anyway, just in my apartment looking around for hidden cameras or listening devices. He was certain he wouldn't find any, but insisted on looking anyway. It didn't hurt to be vigilant, and it kept him busy for a while.

He stepped through the doorway a couple of minutes later, followed by Cooper.

"Hey," Cooper greeted the newcomers warmly. "Long time, no

see." He offered his hand to Paxton and Harmony before introducing himself to Jordan.

All the while, Ben stood near the doorway. He looked composed but wary. He must have caught some inkling of what was going on. Finally, he moved over to stand beside me, almost close enough for our hands to touch.

I sensed he wanted to lace his fingers in mine, but he didn't.

"What's going on?" he asked softly.

"They're here to break the bond," I said as lightly as I could.

It took him a moment to realise what I said. Surprise and hurt crossed his face and flooded through the bond.

"Can we talk about this? Alone?" His eyes pleaded with me.

I thought about refusing, but I owed him that much. "Cooper, offer our guests a drink. Ben and I will be back in a minute."

I gestured towards the door and waited for him to walk through first before I followed.

He led me all the way to the apartment and closed the door behind us.

He turned to face me. "Do I get any say in this?"

Through the bond, I felt his need to reach out to me. To hold me. Only his practiced restraint held him back.

"It's the best thing for you too," I said. "It's not healthy for you to be connected to me like this. It's only been a few days and I'm surprised you're not insane already." I was only half joking. "Or tired of me."

"You know how much I hate magic," he said softly. "But having the connection to you has been..." He searched for the right words. "Enlightening. Weird. Wonderful. Feeling you enjoy it when I touched you was... Fucking hot. It was a whole new level of intimacy."

"It was," I agreed. "But it's not appropriate between a boss and her employee."

He brushed his knuckles lightly over my cheek. "We're more

than that. You know how I feel about you. I know how you feel about me. Even without the bond, we share something."

I wanted to melt into his touch. Let Cooper entertain our guests for an hour or two, while we entertained each other.

Instead, I stepped away from him.

"What we *had*. We have to forget about it. We're back home now. Things have to go back to the way they were."

"I can feel how hard you're trying to convince yourself of that," he said. "But I can also feel that you don't believe it either. I know you're trying to distance yourself from all four of us to protect yourself. And to protect us. But we're all big boys, we can protect ourselves. And you."

"The fact that you say all of that is another reason to break the bond," I said. "Do we really need to know what each other is thinking? Or feeling?" I shook my head. "It's not normal. If nothing else, women are supposed to be mysterious. The bond is fucking with that."

"You're still mysterious," he assured me. "I knew you were planning something, but not that it was this."

"It's reassuring to know I've managed to keep some things a secret, but I'm still doing this," I said firmly. "It's the right thing to do. And you said yourself you hate magic. I'm surprised you didn't suggest breaking it."

"I *do* hate magic," he said. "Very much. What does it say to you that I would keep a magical connection in spite of all of that?"

"It says you take your job too seriously. You need a holiday," I said dryly. "Don't make me insist."

"If I *consent* to this, you won't insist on me taking time off?" he asked.

His deliberate choice of words left me breathless. His eyes snapped with a rare display of anger which quickly dissipated into regret.

"I'm sorry, that was—"

"Yes it was," I snapped. "The fact that you would, for a moment, compare this to what Alistair Dagen did to me..." The worst part about it was that he was right. If I wasn't doing this with his consent, then I was as good as forcing it on him. I never said I wasn't an asshole, but to compare myself to someone so irredeemably disgusting was a whole new low.

"I'm sorry," I said finally. "I had no right to spring this on you. I should have warned you."

He drew himself up, his bodyguard mask firmly in place. "You're the boss. You get to do whatever you want. My job is to make sure no one gets in your way. Including me. I apologise for arguing. It was unprofessional."

I knew that wall he put up around himself all too well. I had no right to feel hurt about it, but I did. Dagen was like the opposite of King Midas. Everything he touched turned to shit. Or maybe it was just me and I was looking for someone else to blame. Either way, a perfectly good working relationship was now tense and I wasn't sure if we would ever be able to go back to the way things were.

"Ben." I wasn't sure what I was going to say. Really, what could I say that would make this any better? "Let's get this over with." I wasn't going to change my mind but the longer we put it off, the harder it would be. There was no point in prolonging this any longer than necessary.

"Yes, boss." His response was almost robotic. Did I sound like that when I was trying to shut everyone out? Probably.

I couldn't look him in the eyes anymore, so I kept my gaze on the floor as we walked back to the office.

We needed to get rid of this bond because, if nothing else, I didn't need him knowing how close I was to crying.

Ivory didn't cry. Ivory was unbreakable. Unshakeable. Nothing got to me. No one got to me. I played those words over and over in my head like a mantra.

"We're ready," I said as we stepped back into the office.

Judging by the expression on Cooper's face, he'd thought we'd gone next door for a quickie. When he saw us back so soon and both with similar expressions, he looked worried.

"Are you guys okay?" he asked. "Did you have a fight?"

"We're fine," I said, my voice tight.

"Nothing to worry about," Ben agreed. To our guests he said, "If you don't mind, my boss would like to get this bond broken." He looked like he wanted to elaborate, but he didn't. Any of the other guys probably would have added something sarcastic, but that wasn't how he rolled.

Harmony rose from her chair and moved to put a hand on my arm. "Are you sure about this?" she asked softly.

"Yes," Paxton agreed. "Be certain, because once this is broken it can only be restored the way it was made in the first place. Bonding stones are hard to find and cost— You could afford it. But they're still hard to find."

"We're sure." I forced myself to look at Ben.

His jaw was set firmly. He could have been the male version of me right now. Maybe stone instead of ice.

"It's been decided," he said.

I felt a flutter of nerves through the bond. For him, it wasn't just about breaking it, it was the proximity to the three witches. He wanted to be anywhere right now but here.

"This shouldn't take long." Paxton took Harmony's hand, and she reached for Jordan's. The air tingled even before Paxton put a hand on my arm. "Take Ben's hand."

I did as he said and noted the look of relief in Ben's eyes that he wouldn't have to touch any of the witches directly. I felt like on some level, I should try to help him get over his prejudice. On the other hand, I didn't trust any black wolf as far as I could spit them. I had no desire or need to get past that prejudice.

I squeezed Ben's hand to reassure him. He squeezed mine

back. I knew he would have preferred to snatch his hand back and leave the bond in place. He didn't. He stood perfectly still while Paxton frowned and muttered to himself.

"This is a kind of reverse healing," Paxton said. "Instead of putting things back where they go, I'm taking something away that shouldn't be there. Or at least, something that was added to both of you."

"Is this going to cause any damage?" Ben asked.

That was a good question. One I should have asked before now. Just because Paxton was a doctor didn't mean I could trust him.

"It shouldn't," Paxton said. "If I think it will, I'll stop and you'll be stuck with the bond forever. You'll have to deal with it."

For a doctor, his bedside manner was shit. On the other hand, it was better than sugar coating things, or flat out lying.

I glanced sideways at Ben. It didn't take a genius, or a bond, to know he would be okay with Paxton failing. Honestly, it wouldn't be the end of the world if we were stuck with it. I mean, they were worse things than a bodyguard who knew exactly where you were at all times.

Now I thought about it—

The bond evaporated and I could no longer feel Ben's emotions. For some reason, I expected it to be a gradual reduction, not the hard slice it was. He was there in one heartbeat and not in the next.

It left me feeling strangely empty.

You know what they say. Be careful what you wish for, you might just get it.

Ben sharply sucked in a breath. Obviously he felt the same immediate response I did.

Paxton lowered his hand and moved away. "There. Done. No damage. You're free to get on with your lives."

Right. No damage. Then why did I feel so empty inside? I couldn't bring myself to entertain the idea that breaking the bond was a mistake. Firstly because I didn't like to second-guess myself, but mostly because it was the right thing for Ben, as far as I was concerned. He might not believe me, or agree, but I did this for him. Because he deserved better than to be stuck with me and my moods.

"Thank you." I let Ben's hand slip out of mine. Something about it felt horribly final.

That was fucking stupid, I told myself. No one should have an empathic link to their employee. Nothing good could ever come of it.

"Ivory," Harmony said tentatively. "Can I have a word with you please? Alone." She gestured towards the other side of the room, which was about as alone as I was prepared to do.

I thought about saying no, but I nodded and stepped over away from all the guys. "What did you need to talk about?"

"I just wanted to be sure you're all right," she said. "You went through a lot and—"

"I'm absolutely fine," I lied. "Now this is done, I can get on with everything. It's nice of you to be concerned about me, but I'm okay."

She gave me a look that clearly said she didn't believe a word of it. She was just as clearly undecided as to whether she should push me or not. On one hand, I could decide she didn't need to walk out of here alive. On the other hand, most women who went through what I did, needed a friend. Most men too. I knew Ben and Cooper talked about all sorts of things. So did Ben and Jake. Knowing Cooper, he was also an ear for Hutton.

And me, I had no one. Yeah, okay, a lot of that was by choice. Don't cry me a fucking river. But from time to time, it would be nice to have another woman to talk to.

"If you change your mind and want to have a chat, you know

where to find me," she said softly. "If not me, then please talk to someone."

"Maybe I'll get a pet cat," I said dryly.

She smiled. "I hear pets are very good listeners. Better than guys sometimes." She rolled her eyes.

I smiled but couldn't bring myself to laugh. Guys certainly did have their moments.

Her smile faded and she sighed. "I know you're a bit older and probably a lot wiser than me, but I still worry about you. Keeping everything bottled up inside isn't good for you. Being distant from the people around you isn't good either. I know that from experience. Letting people in is scary, but it's worth it."

Oh yeah, I thought sarcastically. Who wouldn't want to end up with someone like Paxton Evans, who kept her locked up in a room for five months? She might need a friend even more than I did. Or a cat. That might be what all of this was about, she needed a friend and was projecting that on to me. That was actually really sad. If that was the case, I felt sorry for her.

There was a good reason I didn't have any friends. I couldn't go for more than a few minutes without questioning their motives. I would always assume they wanted something from me or were trying to advance themselves in some way. I was well aware of my trust issues, but at the end of the day, they kept me alive.

"Just think about what I said, okay?" She patted my arm and moved away.

"We should get going," Jordan said. "It's a long drive back."

"Not until we've experienced the pleasures of the third floor," Paxton said. He gave Harmony a look that would have melted the panties on anyone but me.

Harmony smiled and hooked her arm through Jordan's. "Yes, we can stay a bit longer. You know you want to."

Jordan said not one word of objection as the three of them followed Ben out the door.

"That was really brave of you," Cooper said.

I frowned at him. "What was?"

"Breaking the bond," he said. "It must have been really intense to be connected to someone like that. I love Ben like he's a big brother, but I don't want him in my brain. You know?"

After a moment he added, "I'm not even sure I'd want you in there. No offence. I like not knowing what you're going to say or do next. It keeps things interesting." He looked at me like you would look at a wild animal, not sure if it was going to roll over and show its belly, or claw you to shreds.

At the same time, I could tell he wanted to touch me. He was smart and sensitive enough to understand why I went from so hot to so cold. Unlike Jake, I knew he would stick around whether he was sleeping with me or not. My lifestyle was exciting to him. I was the icing on the cake, but the cake was still pretty tasty.

"I'm glad someone understands," I said. "It was intense."

It was also comforting, and now it was gone, I felt lonelier than ever.

CHAPTER
SEVENTEEN

"Is it safe?" Hutton stuck his head in the doorway an hour or two later.

"Safe from what?" I looked up from my screen. "Or who?"

He stepped inside and strode over, his hands in his pockets. He shrugged. "Everyone. Specifically Jake. He is never going to not hate my guts, is he?"

I sat back and tucked my legs up underneath me. "I don't think he hates you quite as violently as that. It's just— The past was hard for all of us." The present wasn't all that rosy either, to be honest. With any luck, the future would be better.

"Yeah, no shit." He grabbed a chair, pulled it up to the desk and sat on it backwards. He rested his arms across the back. "It wasn't all Vegemite sandwiches and too many spoonfuls of Nutella for me either."

"Just as well," I said dryly. "Nutella is toxic to dogs." That was a shame, because the chocolate and hazelnut-flavoured spread smelled delicious.

"You know what I mean," he said. "Suburban families and all

that shit. Mum and Dad, or Mum and Mum. Or Dad and Dad. Or just one or the other. A pet fish. Friends coming over after school. Riding bikes around the neighbourhood."

I sighed. That was my life for the first eight years. More or less. "Dad and his many girlfriends. Parents fighting. Pressing the button on the answering machine and hearing death threats. Suburban living isn't all rainbows and sunshine."

"All of those things still sound better than being raised to be the enemy to your own people." He rested his chin on his arms. He hadn't shaved in a few days. It was a good look for him.

"Or being raised to roll over onto your back and spread your legs for someone with the last name Dagen." I grimaced.

"I can't imagine you taking that lying down. So to speak." He looked intently at me. "You're made of tougher stuff than that. I doubt they would have gotten out of it without losing a shit load of skin and blood."

"No, they wouldn't have," I agreed. Between Alistair Dagen and his father, life would have been hells.

I cocked my head at him. "You had other kids around you, didn't you?" Hadn't he said he was fostered with a couple of other white wolves?

"Yeah, but everything was a competition. Every chance they got, they pitted us against each other. If we were too slow, we were punished. If we weren't careful enough, we were punished. Eventually, we started to see each other as the enemy. It wasn't that I was too slow, it was that they were faster than me. Maybe they pushed themselves a little harder so I would get punished. Looking back, that seems really stupid. But at the time, that was how it was."

"That sounds lonely," I said softly. That might explain my attraction to him. We both went through things the others would never truly understand. The absolute desperation to survive, but the almost equally absolute certainty the black wolves would destroy us. There were days I almost accepted the future they planned for me. Right up until the moment the hammer fell on my virgin auction. Until I saw the look of fury on Alistair's father's face. He and his son were really good at one thing: assuming they had more time than they actually did. Had they realised it, things would have been worse for me.

Hutton shrugged. "I can deal with loneliness. It was the part about doing shitty things to other white wolves that I struggle with. Sometimes I wished Gus Dagen would beat me to death. So I didn't have to keep doing things." His eyes glazed over as he thought back over the memories.

"Other times, I wished I dared to beat him to death. If the other guys and I got our shit together, he wouldn't have been able to stop us. We were just too fucking scared. Half the time we would jump at our own shadows."

I put a hand on his arm. "I'm sorry that happened to you. I wish I'd been old enough to stop everything sooner."

He snorted lightly. "You changed everything for a generation of white wolves, and you're still not satisfied that you did enough? Believe me, you did plenty. The gods know there were other people who could have done something."

"Like Jake?" I guessed. "He didn't like sitting on his hands, waiting. He hated himself for it. He still does."

"That makes two of us." Hutton grinned.

I socked him lightly on the arm. "Sooner or later, one of you is going to have to let up on the other one. If only so you can work together in peace. I guess I could always fire one of you." I shrugged.

"As long as it's him," Hutton said. "You would come to regret firing me. I'm awesome." He wiggled his brows.

I shook my head at him. "Of course you are."

Guys.

"Seriously though, none of us came through all of that

unscathed. Ben's parents fled the state before they died. Left everything they had behind. They had to start over, in Tasmania. That's the same story for a lot of the staff here. That or they grew up in remote parts of New South Wales, or on the border with other states. Some of them even grew up in Queensland or the Northern Territory, because they knew they'd be safer there than here."

"Desperate times call for desperate measures," he said.

"That they do," I agreed.

"Is that why you're trying to push all of us away?" he asked. "Desperate times?"

"You noticed too, hmmm?" I rearranged my legs so I was sitting cross-legged on the chair. "You of all people should understand why."

"Because the Onyx Ridge pack are experts at pitting us against each other," he said. "You don't want them to do anything to us in order to get to you. Or vice versa. But there's one thing I've learnt in my long, long life, and it's that being lonely sucks. Yeah, there are worse things, but there are better things. You have this whole big bad wolf vibe going on, but I know for a fact that you would prefer to save the huffing and puffing for the bedroom. Or the couch. Or the desk. Or—"

"Okay, okay, I get the idea." I rolled my eyes at him. He wasn't wrong. I much preferred my huffing and puffing to involve cocks and orgasms.

I frowned. "You think everything Asshole has done, and keeps doing, is because he wants me to push you guys away? To isolate me from everyone else?"

"Is his last name Dagen?" Hutton asked rhetorically. "They get off on two things." He held up a finger. "One, power. And two, mind fucks. If they can combine those two into one, then they're as happy as a pig in shit. Let's be real here for a moment. He would have really gotten off on seeing you devastated over me and Ben dying. Ben in particular, because of that bond. That would have given him the mother of all hard ons. If your friends hadn't arrived just in time..."

I nodded. "Yes, I know what would have happened." It would have been brutal. "But caring about anyone sets the stage for that to happen again."

"So does being alone," he argued. "You're stronger with our support than without it. Let me ask you this." He paused for a moment to gather his thoughts. "Could you have done all of this," he gestured around the room, "without Jake's help?"

"Now you want to give him credit," I teased gently. "No. I couldn't have done this without him. Without his money or his support."

"Are you worried that if you push him away hard enough, he could withdraw his support? What if he decided to go against you somehow?" He raised an eyebrow at me in speculation.

"He would never do that," I said with certainty. Of course, now the seed of doubt was in my mind. Jake and I at war with each other would make this thing between Dagen and I look like a water fight. It would be ugly and bloody, and destroy us both.

"Probably not," Hutton agreed. "The point is, when you're all in with someone, you're all in. And as for us four guys, we're all in with you. Whether you want us to be or not. But I hope you want us to be."

He stood and stepped away from the chair. "Just think about what I said. Okay?"

"I make no guarantees," I said. "But I'll try."

"That's all I ask." He slipped back out the door.

I stood and walked over to the window to stretch my legs. At least a million conflicting thoughts bounced around in my brain. That was nothing unusual, but he'd added a couple of extra ones.

Men.

I saw movement in the corner of my eye and Hutton's reflection appeared in the window a moment later. I turned around.

"Did you come back to give me some more pearls of wisdom?" I asked.

"No." He shook his head, then put his arms around me and lowered his mouth to mine. The kiss he gave me was soft, but firm. He tasted of cola and cinnamon. An interesting combination.

He deepened the kiss and slid his hands up my back and twined his fingers in my hair.

Without thinking, I kissed him back. It wasn't the sweet, naïve kisses Cooper gave. Or the possessive alpha kisses of Jake. Or the gentle, steady kisses of Ben.

This was the kiss of a man who didn't want to hurt me or be hurt, but who desperately needed to connect with another person. Someone who had spent most of his life alone and lonely. Someone who, in spite of his probably better judgement, decided to invest his heart in me.

And somewhere deep in that kiss, I forgot to think and just let myself feel.

I have no idea how we got to the couch or which one of us led the other there, but the next thing I knew, he was lowering me onto it.

I lay back without our lips breaking contact for even a second.

He settled in on top of me and knelt between my knees. He slipped his hands under my shirt and pushed it up off my belly. Still without breaking off the kiss, he pulled me up to a sitting position.

Now he only broke off long enough to pull my shirt over my head and toss it aside. He pushed me back down gently and reclaimed my mouth.

I don't know how, but he managed to unhook my bra and slide it off my arms without even lifting my back off the couch again. Later, I would have to figure out how he did that.

His hands wandered lightly up and down my stomach and over my breasts. He traced circles around my nipples without touching them.

Even that light touch was enough to drive me wild. My body was already aching for more.

Finally, he broke off the kiss and worked his way down from my neck, to my chest, to my breasts. There, he traced circles around my nipples with his tongue. Only after a few minutes did he finally take my nipple into his mouth and start to suck.

"Mmm," he murmured against my sensitive skin. "You're so soft."

I hadn't heard that one before, but it was a compliment I could own. When your breasts are a decent size, you might as well. Right?

He lavished so much attention on my nipples, I started to think the bond transferred to him somehow. I put it down to a lifetime of having to be vigilant. With that, comes being obser-vant. I saw it in Ben and now in Hutton. Jake too. Cooper just rolled with whatever felt good. It sucked that anything good came from the past, but that didn't mean I wouldn't enjoy it.

He kissed and licked his way down my stomach, taking a moment to lightly kiss my abdomen. There was no scar there now, Paxton had gotten rid of it, but Hutton had the general area right. And the sentiment.

He hooked his thumbs into the waistband of my track pants and worked them down off my hips and down my legs. I kicked them off my feet. My panties followed.

He slid off the couch and knelt beside it, his hands on my thighs. His brown eyes on mine, he lowered his mouth to my pussy and started to give it the same attention he'd given my nipples. He licked my folds and sucked my clit until my breath was coming in tiny pants.

His hands slid up and down my thighs and around to grip my

ass. He picked it up off the couch and dove in a little deeper.

I pressed my hands to either side of me. Each breath was accompanied by a moan and a rise in my desire.

"I'm going to come," I said.

I expected him to tell me to wait, but his eyes smiled at me and he went on licking vigourously.

I arched my back as the first wave of delicious orgasm washed over me. Followed closely by a second. Then a third. The entire world stopped for a full two to three minutes. The only thing that was left was his skilled tongue and a million fireworks.

Finally, he let me go and I slumped back down on the couch.

"Holy fucking gods," I breathed. "That was amazing."

He crawled back up the couch and once again knelt between my knees. He kissed my mouth and I tasted myself on his lips.

"I wanted to hear you sing and you didn't disappoint," he whispered.

"Is that all you want?" I reached down between us to unfasten his pants and push them down.

"Since you're asking..." He kicked off his pants and revealed a very big, very hard cock.

"What—"

He shrugged. "I hated myself. I tried to think of the most painful thing I could do to myself, that might bring enjoyment to someone else some day."

In a line down his cock were four, no, five, piercings, parallel to each other like a silver ladder.

"Did that hurt?" I asked. I reached out to lightly touch one.

"Not as much as I hoped," he admitted. "It actually feels pretty good. More sensitive and intense."

"It's hot," I told him. My body throbbed just thinking how he'd feel sliding in and out of me.

"You're hot," he replied. He eyed my mouth speculatively.

My response was involuntary, but immediate. I shuddered

and a hint of panic started to rise.

"Oh shit," he said softly. "I'm sorry. I didn't mean to—" He started to roll off me.

I put a hand on his arm to stop him. "You didn't do anything. I want you. Only..." I swallowed. "In my pussy, not in my mouth. Okay?"

He nodded his understanding, but his brown eyes showed a flash of anger. He would tear Dagen in two with his bare hands if he was here right now.

"Okay," he said gently. "Whatever you need. If you want me to stop, just say the word and I will."

I flashed a brief smile, then pulled him back down on top of me and hooked my legs around him. "If you do anything I don't like, you will hear about it." That went for in and out of the bedroom.

He chuckled. "I have no doubt about that, babe." He wriggled his hips a little to get himself into position, then carefully, with his eyes on mine to engage my reaction, he pressed his thick, laddered length into me.

The moment my eyes widened, he stopped to let me adjust to him. He was definitely the biggest guy I ever fucked, even without the piercings. My muscles took a few moments to stretch and relax.

When I finally did, he slid in a little further.

"Gods, you feel so tight," he said breathlessly.

"You feel so big," I replied. I had never felt quite this full before. It was pretty wonderful.

"I don't want to brag." He grinned. "Are you okay?"

There was that question again. I didn't mind it so much in this context. I was lying naked on a couch with a hot guy on top of me, his cock deep inside my body. I was more than okay.

"I'm wonderful," I said.

"Yes you are." He kissed my mouth, then slowly started to

thrust, his eyes half closed in obvious appreciation. "Absolutely perfect." Gradually his strokes became faster, but never rushed. Either he was the kind of guy who likes to take his time, or he wanted to be sure not to hurt me.

Maybe both.

His piercings felt like ridges, which massaged my slick core with every movement. I never felt anything like it before. It was pretty fucking amazing.

I rocked my hips in time with his and clenched my muscles around him.

His breathing became ragged.

Careful not to dislodge him, I rolled us both over so I was straddling his hips.

He put his hands on my waist and didn't even break his rhythm.

I pressed my palms to his muscular chest, half closed my eyes and rode him with his cock so deep it almost hurt. His ladder rubbed my g spot inside, and at the same time, my clit rubbed against him on the outside. It was like the world evaporated, leaving behind one one sense; that of touch.

Feeling.

Heightened, intense, deep desire.

"Mmm, yeah." His breathing was deeper and faster. Every so often it would hitch. He was close to coming himself.

I watched his face. I wanted to see him and feel him come. I loved knowing I could do that to a guy.

Especially like this. I was in complete control. He surrendered everything willingly, with no reservation.

I slowed down a little to draw out his pleasure.

One of his eyebrows rose in response, but he didn't say anything. I wasn't sure he was capable of words right now. Neither was I.

I tried to stop myself, but I came again.

If the first three were fireworks, then the fourth was New Year's Eve, with a dose of Australia Day thrown in for good measure. I was absolutely lost in the rush of heat and blood and pleasure.

Through the pounding in my ears, I heard his groans and grunts and felt him grind up into me as he came.

When he managed a word, it was just a long, low, "Baaaaabe."

Maybe I didn't mind him calling me that after all.

Finally, I sagged down onto him, panting and sweaty.

"Wow," he said breathlessly. "You're even more amazing than I imagined. And what I imagined was pretty fucking incredible."

"Thank goodness for that," I said softly. "I would hate for you to hype me up to yourself only to find out I'm a bad fuck." Yeah, that would suck. I had some pride left.

He chuckled. "That is something you could never be. You're far too wonderful."

"You're going to make me blush," I said to his chest. I could lie there all day. Maybe sleep there all night. Unfortunately, I couldn't. We had plans tonight. An event I couldn't miss, as much as I wanted to.

"We should probably get up and have a shower," I said reluctantly.

"Together?" he asked.

Okay, maybe I could get up after all.

At some point though, I was going to have to figure a few things out. A lot of things.

For one thing, Hutton was right about Dagen wanting me to push the guys away and isolate myself.

On the other hand, I made that choice for a reason. The fact I was lying here right now with Hutton strongly suggested I wasn't very good at sticking to the choices I made. Or maybe subconsciously I knew they were shitty choices.

Yeah, I really had some thinking to do.

CHAPTER
EIGHTEEN

All five of us were absolutely smoking hot that night. The guys wore dark suits and crisp white shirts. Cooper wore a brightly coloured tie, while the other three had more subdued colours. They even had shiny shoes on.

I wore a long, white gown that shimmered when I moved. It was higher in the front than what I usually wore, but dipped down low at the back. Of course, it had a long split down the side, and the fabric clung to my curves like an opaque condom. Without all the rubber and need for lube.

I straightened my hair and left it out to fall down my back. As always, a pair of designer heels finished the outfit.

"Stay close to Ivory," Jake said. "This might be a charity concert, but there will be a few dubious people here."

"Like us?" Hutton asked.

Jake gave him a dark look, but nodded. "Yes, like us. Just not as hot."

"We look pretty good, don't we?" Cooper grinned.

I glanced at Ben, who hadn't said a word all night. It was normal for him to stay quiet while he was on the job, unless he needed to say something, but I missed the sound of his deep voice.

He gave the slightest nod of agreement, then went back to watching the crowds.

It was warm out tonight. The Harbour looked beautiful. The Opera House, the location for the night's concert, was lit up and shining. A quartet on stage played something by Vivaldi. A shit load of rich people had turned up to raise money for orphaned children. It was a practically perfect evening.

For a while.

That was before I saw Alistair Dagen. He was surrounded, as usual, by a contingent of goons.

Not just any goons, I quickly realised. The three who held me down, and another two who held my arms while their companions chased Ben and Hutton. There was no chance their inclusion at this event this evening was coincidental. It was just another mind fuck.

"You look beautiful tonight, Elodie," Asshole said smoothly. "Although, I'm surprised you came. I thought you would have some rubble to sift through."

"Fuck off, Alistair," I replied. I wasn't even going to bother with niceties. If it wasn't for the fact we were surrounded by a few hundred people, I would shift and rip his head off. The five of us could take on the six of them.

He started to clap slowly. "Well done. Such an intelligent, eloquent response."

I rolled my eyes at him. "I can't be bothered wasting brain cells on a worthless slug like you."

"That's better." He nodded. "Although, your insults could use a bit of work. Maybe I could give you some pointers, bitch."

I bared my teeth at him.

Before I could even speak, he said, "I know, don't call you bitch. But it fits so perfectly. Especially if I add the words 'in heat,' to it. Still fucking your bodyguard? Or just your lapdog? Oh wait, then there's your little virgin boytoy. And Hutton, I'm so glad to see you still alive. That means I get the fun of killing you again."

"Fuck off, Dagen," Hutton said.

"Yeah, what he said." Cooper jerked a thumb toward Hutton. "If anyone is killing anyone else around here, it's me killing you."

Dagen chuckled. "Elodie, you should probably put a leash on that puppy. Or better yet, a *collar*."

Jake yawned loudly. "Are you done? None of us are impressed with your bullshit." To Cooper he said, "You'll have to get in line to kill this asshole. I'm at the front of it."

He turned back to Dagen. "Were you the bully at school too? What kind of man kidnaps women? Oh, right, the kind with a really, really, *really* small cock."

Dagen gave him a nasty smile. "It's not that small. Just ask your bitch there." He turned that expression on me. "That reminds me, when I was going through a bunch of security footage, I found a little something. I thought you'd like a copy." He held up his phone and tapped the screen.

A moment later mine pinged. Every single part of me said to ignore it. Everything except my stupid curiosity. The part of me that assumed he had footage of Ben and I fucking and thought that would embarrass me in some way. Or upset Jake or the other guys.

I pulled my phone out of my purse and clicked on the screen.

The moment I did it I regretted it. The vision was a little grainy but the camera had captured the moment the three goons pushed me to my knees. My eyes were wide with horror. Dagen stepped over to me. Undid his pants. From this angle, no one could tell it was him, but everything else was clear enough.

I closed the screen before I could see any more. My hand was trembling. The air became thicker. No, that was just panic rising, making it harder to breathe. My head felt light.

"You're welcome," Asshole said smoothly. "Then I figured—why not share?" He pressed his screen again.

Jake's phone pinged

Then Cooper's.

Hutton's.

Ben's.

Then all around me, phones were pinging. The sound was like something out of a horror movie.

The guys didn't move, but all around me people looked at their screens, then at me. Some looked disgusted, but one or two looked amused like they thought I got what I deserved.

"Excuse me," I muttered. I turned to shove my way through the crowds, my head down as if that would stop people from recognising me.

I heard the guys calling out after me, but I also heard Alistair Dagen's laughter. That rang in my ears louder than anything.

I hurried towards the car and fished my keys out of my purse.

Barely able to breathe, I unlocked it and slipped inside. I pulled off my heels and threw them over into the passenger side footwell.

"Going somewhere?" Hutton slipped into the passenger seat.

"Away from here." My hand was trembling so hard I could hardly get the key into the ignition. Jake might have a point about cars that start with the press of a button.

"Should you leave your bodyguards behind?" He clicked his seatbelt into place.

"You're here," I pointed out. I managed to get the key in and started the car. I backed out of the parking space faster than I probably should have.

I saw the flash of Hutton's phone screen.

"Just letting them know I'm with you and you're okay," he said. "Whatever he sent, I deleted it without looking. The other guys would have too. And everyone else, who gives a shit what they think?"

"I don't." I wound through the busy carpark and out onto the main road. "I just don't like being humiliated like that. It was bad enough it happened without everyone knowing about it."

No one who actually watched could see his face. I couldn't even point the finger at him. Even the faces of his men weren't clear. Just mine.

Rain started to sprinkle, covering the windscreen in glittering drops. I turned on the windscreen wipers.

With any luck, it would pour and Asshole would get drenched.

I wished he *had* shared footage of Ben and I together. That would have been humiliating for us both, but at least it wasn't evidence I wasn't invincible. Everyone would look at me differently now. They knew I had weaknesses. They would try to exploit them.

Or they would look at me with pity in their eyes.

Panic started to rise again, but this time I let it. I couldn't have held it back if I tried. It swamped me like a flood of cold, trembling fear.

I couldn't let him break me. I wouldn't. But he got to me with this stunt.

I wasn't sure who I hated more right now, him or myself.

"Maybe you should slow down a bit," Hutton said.

"Maybe you shouldn't have gotten into the car with me." Fuck, even my voice was shaking. I felt like a trembling mess coming apart at the seams.

I would make Alistair Dagen pay for this if it was the last thing I ever did. I would make him hurt, make him suffer and then I would kill him. Jake wasn't first in line for that honour. I was.

"What the fuck?" Hutton shouted a fraction of a second before I saw a huge shape step out on the road.

Two enormous eyes turned towards us and blinked.

"Shit." I rammed my foot down onto the break, but we were going too fast and the road was too wet.

The car went into a skid. It hit the side of the road, flipped and started to roll over and over and over.

It finally came to a stop on its roof as the rain started to pour down in torrents.

ELODIE

RUTHLESS CLAWS BOOK 3

ONE

"F*uck!*"

I pressed my foot down on the brake as hard as I dared. Rain fell in sheets, making the road slick. The SUV skidded for a metre or two before its tyres regained their grip on the road.

I turned the windscreen wipers up to a faster setting and focused on the lights of the car in front of me.

The lights of Ivory's much smaller Shelby Cobra. The woman liked her old, expensive toys. That might be why she liked me.

The rain reflected all the city lights, made them longer and made it harder to see.

But I saw when something huge stepped out onto the road.

I saw when she slammed on her brakes.

Her car went into a skid and hit the edge of the road.

Time stopped.

In slow motion, the small white car flipped and rolled several times. I felt every roll right into the deep of my bones. I couldn't watch. Couldn't look away.

Fuck. Elodie! Holy gods.

"Shit!" Ben's body tensed, poised like he was ready to fly right out of the passenger seat while we were still moving.

Shaking like a wet dog, I managed to steer the car to the side of the road and stopped.

I almost got tangled in the seatbelt, but managed to shove it out of the way and throw the door open.

My heart in my mouth, I bolted to the driver's side of her wrecked car. The rain fell so hard I was drenched in seconds. I barely noticed except to wipe water off my face as I crouched down beside the shattered window.

"Oh gods, Elodie." She was upside down, held in place by her seatbelt. Her face was whiter than her hair, except for the blood from a gash on her forehead. That dripped slowly onto the floor of the car. Or roof. Whatever. That didn't matter right now.

"We have to get her out of there," I said. Moving her might be dangerous, but we couldn't leave her to hang like this. We couldn't—

I sucked in a breath through wet lips. What I couldn't do right now was panic. She needed me to be calm right now. Later, when she was okay, I would freak out. Not now.

Gods, please let her be okay.

Ben crouched beside me. He nodded. As always, he was the absolute embodiment of calm. He would be just as torn up on the inside as I was, but he gave away no hint of it. I drew on that, used it to settle my pounding heart.

A groan sounded from the other side of the car.

Over my shoulder, I said to Cooper, "Go and see how Hutton is." Judging by the groan, he was still alive. I wasn't even sure I could say the same about Ivory.

I tried the door, but it wouldn't open. "We're going to have to do this through the window."

I reached inside, not giving a shit that shards of glass sliced my arms. "I'm going to hold her. When I say so, unfasten her seatbelt."

"Yep," Ben said. He wasn't a big talker at the best of times and this was certainly not the best of anything. He put his hands in place and waited. He would hold that exact position for hours and not complain. He gave new meaning to the word stoic. Good man.

I leaned in as far as I could. There was almost no room to manoeuvre in here. All I could really do was support her head and shoulders, and as much of her body as best I could.

"Okay. One, two, release." The moment Ben clicked the seatbelt free, all of her weight dropped. It felt like hardly anything at all. I kept one hand under her head to support it, while we both gripped her arms and pulled her through the window.

I sat down on the wet road and lay her across me, her neck and head on my bicep, the rest of her stretched out over my legs.

Ben shrugged out of his jacket and lay it over the top of her ruined dress.

She didn't move. She was absolutely, completely still. I couldn't even see her breathing.

Don't freak out yet, I told myself. I put my fingers to her neck to try to find a pulse.

"Come on, El," I said softly. "You have to be alive. He doesn't get to win like this." Rain mingled with tears, which slid down my cheeks and onto her face. Anyone who saw it would assume it was all rain.

Until my breath came in a ragged sob.

Ben crouched beside us and ran a hand over his head. He was drenched through, too. His white shirt clung to his upper body. He must have been as cold as I was. Truthfully, I barely felt it.

Not cold from the weather anyway. What I felt was ice cold grief.

He muttered something that sounded like, "It's my fault."

I had no idea how he figured that, but that didn't matter right now.

"Come on," I said softly. "Please don't be dead."

I closed my eyes and hung my head.

"Um, Jake?" Cooper said tentatively.

"What?" I snapped, but it was half hearted. Nothing fucking mattered anymore. Not without her.

I opened my eyes and looked down at her beautiful face.

Her eyes were open, staring at my face. She blinked.

"Oh, thank the gods." I brushed wet hair off her forehead.

"Jake," she said, her voice barely above a whisper. "It hurts—"

"Shhh," I urged. I looked up to the others.

Hutton stood beside Cooper. He appeared to be injured but more or less alive.

I would worry about him later. "We need a witch. She needs to be healed before we can move her more than we already have."

Ben scowled. "I know one who lives near here. I'll get her."

"But you hate witches," Cooper pointed out. He'd grown up since I met him. Was that only a few weeks ago? That's what this life will do to you. Poor fucking kid.

Ben looked down at Ivory, his face full of emotion. "I love her more than I hate them."

I nodded. "Take the SUV. Hutton, go with him. She can heal you on the way back. Cooper, keep an eye out for... anything."

"Got it," Cooper said. In spite of his light tone, I knew he would prefer to sit beside Ivory and hold her hand until the witch arrived. I understood, but right now we needed his vigilance. There would be time for hand holding later.

Ben trotted to the SUV and barely gave Hutton time to slip into the passenger side before he roared away.

I turned my gaze back to Ivory. She didn't look like Ivory right now, head of Ivory Claw, the biggest criminal organisation in the state. She looked like the young woman I met nine years ago.

Elodie Keelan was never as naïve as she looked. Even at eighteen, she was an old soul. She went through hells and came out the other side, but not unscathed. She was a force of nature, like a deadly ice storm, in the body of a goddess. The moment I lay eyes on her, I knew our lives would be intertwined forever, one way or another.

I brushed the rain off her face. "Sorry I didn't think to bring an umbrella."

"Here." Cooper took off his jacket and handed it to me to hold over her face. It wouldn't keep the rain off much, but it was a start. "How is she?"

"She's... She's still with us," I said softly. I smiled at her. "Right? You have to stick around for a long time yet."

She moaned with what may or may not have been agreement. "Jake."

I leaned in. If this was the part where she told me she wanted to sleep, I might not be able to keep myself from freaking out. I would have to. I had to keep my shit together for her. And, to be honest, the way Cooper kept on glancing at her he was ready to lose it too.

"You should be resting," I said.

"I'm sorry," she said softly. Her eyes fluttered shut and for a moment I thought we'd lost her. She opened them again. "I shouldn't have taken off."

I smoothed more hair off her face. "Yeah, probably not. But Asshole also shouldn't have done what he did." I meant both the video and forcing his dick into her mouth. I didn't know if it went any further than that. This was certainly not the time to ask.

"Can you kill him for me?" she asked.

I chuckled. "If you want me to. But I think you would prefer to do that yourself."

She shifted position a little bit and winced in pain. I had no way of knowing what was broken inside.

"I'll help Jake kill him," Cooper said. In spite of the look I gave him, he crouched beside us and lightly kissed her forehead.

She smiled weakly. "Thanks." Her voice sounded more and more faint. "You guys are the best."

"Yeah, we are." Cooper grinned. "But you're the bestest."

"What he said," I agreed. Should I tell her to stop talking? It might be the thing that was keeping her with us. It was certainly the thing that was telling me she was still alive. She probably wouldn't listen to me if I told her to shut up anyway. She was the most stubborn, driven person I ever met. Neither of us would be where we were today if she wasn't.

"Is my car fucked?" she asked.

I looked up at it. "Yeah. I'd say so." From the look of it, the driver's side took the brunt of the crash. It must have impacted there, hard, each time it rolled over. The passenger side was slightly better off. That explained why Hutton was able to walk away.

Figures.

Ivory cared about him. She would want me to give him a break. I had given him a hard time. Still, I would have preferred she be the one to walk away.

If the witch got here soon, she still might.

I glanced over my shoulder as a car screeched to a stop beside us.

For a heart-stopping moment, I realised it could just as easily be Dagen and his goons. Cooper and I could put up a fight, but Ivory wouldn't stand a chance.

The doors opened and a ragged but otherwise healthy Hutton got out, followed by Ben and a woman who looked scared half to death. Presumably Ben hadn't given her a choice in helping us. She was a witch, she could take care of herself.

Ben all but shoved her over to Ivory and snapped, "Heal her."

"Please," Cooper said.

Ben gave him a sharp look, but didn't say anything more.

"We would appreciate it," I said. "I think she's pretty badly injured." It didn't hurt to be polite, especially since a witch could kill as easily as they heal.

She flashed me a brief smile, scowled at Ben, and knelt in the wet road and put a hand on Ivory's forehead.

Ivory twitched at the tingle of magic which I knew passed through her.

"Keep her still," the witch said.

I put a hand lightly on Ivory's chest and held her there while she twitched this way and that in obvious discomfort.

"She has a lot of broken bones," the witch said. "It's her head I'm most worried about. I'm going to heal that first. The bones probably hurt like hells, but her skull is pressing down on her brain. If I leave that, she'll die."

"Do whatever you have to do," I said. "She's tough, she'll handle it." Right now though, she didn't look very tough. She looked like a broken china doll. A fragile shard of ice.

The other three guys crouched around us, as though just by being there could help her to pull through. Judging by the way her eyes swivelled from one to the other, that was exactly what their presence would do.

Or they would all be there at the end...

I pushed that thought away. This couldn't be the end. I wouldn't let it be.

The witch bent and got to work.

Ivory started to thrash. It took all four of us to hold her still, Ben on her legs, Hutton and Cooper with an arm each and me with a hand on her chest.

She screamed out in agony. The sound tore through my ears and made them throb. It must have hurt the shit out of her throat. I would hear the sound in my dreams, but at least she was alive.

"Just a bit longer," the witch said. "I just have to relieve the pressure here... and here..."

The moment she said the last word, Ivory fell still.

The whole world went silent except for the rain falling on the road, and the engine from the few cars that whooshed by without slowing.

"Is she—" Cooper said tentatively.

"She'll live," the witch said. "I cannot guarantee there isn't permanent damage, but I got here quickly so, she should be fine."

Was she actually giving herself credit for getting here so fast? Whatever. It didn't matter how she got here, as long as she did.

"Her bones will be an easier matter." She scooted down to around Ivory's stomach and put a hand on her arm. Whatever she did only made Ivory twitch gently, and moan, and it was over in a matter of a couple of minutes.

The witch sat back and nodded in satisfaction. "She will need to rest, but her bones are knitted nicely." She didn't even seem to notice the rain that dripped off her nose.

I realised then she wasn't much older than Ivory. She must have been scared out of her wits being dragged out into the dark in the middle of the night. Especially by a guy who wore the role of bodyguard like a second skin. If you didn't know he was a gentle giant, you might be intimidated by him. The witch obviously was. I would have to ask him later how they knew each other.

"We owe you one," I said. I meant it. Whatever she wanted, I would try to find a way to give it to her. She deserved it after this.

Even Ben gave her a grudging nod of thanks.

Cooper, being Cooper, gave her a hug. She gave him an uncomfortable hug back.

Hutton offered her a smile. "Thanks for healing me too. I was gonna have a fucker of a headache otherwise."

Any other time, I would have replied to that with a sarcastic comment about him *being* a fucker, but I didn't have the energy or the heart to bother right now.

"We need to get her out of here," I said. "We'll drop you home first," I told the witch. After that, I had a plan. One that would give Ivory all the time she needed to rest, and give us all a chance to regroup. The gloves were well and truly off now. Whatever it took, we would make Dagen suffer for what he did to her. To all of us, but especially to Ivory.

When we were done, the asshole would wish he had never been born.

TWO

IVORY

I woke with a banging headache. Where the fuck was I? My mind was fuzzy. Thinking hurt.

Gradually, I became aware of the sound of an engine and a thrum underneath me. I was covered in warm blankets, but under those I was naked.

Dagen's jet?

My eyes popped open and I started to sit up, cold terror running through my veins.

"Ivory! It's okay." Firm hands held me from sitting all the way up.

It took a good few moments to realise they were Cooper's hands. His face was only a few centimetres from mine. He lay beside me, but on top of the covers.

I glanced around and exhaled in relief before I lay back down and tried to calm my racing heart.

"It's *my* jet." The walls were off-white and smooth. Dark red curtains were drawn over the small windows. A timber door which led out to the rest of the plane, was ajar. Another door, this one leading to the bathroom, was closed.

He grinned. "Yeah. It's something else. I've never been on a plane that had a king-size bed before."

"Yes, well..." I had no response for that. "Where are we going?" And who the fuck thought it was a good idea to put me on a plane without asking me first?

He propped himself up on his elbow. "I have no idea. Jake just told us to grab a few things and get on board or get left behind."

Of course it was Jake. Who else would have done this? I would have a few words with him when I got the chance.

Cooper's expression turned serious. "You gave us all a scare back there. When we saw the car roll—"

"Yeah, I remember," I said quickly. My heart raced and sweat sprang up on my palms. I had a vague recollection of rain and a lot of pain.

And that fucking video.

Dagen and that fucking footage he texted to everyone. When it came to being a motherfucking asshole, he got top points. He even got bonus points for that particular move. He was trying to get to me and it worked. I shouldn't have let it. I was supposed to be tougher than that.

"Jake and Ben pulled you out, but we all thought you were going to die. I mean, *they* did. I knew you would be okay." He wore emotion on his face that was so raw it made my heart hurt almost as much as my head. He was also obviously lying through his teeth. He had no idea whether or not I would be okay.

I rolled onto my side so I could look at him better. He wore a grey T-shirt that fitted his muscular body like a second skin and black track pants. "And then someone carried me onto the plane."

"Ben carried you," he said. "I don't think he trusted you with anyone else. But then Jake wanted to talk to him so I stayed back here to watch over you. Hutton is fine. He was in the car with you."

"Right." I forgot that detail. Thank the gods he was okay. I wouldn't have forgiven myself if I killed him. Unless he pissed me off and I did it on purpose. That was a whole other story.

Cooper looked like he had something to ask, but was too uncertain.

"What is it?" I asked.

"Before the crash, you seemed kinda pissed off at us. I don't mean right before, but the couple of days before that." He looked tentative, anxious.

"You want to know why I was so cold to all of you?" Was that even the right way to put it? I was trying to keep the guys at arm's length, but I still ended up fucking Jake and Hutton. Running hot and cold might be a better way to put it.

"Ben said you needed some space, but he was pretty cut up when you broke the bond with him. He loves you, you know. We all do. I tried not to be too pushy, but it's difficult. I mean, you're you."

He nodded as though that explained absolutely everything. That was Cooper. He was hot, ridiculously hot, smart and uncomplicated. He wore his heart on his sleeve and I knew he loved me with every bit of it.

Well, except for the bit reserved for his love of killing people. That was a whole other high for him.

I closed my eyes. Partly to ease the throbbing in my head and partly to compose my thoughts.

"Hutton told me Alistair Dagen thrives on two things," I said slowly. "Power and mind fucks. He wants to own every building, every business that belongs to Ivory Claw because of the power that would bring. And along the way he's made a game of screwing with my head. I suspect he enjoys that more than anything."

I opened my eyes and looked right into Cooper's hazel ones. "He wanted to divide us. For me to be separated from the rest of you. And it worked. I was so scared of being distracted and vulnerable."

After a moment, I admitted, "I still am. But I can't do this by myself. I don't want to. I care about all of you." Okay, it went beyond caring.

"We're stronger together, if Jake and Hutton can stop fighting with each other." I grimaced.

"Yeah." Cooper grinned. "Sometimes I wonder if they're actually long lost brothers. I kinda feel like they're my brothers. Ben too. Bossy as fuck brothers, but still brothers."

It was good to know that, for the most part, everyone was okay with this arrangement. With a bit of luck, or a whole lot of ass kicking, maybe Jake and Hutton would kiss and make up.

Okay, now I was imagining them *literally* doing that. Oh my, that was a hot mental image. One that reminded me that I was definitely not dead.

"Did you watch the video?" I forced myself to look Cooper in the face. When his expression filled with regret, I closed my eyes and turned my face away.

"Only the first little bit," he said quietly. "When I realised what it was, I turned it off and deleted it. He's a sick fuck and I'm sorry he did that to you. The four of us are going to personally make sure nothing like that ever happens again. And I'm going to rip his face off and eat it."

I nodded once. As much as I hated the thought of them seeing the footage, I couldn't hide from it.

Honestly, I shouldn't have to. Sure, the list of terrible things I did in my life was long. I've killed a lot of people and had even more killed for me. None of them were innocent and none were undeserving, but I still did it and would keep doing it.

In this case though, I was the innocent victim.

It was probably the first time since I was eight that I could actually claim innocence of any kind. But it was what it was. No one deserved to be violated the way I was.

I was a criminal, but I had some moral standards I lived up to. I refused to let underaged sex workers work in my brothel, or dance in my strip club. I refused to traffic in other people and if any of my employees violated another person, their dead body would be pulled out of the harbour the day after I found out about it. If the victim was a child, then their very badly, painfully mutilated body would be fished out of the harbour.

I was definitely not above torturing people who deserved it. Or, to be specific, letting Jake and Ben do it. Cooper too now, I guessed. They got off on that sort of thing more than I did, so I left them to it.

"So you know that..." Shit, how did I even word this? I swallowed hard.

"Some things are off limits?" he asked gently.

"At least until I'm ready," I agreed. I wanted to suck him off. It was something I got a lot of pleasure doing.

It used to be. Now, the idea gave me deeply conflicted feelings. Somewhere between wanting to do it and not even wanting to think about it ever again.

Cooper looked genuinely confused. "You know none of us would try to make you do anything you don't want, right? I mean, even if we wanted to, we wouldn't dare. You're beautiful, sexy, smart, but you're also the scariest person I know. If I did anything right now that you didn't like, you would call one of the other guys and I would get a one-way ticket to the ground."

"I would never throw someone I care about out of a plane," I said firmly. He was right about the rest of it though. If I didn't care about him and if he tried to hurt me, he would have an uncomfortable landing.

"I guess you wouldn't," he conceded. "If one of us did

anything bad to you, the other three would make him suffer for much longer."

I grinned. "That's more like it."

The smile he gave me was soft and warm. He held back none of his feelings for me. Every single drop of them were written all over his face.

I didn't deserve him, not at all. He was sweet in a way I never was. He was hot enough to nail any girl he wanted, and yet for some reason he wanted me. There was still a boyish naïveté about him that I hoped he wouldn't lose. In time, he would probably end up as bitter and twisted as the rest of us.

I knew when I met him I should have given him the money for the auction, then sent him away. Giving his virginity to me was his choice, but it was also mine. I could have told him no, let him find a nice girl and live his life.

On the other hand, if his fascination for murder spilled into an otherwise ordinary life, things wouldn't end well for him. He was better off with me, killing people who were deserving.

Cooper glanced at the door that led into the rest of the plane. "You should be resting."

"Maybe I've rested enough," I said. "How long was I out?"

"A few hours at least," he said. He glanced at his watch and shrugged one shoulder. "But you almost died, so you probably need more than that."

I rolled over onto my stomach and pushed myself up onto my elbows so he could get a full view of my bare breasts. "Shouldn't I be the one to decide that?"

His eyes widened slightly. "Um. I mean, of course. But..."

"But you think one of the other guys is going to walk in and get pissed off and throw you off the plane?" I raised my eyebrows at him.

"A little bit," he admitted.

"Are you forgetting who the boss is around here?" I asked.

"Nope," he said quickly. "Are you going to pull that out every time we have an argument? Because that kind of seems like cheating to me."

I laughed softly. "I never said I play fair." I was horribly competitive. I was the first to admit that. If I had an unfair advantage, I would use it. He might have a point, though. If this was going to be a thing between me and him and me and the other guys, then maybe I needed to think of them as equals.

Or I could just keep doing what I was doing and keep them on their toes.

I leaned forward to kiss him lightly on the mouth.

"Are you sure this is a good idea?" he asked. "You almost died a few hours ago and, uh—"

He made a funny sound in the back of his throat when I threw off the covers and straddled his thighs. "Or I could just roll with it."

"Good idea." I put my mouth down onto his and kissed him, not like a woman who almost died a few hours ago, but like one who decided it was time to live my best life a whole lot better than I was doing. That included letting the guys in. Starting right now.

He wrapped his arms around me and pressed his hands lightly to my lower back. His tongue explored my mouth, while his hands ran up and down my sides.

"I almost forgot, I have something for you," he said suddenly. "It's in my pants."

I looked down at him. "Yes I can feel it." His erection was pressing into my belly.

He chuckled. "Something other than that." He rolled us both sideways, just enough to get his hand into his pocket. He pulled out a silver chain. On the end was a pendant in the shape of a wolf's head. The black diamond from the box in his uncle's garage shone in the place of the wolf's eye.

"It's beautiful," I said softly.

He undid the clasp and hung it around my neck. "You're beautiful."

I touched the pendant lightly with my fingertips. "Thank you." I tried not to think about where the diamond came from. What mattered now was that it was something lovely from a guy I loved.

There, I admitted it to myself. That was a big step. The biggest I would take for at least the rest of the day.

I lowered my mouth back to his and kissed him until I was breathless.

That was around about when one of the other guys breezed in through the door.

"Well, that's a nice view," Hutton drawled. He ran a fingertip around the curve of my ass.

I shivered and felt myself melt even further. We had barely done anything and I was ready to turn into a puddle. I was no longer in a position to judge anyone for being insatiable. Somewhere along this crazy journey, the same thing happened to me. And I wasn't even mad about it.

"Care to share?" Hutton asked Cooper.

"I'm happy to," Cooper said. "As long as Ivory is."

"I'm good with that," I said and went back to kissing Cooper.

"Good." Hutton sat on the end of the bed and went back to tracing circles around my bare skin. They got smaller and smaller until he slid his hand between my legs and over my rear hole. He lingered there for a moment before he moved down to rub his fingers over my clit and pussy.

I drew up my knees to open myself out to him further.

He responded to that by slipping a couple of fingers deep into me and massaging the inside of my body.

I quivered with desire. I managed to slide Cooper's track pants down his hips to free his erection.

I gripped his hot length and worked him up and down in my hand with a corkscrew motion. I looked up at his face.

His eyes were closed with ecstasy. His cock was almost close enough for me to put my mouth around it, but I didn't. And he didn't ask me to or look as though he planned to.

I suspected he was happy to be here with me and anything else was a bonus.

Hutton worked me a little harder, then pulled his fingers out and slid them down and across my clit.

His touch and the bead of precum on Cooper's tip, drove me a little wilder. I was already as wet as hells.

I didn't realise Hutton pushed his pants down until he gripped my hips. He pulled me up until I was on my hands and knees, Cooper's thighs between them. Hutton straddled Cooper's calves and teased my pussy with his cock.

Cooper opened his eyes and his eyebrows shot up. I didn't think it was possible, but his cock got harder in my hand.

"Whoa, this is hot."

I murmured my agreement as Hutton slowly pressed his thick, pierced length into my body. The friction was immediate. Every sensation heightened a thousandfold by his ladder and this angle.

"Hot is the word," Hutton agreed. He stayed still for a while, his fingers loosely pressed against the skin of my hips.

Finally, he started to move, thrusting with even strokes that penetrated deep inside me. His piercings rubbed up and down every centimetre like ribbed fingers. Somehow firm and gentle all at once.

Cooper reached up and ran his hands around and over my breasts. He gripped my nipples lightly between his thumbs and forefingers and rolled them, then pinched them firmer. His pierced eyebrow dipped in concentration.

I kept my hand curled around his cock, pumping him slowly.

When I reached his tip, I ran my thumb over the top. My hand gradually became slick with his juices.

Hutton slid out of me and guided me back down until my hips were over Cooper's cock. He pressed me down slowly, so I impaled myself on the younger wolf's eager cock.

"Gods, yes," Cooper breathed.

Hutton lay down beside us, and to my surprise he cupped Cooper's cheek and turned his face toward him.

"Hey, I dunno if you're into it..."

Holy shit, was he suggesting what I thought he was?

Apparently he was, because when Cooper moved his face toward him and their mouths met, the whole jet almost burst into flame.

Just watching them kiss made me want to come then and there. The sound alone was... I can't even put it into words.

"Funny, I could have sworn I told them to let you rest." Jake's voice made me jump slightly, but Cooper and Hutton didn't even flinch, much less break away from each other.

I twisted around and shrugged, totally unashamed. "I'm fine."

He leaned against the door frame and crossed his arms over his chest. "Yes, you are."

I smiled sweetly. "There's room for one more." Or two, if Ben wanted to join in.

He cocked his head. "Is there? I might be a hypocrite if I stopped you from resting."

"Your cock says you'll get over it," I pointed out. The front of his pants was so tented he might break a seam.

He shook his head but took my hand when I offered it and knelt down beside me. He caught my lips with his and for a while, nothing else existed in the world but us and our mouths.

And Cooper's cock inside me.

I worked Jake's jeans open and pushed them down his hips.

In the corner of my eye, I saw Hutton and Cooper working on

each other's clothes. Shirts and track pants went flying until they were both naked.

"When in Rome," Jake said against my mouth. He broke off the kiss long enough to pull off his shirt and work his jeans the rest of the way off.

And just like that, I was surrounded by a whole planeload of smoking hot muscle and hard cocks. It's a hard fucking life, but someone has to live it. It might as well be me.

Jake brought his lips back to mine, while I gripped his cock and worked him the way I had Cooper. At the same time, I rocked my hips, riding the younger wolf while he and Hutton explored each other's mouths with their tongues.

Holy gods.

Large hands lightly rested on my shoulders. Jake's eyes flicked over behind me, but his lack of alarm told me Ben had slipped in to join us.

I broke off from Jake and twisted around far enough to press my mouth to Ben's. I would need to have a talk with him too. Breaking the bond was hard on us both, but I wanted things to be okay between us.

I kissed Ben for a minute or two, then turned back to kiss Jake again. Hutton rose to his knees and waited until we came up for air to turn my face and claim my mouth with his. He tasted like coffee and Cooper.

Cooper put his hands on my arms and pulled me down so he could kiss me as well.

I was used to being the centre of attention, but never like this. This was next level awesome and then some. I was more than the alpha she wolf, I was a goddess, and these guys were all mine.

While I leaned over Cooper, tasting his mouth and tongue, Jake opened a drawer beside the bed and pulled out a tube of lube. Silicon based, of course.

He and Ben murmured to each other and someone pressed a

cool, lubed finger to my rear hole. He slipped it in and out, spreading a generous amount of lube.

When one of them pressed his cock into my ass, I had no idea which of them was. I could have turned and looked, but the idea of not knowing was strangely hot.

He waited for my muscles to relax before he pushed in deeper.

Cooper's eyes widened. "Holy shit, that feels so good."

I gave a soft moan in agreement. Two guys deep inside me was quickly becoming one of my favourite things.

The guy behind me thrust slowly and I heard Ben's groan of pleasure. So it was his cock in my ass.

That was confirmed when Jake lay down and propped himself on his elbow so his head was the same height as mine.

Hutton did the same on the other side.

I kissed Jake, long and deep and slow, then turned my head to kiss Hutton. At the same time Cooper and Ben thrust in rhythm with each other.

I felt like the centre of the universe right now, or something. Whatever it was, it felt glorious.

Jake turned my face back to him and while our tongues clashed, he slipped his hand between Cooper and I to caress my nipple.

Hutton did the same with my other breast. I heard the sound of him and Cooper kissing again. I vaguely wondered how far they would go with each other, but I knew this was a first for Cooper, so maybe not far.

Although, he was very adventurous his first time with me, so maybe...

I closed my eyes and savoured the feeling of Jake thrusting his tongue into my mouth, while the two other guys thrust into my warm body. I never wanted this to end but when I came, moaning against Jake's lips, it drew an orgasm out of Cooper. Ben followed half a minute later. Their fast, heated strokes drove me to a second orgasm.

I came down slowly and Ben pulled out of me. He lay down on the bed beside Jake, and wiped sweat off his brow.

I slipped myself off Cooper and he and Hutton made space for me between them.

"Let me clean that up," Hutton said.

I was confused for a moment, until he moved down the bed and gently parted my knees. He bent down between my legs and slowly licked Cooper's cum away as it leaked from my pussy.

Holy gods.

He had me on the verge of a third orgasm when he moved his mouth off me and knelt between my legs. He put his cock into position and slipped into me.

At the same time, Jake knelt beside me and took his cock in his hand. "You always say I make you messy." He grinned and worked his cock back and forth, slowly at first.

Part of me wanted to take him in my mouth instead, but I almost froze at the thought. Instead, I let Cooper turn my face to him and kissed him gently.

The next thing I knew, Ben had moved over closer and took his turn to stick his tongue almost down my throat. My lips might hurt later from all the kissing and stubble on the guys' chins.

I alternated between Ben and Cooper, while Hutton pounded my pussy.

He reached under my knees to bring up my legs to rest on either of his shoulders. With firm, even strokes, he hit me deep inside, hard enough to blissfully hurt.

With a grunt, he came, ejaculating liquid heat into my warm core.

A minute or two later, Jake came. Pearly cum squirted out of the tip of his cock and all over my breasts and belly. It was as warm as blood, but smelled like Jake, and salt, and sex. The feeling made me come one more time, hard and intense, hot inside and out. My back arched, my toes curled.

When I finally sagged back onto the bed, I was exhausted but satisfied. And surrounded by four ridiculously gorgeous, hot, incredible guys.

What more could a girl want?

CHAPTER
THREE

"I want to know what the fuck is going on." I had a quick shower and dressed in a clean skirt and blouse. A pair of heels dangled from my fingers and my arms were crossed over my chest. "Why are we running?"

Jake looked back at me evenly. His posture matched mine and his expression was unapologetic. "We're not running."

I waved an arm around the jet. "What do you call this then?"

The guys were spread around in comfortable chairs covered in butter soft, black leather. Ben was half watching us. Cooper looked like he was asleep and Hutton was engrossed in a book. On the cover was a scantily clad blonde fairy.

I was surprised he was into that kind of thing, but I might steal it when he was finished.

"We're taking a break," Jake said. "Remember the part where you nearly died and need a rest?"

"People will think I'm running away after Asshole shared that video with everyone," I said, my voice tight.

"Since when did you give a shit what people think?" Jake asked.

"Since footage of me looking vulnerable went viral," I replied. "Did you watch it?"

He averted his eyes for a moment before he forced them back to me. "Yes. I didn't want to, but I had to know what we were dealing with. For the record, you didn't look vulnerable, just outnumbered."

"What's the difference?" I asked.

"The difference is, we will never let you be outnumbered again." He grabbed my hand and pulled me down onto his lap. I protested for a moment, but he wound his arms around me and rested his head against my shoulder.

"Not a second will go by for the rest of my life that I won't regret not being with you that night. Cooper and I, we could have killed Haigwood later. He wasn't going anywhere. We should have escorted you to your house and back again. Or sent a bunch of the other guys with you. And girls," he added quickly. "We knew Dagen was going to try something." He sighed regretfully. "I thought he would come after the business."

"He did. He burnt down Scarlett." My favourite restaurant. It was repairable, but that would take time and money. "And he made my house disappear into a sinkhole."

"I put out the order to be watching out for the witch behind that," Jake said. "She will be dealt with. So will Dagen."

"You haven't told me where we're going." I nestled down into his arms. We'd been on this plane for at least a couple of hours. As far as I could tell, I woke up shortly after we took off.

"Would you be annoyed if I told you it was a surprise?" he asked.

"Yes," I said firmly. "You know I don't like surprises." Not even the nice kind, but especially the nasty kind.

He playfully rolled his eyes at me. "Fine. We're in Victoria. I've already let the Quinn brothers know we crossed the border. They're going to come to us in a day or so."

"I would have thought Kian Quinn would want us to go to him, since this is his state," I said.

Jake shrugged. "I impressed upon him the urgency of speaking to you and explained that you were badly injured recently. Personally, I think he would welcome the chance to get out of Melbourne for a while. People seem to try to kill him a lot more often than they try to assassinate you. He'd probably welcome the chance to get away from all of that."

"I wouldn't blame him." I wondered if we could swap him and his brothers for Dagen and his pack. Let the assassins go after Dagen. The Quinn brothers and I could probably carve out some peace and quiet in New South Wales. Until our egos got in the way.

Or their cocks.

"So, we're not going to Melbourne," I reasoned. "That leaves a handful of other places where the jet can land, and we own property."

"Unless we're switching to a helicopter." He looked cagey. "Or horseback."

I snorted. "No thanks. There's only one kind of animal I want between my legs."

He placed his hands to either side of my face and kissed me lightly. "I'll keep that in mind and not suggest it as a pastime." After a moment he added, "Does this mean you're not going to push us away anymore?" He looked adorably hopeful, but I couldn't resist playing with him. At least a little bit.

"That depends," I said slowly. "I'm still a little bit pissed off we're running away, and you won't tell me exactly where we're going."

For a moment, he looked worried I was actually pissed off at him. Then he cottoned on to my teasing.

"I should put you over my knee and spank you," he said. "I would if I didn't think you would enjoy it."

"You would if you didn't think I would have the other three guys throw you out the door," I retorted.

"That too." He grinned like the cocky bastard he was, because he knew the guys wouldn't do that to him. They were as loyal to him as they were to me. They wanted to be *like* him as much as they wanted to be *with* me. Well, except for Hutton. He was happy to be different from Jake.

That brought me to another question. "Are you and Hutton friends yet?"

Jake grimaced and glanced over at the man. Either Hutton wasn't listening or he was pretending not to pay attention to our conversation.

"I appreciate the way he stayed in contact with us while we were following you before the crash. He was texting Cooper. Those two seem to be getting along."

"Don't sidetrack," I said. "If you two are going to kill each other, I'd like to know about it in advance. So I can tell you to stop."

"I swear, I have no immediate plans to kill him," Jake said. "I don't trust him completely, but he seems to care about you."

"I care about him too," I said. "I care about all of you equally."

"But I'm your favourite, right?" Jake grinned.

"I don't have a favourite," I replied firmly. "But you and I will always have a special relationship. We've been through a lot together. Nothing will ever change that." And if he didn't like that, too bad, because that was how it was.

He gave me a sly smile. "Nothing will ever change the fact I fucked you first."

I think he expected me to roll my eyes at him, but instead I smiled softly. "No, nothing can change that. Especially given that Cooper was twelve at the time." Ben was the same age as me and Hutton was a few years older, but Cooper was definitely the pup of this little pack.

Cooper laughed. "Lucky I was too young or you would have had a fight on your hands, old man."

Jake turned to him and gave him a sarcastic smile. "I laugh because I know how much you have in your bank account, Pup. Not nearly enough to buy her virginity."

"How come you had enough?" Cooper asked. "How rich are you?"

Jake shrugged. "I stopped counting after the first billion, but that includes properties and other investments."

"If you keep getting more tattoos, you're going to end up a millionaire," I teased.

"You don't like them?" His brow furrowed.

"I love them," I said. "I just know what they cost. They're worth it though, because you look even hotter with them."

"Should I get a bunch of tattoos?" Cooper asked. He seemed genuinely curious.

"Only if you want to," I told him. "Body art is a personal thing. It's not something someone else should decide for you." Personally, I thought he was already a work of art, but the choice had to be his. I just hoped he never wanted to get any on his pretty face. I wouldn't love him any less if he did. I should tell him that, but the words wouldn't come. At some point, we would have that conversation. For now, it was nice to sit back and relax for a while.

I knew without having to ask, that Jake would have told everyone to contact me through him. I would only hear about anything work-related if he thought I needed to know it. Sometimes his over protectiveness chafed, but today I found it comforting.

The plane banked and started a slow descent towards the ground.

Hutton glanced up from his book. "Looks like we're nearly there."

"No shit," Jake said.

I gave him a sharp look.

"What? Even if we are friends, Hutton and I aren't going to stop giving each other shit. Right, Aaron?" Jake looked around me towards Hutton.

"Probably not, Jacob," Hutton agreed.

Jake grimaced. He was not a fan of his full name. He once said it didn't sound badass enough for him.

He didn't say anything now, of course. If he did, Hutton would keep calling him that until the end of time. But then, he might anyway.

I would leave them to fight it out on that one.

I leaned over to look out the window. There wasn't much to look at, just a bunch of trees. Up ahead was what looked like a small airfield. Big enough for the jet, but not big enough to be used very often.

"We're in the mountains," Cooper said. "I've never seen so many trees."

"I figured you were a city slicker," Hutton teased playfully.

"Aren't we all?" Cooper asked.

Jake chuckled. "He's got you there."

"I'm not," Ben said quietly. It was the first time I heard him speak since I woke up. "I grew up in the country. It's okay." He shrugged.

"Did you grow tomatoes and have chickens?" Cooper asked. "I mean, doesn't everyone do that in the country?"

Before Ben could answer, the jet jolted sideways.

A moment later, it dropped about a thousand feet, leaving my stomach behind.

The pilot's voice, at least as calm as Ben's, came out of the speakers in the roof of the cabin. "You've probably noticed we are experiencing some turbulence. The wind is higher than forecast. I'm going to attempt to land, but if it becomes too risky, we'll do a touch and go and bank for another try."

"Of course a drama-free break was too much to fucking ask," Jake said. He sighed out his nose in frustration.

I kissed him lightly. "Even you can't control the wind. What's the worst that can happen? It will take us a while longer to land."

"The worst that could happen is that we run out of fuel and crash," Jake said.

I cocked my head at him. "Paul is an experienced pilot. He's not going to let that happen. Besides, he's a dragon shifter. If anything bad happens, we can just jump on his back." It was one of the reasons I hired the man in the first place. He was good for defence as well as emergencies.

"He can only take three at a time," Jake pointed out.

"Well *I'll* be okay," I said, only half joking. "Maybe I should figure out now who I'm taking with me." That would be an impossible task, so hopefully it wouldn't come to that.

"Just me," Jake said lightly. "I like to stretch my legs out." He grinned at the other guys.

Without looking up from his book, Hutton flipped him off. "No one else would fit on there with your ego."

"That's true," Jake said. "There's nothing wrong with having good self-esteem. You would have it too if you were as hot as me."

Now Hutton looked up. He snorted. Without saying a word, he looked back down.

I laughed softly. "He told you," I said to Jake. "And for the record, you are all as hot as each other. Okay?"

I clung to Jake as the plane dropped again. We were buffeted so hard to the side, I almost fell off his lap.

"I think it's time for the fasten seatbelt sign." Reluctantly, I slipped off his lap and into another chair. I clicked my seatbelt into place just as the plane shuddered.

I couldn't remember when I ate last. A long time ago. That was just as well because with all this movement, I would have lost it all.

Cooper swallowed hard.

Even Ben looked a little green. I remembered he didn't like flying to begin with and this wouldn't help.

I looked out the window toward the airfield. I was no pilot, but even I could tell we were off course.

The plane banked lightly as Paul pointed the nose back towards the runway. We were almost low enough by now to skim the treetops if any were close enough.

Another gust of wind forced us to the side again.

"It's windier than the Wednesday after taco Tuesday," Jake said.

"Don't talk about food," Ben groaned.

If Hutton or Cooper had said that, Jake would probably have started to talk about hamburgers, pizza, hotdogs and whatever greasy food he could think of. Because it was Ben, he didn't say anything else. That spoke volumes about his respect for the other man. Or maybe just his lack of respect for Hutton and Cooper.

The jet approached the runway at what looked to me like an awkward angle. I wasn't sure we would even touch it, much less be able to land. Or take off again.

I have to admit that in the back of my mind I wondered if somehow Dagen did this. It was a stupid thought, because obviously wind was just a force of nature. On the other hand, so were sinkholes. If anyone would have fucked with us like that, it would be him.

I was almost certain he had done nothing. This time.

The wheels touched the dirt runway with a jarring jolt. Everything outside the windows passed by in a blur. I half expected a wheel to get stuck in a pothole and for the plane to flip, but it didn't. We reached the end of the runway and lifted off again.

Paul spoke over the speakers. "We're going around for another try. If we can't land, we're going to have to head to Melbourne."

He sounded apologetic, but didn't waste time saying sorry. It wasn't as if it was his fault anyway.

The plane banked sharply to the right and came back to face the runway. The wind must have dropped a bit, because we only got buffeted a time or two more. This time, we approached the runway more or less straight.

For the first time, I noticed a couple of white SUVs parked near the airfield. Maybe they had just arrived. I glanced at Jake in question. He nodded.

"They're for us. They're even on our side."

I gave him a dark look. "Don't joke about that." I doubted Dagen would wait until we landed and take us captive again. He would just shoot us out of the sky. I hoped he would anyway. I would rather that than end up in his hands again.

I wasn't sure if the shudder that went through my body was from that thought, or the plane landing on the runway and starting to slow.

FOUR

"If I didn't know better, I would think you've been planning this for a while." The sprawling house nestled in the Grampian ranges was my third favourite place to be, after Crimson and orgasmland.

Now, it was surrounded by a high fence and about a bajillion men and women dressed in Ivory Claw security uniforms. They all watched carefully as the cars approached.

The gates slid open slowly to let us through.

"I might have forgotten to mention putting up the fence." Jake shrugged. "The rest of the operation I put into motion after Dagen took you. I figured we would need somewhere to come for a break. Talking you into it was harder than I thought it would be."

"You didn't talk me into it," I reminded him. "You had to wait until I was unconscious, and basically abducted me." I knitted my brows at him. I didn't want him to think he got off that easily.

Running away from the concert was bad enough, without seeming to be running away from Sydney.

He was unapologetic, of course. "I'll have to remember that for next time."

I socked him hard on the arm. "Whatever you're thinking, don't you dare."

"What am I thinking?" He raised an eyebrow at me in challenge.

"I don't know, but it won't be good," I said.

Cooper, who sat on the other side of Jake in the back of the SUV, said, "I won't let him do anything bad to you. Neither will Ben. Right Ben?"

"Jake wouldn't do anything that wasn't in Ivory's best interest," Ben said from the front passenger seat.

"Whose side are you on? " I asked him. He and Jake seemed happy to decide for me what was in my best interests. Cooper and Hutton too, but those two guys in particular.

"Yours," Ben said firmly. "Always. But Jake is right about needing a break. We all need one."

Sometimes I forgot Ben was also affected by Dagen taking us. He was always so stoic, so chill. It would be easy to pretend nothing ever got to him. But the big bodyguard had feelings just like the rest of us.

Hutton too. He was almost torn apart by black wolves, then nearly killed by my driving. If anyone needed a break, it was him.

I glanced at where he sat in the very back of the SUV. He was still reading. He'd almost finished the book already. I suspected he would have preferred to be in the thick of action of some kind, but maybe this would be a chance for him and Jake to finally get along and put the past in the past. Where it fucking belonged.

As if to punctuate my thoughts, the gates slid closed behind us with a clang. The SUV followed the bend of the curved driveway and stopped in front of the house.

Before I could even touch the handle, one of the security guys hurried over to open the door for me. Another did the same on the other side.

"I feel like royalty," I muttered. "Or a movie star."

"You are royalty, El," Jake said. "You're a queen. And... Anytime you want to be a movie star, I can arrange that." He wiggled his brows.

"Don't make me sock you on the arm again," I mock growled.

"I can take it," he retorted. "Just don't knee me in the groin."

"I make no guarantees." I stepped out of the car and nodded my thanks to the security guy. What was his name? Oh, Malcolm. If I recall correctly, he was also a distant cousin. Then again, a lot of them were. White wolves tended to stick together. Not quite enough for inbreeding to be a problem, but someday it might be.

Not for me, I reminded myself sadly. Dagen took that away from me, my right to choose. Fucker.

I started up the front steps of the house, with all four guys arrayed around me. The way security snapped to attention as we walked past, I felt more and more like a celebrity. I supposed I was, in the way rich and powerful people tended to become famous for just being rich and powerful. Maybe Jake was right and I should put my hand up for my own television show. *Keeping up with the Keelans* did have a ring to it.

Who was I kidding? I was more likely to end up on an episode of *Underbelly*.

"You run a tight ship, Jacob," Hutton said appreciatively.

"Thanks Aaron," Jake said. "Or should I say Edward?"

Hutton winced. "How about you don't?"

"Edward?" Cooper looked confused.

"His real first name is Edward," Jake said helpfully. "Edward Aaron Hutton. What a mouthful."

Hutton opened his mouth, clearly intending to make some remark about his cock size. He glanced at me and closed it again. After a moment, he finally managed to say, "There's a reason I go by Hutton. Aaron is okay, but too many people think they should call me Ed."

"As in dickEd?" Jake grinned.

"This from the guy whose middle name is Lyle," Hutton retorted. "Jacob Lyle Blakesley. It suits you. Not."

"There's a reason I go by Jake," Jake said.

"Do you have an embarrassing middle name? " Cooper asked Ben and I as we stepped through the wide front doors and into the house.

"I don't have a middle name," Ben said. "It's just Benjamin Pellegrini."

"Your last name is Pellegrini?" Cooper asked. "That's so cool. The perfect name for a gangster."

Ben gave him a half smile. "Thanks, I guess."

"Believe it or not, my middle name is Bianca," I said. "My parents might have been obsessed with the colour white."

"That's pretty," Cooper said. "Pretty like you."

We all turned to him.

"What?" He looked around at us. "My middle name is John, but you probably already know that."

"Yeah, we do," I admitted. Jake probably had records on him that went back to his grades for spelling in kindergarten.

"Wow," Cooper said breathlessly.

We stepped from the foyer into the expansive, open concept kitchen, lounge and dining area. Wide windows overlooked the view down the side of the mountain. Fire crackled in a huge fireplace to one side of the room. The wall beside it held the largest sized television in existence.

The gods only knew why. Jake insisted on it. Something about watching football and movies. I didn't remember ever seeing him do either of those things. He was usually too busy torturing and killing people, and other fun things.

"If you're lucky, you'll get to see the first snows here," Ben said. "The view is even nicer then."

Nice was a typical Ben understatement. The view was spectacular on any given day. Snow made it look incredible, but so did thunderstorms and, like today, sunshine.

"Can we ski?" Cooper asked.

"Ski, snowboard, sled, roll around naked and it," Jake said. "The possibilities are endless."

"Jake means rolling around in it in wolf form," I said. Which we did do because we were Arctic wolves after all. We were made for the snow. And then sitting in front of the fireplace with a hot coffee afterwards.

We were also civilised.

The smell of something cooking wafted through the air.

"I brought the chef from Scarlett to work here," Jake said. "I figured it would be better than living on grilled cheese sandwiches."

"You think of everything," I said appreciatively. "Just a wild guess, but there's a nice hot bubble bath waiting for me upstairs?" I batted my eyelashes at him.

"Um. Yes, of course there is," he said quickly. "Just... Don't go up there for about ten minutes."

I laughed softly. He was amazing, but even Jake couldn't think of everything. Besides, if we were delayed, the water would go cold.

That would suck.

While the staff ran around running a bath and sorting out our luggage, I laced my fingers through Ben's and drew him aside gently.

"Can we talk?"

His gaze took me in for a moment. "Sure."

"Don't wander off too far," Jake said. "Remember the rules. Someone is with Ivory at all times."

"Is one of you going to watch me pee?" I raised my eyebrows at him.

"If necessary," he agreed. "Whatever it takes to keep you safe. I trust everyone here, but sooner or later Dagen is gonna try some-thing. We'll be ready."

There was no arguing with him, even if I wanted to, so I nodded and opened the door that led out to a wide deck. It was cold out here, but the wind dropped.

Before I could say anything, Ben said, "You were right. About breaking the bond."

His words surprised me into silence.

He glanced down at the timber decking, then back up again. "When you were lying there by the side of the road, when you almost died... If I was connected to you then, I wouldn't have been able to be objective. I had to be, to go and pick up the witch. I couldn't afford to be hysterical."

I gave him a faint smile. I couldn't imagine him being anything close to hysterical, but I understood what he was trying to say.

"I'm certain you would have been as cool, calm and collected as ever, but I wouldn't have wanted you to feel what I was feeling then." Asshole used the bond as a kind of torture device, and that's what it would have been. It could be something beautiful, but it could be something really horrible as well.

He nodded. "Exactly. I would be lying if I said I didn't miss you in my mind, but at least you're here right in front of me. You're not pushing me away."

I sighed softly. "I'm sorry for that too."

He pressed his forehead lightly to mine. "Don't be. You don't do anything without a good reason and we all understood what that reason was. Just because we didn't like it, didn't mean it wasn't totally legitimate. What happened to us, to you—" He closed his eyes. "No one can go through shit like that and just bounce back. Even you."

"You either," I said. "It was definitely not a highlight of my life. It was horrible for both of us."

"I got to spend a couple of weeks locked away with you," he said softly. "I would have preferred other circumstances, and I hate the things he did to you, but at least I was with you. There are worse things than having nothing else to do but make love to a beautiful woman."

"When you put it that way, I think I'll cancel the therapy sessions I booked for you," I said dryly. "Don't try to pretend you weren't as scared as I was. Dagen's goons would have happily ripped you apart."

"Thinking about what they would have done to you after that would be much worse," he said. "I would happily die for you. You know that, right? Not just because it's my job."

"I know that," I said. They all would. I hoped to the gods it wouldn't come to that. I didn't want to lose any of them. I couldn't.

"So you forgive me then?" I asked.

He opened his brown eyes and looked right into mine. "There's nothing to forgive, but if there was I would always forgive you." After a moment he added, "Within reason."

"That's totally fair," I said. "I'll try not to do anything you couldn't forgive me for." I couldn't imagine what that might be, especially given who I was and the things I did on a daily basis.

"I know you will." He kissed me lightly on the mouth. "I love you."

For a moment, the all too familiar feeling of panic rose in my chest. I was both scared to say it and scared not to say it. I was terrified to feel it. No, I was terrified to *admit* I felt it. Those were three words I had never said to a guy face-to-face. But now I needed and wanted to say it four times over.

"I love you too," I said softly.

There, it was out. I said it. Now I had, I wanted to say it again and again. And I would, because I intended to live a long, long time with these guys.

"Do you think Jake got that bath ready yet?" I asked.

"Probably. Do you need someone to wash your back, or just watch your back?" He leaned his head back from mine and gave me a slight quirk of his eyebrows.

I pretended to think about that for a moment. "Why choose? Do you think you could manage to do both at the same time?"

"Not without getting a hard on," he admitted. "But I think I can manage."

"I'm sure you can." I slipped my hand back into his and we headed back inside.

"You two kissed and made up?" Hutton asked.

"I think we did that on the jet," I said. "But we had a few things we needed to say to each other. And we did that." They all knew about the situation between us, so I didn't need to explain any further. Nor did I mention that we said those three words to each other. We might all be more or less in a relationship with each other, but we didn't need to share every single detail.

"Lunch will be ready in an hour," Jake said. "Is that enough time for a bath?" The look he gave me clearly said he knew we weren't going upstairs just to wash.

For a moment I considered asking him to join us, but as much as I enjoyed threesomes and foursomes and fivesomes, I felt the need to have one-on-one time with each of the guys as well. Right now, I owed that to Ben.

I was relieved he understood about the bond, even though he was obviously clearly still hurt about it. I had considered the possibility he would ask to find another bonding stone and re-bond. Honestly, I wasn't sure what I would say if he suggested it.

Thank the gods I didn't have to make that decision. Especially given the distinct possibility the other three guys would want to do the same. I had enough shit going on in my head, without four others in there as well.

"It should be," I replied. I grabbed Jake's hand and pulled him over for a long, slow kiss. "Thank you for all of this. I know I give you hells for fussing over me, sometimes, but I like it when you do. I feel safer and I feel... Cared for."

"You are loved," he said firmly. "I love you and I would do anything for you. I told you before, you are my universe, and I meant it."

"If I'm a universe, then you are one of my brightest stars," I told him. "All four of you are."

"I'm more of a black hole." Hutton smiled self-deprecatingly.

"Things disappear into you?" Jake asked.

"You like to suck?" Cooper asked.

"Things are irresistibly drawn towards you?" I suggested.

We all looked at Ben, who shrugged. "If the man wants to think of himself as a black hole, then who am I to argue? But I stand by what I said. You might be Jake's universe, but you're my angel."

"And my babe," Hutton said.

"And my..." Cooper frowned in thought. "Dumpling?"

I snorted.

Jake patted him on the shoulder. "Keep trying, Pup."

"But everyone loves dumplings," Cooper said. "They're tasty."

"Not as tasty as Ivory," Hutton said. "Especially with a little Cooper sauce on top." He looked smug.

Cooper's face turned pink. "I never thought I would kiss another guy. But I liked it."

"Of course you did," Hutton said. "It was me." His expression turned serious. "I've always known I was bi, but I've never felt comfortable expressing it until now. It's nice to feel accepted." He shot Jake a challenging look, as though expecting some smart ass remark from the older wolf.

For once, Jake didn't say a word. He didn't look completely convinced either, but he didn't ruin the moment.

401

"It makes sense that you'd feel comfortable," Cooper said. "I mean, it's me." He grinned.

"Exactly," Hutton said. "You're too adorable to resist." He punctuated that statement by kissing Cooper soundly.

"Aren't they both just too cute?" I said to Jake and Ben.

"Definitely," Ben agreed. He didn't look like he was going to kiss or touch either of them any more than Jake was, but he wasn't judging them either.

How did I get so fucking lucky? It didn't really matter how, the fact was I had and I was going to appreciate every moment of it.

"So, about that bath." I squeezed Ben's hand and we turned and headed towards the stairs leading to the upper level of the house.

"Have fun, kids," Jake said. "I'll be down here getting some work done."

I paused and turned around to look back down at him. "If there's anything you need help with—"

He waved me away. "I know you don't understand the meaning of the word 'rest,' but you're going to have to learn. That's all you'll be doing for at least the next few days." He gave me his best 'don't argue with me,' face and turned away.

"You did almost die last night," Ben said softly.

"Apparently you guys have made it your job to remind me of that every chance you get," I said, trying not to sound too bitter. I would relax for the rest of the day, but if Jake thought I'd be out of action for any longer than that, he would have to think again.

I had a black wolf to destroy.

CHAPTER
FIVE

"I wondered why anyone needed a bath this big," Ben remarked. "Now it makes sense. All five of us would fit with space to spare."

"Would you like me to invite the rest of them?" I asked teasingly.

"Hells no." He put his arms around me and tangled his fingers in my hair. "I'm happy to have you all to myself for a while." He gave me a long slow kiss, then stepped back so we could both get undressed.

He slipped into the bath first, then helped me in.

He was right, it was enormous. More like a hot tub than a bath. That was the reason I chose it, but I hadn't anticipated ever being in a position to share it with four guys. Serendipity for the win.

I slowly sank into the heavily scented water, giving my body time to adjust to the slightly too-hot bath.

"Mmm." I leaned against the side and closed my eyes. My muscles were already thanking me for taking the time to do this.

"This is nice," Ben said. He took my hand and pulled me over so my back was against his chest. He placed his hands lightly on my shoulders and started to work out the knots with slow, gentle care.

"I'm not surprised you're so tense, but we should have made you take a break a long time ago."

"It's cute that you think you could have made me have a holiday," I said.

He laughed softly. "Why have this place if you're not going to come here and unwind?"

"I bought it thinking I would do exactly that. I think knowing I could come here if I wanted to is what made me buy it."

How fucking decadent is that? To have a huge house in the mountains just for the idea of owning it. I should probably make time to come here more often.

His hands moved from my shoulders, down my arms and around to caress my wet breasts.

I leaned back against him and closed my eyes as he palmed my nipples. I had no idea how I had any energy, much less the sex drive after the fivesome on the jet, but there it was. I was already ready for more. So was he, judging by the growing erection that pressed into the side of my hip.

His hands ghosted downward, over my belly and thighs. He slipped his hands between my legs and lightly rubbed over my clit with the side of his fingers.

I shivered and parted my legs to give him more access.

He brushed his fingers over my pussy, then turned me around to face him. He kissed me deep and long and slow. His hands cupped my ass. He lifted me up gently until I wrapped my legs around his hips.

I was already wet inside and out. His gentle touch was lovely, but I wanted him to fuck me. I positioned my entrance at the tip of his cock and pressed down, impaling myself on his rock hard, curved length.

He groaned. "You always feel so amazing."

"So do you," I said breathlessly.

He turned us around so my back was pressed against the side of the bath. "I could stay like this forever."

"Me too," I agreed. Maybe I could buy a place like this up in the Blue Mountains and retire there. Let somebody else run Ivory Claw.

That would be heavenly, but I would get bored quickly. I would probably start up a whole new organisation, just for something to do.

Or I could spend the rest of my life with one or two of the guys' cocks inside me. That didn't sound too awful.

He locked his eyes on mine and slowly started to thrust. Lavender scented water slapped between us and threatened to go over the side and onto the floor.

The faster his strokes were, the higher the water rose.

He slipped a hand between us and rubbed my clit with firm fingers in rhythm with his cock. This wasn't going to be a quick fuck. Even as turned on as I was, my orgasm built slowly. It, like him, was taking its time.

My hands wandered all over his body, feeling his ridges and muscles and scars. He was as cut as the rest of the guys, so every centimetre of him was hard as rock. Especially all six, sorry, eight of his abs. Holy shit, he was something else. Hard on the outside, but gentle and soft on the inside. Well, soft when it counted.

"Come for me," he said eventually.

Only then I realised how ragged my breathing was. I was right on the doorstep, with my toes inside. His words made me tumble through into the blissful abyss, where nothing else mattered but his touch.

As I was coming down, he came with a series of fast, frantic strokes. Water surged to the edge of the bath with equal ferocity. As he peaked, it sloshed over the side and splashed onto the tiled floor. The sound was almost drowned out by that of his groans of pleasure.

Finally, he sagged and drew me away from the side of the bath to hold me close.

We stayed like that for the longest time, until the water started to get cold.

"We should get out, I suppose," I said reluctantly. "Before we start to look like prunes."

"Yeah, I guess so," he agreed. We unwound from each other and he helped me out of the bath. He even handed me a white, fluffy towel to wrap around myself.

"Thank you." I dried myself quickly and tucked a section of towel in between my breasts so it stayed up by itself.

I was about to leave the bathroom, when movement out the window caught my eye.

I froze. My blood ran cold.

The bathroom window had a good view out over the road and the driveway leading up to the house. And the three sleek black vehicles driving towards the front gates.

"Fuck," I whispered. Panic started to rise like a tsunami. It was Dagen, it had to be. How had he found us here so fast? How had he gotten cars organised? Questions tumbled through my brain.

"What is it?" Ben came to stand beside me, a towel wrapped around his waist. "Oh." He put his arms around me and pulled me close.

I was struggling to breathe. Was it too late to jump back in the bath and hide under the water for half an hour or so?

"It's okay," Ben said softly. "I'm not gonna let anything happen to you."

I didn't want to look out the window, but I couldn't look away.

Especially when the gates started to open.

My whole body trembled uncontrollably.

"It's okay," Ben said again. He pulled off both of our towels and held me with his warm skin directly on mine. "Jake isn't going to open the gate to Dagen."

He might not, but someone else might be controlling them. But who would do that? Had someone betrayed us?

"Look," Ben said softly. "It's fine."

I forced myself to look. When I finally managed to take a breath, it was with relief.

Jake was trotting away from the house, towards the lead car. His body language didn't suggest he was worried. Cooper and Hutton were close behind him.

Realisation dawned on me. "Fuck. Fuck, fuck. *Fuck.* I should have anticipated he would do this."

Sure enough, when the cars stopped, Kian Quinn got out of the middle one, followed by his brothers, Tyler and Reed.

"They must have gotten into the cars the moment they got the call from Jake," I said. Thank the gods I stopped trembling by now. My mind was whirling instead.

"They thought they would catch us off guard?" Ben asked.

"That's exactly what they did," I said. I ran a hand over my hair. Thankfully it wasn't too wet, but I would have to dress quickly.

"I can go down there and tell them you're sleeping," Ben offered.

I considered the offer for a moment, but shook my head. "I want them to think we knew they were coming today. Kian obviously thought he would have an advantage over us. I want him to see he was wrong. No one takes Ivory by surprise."

Ben nodded. "Then we should both get dressed or they will definitely get a surprise."

I snorted softly. "Yes, appearing naked in front of them would absolutely send the wrong message." That begged the question though, what did I wear? If I wore one of my more revealing dresses, they might take that as an open invitation. Although, if I wore a turtleneck and a skirt down to my ankles, they would also take that as an open invitation.

Before I stepped away to the wardrobe, I squeezed Ben's hand. "Thank you. Even without the bond, you always seem to know what I need."

"That's because I spend more time watching and learning, than talking," he said. "It's a skill that comes in useful sometimes."

He was right about that. I should try it more often myself.

I released his hand and hurried to get dressed and throw on some makeup. By the time I was done, Ben was already dressed in dark jeans and a white T-shirt which accentuated his muscular physique.

I sighed dramatically. "I'm tempted to help you out of that and drag you off to bed."

He smiled. "You can do that all you want, but I'm sure you would prefer to deal with the Quinn brothers first."

"Right," I agreed. "Business before pleasure." That might as well be my motto, I'd spent so much time living by it.

"You look beautiful." He brushed his lips over my cheek. He was smart enough to know not to smudge the lipstick I just smeared over my lips.

"No, *you*." I smiled up at him.

He chuckled. "We're both beautiful. But mostly you." He took my hand and led me towards the stairs. He didn't let it go until we reached the bottom, where Jake had herded the Quinn brothers and their entourage.

Kian stood behind a dark haired woman I didn't recognise. Tyler and Reed stood a little apart, and Reed chewed on a lit cigar.

I waved my hand in front of my face. "Would you take that stinky thing outside my house?"

Reed turned to Tyler and lowered the cigar. "You heard Ivory, she wants you to go outside."

Tyler flipped him off and stepped over to me. He looked me up and down with open appreciation and smiled. "Hey, long time no see." He gave me a quick kiss on the cheek and stepped back.

Kian moved forward to do the same, but he held the woman's hand and brought her forward with him.

"Thank you for inviting us here," he said as if he wasn't two days early. "This is Blair, our girlfriend. Blair, this is Ivory."

Blair offered me a warm smile. "It's nice to meet you. The guys have all told me a lot about you."

"Don't believe a word," I said dryly. *Our girlfriend?* That would explain the vibe I got when I stepped into the room. These wolves didn't need to hunt, because they had prey of their own. From the smell of her, she was a black wolf too. She must be one hells of a woman if she could handle all three Quinn brothers. I hoped she knew exactly what she was getting into.

"Hey," Tyler protested. "We had some nice things to say."

"Ty mentioned you have great tits," Reed said. He still stood puffing on his cigar.

Kian and Blair both gave him a sharp look, but Cooper grinned.

"She does have great—" He caught the look on my face and shut his mouth with a click of his teeth.

"Please," I waved towards the couches over in front of the fire. "Get comfortable. It's so nice of you to have come so quickly." I impressed myself by managing to keep sarcasm out of my voice. Go me.

I sat down in a plush armchair and crossed my legs at my knees.

Jake perched on the arm of the chair. Hutton reclined on a couch. Cooper and Ben stayed standing, as was appropriate for bodyguards.

Our guests sat on the couches. Tyler and Reed managed to manoeuvre so Blair sat between them. Kian gave them both a dark look, but settled into the armchair opposite them.

"Jake said you've been having a bit of trouble with Alistair Dagen, and almost died last night," Kian said. "I thought it was best not to wait."

A bit of trouble? That was an understatement. The semantics didn't matter right now, I supposed.

"I appreciate your time," I said graciously. "He has been causing a bit of trouble recently. He destroyed my home and one of my businesses. He blew up one of his businesses in an attempt to get to me. And he abducted me and one of my employees."

Kian nodded. "So I've heard. He sent us some footage..."

I winced. Who hadn't the motherfucker sent that fucking video to? "Yes. I think he gets off on the idea of other people seeing that."

"That was him?" Kian asked carefully.

I swallowed. I didn't want to talk about this, but it was inevitable the moment he mentioned the footage.

"Yes it was. He also had a doctor perform surgery on me to prevent me from having children."

Blair responded to that with a sharp intake of breath. "That's awful. I can't believe—"

I turned to her. "Believe it. I didn't want to start a war with him and his pack, but he declared war on us."

"You realise what's at stake if we help you?" Kian asked.

"I know it's asking a lot," I said. "If nothing else, I would ask that you don't side with him."

My words were followed by an uncomfortable silence.

It was finally broken by Blair. "If they side with a rapist, I would kick them in the nuts."

"She really would," Tyler said. "She's an even bigger hard ass then Kian. I mean that in a nice way."

I nodded my thanks to Blair. She was easy to like. She reminded me a bit of myself, except the whole thing about being a black wolf, not a white one. Sometimes, we weren't so different.

"If we helped you," Kian said slowly. "What would you want from us?"

It was Jake who responded. "Information. Fighters if you want to send those. A spy or two. Who better to infiltrate the Onyx Ridge pack than another black wolf?"

"I could do it," Reed said. "They would never see me coming."

"You would stand out like a shark in the middle of a school of sardines," Tyler said.

"First of all, thank you for mentioning how big I am." Reed patted his groin. "But that's also the point. I stand out, and they think I'm on their side. They wouldn't need to let their guard down because they wouldn't have it up in the first place."

"You're not going in there," Kian said. "If we help Ivory, we'll do it in a way that doesn't provoke a war between the Ironhide and Onyx Ridge packs."

Reed pouted.

"I hate to say this," Tyler said, "but Kian is right. One of us going in there would provoke the shit out of this Dagen asshole. We have enough trouble already without inviting any in."

"You sounded just like Kian," Reed told him.

Tyler shrugged. "We have to grow up at some point." He was about the same age as me. Kian was a few years older and Reed a few years younger.

"Growing up is overrated," Hutton remarked.

"I think that's the first thing you've said that I agree with," Jake told him. "It really is overrated." He turned to Kian. "We understand you can't offer personal help. The last thing we want to do is start a war that goes across state lines. We just need a little help tidying up our own backyard."

Kian sat back in his chair and ran a hand over his hair. "I could

411

try a phone call to Alistair, to see if he'll back off, but if what you're saying he did is true, it seems unlikely he'll listen, much less comply."

I tried not to bristle at the implications that we were lying. Of course, he wasn't obligated to believe a word we'd said. The fact he was here at all said at least he was ready to listen.

"I think that might provoke him further," I said. "If he knows we spoke to you, he's going to be pissed. He will come after us hard. We need to go after him first."

Kian nodded. "I'd like to talk a bit more and then I'll consider what help the Ironhide pack can give. I'm inclined to at least offer some assistance." He looked thoughtful.

"From what I know of Alistair Dagen, he's not going to stop at taking over your organisation. Before you took down the Onyx Ridge pack, his family was eyeing ours over the border. It's only a matter of time before he does the same. Whereas you, you've been happy to stay in your lane all these years. I would prefer to continue that arrangement."

"Me too." It was news to me the Onyx Ridge pack had looked to take over Ironhide territory, but it shouldn't surprise me. They were nothing if not ambitious. Overstepping was in their blood, along with cruelty.

"So you might say that by overthrowing the previous genera-tion of Dagens, I did the Ironhide pack a favour," I said. I gave Kian my best sweet, innocent expression.

He wasn't fooled for a moment. I wasn't expecting him to be. I mean, I was hoping.

"You might say that," he agreed. "But that doesn't mean I have to do you one in return. Give me some time to think."

"Don't take too long," Jake said. "I can almost hear Dagen planning something from here. If we don't strike before he does, we might all be fucked."

CHAPTER
SIX

"Do you think they'll help us?" Cooper asked.

I looked over to the dining table, where the four of them sat, talking in low voices.

"It's in their best interests to," I said. My phone pinged.

I raised my eyebrows at Jake. If he thought I didn't realise he stashed it in the left back pocket of his jeans, he would have to think again. He kept his phone in the right pocket, so it was obvious what it was. And yes, I was checking out his ass, that was when I noticed.

"You're not supposed to be working," he said firmly when I held out my hand.

"It might not be work," I pointed out.

"What else would it be?" He eyed my hand but made no move to pull out my phone.

"The company I hired to clear out the rubble of my house," I suggested. I wiggled my fingers at him. It was cute that he wanted to take care of me, but I was growing impatient.

"Do you want the three of us to hold him down for you?" Hutton offered.

"Fuck off," Jake told him. Reluctantly, he pulled my phone out of his pocket and tapped on the screen. He pressed his thumb on the fingerprint reader when it prompted him to.

I frowned at him. "Do I have absolutely no privacy?"

"None," he said unapologetically. "It's Freddie Whitlock. One of Harmony's boyfriends. It's work-related, isn't it?"

I leaned over to snatch my phone out of his hand. I would have to rearrange a few settings to lock him out of it. Or maybe I wouldn't bother, because he would find a way around it anyway. Asshole.

I opened Freddie's text message and read. And smiled.

"I asked him to try to access Dagen's systems. Specifically his bank accounts. It took him a while, but he got in. Money will mysteriously trickle out of Alistair's account. Then, when the time is right, bam, it will be gone." I grinned.

Jake smiled appreciatively. "I like it. When in the hells did you get a chance to set that up?"

I shrugged one shoulder modestly. "A few hours before the charity concert." I glanced over to Hutton.

That was what I was doing before we had our conversation that led to us fucking on the couch. After that, I was too distracted to remember to mention it to anyone.

"That's fucking awesome," Cooper said. "Where is it going?"

"Some of it is going into our accounts," I said. "Several organisations who help women escape domestic violence are going to get generous donations." I didn't want his dirty money, so this way a lot of it was going to a good cause.

"I might also need to make a generous donation to the Quinn brothers," I said. I looked over to them. They didn't seem any closer to a decision.

"Wouldn't that be called a bribe?" Hutton asked.

"Of course," I said lightly. "I just thought donation sounded a bit more classy." No one would be under any illusion about what it really was, but it didn't have to sound sleazy.

"I guess you make a lot of *donations*," Hutton said.

"You would guess right," I agreed. Police, politicians, people like that. They were worth every cent to avoid a shit load of hassle. "I'm not above doing what needs to be done to get what I want."

"If we take all of his money, then do we need to attack him?" Cooper asked. "I mean, it's hard to do much of anything without the resources. Right?"

"Chances are that the moment he realises he is losing money, he'll come after us," I said. "We need to make sure our accounts are locked down tighter than a fly's asshole. He'll probably do the same when he realises what's going on. This is a distraction. Unless, of course, we manage to drain all of his accounts."

That wasn't something I could rely on. Alistair Dagen was many things, but stupid was not one of them. This would be a lot easier if he was. I could have ended this a long time ago.

"If we do that, I can buy the Maserati I've always wanted." Jake said wistfully.

"You can already do that," I pointed out.

"Yeah, but it would be much sweeter if I bought it with his money." He grinned.

I laughed softly. "I see your point. You could drive it past the park bench he's sleeping on and rev the engine really hard. That would annoy him." The mental image of Dagen being that far down on his luck was a pleasant one. I made a note to donate some of his money to homeless people. Not because I wanted him to benefit from it some day, but because they needed the help.

"I'd prefer to run him over with it," Jake said. "Several times."

"Can I come if you do that?" Cooper asked easily. "That sounds like fun."

"We could all go," Jake said. "We could make a family outing out of it. Maybe have a picnic afterwards." He grinned.

"How wholesome that sounds," Hutton said. "Do we have to wear matching outfits?"

I snorted. "No matching outfits. Jeans are fine. Hells, pants can be optional as long as Asshole is dealt with."

"Now you're talking," Jake said jokingly.

At least, I think he was joking. As far as I know, he didn't have any particular aversion to wearing pants. Although, he and the other guys seemed more than happy to get out of them around me.

"So this is our battle plan?" Ben said softly. One side of his mouth was turned up slightly. That was the only sign he too was joking. "Running over Dagen with a car?"

"Let's call that plan B," Jake said. "We have to do a lot better than that for plan A though. Something a bit more subtle. And harder for him to get away from."

"We all know what our best option is," I said softly. "We need to draw him out. The best way to do that is with the thing he wants the most. Me."

"Not a chance," Jake said immediately. "I am not going to risk you for anything."

The rest of the guys murmured and grunted their agreement.

"We have to end this," I pointed out. "This might be the easiest, quickest way to do it."

"It might also be the way you end up dead. Or worse," Hutton said. He gave me a long, measured look.

He didn't need to draw me a picture. I knew what he was talking about. Dagen would keep me alive long enough to force himself on me a time or two, then he would kill me.

"That only happens if he manages to take me." I said. "That's what you four are for. To stop that from happening. We only need me to get his attention."

"As much as I appreciate the faith in us," Jake started, "it's too big a risk. I can't ask you to do something like that."

"You're not asking," I said. "I'm telling you this is the best way. Maybe the only way. We might catch him off guard."

I chewed my lip for a moment. I hatched an idea in my mind, but I decided not to go into details yet.

Instead I said, "If we do this right, then there's no risk to me at all." That wasn't true, there was always going to be some risk. But we could minimalise it.

"It's better than sitting around waiting for him to do something." I crossed my arms over my breasts. "I could do this without any of you."

From the expressions on all of their faces, I struck a nerve with that.

Jake even flinched. He knew it wasn't an empty threat. If they tried to stand in my way, I would do this anyway. Not without an army of white or black wolves, because I was pissed off, not stupid, but I would prefer to do this with them. I didn't trust anyone else to have my back the way they did.

Cooper raised his hand. "Is anyone else thinking we should lock Ivory in her bedroom until this is over?"

No one disagreed with that question.

"I will not be locked in an..." I couldn't resist, "an Ivory tower while you guys get on with the job."

"This is usually where she threatens to fire us all," Jake said. "But that won't fly anymore. We've all gone way past being employees." He looked directly at me. "You'll have to find some other way to threaten us. If we have to lock you away to keep you safe, that's what we'll do."

"The fuck you will," I growled. I stood and stalked a few steps away before turning and stalking back.

"Running away was bad enough. I refuse to hide." I placed my fists on my hips. "Has any one of you got a better idea than using me as bait?"

"We could fire a rocket launcher at his house," Cooper suggested.

"See?" Jake said. "That's a much better idea."

"Right," I said slowly. "Do you think the police will turn a blind eye to that? It only takes one dickhead with a phone to film it and we're screwed."

"We will happily go to prison for you," Jake said. "We would probably fight over who used the rocket launcher. That's how much we care about you."

"Rock, paper, scissors?" Cooper asked.

"None of you is using a rocket launcher," I said as they started to stretch their hands out in front of them.

Men.

The smell of testosterone was stronger than ever. Usually I liked it, but today it was almost overwhelming.

They lowered their hands. All four of them looked disappointed.

I closed my eyes and shook my head. "It's decided then. We just need to work out the details."

"Elodie—" Jake stood and put his arms around me. "If anything happens to you, I will never forgive myself."

"I'll never forgive him either," Hutton said helpfully.

Jake flipped him off.

"If you have to do this, then I'm going to be there," Ben said firmly. "In whatever capacity you need me. If this is what it takes to bring down Alistair Dagen, then I'm in."

"Me too," Cooper said. "Can we at least make the rocket launcher plan C?"

"Since we won't get down that far, you can make it plan whatever the hells you want," I told him. I almost managed to ignore when he punched the air in triumph.

I was surrounded by hot, muscular little boys. I wasn't exactly saying I wanted them to grow up, but hopefully they would show a little bit of maturity during this operation. Playing around could get them killed. Worse than that, it could get me killed. No one would forgive them for that, especially me.

Jake leaned his head on my shoulder and sighed. "Since you're going to do this with or without me, I guess I better be in as well. If I leave it to these clowns, they'll probably fuck it up somehow."

"We love you too, Jake," Cooper said. "We're a team and we couldn't do it without you. We need your badass skills."

"You'll need mine too," Hutton said. He looked less than thrilled with the idea of going after Dagen like this, but he was as determined as I was to put a stop to all of this. "I don't suppose —" He shifted in his seat. "We could use me as bait instead. He wants me dead as much as he wants you dead."

"Now there's an idea I could get behind," Jake said.

Hutton shot him a look and rolled his eyes. "He wants you too."

"I will happily take Elodie's place," Jake said easily.

"He would have both of you killed before you got anywhere near him," I pointed out. "He wants to toy with me. That gives us time."

My stomach turned violently at the idea. I had to shove down the starting edge of a panic attack. If we did this right, the guys would be there before the whole thing went sideways. If we messed it up, I would have to live with the consequences of that. Assuming I got to live at all. If I didn't, then Jake and my sister might have to finish what I started.

"I hate to say it, but she's right," Hutton said.

Ben nodded his agreement. "He only kept me alive to screw with Ivory. I doubt he will make the same mistake again."

"He kept me alive because the idea of a white wolf working for him amused him," Hutton said. "And so he could test my loyalty to him. Which I failed, as you know. My loyalty is with Ivory. He knows that for certain now. He's definitely not going to let me near his organisation again."

"No, he's not," I agreed. "He would prefer to work with witches than other wolves." I wrinkled my nose.

"Most of the wolves don't want to work with him anyway," Ben said. "Otherwise why would he lower himself to work with witches?"

"Some witches are okay," I pointed out. While I understood his hatred, in the long run, he was only hurting himself by holding onto his anger. "Like Harmony."

"She's a half demon," Ben pointed out, as if that somehow changed everything.

I wasn't going to pretend to understand the difference. Magic gave me the heebie-jeebies, regardless of who was doing it.

"A witch saved Ivory's life last night," Cooper said softly. ""I know you don't like them, but if it wasn't for her..."

Ben grunted. "Okay, she's one exception. The one Dagen has working for him, Irina, has done some really shit things. She's as complicit as he is."

I stepped away from Jake's arms to sit beside Ben and lean my head against his bicep. "Yeah, she did and she is."

Like her part in the surgery. And then making a sinkhole under my house. I was still salty about both of those. I would be for a long time. If I found her, she would become part of the foundations for my new house. If she was really lucky, I would kill her before she was encased in concrete.

That thought cheered me up a bit.

"It would probably be a good idea to have a witch or two on our side," I said slowly. "If only to stop the ones who work for Dagen from doing anything to us."

Ben's body stiffened. "You're right, we should," he said reluctantly. "I know a couple who don't have a high opinion of black wolves in general. Or white ones, but they'll help if I ask them to."

It wasn't lost on me how big an offer he was making. If this was a step towards his healing, then that was even better.

"Yes, please do ask," I said. "Thank you."

I remembered his words when I was lying by the side of the road in the rain. 'I love her more than I hate them.' That was what all of this was about.

I didn't know what I did to deserve any of these guys, but I wasn't going to throw their love back in their faces anymore. And I wasn't going to take them for granted ever again. These four guys were the best people I knew and I was a better person for knowing them. A much better version of myself.

"I would do anything for you," Ben said softly. "I know I've said that before, and I will say it again, and again, and again until you believe it. There is no one in the world like you and there never will be."

He meant that as a compliment, but it was probably a good thing. Even the best version of myself was still a fucked up killer. On the other hand, I was surrounded by fucked up killers. Maybe they were the best kind of people and not the worst.

"There is no one in the would like you either," I said. "Like any of you. You're next level amazing and I love all of you."

"We love you too," Jake said.

"Yes we do," Cooper agreed.

"What they said," Hutton said.

"Same with me," Ben said softly.

I smiled at each of them in turn and kissed Ben lightly on the mouth.

"It looks like we're about to get our answer," Jake said.

I looked over as the Quinn brothers got to their feet.

Kian walked over to us. Tyler and Reed followed along behind like they were more than happy to let their brother do the talking. What must it be like to work so closely with siblings? They didn't always get along, but at the end of the day, they had each other's backs. It sounded like both the best and the most infuriating arrangement imaginable.

"We've decided we will help," Kian said. "You look as though you have decided on some sort of plan."

I wondered if they spent all that time conferring, or just waiting for us to get our shit together.

Either way, I nodded.

"Yeah, we've come to a decision. Not everyone agrees with it, but it's what we are going to do. Your help would be very much appreciated, and useful."

Kian nodded. "What do you need?" He spoke carefully, as though he still hadn't quite decided the extent of his assistance.

"That's easy," I said lightly. "I need you to declare war on us."

CHAPTER
SEVEN

"Are you sure about this?" Jake asked. "It seems a bit... extreme. Even for us." The wry expression on his face said it all. That was saying something. We'd done some pretty wild things over the years.

Selling my virginity so I could raise the money I needed to get away from Helen Dagen was only the beginning. I had no idea then, that my dreams of building my parent's empire back up would actually happen, much less on the scale it did.

I also had no idea that along the way, I'd meet four incredible guys, much less give my heart to all of them. Wait, did that mean I actually had a heart after all? I guessed it did. The jury was still out on whether or not I had a soul.

"It's very extreme," I agreed. "But it's necessary. It'll work." It had to. Plans B and C weren't options, as far as I was concerned. I didn't get where I was without taking risks from time to time. Sometimes all you could do was roll the dice and hope you got the right pips face-up.

"I hope you're right." He clearly didn't like it, but he didn't argue against the idea either.

"I am," I said firmly. "Would I lead you astray?" I cocked my head and gave him a sultry smile.

"Gods, I hope so." His expression melted into a smile. The worry took longer to leave his eyes, but when it did, it was replaced with a heated look that melted my panties. We were clearly on the same page now.

I stepped towards him. "When you put it that way, how could I resist?" I put my hand to the back of his head and brought his mouth down toward mine.

Before he kissed me he said, "The cars will be here to take us to the plane in an hour." Always the practical one.

"Perfect," I said against his mouth. "That's just enough time, if we hurry."

That was bogus, of course. The cars and the plane would wait until we were ready. Still, it was fun to tease.

"An hour?" he echoed. "How fast do you think I am?" He kissed me, then left his lips to linger on my mouth.

I laughed. "Not just you. *All* of you. One at a time."

He pulled away, his eyebrows raised. I could see him thinking that nearly dying must have ramped up my sex drive to overdrive.

So maybe it did. Sue me. Or better yet, fuck me.

He didn't look as though he minded too much.

He glanced at the other guys. "Fifteen minutes each? Challenge accepted." He placed his hands on my waist and pulled me to him. He slanted his mouth over mine and claimed my lips in a kiss that melted my entire body against his.

He caught me up, lifted me and carried me over to the wide bed. For a moment, I thought he might throw me down. At the last moment, he lowered me gently, then lay on top of me with his legs on either side of mine.

The bed dipped as Hutton sat on the side of it. He made no move to interrupt. Instead, he silently stripped off his clothes down to his boxers and watched.

I didn't know which was hotter, him, or him watching. Either way, my overdrive switched up a gear. I needed to be touched and I needed it now.

After a minute, Cooper stripped down too and sat beside Hutton. Oh yeah, it was definitely getting hotter in here.

Ben hung back a bit, like he felt the need to watch over us all. His pants were stretched almost to breaking point at the front.

Jake slipped his hands up my blouse, pushing it up off my breasts. He teased one of the cups of my bra down and tickled my nipple with the tip of his tongue.

A quiver passed all the way through me. If my pussy wasn't already slick before, it was now. Dripping with molten heat.

Jake pushed himself to kneel beside me and pulled my blouse up over my head and off. He tossed it aside and unhooked my bra to free my breasts.

"I'll never get tired of doing that," he said with a satisfied smile.

"I'll never get tired of watching it," Hutton said. "Or doing this." He placed his hands on the back of Cooper's neck and brought him in for a deep clash of lips and tongues.

Holy shit.

Ben sat down on the other side of us now. I guessed he could only watch from afar for so long. He took his shirt off, but he only had the front of his pants open. His curved cock was free from his boxers, but he only touched it lightly. For now.

Jake pressed me back gently and tugged my skirt down. He pulled it off my legs and left me in my damp panties.

He straddled my hips and reclaimed my lips. His tongue tasted all of my mouth, even my teeth, before he moved back down to graze his own teeth over my nipples. While he lavished attention on my breasts, he slipped out of his pants and bright blue underpants. His cock was one of the few places where he wasn't tattooed.

Yet.

He grabbed hold of the sides of my panties with both hands. Just when I thought he was going to tear them in two, he slid them down my hips gently instead.

"If I tear too many pairs, you might spank me," he said teasingly.

I smiled. "I might spank you anyway." I mean, if that was what he wanted...

He kissed his way back up to my mouth. "You're so beautiful," he whispered as he eased my legs apart with his knees.

I had no answer but to sigh as he slid the length of his cock into my wet heat. This was something I wouldn't get tired of. Not for as long as I lived. I would never deny this to either of us again.

I half closed my eyes and enjoyed the feeling of Jake filling me, before he started to move slowly, taking pleasure from my body as well as giving it.

Beside me, Cooper and Hutton kissed so deeply I wasn't sure if they'd stopped for a breath in the last few minutes.

Watching them was so fucking hot, I moved my hips in rhythm with them, driving Jake harder as he pounded all the way into the centre of my core. He panted out his nose a couple of times before his breathing turned to grunts from between his slightly parted lips.

"Gods, El, you feel incredible. I could take the whole hour—"

Ben groaned. "Please don't."

His voice was so strained, he pushed me to the edge of orgasm, but not quite over.

Jake, on the other hand, came hard, with long, fierce strokes which pulled all the way out, then slammed back in and ground his balls against my pussy.

He let out a loud cry like a warrior defeating his prey. A few more gentler thrusts and he sagged, panting beside me.

He was barely out of me before Ben grabbed my hips and

rolled me so I straddled him. I smiled down at him before I lowered myself onto his hard, curved length.

He shivered from head to toe as he slid deep into my body. The groan that slipped from his mouth was guttural, animalistic. For a man who was almost always in control of himself, this was when he let go. Nothing mattered right now but the way our bodies joined and how we made each other feel.

I placed my palms on his chest and rode him slowly, rubbing my clit against him. I kept my eyes locked on his face, even when he closed his eyes. His mouth curved up into a smile of pure bliss.

It faded when I rode him faster and harder, becoming a frown of concentration instead.

"Mmmm," he moaned. "Gods, yes, angel."

I smiled and brushed sweaty hair off my forehead. I doubted I looked much like an angel right now, but I'd take the endearment.

He put his hands on my hips and helped me to rise and fall higher and faster. The friction against my clit pushed me all the way into my first orgasm; a shower of multicoloured fireworks and soft moans.

Ben followed a moment later, bucking hard into my wet pussy. His hot cum made me wetter still. For some reason, that made me aroused all over again. I mean, what could be more enticing than having the juices of two guys inside me, and two more to come? Literally.

Ben fell still, panting before he helped me off and onto my back beside Cooper and Hutton.

I looked up at them both as they broke off the kiss.

They glanced at each other.

"If you're about to do rock, paper, scissors..." I growled.

"No," Cooper groaned. "I've already got rock covered."

I grinned. His cock was certainly so erect it looked painful.

He rolled me onto my side facing away from him and bent my

leg at the knee. He positioned his cock at my entrance and slammed into me with so much force I cried out.

"Gods, sorry." He put a hand on my hip and for a moment I thought he was going to apologise again and maybe pull out. Instead, he pounded into me as violently as the first stroke.

I watched Ben watching me as I took every single firm thrust and gave it back with a roll of my hips. On the other side of Ben, Jake propped himself up on his elbow and was also watching, a smile on his face.

I smiled back briefly, then closed my eyes and savoured the exquisite pain of Cooper ramming himself deep into my body.

His breathing was quickly ragged. He was close to coming. He pulled himself out and quickly rolled me over to face him. He hooked my leg over his hips and thrust into me like he hadn't even stopped for a breath. His hazel eyes were half closed and his lips slightly parted. He was always so fucking gorgeous, but even more so right now, lost in a world of love, lust and heat.

All the good things.

"Gods, Ivory." The words slipped out of his mouth, followed by a series of groans that sounded almost like he was in pain. He gritted his teeth and ground out another groan as he came. Every muscle in his body seemed to tense up, except those in his hips which ground him against me harder than ever. Finally he managed to suck in a breath and that triggered a series of pants before he blew out through pursed lips and relaxed.

"I will never, ever get tired of doing that. You are fucking amazing." He placed a gentle, lingering kiss on my lips, then pulled out of me and rolled aside to make room for Hutton.

"Lucky last," Hutton said with a smile. He pulled me up into a sitting position and sat facing me. He grabbed my legs gently and pulled me so my thighs were resting over his and my feet were on either side of his ass. He positioned his laddered cock at the entrance to my pussy and slid in slowly and gently.

I leaned back on my hands and lifted my hips up a little more to meet him.

This was a much slower way to fuck, but with his Jacob's Ladder massaging the inside of my body, it was no less intense.

I matched his rhythm. My breasts bounced with every buck. I leaned back on one hand and put up my other to hold them in place. At least that was the idea. I ended up teasing my nipple with the tips of my fingers. Between that and his cock, not to mention fucking three other guys before him, I rushed towards an orgasm and over.

Where the first was like multicoloured fireworks, this was like a shower of silver and gold. My back arched further, pushing me onto him even more.

I dropped my head back and moaned loudly, before I said, "Hutton," in a choked, breathless voice.

He responded with, "Babe," and bucked his hips frantically as he came, driving forward, then back onto his hands, then forward again. He was the last to spill his hot cum into me. And the last to sag and slide his cock free.

I flopped back on the mattress, sweating and staring at the ceiling. It was a good thing the cars would wait, because I needed a shower after that.

EIGHT

"Have I mentioned recently that this is a bad idea?" Jake asked.

"Not in the last hour," I said. Truthfully, I was starting to think the same thing. This whole thing could go really, really bad for me.

"In that case, let me say how reckless this is," he said. "In all the time I've known you, this rates somewhere in the top five craziest things you've ever done."

"What were the other four?" I looked at my reflection in the full length mirror. My crimson coloured blouse complimented my white hair and contrasted with the black skirt that fell to my ankles. Black kitten heels completed the outfit.

"Offering yourself up for auction is right up there," he said. "Taking on the Onyx Ridge pack in the first place. I don't know what else, but I'm sure there's at least two or three more."

"Compared to those, this should be a breeze," I said. I pulled out a stick of lipstick the same shade as my blouse and applied it to my lips.

He stood behind me so I could see and talk to his reflection. He looked more worried than I had ever seen him before. "I'm starting to think I should lock you in your apartment and leave you there until we get that rocket launcher."

I placed the cap back on the lipstick and put it down beside the sink. "You wouldn't do that unless you lock yourself in here with me. Then you would miss all the fun of blowing up Dagen's house."

His reflection smiled. "I don't mind missing all the fun if I get you all to myself." He put his hands on my shoulders and leaned forward so his cheek was pressed against mine.

"I *almost* believe you," I told him. "But we're talking rocket launcher here."

"I would prefer to have you play with my rocket launcher." He grinned.

I groaned at his pun. Personally, I would much rather stay here and ride his cock, but this needed to be done. When this was over, we would have all the time in the world for fucking.

I turned around to face him. "Is everything in place?"

His expression was immediately all business. "Yes. Everyone knows what they are supposed to do and where they are supposed to be. There is one major flaw in this whole plan."

"Only one?" I asked. "That's better than I expected."

The sides of his mouth drew back. "There's probably a shit ton, but there's one in particular I can think of. The last two times you drove yourself somewhere, things didn't go very well."

"Third time's the charm?" I asked lightly. I was torn between growling at him for commenting on my driving skills, and being nervous for the same reason. I couldn't help what happened the first time, when Dagen's goons ambushed Ben and me. It wasn't raining today, but it still wasn't a very good track record.

And, honestly, I couldn't rule out the possibility that someone in my organisation might betray me.

Like everything else I was going to do today, that was a risk I had to take.

"Elodie." He cupped my cheek with his hands and kissed my forehead. "I love you. Whatever happens today, I want you to know that."

"I love you too," I said softly. "I intend to be back here tonight for dinner. I'm sure you've already worked out something with the chef. Something healthy, no doubt."

"I might have." He looked cagey. I doubted he'd even thought that far ahead. Not today, when the way things might end was so uncertain.

"I'm sure it will be fabulous." Now I was just talking to put off having to leave. "You should get into place."

He sighed. "Only if you're really going to do this. It's not too late to change your mind."

"I'm doing this," I said firmly. Hutton, Cooper and Ben should all be in their places by now. I needed to get going before anyone wondered why they were where they were.

He looked like he had a thousand things he wanted to say, but the only thing that would come was, "Stay safe."

"You too." His role in this was only slightly less risky than mine.

"Always. That's basically my middle name," he said. "It's better than Lyle."

I laughed softly and hooked my arm through his. Together, we walked to the elevator and headed down to the ground floor of Crimson.

Staff bustled around, blissfully unaware of what their bosses were up to. I saw a couple who had worked at Scarlett, but who took jobs here while the restaurant was being rebuilt. None of them was left without a job. Most of them worked behind the bars, but one or two opted to work in the strip club, once they found out how much extra money they stood to make. They got absolutely no judgement from me. No matter what position they were in—no pun intended—my staff always got looked after.

Confident that everything was running smoothly, I left Jake there and took the elevator down to the basement garage.

Is there anyone on the face of the planet who likes walking around in these places by themselves? Even Ivory, the big bad wolf, who could look after herself most of the time, didn't like being in here alone. It was dimly lit, cold, and every sound echoed. If anyone was going to get the jump on me before we got this operation underway, they would do it here. At least in theory.

My car of choice today was a convertible MG, white of course, like the rest of my vehicles. For no particular reason, it was one I rarely drove. I made a mental note to drive it more often. It was a cute car, suited to zipping around the city.

I checked to make sure the back seat was empty before I opened the driver's side door and slipped inside.

It didn't explode. Bonus.

I slipped the key into the ignition and turned it over.

When it still didn't explode, I backed the car out of the parking space and pressed the button on one of my keyrings to open the garage door to the street.

The street seemed quieter than usual, but that was probably my imagination. Under the circumstances, it wasn't surprising if I jumped at shadows.

"Pull yourself together," I told myself. I couldn't afford any panic attacks, changes of heart, or anything that might fuck this plan up. "And keep it together." I could flip out when this was over, and I was alone, in private.

The drive was a short one. I could have walked, but we agreed on this instead. I pulled into a parking spot as another car pulled out of it. One hour parking should be more than enough. If not, I would pay the fine. It wasn't like I couldn't afford it.

I ignored my racing heart as best I could, and got out of the car. *See Jake*, I thought, *I can drive from one place to the other without getting into trouble.*

I waited, just in case my thought was premature. No one shot me, nothing exploded and no sinkholes opened up underneath my feet.

So far so good.

I locked the car and walked down the street a block. I passed several people who were heading in the opposite direction. A couple of them glanced at me, but most of them were engrossed in their phones or chatting to each other. None of them met my eyes. None of them looked twice.

I ignored them as well.

I also tried to ignore the sweat that sprung up on my palms as I approached the Lair. I paused long enough to nod at the bouncers who stood to either side of the door.

They both looked surprised and anxious, but neither made any move to stop me.

My chin raised with as much confidence as I could muster, I stepped inside the club.

The place was empty except for Luca Fisher, who sat at the bar smoking a cigarette.

"I'm pretty sure it's illegal to smoke in places like this." I slipped into the stool beside him.

He turned towards me slowly as if he just became aware of my presence. "I have to say, you have bigger balls than Alistair Dagen."

"Would that be difficult?" I asked.

He shrugged. "I dunno. Haven't seen his. Consider it an educated guess." He tapped the ash of his cigarette into an empty glass, while he took a sip on his drink. It looked like whiskey and ice, but it was probably apple juice. Sometimes we shifters like to pretend we're the cool kids.

"Where is the asshole?" I asked.

Luca took a puff of his cigarette. "Around. Like a cockroach. He'll turn up again sooner or later."

"He knew I was coming?" I asked.

"He suspected it, but he likes to cover all his bases." He finished his drink and walked around the bar for a refill. Just as I suspected, he pulled out of a bottle of apple juice and filled the glass to the brim. "Would you like a drink?"

"No thanks." I trusted Luca more than I trusted Alistair, but he was still a black wolf and an assassin.

"Suit yourself." He put the bottle back in the fridge and slipped back into his stool.

"I'd like to go on the record as saying I didn't hire you to kill me," I said. "At Dagen's country house, when I asked if anyone had ever hired you to kill them, I wasn't in my right mind at the time."

He nodded and lit up another cigarette. "Noted. And now you're wondering if someone else hired me to kill you."

"The thought crossed my mind," I said. "Would you tell me if they had?"

He considered the question for a moment. "I like you, but even us assassins have rules we have to follow. I can tell you this though, if I was, you wouldn't see me coming. So you're safe. For now."

"Good to know." I leaned my elbow on the bar. "I wondered what happened to you after the bush mysteriously caught on fire."

He chuckled. "Very mysterious. Alistair was pissed, to say the least. The whole place burned to the ground."

"Good," I replied. "It's a shame he didn't go up in smoke with it."

"Like I said, he's like a cockroach. He'd probably step right out of the ashes, good as new." Luca sipped his drink.

"You don't like him very much, do you?" I asked. "Have you

ever considered hiring yourself to kill him? You could save a lot of people a lot of hassle."

"Who would pay me?" he asked. He actually seemed to consider the idea.

"I would be more than happy to," I said. After a moment I asked, "What would the rest of the pack think of that?"

He tilted his head back and blew a smoke ring into the air. "This might come as a surprise to you, but I don't really give a shit what the rest of the pack thinks. Like you, I make my own rules and live by those. But I'm not gonna take that job. Want to know why?"

"Of course I do," I said. I hadn't expected him to take me up on my offer, but it would make things much easier. Alistair Dagen could be dead by morning. We could all sleep better then, especially me.

"I won't take it because you don't do things by sneaking around in the dark. That might be Alistair's preferred method, but it's not yours. When you take out Alistair, you'll want it to be in a way that ensures everyone knows who did it. The problem with hiring an assassin is that there is often a question mark over who paid for it. Believe it or not, there are some black wolves who would be happy to see him gone. Some who might be worse than him, so be careful what you wish for."

That was a risk I considered, but also one I had to take. If I cut off the head of the snake and another one popped up, it would take time for them to consolidate their power and repair whatever damage Dagen and I did to the pack. That would give me time to decide if they were a threat or not. If they were, I would end them. I wasn't going to let another Dagen rise up in his place.

I cocked my head at Luca. "You said *when* I take him out."

He feigned innocence. "Did I? How about that? Like I said, you have bigger balls than he does."

436

"You never told me how you got out before the house burnt down," I pointed out.

He put out his cigarette in the bottom of the empty glass and lit another. He took a puff and looked chagrined as he blew it out.

"Here's where I'd like to say I sprinted over to my motorcycle, threw myself onto it and wove through smoke and blazing trees. Somewhere in there, I jammed on my helmet, because safety first."

Ironic for a man who was on his third cigarette since I arrived.

"Let me guess, none of that happened," I said.

He sighed dramatically and blew another smoke ring or two. "Naw, I managed to get on board the helicopter before it left. I had to leave my bike behind. It's toast."

"Oops, sorry," I said. "I'll buy you a new one." Maybe I should feel bad, but I didn't. It was only a motorbike after all.

He waved his hand in dismissal. "Don't worry about it. I've replaced the old girl already. She was just about on her last legs anyway. But if anybody asks, I escaped on her and not on the helicopter like a fucking coward."

"At least you're alive," I said.

"Yeah. That's what matters." He breathed out a long line of smoke. "You know, for a white wolf, you're okay. Under other circumstances, we might even be friends. Or more." He winked at me.

Once, before I was involved with my four guys, I probably would have been interested in pursuing something with him. Just a night or two, nothing more than that. He was an attractive guy, smart and funny.

And a good judge of character since he obviously liked me more than Alistair Dagen.

I mean, it didn't take a genius...

"For a black wolf, you're not so bad either," I said. "There's still plenty of time for us to be friends though. Or at least allies.

Do you have family or friends who work for Dagen? How many of those will die if we end up in a full-blown war?" It wouldn't be a war like humans knew them. We would fight tooth and claw, not with tanks and guns. It would still be bloody, but with much less collateral damage inflicted on children or innocent buildings.

"You said you don't care what anyone else thinks," I continued. "So you shouldn't feel too bad about saving their lives by taking sides with the white wolves."

"Most of my family are assholes," Luca said. "Any wolf who dies defending Dagen probably deserves it."

"So you won't die defending him? " I asked.

He barked a laugh. "Fuck no. I'm only here today as a favour and because I'm between jobs right now. Not to defend him. Not to attack you either. I'm just...passing the time."

He cocked his head at me.

Once again, I had the thought that if I wasn't with the guys, I would be interested in him. Most hot-blooded women would be. He had the kind of hair a girl could tangle her fingers in. Right now, he had it tied back in a ponytail. He was no muscular beef-cake, but rather an enigmatic, charismatic guy.

"You look like you have something to ask me," I said.

"We know why I am here," he said. "But why are you here? Most people don't walk right through the front door of the enemy's territory."

"First of all, the Lair is my territory," I said slowly. "Or it will be as soon as Alistair is dealt with. And that leads me to my second point. I decided not to sit by and wait for him to do something. I thought I would come and have a chat with him."

"And by chat you mean..." Luca put out his third cigarette, pulled out another and held it in his hand.

"Just a chat," I said lightly. "I might give him the chance to surrender. There's still time for him to buy a little house in the country somewhere and fuck off out of our way."

"You know the chances of him doing that are none and zero, right?" he asked.

"I know," I admitted. "But it seems like the classy thing to do would at least be to offer. He wanted me to sign my organisation over to him. There is no reason why he can't do that for me. Imagine the power both of them combined would bring."

Luca made a face. "Too much power for one person. Even if that person seems to be not too shit."

I snorted softly. "I think that might be the nicest compliment I've ever received. Not too shit. I wish I could say the same for Alistair." This would be a lot easier if he wasn't a massive asshole. How different things might be if his parents weren't assholes too. My parents might still be alive. Divorced, for certain, but still, alive. Where would I have ended up then? I couldn't shake the feeling I still would have found my way to the guys, but everything else would have been very different.

"Well, if it isn't the Ice Bitch," Alistair Dagen's voice came from the doorway.

CHAPTER
NINE

I turned around slowly, as though I wasn't even slightly concerned by his presence. I congratulated myself for not having a panic attack this time. Instead, the moment I saw his face, I wanted to punch him in it. Or better yet, scratch his eyes out as he was raking his gaze up and down my body.

"Alistair. You're looking well. What a shame. I was hoping you would be in a shallow grave by now." I gave him a sarcastic smile.

"I could say the same about you." He stepped further inside, followed by four of his goons. Two I recognised, two I didn't. "Have you come to surrender or suck my cock again? Or both?"

It took everything I had not to react, except to say, "If you bring that thing anywhere near me, you'll lose it." Even if I had to bite it off.

He crossed his arms over his chest. "I'm surprised to see you back. I thought you'd run away for good."

"I didn't run away," I said smoothly. "I just took a break for a couple of weeks. I work hard, I deserve it. Maybe you should try it sometime. Have a break for a decade or seven." That should just about do it.

His gaze flickered over to Luca and he frowned. He clearly didn't miss the fact we had an amicable chat. Did he expect Luca to kill me when I walked through the door? I didn't mind it one bit if he was disappointed to find me alive. I planned to keep on disappointing him for a long, long time.

He turned back to me and smiled. "Have you been enjoying the presents I've been sending you? I know I have. I think my personal favourite was the sinkhole. Or maybe the footage." He shrugged. "I can't decide. Maybe it's a tie."

Maybe I should grab his tie and strangle him with it.

"My favourite was when my friends burnt your house down," I retorted. "You wouldn't know how that feels because you don't have any friends. Only lackeys."

He laughed. "That's ironic. You've surrounded yourself by a man you bought," he counted them off on his fingers, "one who bought you, a traitor and an employee. You call them friends?"

"No." I shook my head. "I call them lovers. It's the powerful witches I call friends." Close enough anyway. "You only have witches on your payroll, don't you Alistair? They wouldn't come and help you if you needed it."

"I wouldn't put myself in a position where I needed help," he said smoothly. "Whereas you seem to enjoy playing the damsel in distress role." He stepped closer to me. "Some people like being the victim. Like you. You seemed to quite enjoy being locked away. You and your bodyguard. You both got off on it."

"Keep telling yourself that," I said. "If you'd like to experience it for yourself, I'm sure I could find a nice, enclosed space for you."

"Are you offering to lock yourself in there with me?" He seemed amused by the idea.

I smiled sweetly. "No. But I'd happily lock you in there with Ben. He enjoys killing people. Slowly if preferred. Cooper too. The three of you would have a lot of fun together."

"You accuse me of having lackeys, but you won't kill me your-self?" he asked. "That seems a bit hypocritical, wouldn't you say?"

I gave him a smile that was all the more brutal because I smelled a hint of fear on him. It wasn't immediate, as though he thought I was about to lunge at him. It was more a general fear of death.

"Oh, I am more than happy to kill you myself," I said lightly. I turned my head slightly, while still keeping my eye on him. "Luca, is there a knife behind the bar?" There should be, for the staff to slice lemons to put in people's drinks.

"Yeah but it's a bit blunt," Luca replied. "It'll take a lot of upper body strength to finish him off."

While Alistair looked at him in outrage, I nodded. "His goons would probably step in before I got too far." I eyed them. The two I recognised looked like they wanted to use the blunt knife on me. The other two looked indifferent. They might not help me, but they might not stop me either.

Luca was right though, I couldn't overpower Dagen by myself. Not in person form anyway. Okay, not in wolf form either.

"You still haven't told me why you're here," Dagen snarled. He was clearly losing his patience and his temper with it. "Are you really so stupid that you would walk into my club alone? You're surrounded by six black wolves who could tear you apart in seconds." His anger melted into a dark smile. "Or have some fun with you first."

I rolled my eyes at the ceiling. "Threatening rape, how origi-nal. What happened to wanting to break me?"

"That's still on the table," he said coldly. "Maybe I'll start with your sister, Stella."

I managed to keep most of the cold shock that went through my body off my face. But I knew my eyes widened enough for him to see.

He didn't bother to contain his look of triumph. "You thought you could hide her presence from me? You should know better than that by now."

I probably should. "If you know she exists, then you must know she's my half-sister and we're not close. If this is the part where you threaten to hurt her in return for me doing something, then this is also the part where I remind you that you coined the nickname Ice Bitch. I don't give a shit what you do to her."

Most of that was true. We weren't close and probably never would be. If he somehow made her sign over any part of the organisation, I would be pissed. It would be nothing without my signature and Jake's, so it would be mostly meaningless. On the other hand, I objected to the torture, abuse or coercion of any woman, no matter who she was.

"I guess we'll find out," he said smugly.

My phone vibrated in my pocket, just once. That was a signal from Jake that he heard and would act on what Dagen said. He would send somebody, probably a group of them, to find and protect Stella.

"I guess we will," I replied.

Luca cleared his throat. "That's my cue to get out of here. Before blood starts to flow."

Neither of us was willing to take our eyes off each other long enough to acknowledge Luca leaving.

I wasn't sure what it meant though. I didn't think he factored into the number of wolves who would tear me apart if Dagen gave the word, but I also didn't think he would try to protect me. Why should he? He was in a sweet position where he was. Dagen trusted him, more or less, and I had no particular reason to turn my people on him. And it seemed like he followed his own rules most of the time. I wouldn't fuck with that either if I was him.

I leaned back against the bar and crossed my arms. "The reason I'm here is to give you a chance to surrender while you can. I don't see any reason why we can't sit down and talk like civilised adults, do you?" Except that he was not particularly civilised. Nor did he act much like an adult. More like a spoilt child.

"Let me see," he said slowly. "We're equal when it comes to destroying houses. I am one up on you when it comes to destroying businesses, one up on fucking that pretty little, hot mouth of yours, and one up on making you run away from that charity concert. It seems like I'm winning the war to me."

The side of my mouth twitched. "It might look that way on the surface, but if you look underneath that you would find out how fucked you're about to be. Not literally, because the last thing I would want to touch is your mouth. Sorry, second last thing."

The last thing was his cock, of course.

"You talk a good talk for someone who is as outnumbered as you are," he said.

I smiled. "Are you sure about that? You said it yourself, I would be stupid to come in here alone."

"Or arrogant," he said. "I have another one of those shifter dampening collars in my office. I should just snap it around your neck and see how long it takes to break you."

I held up my wrist and let my sleeve drop down far enough to show him the bracelet wrapped around it.

"I'm so sorry, but I came prepared. This will stop any magic, including artefacts like that. Not even a bonding stone is getting past this baby." I couldn't be healed with it on either, but that was a risk I had to take. If I was so badly injured I couldn't take it off myself, he could pull it off me anyway.

He actually looked disappointed. It was glorious, but it didn't last long.

"I can still break you, no matter what form you're in," he said.

I pretended to yawn. "You're repetitive, you know. Have you ever stopped to think about what would happen if we actually joined forces? We could be unstoppable."

"Why would I join forces with you when I've already joined

them with the Quinn brothers?" He looked smug. "I'm sure you were upset when you heard about that. The Ironhide pack has been very generous in sending men to help in the fight against you. When I said you were outnumbered, I didn't just mean here, in the Lair. I will give you one last chance to sign over all of Ivory Claw's assets. This could still be a bloodless takeover. If you refuse, then we will put down every white wolf in the state."

"Huh." I pretended to examine my fingernails. "Kian didn't seem that ambitious when I spoke to him last. His brothers either."

"Kian mentioned that he visited you in your home in Victoria," Dagen said. He looked like he couldn't decide if he was annoyed that Kian wouldn't tell him where that was exactly, or smug again because he apparently knew something he wasn't supposed to.

"Desperate times, desperate measures," I said. "You know how hard it is to get any of the wolf packs in the country to involve themselves in anyone else's problems. The grey wolves and the dingoes keep to themselves. The other white wolves prefer to keep their noses out of the way. The Ironhide pack was our last chance to gain allies against you. At best, I hoped to convince them to stay out of it."

Dagen was very pleased to hear all of that, of course. He took a few steps towards me. "So, you find yourself very much isolated. You know what I think?"

I raised a dark eyebrow at him. "I'm sure you're going to tell me."

And that was what he did. "I think you know you've lost. Maybe you can't bring yourself to admit it, but you know. You don't want to hand everything over to me because that would be an admission of defeat." He stepped closer. "Your pride won't let you face that."

He ran the back of his knuckles over my cheek. "I think you've come here because you want me to force you to give in to me. Because that is the only way you save face."

I stood frozen. The only thing I wanted to do right now was vomit on his shoes. His touch felt like acid on my face, burning and destroying.

He gripped my throat lightly, leaned in and whispered in my ear. "You want me to break you."

I should have grabbed that blunt knife from behind the bar when I had a chance. I could stab him right in his groin with it.

"I want you to die in the cold fires of the seventh hell," I said.

He chuckled. "You first." He tightened his grip on my throat and shoved me back into the bar. His erection dug into the side of my leg. His breathing was already ragged.

"You pretend you don't want this," he said, "but I saw your face in that footage. You came here today because you want more. I'm going to give you exactly what you want. I'm going to tear your pussy to shreds and leave you bruised and bleeding. And after that, you will still beg for more."

That sounded like a roundabout way to say he had no clue how to satisfy a woman.

His phone rang.

At first he ignored it. He held me in place with one hand, while groping at my breast with the other.

It was getting harder to breathe. All I wanted to do was scream.

His phone stopped ringing for a moment, then started again. He swore under his breath and shoved me away.

I staggered back and put a hand to my now tender throat. I should run, but it wasn't time for that yet.

He pulled out his phone and mashed his finger against the screen. He put it to his ear and barked, "What?" He listened and frowned. After a moment his frown turned into a scowl. "What the fuck? I'm on my way."

He turned his furious look on me. "I should kill you and be done with it, but..." He turned to his goons and nodded. "We have to go *now*."

I was going to comment that whatever was going on was obviously not good, but I was trying to hold back a laugh at the look on Dagen's face. I bet one man's cock never got so soft as his did right then.

To me he said, "This isn't over." He stabbed a finger in the air towards me.

Without another word, he turned and stalked out the door.

The moment he was out of sight, I sagged against the bar.

It took me a while to catch my breath and for my heart to stop racing. That could have easily gone horribly wrong. For a few moments there, I was starting to think Jake was right, that this plan was insanity. If the phone hadn't rang when it had, blood would have been spilt. At least some of it would have been mine.

I pulled out my phone and checked the screen as I started towards the door. There was a message from Jake that read, *Trying to find Stella. No luck yet.*

Just as I finished reading that, another one popped up.

This one was from Ben. *Target in sight.*

Following that was a text from Cooper. *Can I kill him now?*

I respond to that with a succinct, *No.*

He replied back a moment later with a pair of crying emojis, then a pair of smiling ones.

The next message that popped up was from Hutton. I opened it and was just about to read when I almost walked right into him.

He put out his hands to stop me, then drew me into a hug. "You definitely have bigger balls than Alistair Dagen. You might have bigger balls than I do."

"I'll settle for having a cast-iron uterus," I said without thinking. I sighed. "Proverbial uterus."

Hutton kissed my forehead. "We should get out of here, just in case he realises what's going on."

"Yeah," I agreed softly. What was going on was probably something I would need therapy for later. Not that any therapist would believe any of this. Certainly not a human one.

"Do you trust me to drive?" I expected him to say no, or laugh, but he nodded instead.

"You haven't held my past against me," he pointed out. "I'm not gonna hold one accident against you."

He stared at me when we stepped out into the sun. He stopped me and looked sideways at my throat. "Did that motherfucker—"

I touched my fingers lightly to my neck. "It's fine. Nothing I couldn't handle."

"Babe." He shook his head. "That's another reason why I want to rip off this guy's nuts and shove them down his throat. No one should be that rough with a woman. Unless she wants him to." His expression went from anger to wiggling eyebrows in the blink of an eye.

"I didn't want him to," I said. "But you—that sounds like an offer I can't refuse."

"You can totally refuse," he assured me. "But we can have a lot of fun if you don't."

I glanced up and down the street, but there was no sign of Alistair Dagen or his henchmen. They must have taken the bait. If they were lying in wait for us, Ben would have said so.

Assuming he was able to.

I shot off a text message to Ben and waited. When he didn't reply, I frowned at the phone for a moment, then sent a text to Jake.

Again I waited.

Nothing.

I shook my head and sent one to Cooper.

He responded a moment later with a shrug emoji and the words, *I haven't seen either of them.*

I looked up at Hutton with worried eyes. "What the fuck is going on?"

Hutton glanced around, then hurried me towards the car. "I don't know, but I have a bad feeling about this. We need to get the fuck out of here and regroup."

"Yeah." I let myself be herded, but I shared his bad feeling.

Something was fucking up and badly.

TEN

We reached the car without seeing more than a couple of apparently oblivious humans.

What must it be like to live in their world? To be completely unaware of magic, shifters, demons and the fact we basically ran and dictated everything that ultimately impacted their lives. They were probably better off not knowing.

I stood beside the car and tapped my fingernails against the window. I couldn't bring myself to get in, not yet. The guys wouldn't leave without me and I didn't want to leave without them. We could wait a few minutes.

I looked around me and smelled the air, but there was no immediate sign of any of them. Just Hutton and me. I managed to stop myself from chewing my lip. I was so anxious right now I would probably draw blood.

"They probably can't respond," Hutton said. "They're supposed to be keeping things quiet on their ends, right?"

I nodded. "You're right, of course." In answering me they might reveal themselves to Dagen. That would definitely defeat the purpose. The reminder didn't do much to ease my tension though.

"Are you okay?" Hutton moved around to stand beside me. He tangled his fingers in my hair and lightly kissed my temple. "It sounds like things got pretty intense in there."

"You could say that," I agreed. I was rattled, I didn't mind admitting that to myself. At the end of the day though whatever happened would have happened. Whatever sacrifice I had to make to secure my legacy for the rest of the white wolves and all the others who worked for Ivory Claw, I would make.

Some days I felt a whole lot fucking older than I really was. Like right now.

I was ready to give up everything to keep Dagen from taking anything from me. My body, my life, whatever it took. That was probably not a choice someone should have to make when they were still in their twenties, but here we were.

"I hope you realise how close I was to walking in there and ripping his throat out," Hutton said. "The only reason I didn't is because I knew you would be pissed at me." He gave me a level look. "Would you have really let it go as far as it almost did?"

I met his gaze. "If I had to. I knew when I made this plan what might happen. We all knew it."

"We didn't like it," he said. "If it was up to me, I wouldn't have let you near him."

"I know you wouldn't," I said. "I wouldn't have wanted any of you near him either. Sometimes in war you have to make the hard calls. What kind of general would I be if I let my troops take risks I wouldn't take myself?"

"An alive one," Hutton said. "One without a throat which is already starting to bruise."

"Bruises fade," I said lightly. "Dagen carrying out his threat of annihilating all of us would have a much more lasting impact. I will always do whatever I have to, to prevent the genocide of my pack. Wouldn't you?"

"That's the only reason I didn't storm inside and rip his head off his neck," Hutton said. "I have done some hard shit in my life, but listening to that was one of the most difficult. Listening and not acting. Imagining what was going on. It was probably worse than my imagination."

"It wasn't that bad," I lied. "Mostly just a bunch of threats and the throat thing. Nothing I couldn't handle." I doubted any amount of washing would get the smell of his hand off the front of my blouse. The memory of his fingers digging into my breast was seared into my mind, but it really could have been worse.

He could have ignored the phone.

I swallowed down my breakfast when it threatened to come back up. I had vomited enough meals because of that man.

"You're a very good liar," Hutton said. "But I can still tell you're not being honest with me. Or yourself. It's okay to not be okay. If that slime ball touched me, I wouldn't be okay. In fact, I'm not okay that he touched you."

I cocked my head at him. "Is this where you say you don't want anything to do with me anymore because I'm tainted by him?"

"Fuck no," he said quickly. "Nothing would make me stop wanting to be with you. Hells, if Jake can't scare me away, then Dagen sure can't. The only one who can do that is you." He gave me a lopsided smile.

"Good to know," I said. I wasn't planning on scaring him away any time soon. Not anymore.

I lightly kissed his mouth, but drew away as a car slowly drove past us. They kept on going and turned at the end of the street, but for some reason I felt even more on edge.

"One of them should have reported back by now," I said. "How long has it been?"

"About ten minutes," Hutton said. "It feels like a lot longer."

"It does," I agreed. It felt like about nineteen years. If they took any longer, I was going to get grey hairs... Oh, right. My hair was white anyway, no one would notice. In that case, I would get wrinkles. Lots of them. Not the laugh line kind either. The type that appeared when you frown too much.

"Maybe we should leave," Hutton said. He looked as anxious as I felt. His eyes kept darting up and down the street. "Sooner or later someone is going to notice us standing here and wonder why."

"It's obvious," I said. I put a hand on his arm. "We're standing here doing this." I slanted my mouth over his and kissed him deeply with my lips and tongue.

He wound his arms around me and kissed me back. He turned us both and pressed my back against the car. One of his hands wandered down my side and cupped my ass.

He pulled back for long enough to say, "If it wasn't broad daylight..."

"Who cares if it is?" I pulled his lips back to mine.

"Just in time to join in," Cooper said.

The sound of his voice made me jump and pull away from Hutton.

"Where the fuck did you spring from, Pup?" Apparently Hutton had taken to using Jake's nickname for Cooper.

"Out of the alley just there." Cooper waved a hand. He glanced around. "Where are Ben and Jake?"

"You still haven't seen them," I said rhetorically. Obviously hadn't, or he wouldn't be asking us.

Cooper shook his head. "Nothing since I texted you. Ben is probably still following Dagen." He looked at me with worry. "Are you okay?"

Oh, wonderful, I had invited a whole new round of being asked that question.

I smiled and tried not to look annoyed. It wasn't as though he did anything wrong. He just loved me, that was all. I was grateful for that. More than he would ever know.

"I'm fine," I assured him.

He tilted his head and looked at my throat, but didn't say anything. Maybe he assumed the bruises were from Hutton during the ten or eleven minutes we were alone. That would be a fair enough assumption to make. Much better than the truth.

"Are you okay?" I asked him. His job was to stay out of sight and let Ben and Jake know if Dagen walked past. And then meet me back here. He was disappointed to be doing the least risky job of the plan, but I assured him that at some point he would get to kill someone. Even if I had to find someone for him to kill.

He shrugged. "Yeah. He walked by without stopping. He looked pissed." Cooper seemed like he wanted to say something else.

"I know you wanted to jump out and kill him," I said. "But that wasn't the plan." I cupped Cooper's cheek and gave him a quick kiss.

"I know," he said. "I'm supposed to be the assassin. Sneaking around and killing people that way, not jumping out of alleyways and tearing them apart. Except for those cops." He grinned at the memory and I noticed the front of his jeans got tighter. The guy really did get off on killing. He was something else.

Luckily I liked something else. A lot.

I kissed him again, deeper this time. I couldn't help being turned on by seeing him turned on. But my worry about Jake and Ben overshadowed all of that and I pulled away reluctantly.

"I should see if Luca Fisher would help with your training," I said. When Cooper looked at me questioningly, I added, "He's one of the best assassins around. You have to be the best to be the kind of killer people know by name and on sight. He only sneaks around when he's working. Most assassins don't like their names being publicised, in case someone comes after them. No one with even a drop of sense would go after Luca."

Cooper's eyes widened and I knew he had another source for his hero worship. And another goal.

"I'd like to be like him someday. And like you. With a scary reputation."

He would have to harden a lot to achieve that, but it certainly wasn't out of reach. I would help him to do that in any way I could.

"Then that's exactly what you'll be," I assured him. "I'll introduce you two if I get the chance. *When* I get the chance," I corrected myself. As soon as I dealt with Dagen, I had a feeling I would be seeing Luca around.

"That would be amazing," Cooper said. "You're the best." He gave me a big, squishy hug. The kind that let me know I was loved and appreciated.

I hugged him back. "You're pretty amazing yourself."

"While this is all very nice, we really should get out of here," Hutton said. "My bad feeling hasn't gone away yet. If anything, it's worse now."

It wasn't until he said that that I realised I had the same feeling. It went beyond worry or even fear. I don't want to use a melodramatic term like impending doom, but that was what it felt like.

"I don't want to leave yet," I said with a shake of my head. "They might need us."

"I'll go and find them," Cooper offered.

I considered his offer seriously, I really did. But in the end I shook my head again. "I think it would be better if we stay together now." I didn't want to let either of them out of my sight, and I suspected they both felt the same way. Not to mention that if something bad happened to Jake and Ben, I might be sending Cooper in to meet the same fate. That would be stupid at best and devastating at worst.

"Okay," Cooper said lightly. He must have also been in two minds about leaving me and Hutton anyway. He never argued with me the way Jake and Hutton did. Like Ben, he usually just did what I asked him to.

I hoped he realised he had a voice and that I would listen if he had anything to say. There was a fine line between being treated like the boss and being treated like a lover. I was happy to wear the figurative pants in the relationship, but I didn't want complete control all the time. That would start to wear on us both eventually.

"We should at least not stand out in the open," Hutton said. "Let's find an alley or an abandoned building or a place you own or— Somewhere. Whatever. As long as it's a place we can't be easily seen. And attacked."

"Hutton is right," Cooper said tentatively. "Anything could happen to you out here."

Anything could happen to him too, but it was sweet of him to think of me first.

"Okay," I agreed. "You're both right. We are vulnerable out here." I couldn't guarantee that Dagen wouldn't walk back past us. I doubted he would fall for another phone call.

We could deal with him and four goons, but he might have picked up another few along the way. That would mean we could end up screwed. I preferred to know exactly what we're up against, and right now, I didn't. That was unnerving at best, and made me slightly cranky. I thought we'd considered everything that might go wrong in this plan, and put contingencies in place.

Okay, I wasn't that naive. There was always room for unexpected fuck ups.

"We don't own anything on this street, believe it or not." I squinted at the buildings which lined the road. As far as I could tell, none were abandoned, but it was difficult to see inside most of them.

"Want me to break a door down?" Hutton asked. He rubbed his hands together like he was ready to do just that.

"Nothing says subtle like breaking down a door," Cooper commented.

Hutton frowned at him. "If I didn't know better, I would think Jake is starting to rub off on you."

Cooper cocked his head adorably at the other guy. "I'm sorry, I didn't mean to sound sarcastic." He gave Hutton a quick kiss on the mouth that almost set my panties on fire.

Damn.

I cleared my throat. "Cooper is right, though, it wouldn't be subtle. Let's try to find a place and hunker down for a while." That was appropriate, considering they were both hunks.

"The alley I was in might be safe enough," Cooper said. "It was smelly enough."

I realised he was right. He must have been closer than I realised the whole time, but I couldn't smell him. In wolf form I probably would, but in person form my senses were not as sharp.

"A nice, dark alleyway." Hutton wiggled his brows at me.

"What?" I asked him. "I was the one who wasn't bothered by fucking out in broad daylight. If Jake and Ben would just text me back..." I glanced at my phone. Still nothing.

"They'll be okay." Cooper slipped his hand into mine. "They're both careful and probably invincible."

I knew they were the first, but I wasn't so sure about the second. I would feel a lot better if they were.

The problem was, none of us were invincible. The upside of that being that neither was Dagen. At least, I hoped he wasn't. I heard rumours once about paranormals who, while not exactly invincible, were long lived and extremely powerful. That same rumour said they were rounded up by the Witch's Council and killed, or taken away somewhere. Apparently they thought they were demigods of some kind. That would explain why the council wanted to get rid of them. Most witches I knew thought they were only half a step below being gods themselves. They wouldn't want anyone else to threaten their existence or egos.

At any rate, I was almost certain Dagen wasn't any kind of demigod. He was just a regular, asshole shifter.

"If anything happened to them we would know, right?" Cooper asked.

"Of course we would," Hutton said quickly.

Yeah, I would know exactly what was happening with Ben if I hadn't had Paxton break our bond. I still couldn't quite bring myself to regret breaking it, but it would have come in useful right about now.

"We would absolutely know," I agreed. There was no way any of my guys could die without me knowing it. There must be rules about things like that, surely? If not, then there should be.

I wrinkled my nose as we stepped into the alley. Cooper wasn't wrong about the stink. If I guessed correctly, something died in here, possibly not recently. Maybe several somethings. While I liked the smell of blood and wasn't bothered by death, the stench of decay was revolting.

"No wonder I didn't know you were here," I said to Cooper. "I feel like I should apologise for putting you here in the first place."

He shrugged. "It was Jake who put me here. It doesn't bother me too much. I've smelled worse things."

"Like what?" I couldn't think of anything worse than this.

"Reed Quinn's cigars," Cooper said. "Rotting potatoes. Some people's armpits. Not yours, of course," he added quickly.

"Of course," I echoed. I would have been offended if he hadn't clarified his comment. No one wanted to think they were on par with an alley full of decay, especially me.

"This is the least sexy place I've ever been," Hutton remarked. "And that's saying something considering I've been basically in hiding for the last few years. I've seen some pretty shitty places."

He sounded so sad I put my arm around him. He rested his head lightly on top of mine.

"Like where?" Cooper asked. Apparently he hadn't picked up on Hutton's vibe.

"I'll tell you about it later," Hutton said. "It's a long, ugly story. I wish I had come back to the pack long before this. If I thought it would go the way it did, I would have."

I squeezed him a little tighter. We all had stories to share, some less pretty than others. When this was all over, hopefully we would have a chance to tell them and to listen. Or at least to be there for each other. Not all stories needed to be told. There were things about me even Jake didn't know, and never would. That went both ways. And that was okay.

"You're here now and that's what matters," I said. "I love you."

"I love you too," Hutton and Cooper both said at the same time.

We all laughed.

"Awww, you love me?" Hutton said to Cooper. He only seemed to be half teasing.

"I—" Cooper swallowed. He looked at me. "I mean..."

"It's okay if you do," I said lightly. "If I can love four guys, then why shouldn't you love each other? Love isn't a cake; once it's cut up into slices, that's it. Love is bigger and more flexible than that. Love is whatever you want it to be."

"That's beautiful," Cooper said softly. "I—"

Whatever he was about to say was interrupted by the sound of my phone ringing.

ELEVEN

I almost jumped out of my skin. I glanced at the guys before I tugged my phone out of my pocket and looked at the screen. I was expecting to see Jake's or Ben's names under the tempered glass screen protector.

Instead, it was Dagen's.

"Fuck." I was tempted to ignore it. I didn't want to hear the sound of his voice or the bullshit that was bound to come out of his mouth. He probably wanted to thank me for turning him on or some shit. Ugh.

On the other hand, talking to him might distract him long enough for Ben and Jake to carry out their part of the plan. If they could get close enough and everything else was in place...

I sighed, accepted the call and put the phone to my ear.

"Alistair. What the fuck do you want?" I asked.

He clicked his tongue. "Elodie, can you not be classy once in a while? Or at least more friendly to a fellow businessperson. You're always so aggressive. It's not attractive in a woman."

"We're not friends," I said coldly. "I have no reason to show you any kindness or respect."

I thought of him more as something I would scrape off the bottom of my shoe. That was appropriate given the stink in the alley. I might have to throw away my shoes after this. That was a depressing thought but I replaced it with a more pleasant one; that the smell of rot and decay would soon come from Dagen's body.

"I certainly don't want to attract you to me." I grimaced in revulsion. His apparent obsession was bad enough.

"I don't want your kindness or respect, bitch," he said. "I much prefer you to fear me. That's a lot more fun, wouldn't you say?"

I rolled my eyes.

Hutton and Cooper gave me questioning looks.

I shook my head and shrugged. "What do you want?" I asked again. "If this is just a nuisance call, I'm going to block you. I have better things to do than deal with your shit."

"You'd much rather deal with me in person, wouldn't you?" he asked. "The phone is so impersonal. Although I would be happy to send you dick pics. I know that's your favourite part of my body. Especially near your mouth."

I pulled the phone away from my ear and made a gagging face. "Unless you carry around a microscope, then it would be hard to take a photo of that."

"Hard is the word, Elodie," he said. "Don't pretend that isn't the way you like me."

"The only way I would like you is if you were dead," I said dryly.

"So that was your endgame today was it?" he asked. "I have to admit, I should have realised you had some silly little plan you were trying to carry out. That phone call that drew me away just in time. I should have known that wasn't coincidental. But I bought it. Shame on me. I should have ignored it and fucked you instead."

He paused for a moment before he added, "I'm sorry for that. I'm sure you're disappointed to have had our time cut short."

"Absolutely devastated," I said sarcastically. "I'm not sure I'll ever recover from the disappointment."

"Luckily we have plenty of time to recreate that magic," he said. "Where are you?"

I snorted. "As if I'm going to tell you that."

"I know you're not far," he said as though he hadn't heard my answer. "I would have heard your car."

I frowned. My car wasn't that loud. What the hells was he talking about?

"I can almost hear you thinking," he taunted. "No, I'm not talking about the car engine. I'm talking about the explosive my people put under it. If you turn the engine on, you'll see what I mean. Although, if you're going to do that, let's say our goodbyes now."

I glanced at Hutton and made a face. There was a possibility Dagen was bluffing, but if he wasn't, we came close to being blown to smithereens.

"I have an idea," I said lightly. "How about *you* turn the engine on? If you don't explode, then I know I can kick you out of my car and onto your ass. And if you do, well, no loss. Except my car. I'm fond of her."

"I have a better suggestion," he said. "Have your traitor or your boy toy start the car. There's a camera across the street from it, so I can enjoy watching *them* be blown up."

"You have a fucked up idea of entertainment," I remarked. "I'm starting to think Dagen blood is tainted by psychopathy. Both of your parents had it. Your aunt and uncle certainly did. You have it. Putting you down might be a kindness."

"Psychopathy," Dagen echoed. "That's a long and educated word for a woman who made her fortune by spreading her legs."

"I guess I better hang up to give you time to look it up and see what it means," I said. "Or better yet, I'll just tell you. It means you're a fucking psychopath. Or in terms you can understand, a nut job. Should I dumb it down a bit further?"

"No," he replied. "I think we are now at a level you can understand as well. And your boy toy. Oh, wait a minute. He is better educated than you are, isn't he?"

"There are all different kinds of education," I said. "Some of us learn at school, and some of us learn from life. Plenty of people have expensive educations and are still as dumb as fuck. Like you, Alistair. Didn't you go to the most exclusive boys' school in the state? And the best university as well? The things money can buy."

If I recalled correctly, he did a degree in English literature or something like that. Cool, I might make him quote Shakespeare while the guys tortured him. His last hours would be classy and educational. Win-win.

That was probably just as well he studied literature, really. The idea of him as a doctor or some kind of scientist was scary as hells.

"Money bought you," he pointed out. "And your boy toy. Tell me, does he resent being owned?"

I rolled my eyes again. "He's not owned. He is with me because he wants to be. Because I don't have to force myself on anyone."

"If you say so," Dagen said. "You might want to have a talk about that later, just to be sure. I mean, he probably feels at least obligated. Although, you are undeniably a beautiful woman. You certainly have a beautiful, tight mouth. Why would he not want to stay around a slut like you?"

I heard a strangled sound of anger in the background of the call. I frowned. I knew he wouldn't be alone, because he was always in the company of his goons, but that sounded like...

"Someone doesn't agree with you," I said carefully.

"Ahhh, I almost forgot. I have a couple of your friends here with me," he said.

His words chilled me all the way down my spine. My stomach turned to water.

"What are you talking about?" I asked.

"Let me show you," he said.

He hung up the call.

I pulled the phone away from my ear and looked at the screen as the request for a video call popped up.

I glanced at the phone with trepidation, a word which, in spite of Dagen's digs, I actually knew how to spell.

Cooper and Hutton arrayed themselves behind me, so they could see the screen as well.

"What is it?" Cooper asked.

"I don't know." I tapped the screen and Dagen's face appeared in a square in the centre. He looked even more smug than usual, which was saying something. He pretty much wrote the book on smirking. He should have gone into politics.

He illustrated that point by giving me a smirk. "There you are. And your traitor and your boy toy as well. How nice. You know, you should smile more often."

"I smile all the time," I said. "When I have something to smile about." There was nothing about looking at him that made me happy.

"Well, you'll definitely smile about this." He must have flipped the camera on his phone to the back camera. Instead of his face, I saw the side of a building.

He lowered the phone and my heart stopped.

Cooper let out a little choked noise and Hutton sucked in a breath.

Inside the square on my screen were Jake and Ben. Both were on their knees, their hands clasped behind their heads. They wore matching, steely expressions, which gave away little about the way they were feeling. Except for an edge of anger around Jake's eyes. And half a drop of fear in Ben's.

I stared. I couldn't get my head around what I was seeing. Thank the gods they were alive. They seemed to be unhurt, but... My heart raced and my palms started to sweat.

This was definitely *not* part of the plan.

"I'm sure you were wondering where they got to," Dagen said. He turned the camera back to himself. "When I realised you were up to something, it didn't take much thought to realise they were lurking around. It was just as easy to get them on their knees as it was to get you on yours. Maybe they also like sucking cock. Unfortunately for them, neither of them is my type."

"What do you want, Alistair?" I asked. "Do you want me? Fine. I'll swap them for myself. I'll do whatever you want as long as you don't hurt either of them."

Both through the phone and from the guys behind me, I heard mutters of outrage.

"You can't," Cooper whispered.

"Elodie no," Jake said. He sounded frantic. Of course he would. He would give up his life for me. But I would do the same for him. And for Ben.

"Keep him down," Dagen snapped. One of the guys must have tried something.

I heard a grunt of pain and Dagen nodded in satisfaction.

"Who said it's hard to get good help? I haven't had any trouble at all. It might interest you to know that several of the men with me right now work for the Quinn brothers. They sent them up to help me. They've been very useful."

"I'll remember to kill one of them the next time I see them," I said darkly. "Or one of my people can. I'm sure you don't plan to keep me alive for very long if I give myself up to you."

"Only for as long as we're having fun," he agreed. "Or more to the point, as long as I'm having fun. I don't give a fuck about your pleasure."

I would have made a joke about his lack of skills as a lover, but none of this was funny right now.

"Just tell me where to go," I said. "Let them go and I'll meet you there. No tricks. No nothing. Just me. That's what you want isn't it?"

I wouldn't cry or panic. I put on my best ice wolf calm, lifted my chin and stared right into the phone at his repulsive face. The face that would have been handsome if he wasn't such an evil son of fuck.

"It might be," he said smoothly. He looked like the proverbial cat that got the cream. Or the dog that got the juiciest, fattest steak. Or the... Whatever.

What mattered right now was that he let the guys go. They would deal with him later, without me. I had no doubt of that. I didn't even care what Dagen did to me anymore. I would lie there and take it, as long as Jake and Ben were okay. That was all that mattered.

"Maybe I would prefer to have you *and* them," he said.

"The whole organisation will fall apart without me," I lied. "You get me, you win. I'll sign over everything. I'll suck whatever you want me to suck." It was hard not to shudder at that.

Okay, maybe I wasn't all right with him doing whatever he wanted to me, but I would still make that sacrifice for my guys.

"Babe," Hutton said softly, "we can't let you do this. You know Jake and Ben won't want you to do it either."

"Hutton is right," Cooper said. "Ben told me once that you're more important to him than his life. I know Jake feels the same way. Ivory Claw needs you. *We* need you."

By the time he got to the end of that, he was begging. He sounded like he was about to cry.

Hells, *I* was about to cry. I couldn't. I had to hold it all together.

I lowered the phone and turned to face them, chin raised. "I am still the boss around here. If I decide to sacrifice myself to save my people, then you have no choice but to respect that. What kind of leader would I be if I left them to die?"

"An alive one," Hutton said dryly. "One with an organisation to run and a shit load of other hard choices to make. We all knew what we were getting into. Especially those two guys. Do you think either of them will forgive themselves if they go free and you don't?"

He gave me a harder look than I had ever seen on his face before. "Do you have the right to make that choice on their behalf?"

"Yes, I do," I said firmly. "I have every right. I have always taken responsibility for the choices I've made, and that will never change. Not ever." Even if I woke up the next day chained to Dagen's bed and bleeding from all my holes. As long as the guys walked away from it, then it would be worth it.

"Isn't that sweet?" Dagen said sarcastically. "How about all three of you come here? There is no reason why we can't all have a good time together."

"Not going to happen," I said.

"What if I take Ivory's place?" Cooper offered. "I'll even sell my garage to you instead of her."

Dagen snorted derisively. "I have no use for that shit hole. I only wanted to buy it to piss Ivory off. I will take you as well as her. It might be fun to see how many toenails I could pull off you before you scream."

Yep, he was mentally healthy. *Not.*

Okay, I admit I would have a good time finding out how many toenails I could pull off Dagen's feet, but I didn't go around threatening people with it. That was totally not the same thing at all. Right?

"Probably one." Cooper scratched the side of his head. "I have a very low pain tolerance."

"What a surprise," Dagen said sarcastically. "You're a pathetic ballsack."

At least he didn't call Cooper a pussy. Those are way stronger than any balls. As insults go, it's not a good one.

"I'm starting to think this guy isn't very nice," Cooper remarked.

"Right?" I agreed. "This is what I've been telling you since we met. And exactly why I need to get Jake and Ben away from him. At best, Dagen will bore them to death by reading some two hundred year old poetry."

"I prefer Gothic horror," Dagen said. "'Quoth the raven, nevermore.'"

"I've met Raven," I said. "I've never heard her say nevermore." Raven was the head of an organisation called Raven's Gate. They took in young, often homeless paranormal people and trained them to use their skills and be productive members of society.

Raven was a title, rather than her name, but who knew what her actual name was? Like me, she preferred to keep that detail a secret. Every so often, she would request a meeting to ask for help with a young shifter whose skills I could make use of. In return, I helped fund her organisation. Without them, there would be any number of shifters, witches and demons running around out of control. Or worse, working for people like Dagen and Zeta.

"It doesn't surprise me that you like horror though," I added. "You seem to enjoy creeping people out."

"I like to keep people on their toes," Dagen agreed. "Which is why I considered your gracious offer of surrender. But I'm not sure I want to accept it." He looked squarely down the phone at me.

"Your bodyguard was supposed to die a couple of months ago. It doesn't seem fair that he cheated that fate." He turned his face away.

I assumed he was looking towards my guys.

"As for you, Jacob Blakesley, you've been a thorn in my side for the better part of a decade. As much as your bitch has been. I call you lapdog, but I know you're just as much behind everything she does as she is."

"Don't call her bitch," Jake growled. "I don't care what you do to me, cunt, but you're not going to lay a hand on her ever again."

If Jake's tone didn't tell me how angry he was, his use of *that* word was. He knew how much I disliked it, especially to describe someone like Alistair Dagen. He didn't deserve to be called a woman's body part, especially something as badass as a pussy. Ballsack was much more accurate.

"How funny," Dagen said. "You actually think you can stop me, don't you? You all do. It's long past time for a wake-up call."

He came back into view and reached for something.

I squinted. It was a gun, handed to him by one of his men.

Holy fuck.

My heart stopped cold. "No. Tell me where to go. I'll come to you. I'll do whatever you want, I swear." I blinked back a haze of tears. Oh gods, this couldn't be happening. "Please."

"You'll do that anyway," Dagen said. He gave me a last smirk and ended the call.

"Wait. *No.*" My hand trembled.

Everything was silent for several heartbeats.

Then somewhere out in another street, the sound of a gunshot rang out.

A moment later it was followed by another one.

CHAPTER
TWELVE

I stood frozen for what felt like the longest time. It was probably no more than a handful of seconds.

Then I started to crumble.

Hutton grabbed my phone just before it slipped out of my fingers. "Babe."

Whatever, who cared if it fell on the ground and shattered to a thousand pieces? My heart was in at least as many as that right now.

My knees buckled under me. If Cooper hadn't caught me, I would have collapsed onto the filthy pavement.

Instead, he sat and pulled me onto his lap.

Together, we sat in stunned silence.

I couldn't even begin to get my head around it. This couldn't be happening. I must have imagined it. None of this was real. It couldn't be.

But the sound of gunshots rang in my ears. Until the day I died, I would hear them, one after the other.

Bang.

Bang.

I didn't need the bond to tell me Ben was gone, I would hear it every time I closed my eyes.

And Jake...

I couldn't start to fathom how I could possibly go on without him. He knew the ins and outs of the organisation, probably better than I did. I was the boss but he was the keystone that held the whole thing together. Without him, what was the point of any of this?

What was the point of living?

I gradually became aware Cooper was shaking. No, not shaking, sobbing. He was silent except for the occasional hitch of his breath, but he wasn't holding back his grief.

Hutton crouched against the wall beside us, massaging his forehead with his fingertips. "Fuck," he said softly. "This is some next level fucked up shit."

"Yeah," I whispered. This clearly hit both guys as hard as it hit me. We all became closer over the last month, even Jake and Hutton. They still bickered like children, but I had sensed a growing respect between the two men.

Maybe because I told them if they didn't get along I would bang their heads together. They were a little nicer to each other after that. If I had done that sooner...

Hells, it wouldn't have changed anything that happened today. Nothing.

I wanted to cry as hard as Cooper was, but all I felt was numb. The tears that trickled down my cheeks when I was talking to Asshole had dried. The salt felt like a crust on my cheeks. Or maybe my face was numb as well. I didn't know. I didn't care. Nothing fucking mattered anymore.

I leaned back against Cooper. He put his arms around me. I closed my eyes. Maybe, just maybe, if I never moved from this spot, then I wouldn't have to accept any of this was real. Surely it was all a nightmare? I would wake up and find myself in a nice, comfortable bed surrounded by my four guys.

"Now can I kill him?" Cooper whispered.

I took a moment to respond, because answering might make all of this real. I didn't want it to be real. It couldn't be. If it was, the hole in my heart would never heal. I would be missing two big parts of myself forever. The jagged edges of that wound would always cut me to my core.

Fuck, I couldn't hide from the truth either. The cold, hard, shitty truth was they were gone. Somewhere is a street close to where we sat, Jake and Ben's bodies were already starting to cool. Their blood was pooling on the ground beside them. And Alastair fucking Dagen was probably laughing his head off. Shitty ballsack should have been strangled at birth.

"Of course you can," I said finally. "You can kill anyone involved in..." I couldn't say it. "Anyone involved."

I should have killed Alistair Dagen while I had the chance. That was the end game of the plan, but not the whole of it. We wanted to destroy the whole snake, not just the head. Just killing him would ultimately have served no purpose. Or so it seemed at the time.

That was a miscalculation I would regret for the rest of my life. It was one I would have to live with. I made the call. I had to own it. I would have to be the one to explain everything to our staff. I would take full responsibility for it and for the consequences of it.

Okay, I would put some of it on to Asshole. After all, I hadn't pulled the trigger.

But I might as well have.

I put a hand over my mouth and forced a few breaths in and out of my nose.

Could I have been more arrogant? I knew he wanted me, but I also knew he wanted Jake dead. And Ben too, if only because he knew what it would do to me. I shouldn't have let either of them get involved in this plan. Or Cooper, or Hutton. He would kill them too, if he got the chance. I should send both of them far away, right now. For their own safety.

"Babe, listen to me," Hutton said softly. "None of this is your fault. No, don't argue with me. I can see it on your face. This is all Dagen's doing. Every single bit of it. Remember what I told you. He likes screwing with people. Right now, he's laughing because we're devastated. Because that's the kind of piss weak prick he is. He's hoping we'll fall apart, so he can step in amongst the ashes and take everything from us."

He put his knuckle under my chin and lifted it so I was looking him in the eyes. "We are *not* going to let him win. Okay?"

I had no words to respond to him. Not right now. I shook my head and slipped my chin away from his touch.

Right now, I would be happy to jump into my car and start the engine. If what Asshole said was true, and there was a bomb under it, I didn't give a shit. With any luck, I would reach the first hell at the same time as Jake and Ben.

Although, knowing my luck I would go there and they would go to heaven, if there was such a place. I really didn't believe in any of those things, but I had to cling to the hope I would see them again some day.

Right now that felt like the only hope I had left.

Cooper was sitting perfectly still now. He leaned his head forward and rested it on my shoulder.

"Killing isn't so much fun when it's someone you love," he said softly.

It didn't surprise me that he loved Jake and Ben as well. The guy might have the biggest heart of anyone I ever knew. He would be so much better off if he never met me. Some pretty socialite might have bought his virginity. He could be spending his nights at parties instead of in a cold, smelly alley, surrounded by death.

"Death is bullshit when it's someone you love," I agreed. After my parents died and my heart turned stone cold, I thought I would never feel like this again. I didn't want to, it hurt too badly. Yeah, big, bad Ivory was scared to face loss. It was so much worse than any physical pain.

But then, I let myself care about Jake. I kept him at arm's length so I wouldn't have to face the pain of losing him someday. That was naive, of course. There was no way losing him wouldn't rip my heart out, even if we had just stayed friends.

When I admitted to myself how I really felt, I opened myself up to the chance of getting hurt. I let myself fall in love with all of them. Now I had to deal with the pain of losing two of them. It was so much worse than I ever could have imagined. A red hot poker through my heart would hurt less than this.

This... this was beyond any kind of agony I could ever imagine. And it hadn't even started to sink in yet. When it did... I shook my head. I wasn't sure I could face the next few days.

In spite of that, I wouldn't push Hutton and Cooper away again. Not now. I was done with doing that. Just because my heart was broken into a bajillion pieces didn't mean I was going to hide from my feelings anymore. If nothing else, we needed each other to get through this.

I needed them.

"Are you going to growl at me if I ask you if you're okay?" Cooper asked gently.

For a moment I considered doing just that, but then I shook my head. "I won't growl at you, but no. I'm not okay. I don't think I'm going to be okay for a while."

"Me either," Cooper said. "It's all right to not be all right though. Right?"

"Under the circumstances it is, yes," I said.

"Hutton, are you okay?" Cooper asked.

"Not really," Hutton said. "I know I've said this before, but we should get out of here. Regroup or... Whatever." He rose to his feet and offered me his hand.

I took a moment to collect myself, then accepted his hand and a gentle shove from Cooper. I wasn't sure if my knees would hold me, but they did. The moment I was upright, my Ivory persona snapped back into place.

Elodie could sit on the ground and wallow in self-pity, but Ivory had a job to do.

Hutton helped Cooper up as well. The pair hugged, then they both reached out and drew me into their circle.

I put an arm around either of them and leaned in.

"We'll get through this," Hutton said. "We're still a badass team."

"Yes we will," Cooper said. "We're Ivory's badass team. Dagen will regret the day he ever messed with us."

"He'll wish he was never born," Hutton said.

"I certainly wish he never was," I said dryly. That would have made all of this a whole lot easier. Or not, because someone would have taken over the Onyx Ridge pack in his place. We could have ended up with Gus or Helen Dagen in charge instead. Or someone like them. There were plenty of bad puppies in that litter.

"If I could go back in time I would make that happen," Cooper said.

"I would settle for going back an hour and making sure you all stayed back at Crimson," I said. "Even if I had to tie you all down."

"You would have had to," Hutton said. "There was no way any of us were going to let you do this by yourself." In spite of his words, he sounded regretful.

"I know," I admitted. "You're a bunch of stubborn bastards, aren't you?"

Hutton smiled faintly. "That's one of the things you love the most about us."

I tried to smile back, but he was right. I did like that none of them let me walk all over them, but it got Ben and Jake killed. Stubborn could only get a person so far.

"What are we going to do?" Cooper asked. "You want me to go and see if there is really a bomb in the car?"

I could hardly believe he would suggest such a thing.

"I'm not going to risk losing you too. That's exactly what Asshole wants." Even as I said the words, they sent a chill up and down my spine. If anything happened to Hutton and Cooper, I would be alone.

Vulnerable.

I didn't know what was worse, the fact I had become so dependent on them and their presence, or the idea of how fragile I would become if I lost them too.

Was it better to love and be vulnerable, or close yourself off and be tough? I decided that I didn't want either. I wanted to love and be tough at the same time. The three of us would draw strength from each other.

Together, Dagen wouldn't see us coming. Not this time.

Some day, the gaping hole in my heart left by Jake and Ben might even heal.

Who was I kidding? That would never heal. I doubted there would ever be a day when that wound wasn't raw and bleeding.

I swallowed back tears because Elodie cried. Ivory did *not* cry. Ivory focused and got shit done. No matter how hard it got.

I had to do just that right now.

I lowered my arms from the guys and took my phone back from Hutton.

"Enough feeling sorry for ourselves," I said coolly. "Our plan had a setback—" I gave Cooper a stern glance when he looked like he would argue with my wording. "A *big* setback, but we're not done yet. We have to finish this. Now."

I turned on my phone and opened the screen Jake set up a

couple of hours ago. I swallowed down a bitter knot of grief and anger. I could tap into that well of fury soon, but I needed to keep a cool head for the next while.

I pressed a button on my phone.

"This is the beginning of the end, Asshole."

CHAPTER
THIRTEEN

Against my better judgement, I stripped and shifted in that dank, stinky alley. The smells, which I almost got used to, hit me even harder when I was in my sensitive wolf form. So much so, I was able to tell the dead animal was a possum. Part of it anyway. Something had snacked on it.

I nudged my neat pile of clothing deeper into the shadows and hoped my mother's watch would stay hidden in the pocket of my skirt. It wouldn't be the end of the world if somebody stole it, but I would be pissed off. It was just a thing, a possession, but it was the last thing I had of my mother now the house was gone. Well, that and her good looks. I got my uncompromising stubbornness from my father. And, apparently a thing for having multiple partners.

With Cooper and Hutton on my tail, I slipped out of the alley. I took a moment to step over to my car and sniff the underside of it. Sure enough, there was something out of place there. Something metallic.

I would have someone deal with that later.

I trotted away and sniffed. The sulphuric smell of gunshots still hung heavily in the air.

I turned my muzzle this way and that, searching for the right direction. When I was sure I found it, I headed off at a swift walk.

Fortunately there is nothing better than the sound of gunfire to clear the streets. There was no one to see three white wolves slinking through the city of Sydney. The sun would set soon, which would give us a slight advantage but the black wolves an even bigger one.

Sometimes I regretted not being a black wolf myself. Or a grey or brown one. Of course, white wolves were the most magnificent, but we also stood out. Unless we were loping through the snow, then it wasn't a good thing.

We kept to the shadows as much as we could, sneaking behind parked cars and stopping in darkened doorways to sniff again.

At one point, I thought I lost the scent of those terrible gunshots. They got weaker and weaker as the minutes passed. I cursed myself for taking so long to reel and grieve. We should have acted immediately. That was another stupid miscalculation I had to own.

Hutton stopped at a narrow side street and whined.

I whipped around so fast I almost hit Cooper in the face with my tail. I trotted back to Hutton and bobbed my head.

He was right. The smell was down this way. Fainter, yes, but discernible.

I wound my way down that side street, stepping carefully. The sulphuric smell wasn't the only one I sensed now. I caught the edge of the smell I knew all too well. Black wolf. Lots of them.

The further I went, the more overpowering the smell was. Gradually it became stronger than the smell of nitroglycerin.

It didn't matter, I knew we were headed in the right direction.

I kept all my senses open, and moved more slowly. With the

number of black wolves I could smell, the chance of discovery was greater. We were too close to fuck up now.

I paused with one paw in the air and wondered if I should make Cooper and Hutton leave. They could get away from here while they had the chance.

The problem was, Hutton was right when he said the only way to leave the guys behind was to tie them up. If I tried to make them stay behind, they would probably wait a minute or two and then follow me anyway.

Stubbornness was both a blessing and a curse.

I resumed walking slowly, sniffing the air and listening carefully. Like any city, it smelled of human waste, exhaust fumes and food. The strongest sound was that of cars and trucks roaring past on nearby roads.

I darted behind a car when a bus rattled past.

Someone a couple of blocks away was playing music loudly. A band practicing, if their stopping and starting was an indication. They weren't bad. Another time, I might track them down and ask them to play at one of my clubs.

Those were the only signs of life in this part of Sydney. People must be hiding in their buildings, hoping there wasn't a shooter roaming the area. With any luck, no one bothered to call the police. That wouldn't surprise me. People often assumed somebody else we deal with a problem. If that was the case, then that would help us to stay unseen.

On the whole, the humans around us were totally oblivious.

We drew closer to the black wolves.

My nose twitched. I drew my brows in a frown.

Something was missing. Something big. Significant.

Blood. I couldn't smell it.

Were there so many black wolves they overpowered the smell of Jake and Ben's blood? Or had Dagen removed them that quickly? He probably had a black SUV handy to do the job.

Fucker.

I swallowed at the idea. Part of me would only believe they were dead when I saw them. If he removed and disposed of their bodies, I may never get that chance.

An edge of panic started to rise, but I shoved it down. In my line of work, I couldn't always expect closure. That was a luxury for people who kept out of trouble. And then not always. Life was never that predictable.

Hutton caught up with me and nudged my muzzle.

I didn't need words to understand his meaning. *We are close and I am here.*

I nudged him back. Unless I missed my guess, Dagen was at a small park at the end of the street. The kind where workers sat to eat their lunch and stare at their phones.

We could approach the park from several different directions, but I kept heading straight forward. I only needed stealth until we actually got into visual range of Asshole.

Then it didn't matter anymore.

I quickened my pace toward the corner and around it. The park was directly across the street.

I froze.

What the hells?

My heart stopped. When it started again, it rose.

Then it sank.

Dagen stood in the centre of the park surrounded by more men in black suits than I ever saw in one place before.

Kneeling beside them, their hands still clasped behind their heads, were Jake and Ben.

Alive.

I let out a sobbing whine of relief. The sight was the single, most beautiful thing I had ever seen in my life. I was so sure they were gone. Of course, I should have realised it was another mind fuck.

Fine, take that fucking point, I don't care. The guys were alive, that was all that mattered.

If I wasn't careful, my relief would be short-lived.

I lifted my head and trotted across the street in full view of all of those men.

Hutton and Cooper followed right behind me.

Jake and Ben watched our movements. They both wore the same expression on their faces.

I didn't need a bond to tell me they wished I'd stayed away. I was safe where I was. Now I stood right on the doorstep of the enemy's camp, as it were.

But this was still my territory, and I wasn't going to let Dagen dictate the terms.

I bobbed my head at them both and hoped I was able to convey my feelings with my dark brown eyes.

Judging by the expressions on their faces, they understood what I was trying to say. I saw the same look in both of theirs. Love.

I turned my attention to Asshole.

"There she is," Dagen said cheerfully. "You took longer than I expected. Did you take some time to cry?"

I stopped on the grass and looked back at him with cold, predatory eyes.

He no longer had a gun in his hand. The smirk hadn't left his face though. He looked more smug than ever.

"You're as predictable as ever, bitch," he said. "Did you really think I would make it that easy for these two?" He waved his hand at Jake and Ben. "I'm not going to say I wasn't tempted. A bullet to the head would rid me of two major problems. But where would the fun be in that? Now here all five of you are. Right where I want you."

He stepped away from his men and rubbed his chin. "Do you know what the funny thing is? You still look like you think you're in charge here. Like you still might win. Look around you."

He raised his hands. "You are more outnumbered than you have ever been. I hold all the cards. And the pack." He seemed to find his own pun hilarious.

I rolled my eyes at him, but he was right. We were very outnumbered. Jake and Ben knelt in the middle of a sea of dark suits. Had they bought out a bridal store? I certainly wasn't the bride, in spite of my white fur.

"I can see you thinking," Dagen continued. "You're hoping to try to find an advantage somehow. Maybe you're hoping to distract us long enough for these two losers to shift and run away. You might be hoping for an army of white wolves to come and rescue you. I assure you, I have people on every access point. If they see a hint of white wolf, I'll know about it. But so far, there is none. Why is that? Did you think five of you were a match for me?"

I stared back at him. I knew very well no one was coming. That wasn't part of the plan. Maybe that was another miscalculation on my part, but I couldn't change it now. My arrogance was definitely getting the better of me today.

"I like this side of you," Dagen said. "No smart ass comments. No insults. Just you listening attentively to me. Just as you should. I like my women well-behaved and meek."

That didn't surprise me at all. He would enjoy the type of women who would do whatever he said whenever he said it. Who would fawn over him and tell him how wonderful he was.

I wouldn't judge any woman for behaving that way, but it certainly wasn't my cup of tea.

"In case you're wondering, those gunshots went into the sky. Before that though, you swore something to me. Something about an unconditional surrender." He raised his eyebrow at me. "I'm sure you realise by now I don't need you to surrender. I have everything I need without it. The lapdog, the bodyguard, the traitor, and the boytoy. And the slut."

I was starting to hate that word more than I hated the word bitch. Just because I loved four guys and had sex with them all didn't make me any less of a woman. It didn't mean I was dirty, or tainted, or wrong. It meant I had more love to give than I realised.

"If you lay a hand on her—" Jake growled.

Dagen half turned around and chuckled. "What will you do? You aren't in a position to do anything. Speaking of positions." He turned back to me. "You swore to do whatever I wanted. Are you a woman of your word, I wonder. Shift and let's find out. You can prove you will do what you said you would do, right here, in front of all these people."

The motherfucker must have a short memory. I swore I would do whatever he wanted if he let Jake and Ben go. If he wasn't going to do that, then he could fuck himself.

I still stared back at him.

His expression darkened. "Shift," he demanded. "It's not too late for a bullet through one of their brains." He made no move to get another gun from any of his goons. "Shift." He was getting more and more angry.

I stepped closer to him. He took a step back and stopped. I would have won the staring competition, but he was right. I had run all my options through my head and had none left. I lowered my head and exhaled out my snout.

As I lifted my head back up, I shifted.

Dagen smiled. "That's better." He didn't even pretend he wasn't ogling me. His gaze took in my breasts and pussy, lingering on both before he bothered to look back at my face.

"That wasn't so difficult, was it?" he asked.

I tried not to look at the way his pants got tighter. "A gentleman would offer me their jacket. It's cold out here."

"We both know the cold isn't the reason your nipples are hard," he said.

Actually, that was *exactly* the reason. This man was fucking delusional.

I'm not going to lie. Standing there naked in front of at least two dozen men was intimidating. Some of them looked at me with open lust or disgust, depending on how pissed off they were at me in general.

Others looked away, some with respect and others with discomfort. Apparently not everything was rainbows and roses at Onyx Ridge pack HQ.

I caught Jake's eye. He looked pissed off, like he wanted to jump up and rip off Dagen's balls with his bare hands. That was probably exactly what he wanted to do.

I didn't blame him. I didn't want to touch Dagen's balls with my bare *anything*, but he deserved to have them ripped off painfully. Maybe slowly.

I gave Jake a smile and moved my gaze over to Ben.

He looked as cool and calm as ever. Did anything ever ruffle the man? I noticed a tightness around his eyes. There it was. The first sign something actually was able to get to him. Something that was definitely not good.

I gave him a smile too. They knew me well enough to see past my composed expression. They would know how happy I was to see them both alive. No, not happy, ecstatic.

With a whole lot of luck I would be able to growl at them later for giving me such a scare.

And then fuck both of their brains out.

I turned my eyes back towards Dagen. "The only way I'm going to cooperate with you is if you let Jake and Ben go." I surprised myself with how calm I sounded. "Hutton and Cooper have to be a part of that deal as well."

I didn't dare to look away from Dagen for long enough to see if the guys were still in wolf form or not. I assumed they were.

Dagen laughed. "You don't get to make any deals, bitch. Have you not realised that by now? You must be stupider than I thought you were. Fortunately, I don't give a shit about your brain. It's the rest of you I plan to fuck with." He gave my breasts a long look, one that would be considered inappropriate by most people.

Most *decent* people anyway.

Jake growled. "I swear to the gods, if you touch her, or even one hair on her head, I'm going to shove your head up your ass so far it will come out the other side."

I couldn't help but smile. I had to give Jake bonus points for creativity. He would probably do it too, or at least try.

Dagen snorted. "Is that the best you can do?" To me he said, "Your lapdog's insults are lacking."

I shrugged one shoulder. "I thought it was a pretty good one. But what he lacks in insults he makes up for in *so* many other ways." I forced myself to look in the direction of Dagen's groin. Ick. I felt like I needed a shower after just doing that.

Apparently that prompted Dagen to step closer to me. Close enough to touch my cheek with his knuckles. Close enough to whisper in my ear.

"How does it feel to know mine is the last cock you will ever have inside you?" he asked. "The last hands that will ever touch you? I hope you got your fill of them, because they will never fill you again. I can promise you that."

I forced myself not to shrink away from his touch, although it made me want to vomit. It went a long way past revulsion. My memory was kind enough to remind me of the way it felt to be on my knees in front of him. How it felt to be held down by three other men. The feel and the taste of him...

I don't know how I managed not to vomit on his shoes. Somehow, I even managed to keep the panic at bay. For now.

I swallowed hard. "Jake, Ben, Hutton, Cooper. It's time for you guys to go. Alistair won't stop you. Will you Alistair?"

Dagen glanced around at Jake and Ben. "Don't move. I will deal with you later." He turned back to me. "You will never stop being an arrogant bitch, will you? Right up until the end. Or do you have some delusion that I will let you walk away from this? That I would let *them* walk away from this?" The smile he gave me was nasty.

It soon faded, replaced by anger. "You have *lost*, bitch," he snarled.

I managed to keep my gaze and tone even. "I swore I would do whatever you want as long as you let them go. That's the deal. Take it or leave it."

I could almost see the wheels in his brain turning. He was almost absolutely certain I was bluffing, but there was a small hint of doubt in the back of his mind. He was clearly running possibilities through his head. He knew he had all his bases covered and it didn't take him long to dismiss his own misgivings.

He smiled slowly. "I have to give you credit for at least trying. If you were the sort of person who gave up easily, then this whole game would have been no fun. You haven't given up the fight. I like that." He leaned in and whispered in my ear again. "I like women who fight. The bruises around your throat right now are particularly charming."

"Fuck off," I told him. Of course, I realised he didn't like his women meek. At least at first. He liked them shattered. And he liked to be the one to shatter them. Fucking coward.

He chuckled. "That's exactly what you're here for, yes."

He stepped back, his eyes on my mouth, and spoke loud enough for everyone to hear. "Get on your knees."

CHAPTER

FOURTEEN

I regarded him for a moment, my back straight. Slowly, I bent my knees as if I actually intended to kneel in front of him.

The triumphant look on his face was sickening, but short lived.

I stood back up, looked around at all the black suits and nodded.

A bit over half of them threw off their suit jackets and shifted. Including the four who arrayed themselves behind Jake and Ben.

I caught a glimpse of a grin on Jake's face before he also shifted. Ben followed half a second behind.

"What the fuck?" Dagen stared at the black wolves around him, his hands outstretched as if that would somehow ward them off.

Several of them stepped towards him and growled.

It took him at least a good half a minute to comprehend what was going on.

"Fucking traitors," he snarled.

I smiled. "Not traitors. Ironhide. The Quinn brothers decided not to side with you after all." I spread my hands. "Surprise."

If I had my phone on me, I would have taken a photo of the expression on his face. It was a mixture of anger and fear. It was fucking gold.

He pulled himself together a moment later. "What are you waiting for?" he asked his men. "Deal with these traitors."

Being the fine, brave person he was, he shifted. He got a leg caught in his suit pants, but he managed to shake it off and literally turned tail and ran.

"Let's get this asshole," I said. I shifted back into my wolf form and found myself surrounded by my guys. All alive and more or less unhurt. I watched past Jake as Dagen's men also shifted and threw themselves at the Ironhide wolves.

They clashed with teeth and claws, and vicious growls.

I hesitated, torn between helping to take down the rest of the Onyx Ridge pack and wanting to go after Dagen.

Ridding ourselves of as many people loyal to Dagen as possible, was the crux of the plan to begin with. Of course, that included him, but he would be a lot easier to deal with without the rest of them.

The smell of blood and the sound of tearing flesh made it harder to think. My wolf instincts were kicking in hard. I wanted to join in so badly. To rip and tear and claw and bite and kill.

I could tell from the smell of them that the guys were feeling exactly the same way. Especially Cooper. He was barely hanging on to his own self control. If I wasn't there, he probably would have lost it.

Two black wolves right in front of us snapped at each other. They circled slowly around, teeth bared, hackles raised. Each searching for the right moment, or a weakness in the other. They were evenly matched.

To anyone who didn't know better, they might look almost identical as well. To me and the other wolves though, they smelled so different it was easy to tell who was an Onyx Ridge wolf and who was an Ironhide wolf.

The Ironhide wolf took a few steps back like he was being forced. The Onyx Ridge wolf, apparently sensing that he had the advantage, got cocky and lunged. The Ironhide wolf leapt aside and let the Onyx Ridge wolf land hard. He twisted and lunged, grabbing the Onyx Ridge wolf by the throat. He gave him a bone-snapping shake. Blood flew everywhere.

I couldn't tell if the Onyx Ridge wolf was dead or dying when he was dropped to the ground, but he was done for either way. Not even a witch could have fixed his wounds.

The Ironhide wolf bounded away to find another Onyx Ridge wolf to kill.

Jake butted me in the side of my head, just under my ear. He jerked his muzzle in the direction Dagen went.

It was clear what he wanted to do. Leave the Ironhide wolves to it. If I timed everything right, a contingent of white wolves was due to arrive any minute now anyway.

They could deal with what was left of Dagen's loyal goons. If there were any left by then. I had to give credit to the Quinn brothers men, they were fierce fighters. I had no doubt the women were too, but they had only sent men because Dagen wouldn't have let a woman infiltrate his organisation. The bastard was so convinced the Quinn brothers were on his side, he let their men work side-by-side with his.

Truthfully, until they shifted I wasn't entirely sure that Kian's assurance that he would help was legitimate. He could just have easily been playing me as Dagen.

I hated to think how big the favour Kian asked for in return for this would be. It was going to be huge, but I'd pay it. It would be one hundred percent worth it.

I bobbed my head to Jake and followed him in the direction

Dagen disappeared. The scent of him lingered in the air like a bad smell, but it wouldn't last.

Dagen was a coward, but he wasn't stupid. He would find a way to cover his tracks as soon as he could. What would he do then? That was anyone's guess. My only concern was that he had a backup plan of some kind. An escape route, another pack up his sleeve, so to speak. He might have anything and he might have nothing. When he ordered me to kneel, he seemed certain he won. Right there, in front of everyone, he would show them he had beaten me.

At this point I would rule out nothing.

I trotted between Ben and Jake, my head level with their front legs. Cooper and Hutton trotted right behind us. Honestly, I would have been happy to drag them all aside, shift back into person form and fuck them all silly. If it was anyone but Alistair Dagen we were after, I might have. I was absolutely determined that he wasn't slipping away. Not again. By the end of this, one of us would be dead.

I mean, he would be dead. I had no intention of it being me. Obviously.

Ben paused mid-trot, his muzzle in the air. He swung it this way and that, seeking the scent.

The rest of us stopped as well.

I sniffed the air and frowned. The stink of Dagen lingered, but now there was something else. Something I couldn't put my toe beans on. I looked questioningly at Ben, then at Jake. They both looked as confused as I was.

I nodded my head in the direction we were going before we stopped. Should we keep going after Dagen?

Jake hesitated for a while longer, then bobbed his head and continued down the street.

We moved more slowly now, careful. Mindful that it might be

a trap. Only because we were being so careful did we first feel the ground shake under us.

Following Jake, we all darted for cover under a truck parked by the side of the road.

I tucked my tail in tight to my back legs and let the guys press themselves in around me.

We fell still as something huge stomped around the corner.

Taller than the truck, the creature looked like something out of a science fiction movie. It had a brown hide like leather and huge, round eyes.

It might be something out of a nightmare, but it was also something out of my memory. Judging by the way Hutton froze beside me, he remembered it too.

The thing that stepped out in front of us in the rain.

The moment I realised that, I understood what the smell was. Magic, and a lot of it.

Dagen did have a backup plan. His witch. She created this monster.

I knew a few things about magically created creatures like this. Firstly, they could be conjured from a tattoo, a picture or a photo.

Secondly, they weren't permanent. They only lasted as long as the witch's power could hold it. That could be anything from a minute or two, to half an hour.

Thirdly, although they were little more than a sophisticated illusion, they could still kill us. And lastly, if we killed the fuck out of Irina, then this monster would disappear as well.

Since killing her was high on my list of things to do, that suited me fine.

The monster stomped closer to us. Since it seemed to know where we were, the witch must be close by.

I stuck my head past the truck's tires and sniffed deeply. The smell of magic was strong, strong enough to almost mask the smell of Dagen and the witch.

Almost.

They weren't far away.

Jake lifted a paw and pointed towards Ben, then Cooper. Then towards the monster, and down the street.

The message was clear. He wanted them to distract the monster and draw it away from me, him and Hutton. He sketched another motion in the air to give his orders as to what they should do next.

Both of them nodded. Side-by-side, Cooper and Ben darted out from under the truck and into the path of the monster. They stood in the middle of the street, taunting it for a while before they turned and bolted away.

The monster paused, clearly waiting for direction from the witch and Dagen.

Finally, it resumed its stomping toward the truck and us.

I cursed mentally. It hadn't taken the bait.

The monster leaned against the side of the truck and shoved. It rocked violently above our heads.

I pressed myself down as low as I could go, but kept myself ready to jump and run.

It shoved again, harder this time. The truck teetered to the side, but didn't fall. Again and again, the monster drove itself against the side of the truck.

Bits and pieces started to fall off it. A side mirror, chunks of the side door. The windows cracked and started to break. Glass rained down on the road beside us. If the monster didn't push the truck over, then it was going to collapse on top of us.

I was starting to think it would have been safer to stay and take on the rest of the Onyx Ridge pack, but the choice was made now. We would deal with this as we had dealt with everything else. Or die trying.

Jake looked directly at me and waved his paw towards the other side of the truck.

I shook my head. I wasn't going to run away and let him and Hutton stay here to be killed. Frankly, I might never let Jake out of my sight ever again. Or Hutton. Or Ben and Cooper once they were back in my sight.

Jake growled at me, but I stood my ground. I licked his muzzle in apology, but like it or not, I was staying.

Jake waved his paw again, this time to indicate that we should all be ready.

Now this I could agree with.

The monster bashed itself repeatedly against the side of the truck, almost in rhythm like it rocked back and forth. If we didn't know before that it was made of magic, we would know now. If it was alive, it would be in a lot of pain.

I almost felt sorry for it, as irrational as that was. It didn't have a brain, it was just a bunch of magic working to order. It had absolutely no control over its actions. What a shame we couldn't turn it against its maker.

Was that even possible? I didn't know. Honestly, I didn't really care. I already knew more about magic than I wanted to.

The monster stepped away a metre or two, then hurled itself back into the side of the truck. This time, it leaned heavily to the side. It teetered for a moment, balanced on its tyres, before it came crashing down onto the sidewalk.

The three of us bolted before the truck even stopped moving.

We loped to the end of the street and veered around the corner the monster appeared from.

The monster pounded up the road behind us, its footsteps shaking the ground and rattling windows and doors. If no one looked outside, they would assume the city was in the grip of an earthquake. A small one, thankfully, otherwise we might have faced dozens of people coming running out and getting caught up in our shit.

I hoped to find somewhere else to hide until the magic dissipated, but there were no parked cars here, no open doors leading into abandoned buildings and, unfortunately, no army of white wolves to back us up.

Just an open street leading through the city.

We were faster and more agile than the monster, but it kept coming. Eventually, we would tire but it never would. I made a mental note that when we got out of this I would get a couple of witches on the payroll who knew how to make monstrosities like this. A couple of oversized gorillas and a Godzilla or two would come in handy right about now. They could smash the shit out of the monster and then go after Dagen and the witch. All without breaking a sweat.

Hells, at this point I would welcome a dragon or a phoenix or two as well. Just because wolves were clearly superior didn't mean I should rule out working with other shifters or other kinds of paranormal people. Even demons had their uses from time to time. Especially powerful half demons like Harmony.

I kept on Jake's tail as he ducked into a side street, then around the corner into another one. It took me a moment to realise what he was doing, but I followed him around another corner and darted past the street the monster was lumbering down. Without anyone to direct it otherwise, it just kept going.

Interesting. Dagen wasn't close enough to see our change of direction. Where was he then?

We loped back until we got to the wrecked truck, then stopped for a few moments to catch our breath.

We seemed to have lost the monster. For now. The ground still shook, but it was a block or two away. Good, that would keep the witch busy.

Now we just had to find the other monster; Dagen.

I sniffed the air but found no sign of him and only a faint scent of the witch. What would I do if I was a cowardly piece of shit? Well obviously, I would leave her to deal with us and run away. That left us with three choices: go back and help the Ironhide pack with the Onyx Ridge pack, try to find Dagen, or deal with the witch.

I quickly ruled out the first option. They didn't need our help all that much and the other two options were more pressing. Reluctantly, I had to rule out the second option as well. Without his scent, Dagen could be anywhere.

But we knew where the witch was. Her mistake.

I trotted off in that direction and left the guys to follow me.

I knew very well how dangerous this was. It could be the fatal miscalculation that actually turned out to be fatal, but it was something I needed to do. The witch stood by and let Dagen abuse me in the worst possible ways, and then didn't even heal me properly. I don't know what, if any, attachments she had to Alistair Dagen, but she was dangerous.

And I held a grudge.

Her scent gradually became stronger. She was only half a block away. The ground stopped shaking. The magic that held the monster together must have dissipated.

I caught sight of movement up ahead and crouched behind a couple of rubbish bins.

It was her. Irina. She stood scanning the street carefully, but it was obvious she didn't know where we were. She had that cocky, arrogant bearing witches so often have. The confidence they were so powerful, they were all but invincible.

Anyone but a witch would have left the scene by now, but not her.

That, I decided, would be her fatal miscalculation. I could almost taste her blood on my tongue.

Jake placed a paw on my leg and nuzzled the side of my face with his muzzle.

I got the message loud and clear. Don't let anger get in the way. Don't go in half cocked and take an unnecessary risk.

I nuzzled him back. He was right. I was ready to bounce out from our hiding spot and run right at one of the most powerful paranormals in existence. Sure, I had claws and sharp teeth, but her magic could do any number of horrible things to me. Harmony, I knew, was able to incinerate things with only a moment's notice. I would really prefer that didn't happen to me.

I sketched out a plan with my paw.

Jake and Hutton nodded.

I checked to make sure the witch was still there, then indicated that we should enact our plan.

Hutton darted out first. He stood in plain view of the witch and growled.

She turned to face him, her hands outstretched. What looked like lightning arched out of her fingertips. That would be fucking cool if it wasn't so terrifying.

At the last moment, Hutton threw himself to the side and rolled out of the way.

Simultaneously, Jake darted out of our hiding spot.

Lightning flashed towards him, but only connected with the parked car he pounced behind. It flashed so bright I had to close my eyes for a moment. The smell of burning metal filled the air.

I sniffed back a sneeze and trotted out into the open.

FIFTEEN

For the second time in an hour or two, I stood out in the open, vulnerable. I felt less vulnerable than when I was naked, but that was an illusion.

Surrounded by my guys and those loyal to the Quinn Brothers, I was safer standing naked in front of Dagen than in wolf form in front of a witch. Still, this was much more within my comfort zone.

I raised my hackles and growled at her while I stared her down. In spite of how difficult it was for people to tell us apart on sight, I sensed she knew exactly who I was.

Arrogance warred with fear on her face.

Yeah, you better be scared, I thought. We were about to find out what happened when lightning met an ice storm.

I stalked towards her, growling harder.

Before she could raise her hands, Jake and Hutton slipped back out from behind their respective cars and took a place on either side of her.

Some witches could attack two enemies simultaneously, one

with each hand. But not three. Her arrogance hadn't slipped, but she was starting to realise the predicament she was in.

On the very edge of my senses, I recognised Dagen's presence. He was close enough to smell now, but not see.

I knew with absolute certainty he was not going to come out and rescue his pet witch.

Welcome to my world, I thought. *Sucks to be you.* I almost felt sorry for her, because I knew how it felt to be outnumbered and pretty sure you were more or less completely fucked.

If she had made better life choices and not screwed with me, I might have let her go. But no one fucks with me and gets away with it. If nothing else, I had to make an example of her. I wouldn't tolerate witches working against Ivory Claw.

She took a step back as we closed in on her. She was clearly thinking through her options, and hoping like hells help was coming.

I matched her step back with a step forward. Then a handful more.

I was within a metre or two of lunging at her when a large white shape streaked towards her from behind.

Ben leapt at her, knocking her to the ground before his powerful jaws snapped around her throat.

The witch let out a pitiful cry before he tore into her neck.

Not loud enough to cry wolf.

Cooper was half a second behind Ben in bounding on the witch. Between them they tore her apart.

I was only a little bit annoyed they didn't leave any for me. I didn't want to fill up on a snack when the main meal was so close I could taste him.

I cocked my head and watched the guys tear into her. Ben really, *really* didn't like witches, did he? And Cooper, he looked like he was having the time of his life.

I let them indulge their fun for a while longer before I let out a soft bark to indicate that we should keep moving.

Neither hesitated to lift their muzzles and step back into their loose formation behind Jake, Hutton and I. Honestly, there wasn't much of the witch left anyway. If anyone came along they would find nothing more than a few bones and a smear of blood on the road.

I would send somebody to clean it up when we got the chance.

Before we continued after Dagen, I took a moment to lick blood off Ben's muzzle. Partly to thank him for dealing with the witch and partly to let him know how relieved I was he was alive and safe. And maybe just to get a little taste of her blood. It was delicious.

Ben nuzzled his face against mine, then moved back at a bark from Jake. Right, we had time for this later. We had Dagen to deal with first.

We moved in a tight pack with Jake in the lead, all of our senses as open as possible. The smell of Dagen was faint, but still present. Without the overpowering stink of magic, it was a lot easier to follow.

I absolutely didn't rule out the possibility he had another backup plan. I knew that was uppermost in the minds of all the guys as well. We couldn't lower our guard for a moment. Nor would we.

We moved carefully, following the scent while slinking from one parked car to another.

We crouched down low when a bus rattled past, but it kept on going without stopping or even slowing. If any of the passengers saw us, I have no idea. No one would have believed them anyway.

I mean, a pack of white wolves trotting down the streets of Sydney? Most people wouldn't believe it even if they saw us with their own eyes. That was just as well. If they saw us, we might have to kill them.

The scent grew stronger, then weaker, then stronger again. He must be moving, slinking around, hoping to throw us off the trail.

A couple of times we lost it, but managed to find it again. Once or twice, I caught the smell of something else; some other kind of shifter. A tiger perhaps? Maybe a fox?

Whatever, as long as they had the sense to stay out of our way. Most of them did. Cat shifters and dog shifters tended to get along better than the other animal varieties. Mostly because no one wanted to start trouble between different breeds and across species. Wolves versus wolves got ugly enough.

Jake stopped and pointed his muzzle to a darkened doorway up ahead.

At first, I thought it was an abandoned building. I quickly realised it was a construction site. No one was working on it today, because it was a Saturday. How fortunate for Dagen.

It was also the perfect place for him to make a stand, especially if he had a backup plan. Lure us into a dark, half-built place and potentially trap us under falling scaffolding, or the gods knew what else.

I followed Jake inside and we stopped to look around.

Ben moved to stand beside us.

I didn't question his presence at my shoulder. He was the most observant person I ever met. If there was a trap here, he would see it before we did.

In the end, none of us needed to see it. The sudden smell of more black wolves was overpowering.

Three of them. No, four. They must have come in through a back entrance.

Still, the smell of Dagen was easily discernible from the others. He wasn't far, possibly tucked into a corner like the cowardly piece of shit he was.

I pictured him cowering and bared my teeth at the idea. It was as close as I could get to a smile right now.

Jake gave me a stern look which was easily interpreted. He wanted me to hang back and let the guys deal with Dagen.

I snorted in response. *Good luck with that, buddy*. I hadn't come this far to stay out of it at the last moment.

He sighed and gave me a nudge with his muzzle. I nudged him back. I don't know what I would have done if I was standing here in this moment without him and Ben. Or Hutton and Cooper for that matter. I would have been a lot angrier than I was. That isn't to say I wasn't pissed off, I was. But having them there with me made it all a lot easier and a lot more fun.

This was what pack life was all about. Hashtag wolf reverse harem goals.

What was the point of any of it if you couldn't chase down a baddie once in a while? Okay, there was all the really amazing sex as well. And the love and support of four incredible guys. When I thought about it, I was a lucky girl.

I would be even luckier when Dagen was dead.

I stayed back a little, with my head beside Jake's shoulder. Ben was close beside me on the other side. Hutton was a little in front and Cooper a little behind.

Something scuttled across our path, but only smelled of rat or mouse. The animal kind, not a shifter.

Yes, there are rat and mice shifters. I wasn't sure if I should feel sorry for them for being a rodent, or envious they could scurry and hide in small spaces. Either way, I wouldn't swap being a wolf for being a vermin of any kind.

The closer we got to Dagen, the stronger the smell of the other four black wolves became. They were closing in on us while we closed in on Asshole.

In the gloom of the enclosed site, it was harder to see much of anything, much less a black wolf. The five of us probably stuck out like sunlight through the clouds. We couldn't help that.

There was also no chance that the other wolves hadn't smelled us coming, so there was no point in hiding anyway.

We walked carefully around stacks of lumber and broken tiles. I stepped on a shard of ceramic and winced as it stabbed into the bottom of my paw pad.

The guys all stopped and immediately turned to make sure I was okay. I lifted up my paw and Cooper stepped closer to lick it quickly. There was no blood, not even punctured skin, but I appreciated the attention. They were adorable to care so much. I bet they'd fuss over me endlessly if I ever got a cold. Fair enough, I'd fuss over them too. They deserved it.

I lowered my paw and nodded that I was all right.

We all walked a little bit more carefully after that.

We approached the corner where Dagen's scent was strongest, and spread out a little. There was no way he was getting past us, not now. We were too close to let him slip through the net.

I took a handful of steps forward and peered into the gloom. *Gotcha.*

Dagen was still in wolf form, huddled against the wall. If I didn't know better, I would think the smell around him was his own urine. Oh, right, it probably was.

When he saw us, he scrambled to his feet and raised his hackles. He let out a low growl.

I have to give him credit for not giving up even when he was screwed. I growled back at him. For some reason, it felt good to do that. Maybe because he was outnumbered. Maybe because I knew the next blood I would taste on my tongue would be his.

He stepped back and straightened up.

That was when I became aware the other black wolves caught up to us. They arrayed themselves around behind us.

I glanced over my shoulder as the biggest one let out a deep growl. *My thoughts exactly*, I thought.

I turned back to Dagen. He must have been absolutely

convinced there was some chance his allies would still stand by him. Sucks to be him.

Mindful of exactly who I was shifting in front of, I shifted back into person form.

"Shift," I ordered Dagen. "You know you're outnumbered. Five Ivory Claw, the Quinn brothers and their girlfriend. Against you."

I stood with my back to the black wolves, absolutely certain I could trust Kian and his brothers. The way his men had turned on the Onyx Ridge pack was clear evidence of that.

"Shift." I planted my fists on my hips.

Dagen withdrew into himself, so that when he did shift he was sitting with his knees almost to his chin.

"I beg for mercy," he said, his voice small.

I laughed. My voice echoed back at me. "Like you gave me? Why should I give you even a moment of anything other than torture and death?"

"Because I'm asking for it," he said.

Honestly, if the next words out of his mouth was that *I* was asking for what I got from him, I was going to slap him silly. With a brick.

"You gave people mercy when you overthrew my pack the first time," he added. "And we gave you mercy. My parents could have killed all the children, but they didn't."

"Give them all a fucking sainthood," I snarled. "They only did that so they could look good. I only spared who I spared because I'm not an asshole." I gave him a look, challenging him to refute that statement.

He surprised me by agreeing. "No, you're not. That's why I know you're going to let me live." Reluctantly he added, "It's my turn to swear to do whatever you say. I'll sign away all my assets if I have to."

I smiled. "You mean the ones that are all forfeit now?" I took a moment to celebrate the fact the Lair was finally mine. It better be worth it after all the work I put into securing it. I knew just the person to run it...

I stepped towards him.

Even now, surrounded by the enemy, he glanced at my breasts. If they were the last things he ever saw, then he was luckier than he deserved to be.

"Alistair," I said slowly, "you have nothing I want or need except your death."

He swallowed audibly. "Are you sure about that?"

I cocked my head at him. "If you can think of anything, now would be a good time to bring it up. I have a pack of very hungry wolves with me and I don't know how much longer I can keep them contained. Except for Ben and Cooper. They had a good snack on your witch. You probably smelled her blood from here."

Judging from the way he shifted from foot to foot and looked increasingly anxious, he had. He must have felt his last chance wither away.

That begged the question. "Why didn't you run when you knew she was dead?"

He shrugged one shoulder. "Where could I go so you wouldn't find me?"

"That's true," I conceded.

"Besides, as soon as my men dispatch the traitors, they will come for me." He seemed sure of that.

"I don't see them." Jake shifted too. He stood with his arms crossed over his muscular chest. Gods, the man was hot, especially when he had that whole alpha male, winner winner, chicken dinner, look going on. Not smug, just confident and comfortable.

Only now I had a craving for chicken.

I glanced down towards Ben. "Can you smell any more black wolves coming?"

He made a show of sniffing the air, then shook his head.

I turned back to Dagen and shrugged. "You seem pretty fucked to me. As a matter of fact, I think your whole pack is fucked. Even if they're not, they're not going to get here in time. Let me guess, you hoped we would let you stay alive long enough for them to save the day?"

"Isn't that what you would do?" He narrowed his eyes at me. "You would even go so far as offering me your body as a distraction. At least I have more dignity than that."

I eyed him with the utmost scepticism and clicked my tongue. "Alistair, Alistair. You wouldn't offer me your cock if it would save your life?"

Jake made a funny sound in the back of his throat and looked sideways in the direction of Dagen's groin. "Would you want it?"

I smiled at him. "Fuck no. Why would I want what he has, when I can get all of that?" I nodded towards Jake's dick, which was considerably more substantial than Dagen's.

"And all of that." I jerked my head towards the other three guys.

"The point is, I'm certain there's nothing you wouldn't do to convince me to spare your life." I jerked an eyebrow speculatively at Dagen. His suggestion that he still had something I wanted had me curious, but little more than that.

Dagen's tongue darted over his lips. I could almost hear him thinking. He was desperate enough to offer anything to save his own ass. If his mother was still alive, he would probably offer her.

He lifted his chin. "When the doctor did the procedure on you, he extracted an egg. Several in fact. Stimulated by Irina, the witch you just killed. On my orders, they were frozen. They were removed before the fire just in case of a scenario just like this. I can tell you where they are. If you kill me, you'll never know." He shrugged.

His words knocked the breath right out of me.

"You're bluffing," I whispered.

506

He pulled himself up a little taller. "Not at all. Of course, you can't carry them yourself, but with a surrogate you could have several children. Maybe one for each of your so-called lovers."

Jake was staring at me.

For the longest time, I had no idea how to respond. If I bought what he was selling, then I ran the risk of him escaping at a later time. The remains of his pack might come for him. Or another pet witch.

But if I didn't, I lost what might be my last chance to have my own, biological children. Not just that, I would take away the guys' chance at fathering children. There might come a day when they decided that was what they wanted and they would end things with me.

Okay, I couldn't imagine it, but that might be because I didn't want to. I didn't want to think something like that could drive us apart.

"El?" Jake said softly. I wasn't sure if he was begging me to ignore Dagen or asking me to at least keep him alive for much longer.

I licked my lips. There was a very good chance Dagen was lying anyway, so all of this speculation might be a waste of time.

"What proof do you have that you're telling the truth?" I asked.

"None," he admitted. "You'll have to believe me. Or not." There was more than a little hint of desperation in his eyes.

It probably matched mine. He wanted to live and I wanted to know for sure whether or not I could ever be a mother.

I looked down at the ground.

At the end of the day this was about more than just me. This was about all the children who wouldn't grow up under the shadow of the Onyx Ridge pack because of me. This was about continuing to keep them safe. The existing children had to matter more than children I may or may not ever have.

Besides, I could always adopt.

"Kill him," I said softly.

Jake and I both shifted back at the same time and leapt toward Dagen. The rest of my guys, and the Quinn brothers and Blair, all joined us.

Later, I wouldn't remember who delivered the killing blow or whether it was Dagen's arm or leg I chewed on. It didn't matter.

What mattered was that he was gone and we were united.

CHAPTER
SIXTEEN

I leaned back in my chair and swallowed down a mouthful of apple juice. Who needed alcohol when I had the rush of vanquishing my enemies? I couldn't compare it to getting drunk, but I was pretty sure it was a lot better.

"This place is going to take some work." Jake looked around at the inside of the Lair and grimaced. "And a shit ton of money."

I shrugged one shoulder. I was too relaxed to bother to shrug the other one. "We have plenty of time. And plenty of money." Once Dagen was dead, there was nothing to stop us from funnelling the rest of his money out of his account and into much better places.

"You can't spend all of it on this," he reminded me. He glanced at the smartwatch on his wrist. "The next group is due here in about—"

He stopped talking when Cooper showed the latest group through the doors.

"This is Gunter and Carol Frankston," Cooper said. "And the children." All six of them. "I told them to leave their staff outside."

I nodded my thanks and turned to the newcomers. They both looked nervous. Anxious.

Hells, I'd be anxious too if I was a black wolf in Sydney today.

Unless my last name was Quinn, or I was dating four of them. Or if I worked for the five of them. They would get nothing today but my undying gratitude.

I turned my attention to Carol Frankston. Judging by the way her husband was looking at her, she was the one in charge in their family.

"Thank you for coming." I uncrossed my legs and crossed them again the other way. "I understand you have something to say?"

Carol stepped forward, her chin raised.

I gave her credit for having some pride left, and not being afraid to show it.

"My husband and I run the Roam hotel two blocks down from here," she said. "We've never been supporters of Alistair Dagen or any member of the Dagen family." She glanced back at Gunter, who nodded to her.

She turned back to me. "We've always kept peace with Ivory Claw and would like to continue to do so."

I had heard the same message spoken umpteen different ways all morning. Every black wolf wanted to be quick to let me know they had nothing to do with the late, not so great, Alistair. Or any of the people who were loyal to him. I believed some of them. Others were blatantly lying.

They would have been just as happy if I was the one lying dead. Happier maybe, if it advanced them in some way. Those, I would keep an eye on. People like the Frankstons, who had worked in the area for years, and whom I knew on sight, were more or less harmless. They just wanted to get on with their lives and raise their children.

Of course, I couldn't make it that easy on them.

"I know you are," I said coolly. "Did any of you take any action in the past to stop the Dagen family?"

Carol swallowed visibly. "No, Ivory. We tried to stay out of... any trouble. Dagen wasn't known for being forgiving if anyone spoke out against him. Even if they were black wolves too."

Yeah, I couldn't argue with that. Alistair was a pissy little coward, even as a child. He always liked to get his own way. I mean, me too, but at least I was reasonable about it. Mostly.

I leaned forward. "Did you ever help him in any way?"

She looked even more uncomfortable now. "He stayed at our hotel once or twice. We couldn't really turn him down, considering who he was. He would have had us—"

"Yes," I interrupted. "Yes he would have." Just like I had Jake and Ben kill Silas Wheeler and Jefferson Haigwood, Dagen would have had his people kill anyone who pissed him off. I would be a hypocrite if I held it against her.

"We don't want any trouble," Carol said quickly. "Whatever it takes to avoid that, we will do it."

Gunter looked like he was going to choke on air, but he still nodded. "Yes we will."

"Do you have room for more staff?" I asked. "I have a couple of very good cleaners who need steady employment." And of course, they would report back to me. Wherever possible, I was inserting white wolves into businesses owned by black wolves. If they tried anything, I would hear about it long before it became a problem.

"We can make room, Ivory," Carol said respectfully. "If they come with your endorsement, then they must be very good."

Was that sarcasm or scepticism I heard in her tone?

"Believe it or not, I want us all to succeed." I set aside my empty glass on the table. "There's been more than enough animosity between white wolves and black wolves. It's time for us all to come together and put the past behind us." With me in charge, of course. That was the best way to ensure peace.

"Yes, Ivory," Carol agreed. "I would like my children to grow up without having to worry about getting caught up in a war." She was maybe ten years older than me. Old enough to have seen how ugly things got. Old enough to remember them. And old enough to appreciate the relative calm in the city since I took over.

I nodded and gave her a sincere smile. "That's what I want too." Not for my own children, of course, I sighed. I would be happy if other people's children enjoyed some quiet for the next hundred years or so.

I could only hope to leave a lasting legacy beyond that.

She returned my smile and said, "Thank you," before she backed away and herded her family out the door.

Cooper made sure they got out and came back to stand behind my chair. He put his hands on my shoulders and started to massage them lightly.

"Just when I think you can't get hotter, you do," he said in my ear.

"Oh? I do?" I asked. "How is that?"

"I don't know. I guess I just find this whole boss lady thing a turn on. I mean, I kinda like the fact that you haven't just made us go out and kill every black wolf we could find. Instead, you're making sure they know exactly who is boss and everyone knows what will happen if they step out of line."

"I would have thought you liked the idea of killing them all," I said lightly.

"I've been talking to Luca." His tone spoke of a clear case of hero worship. "He told me it's much more fun killing people if they really deserve it. Those people who left, they're just regular people, y'know? And they have kids. They just want to raise them and work hard and stuff. But then there are people like Dagen, who deserve to have their throats cut in the dark or whatever. Luca said it's much more rewarding."

"It sounds to me like you found your calling in life," I said.

"I'm glad. You could have worse mentors than Luca. Just make sure you pay attention to Jake, Ben and Hutton as well. They all have plenty of good things to teach." Each one had a unique set of skills and they all seemed happy to pass them on to Cooper. He would be formidable in another decade or so. Luckily he was on my side.

"I will," Cooper assured me. "And I'll learn from you as well. Lots of things." His hands slipped down to the top of my chest and caressed softly. "Like how to stay classy while dealing with an archenemy."

I laughed at that. "I try."

He leaned in to kiss the side of my face. "You succeed. Every day." He slipped his hands down the front of my blouse, under the silky fabric of my bra. He ghosted his fingertips over my nipples and made me shiver. White hot heat went straight to my core.

"If you keep doing that, the next people through the door are going to get a show." Not that it bothered me, depending on who the next person was. If it was one of the guys, they could join in.

"They might—" Whatever Cooper was going to say was interrupted by Luca strutting through the door, followed by a blonde woman about four years younger than me.

In front of Luca, I might have let Cooper keep doing what he was doing, but I put my hands on his wrists and said, "Stella."

Cooper jerked his hands out so fast I thought he might tumble over backwards. "Um, hey."

Luca chuckled.

Stella looked less than impressed. She glanced around the inside of the Lair. "What a dump." She looked squarely at me. "Did you summon me here for some reason?"

I stood and offered my half-sister a smile. "You weren't summoned here," I corrected. "I *asked* you to come here because I have an offer for you."

She and I had never been close. A lot of that was for her own safety. Okay, a lot was also because I never knew how to deal with her. We shared a father and a last name, but that was all. I barely knew anything about her. Her likes, dislikes, hobbies, pet peeves.

If I knew Dagen was already aware of her existence, I might have tried to remedy that sooner. I assumed we had done a good job in keeping her hidden, but evidently that assertion was wrong.

Now I hoped she would give me a chance to get to know her.

Stella looked at me like she thought I was full of shit. She jerked her head towards Luca. "That wasn't what he said. He said he was sent to keep me safe until you summoned me."

I raised an eyebrow at Luca.

He shrugged. "I embellished a little. Not the part about keeping her safe." He loudly whispered, "She's outspoken, isn't she?"

"I'm right here," Stella snapped.

"Yeah," I agreed. "She's nothing like me at all." Only a lot. She also inherited our father's stubbornness.

I grabbed Cooper's hand and pulled him forward. "This is my sister Stella. Stella, this is one of my boyfriends, Cooper."

She mouthed, "One of?" Out loud she added, "He's a bit young for you, isn't he?"

"I'm twenty," Cooper said. "Well, almost."

Stella snorted. "What do you want, Elodie?"

I waved my hand around our surroundings. "I need someone to run this place. I know you have experience in running a bar. I thought this might be a challenge you would enjoy."

She frowned at me like she was certain I was up to something, but couldn't figure out what. "This place? Why?"

"Why not?" I asked. "I don't have time and I thought you might like the challenge. I can give you all the money you need to fix it up. You can do what you want with it."

Her eyes narrowed further. "Can I change the name?"

"Of course," I agreed. I wasn't particularly attached to the name the Lair anyway. "You can call it whatever you want."

"Even if it's nothing red?" She looked at me sideways.

"You can call it something green for all I care," I said lightly. "Or pink. If you want to call it Fandango, then go ahead. I just want someone I can trust in charge of the place."

"You can't trust your boyfriend?" she asked.

I glanced at Cooper and gave him a soft smile. "He has other duties to keep him busy. A new career he's training for."

He gave me a loving smile in return.

"And he's supposed to be outside making sure riffraff doesn't walk in," Jake said, as he walked through the door.

"Too late," Hutton said as he followed on Jake's heels. "We're already here." He snaked an arm around my waist and kissed my mouth.

"Want me to throw them out?" Ben asked. He stepped to the other side of me and kissed me after Hutton and I came up for air.

Apparently feeling left out, Jake snuck in and did the same.

Stella's eyes were wide. She'd met Jake and Ben on previous occasions, when we needed to keep her updated with something related to the organisation, but the guys were nothing more than professional then. She clearly didn't miss the fact things had changed significantly.

What she thought of that little surprise, I couldn't tell.

"Who are you throwing out?" Reed Quinn drawled. He too stepped through the doorway, followed by his brothers and Blair.

I smiled sincerely and without reservation. "Not you four, that's for sure. I owe you a really big favour. I hope I can repay it someday." And that it wouldn't cost me too heavily.

"I can think of a few things you could do." Reed gave me a wink and smiled at me until Blair smacked him on the chest. "What?" He grinned.

She rolled her eyes at him.

"You've definitely got your hands full with these guys," I told her.

"With those two anyway," Kian said, giving his brothers the side eye. "Some of us know how not to be pains in the ass."

Spontaneously, I walked up to him and gave him a hug and a kiss on the cheek. "I owe you the biggest thanks. You could easily have said no and walked away, but you didn't."

To my surprise, he hugged me back. "I didn't want to have to deal with Dagen on my northern border in a year or two. I know I won't have that problem with you."

"I give you an ironclad guarantee that you will never have that problem with me," I assured him. "And I know I have your guarantee I won't have problems on my south border."

He nodded and stepped back. "Ironclad or Ironhide. Either way, you won't have any trouble from us."

"We can't guarantee Reed won't stick his cock in where it's not supposed to," Tyler said.

"Fuck off," Reed told him cheerfully. "I'm tame now. The only one who gets my cock is Blair. Now and forever." He gave her a smile which mirrored the ones my guys gave me. Who knew Reed Quinn could actually fall in love? It was almost as unlikely as me falling in love.

Kian shook his head at his brothers. "Anyway. We just came to say goodbye and that we only lost five men yesterday. The Dagen clan is down by a couple of hundred. If they ever rebuild, it's going to take them a long time. Hopefully not in our lifetime."

"Hopefully not," I agreed. "Thank you again." I watched them walk out the door and turned back to Stella. "Will you at least think about taking on this place?"

"I have no interest in becoming a part of Ivory Claw," she said coolly.

"I'm not asking you to," I said. "Just run this place. You can be the owner if you'd prefer." That earned me a look of surprise from all of my guys, especially Jake. He knew how long I'd been trying to buy the Lair, only to now give it up? If it went any way towards building a relationship with my sister, then I would let her have it in a heartbeat.

"I'll think about it," she said finally. "But if I say no, I want you to accept that. You might own everything else around here, but you don't own me."

"I didn't think for a second I owned you," I told her firmly. "I certainly don't want to. I want us to have the chance to get to know each other. And let's face it, this place could really use a facelift."

"That's for fucking sure," she muttered.

"If you're done," Jake said carefully. "We have a surprise for Elodie. Over at Crimson." He jerked his head towards the doorway.

"Go ahead," Stella said. "I might take a look around for a while and see if I like the place or not."

"Of course." Jake slid his hand into one of mine and Ben took the other. I gave them a smile, one after the other. How did I get so lucky?

"I'll stick around for a bit too," Luca said. "Make sure nothing happens to Stella."

I gave him a speculative glance. I had a funny feeling he was interested in more than her safety. I wasn't sure how I thought about that. At the end of the day, she was a white wolf and he was a black wolf. Well, no doubt they would work it out between themselves.

"Okay," I said finally. "I'll see you both later." As we headed towards the door, I looked around my guys and asked, "So what is this surprise?"

CHAPTER
SEVENTEEN

When I stepped through the doors into the apartment, it was like stepping into a wonderland. Every spare surface was covered with candles. Some sat on top of tall candlesticks and others floated in bowls of water.

Scattered here and there were bunches of lavender and scented roses. Not enough to be overpowering, but enough to make the place smell divine.

"What is all this for?" I asked.

"Because you are a goddess," Jake said. "You are *our* goddess. You deserve to be spoilt once in a while."

"You don't think I'm spoilt enough?" I asked lightly. "I have the four of you and all of this." I waved towards the large window.

The sun had set and the city lights glittered across the harbour like a crown.

"There is no such thing as spoiling you too much, babe," Hutton said. "We decided we would devote the rest of our lives to reminding you of that. Every day. And if we miss a day, you get to kick our asses."

I laughed. "That sounds like a lot of work."

"You're worth it," Ben said softly. I hadn't had much chance to talk to him since we killed Dagen, but he looked like the weight of the world was off his shoulders for once.

"I think *you're* worth it," I told him. "All of you." I frowned for a moment. "Wait a minute, is this where you say you get to kick my ass if I don't tell you every day?" I grinned to show I was joking.

"Just being around you is enough of a reminder," Cooper said firmly.

"And having you around," Jake started. "For a while there, I didn't think we'd have that." His eyes were actually glassy with emotion.

"I thought the same about you," I said softly. "I could have lost all of you yesterday. For a while there—" My voice caught in the back of my throat.

Cooper put his arms around me and gently pulled my face to his shoulder. He rubbed his hands up and down my back slowly, soothingly. If anyone could see him now, they would never think he liked to kill people. With me, he was always gentle and loving.

"When he got out that gun, I thought we were fucked," Jake admitted. "If he didn't like playing games so much, we would be." After a moment he added, "I would be. The Quinn brothers' men would have stopped him before he killed Ben."

"Maybe," Ben said softly. "It doesn't matter now."

"Of course it doesn't matter, you would have survived," Jake said teasingly.

Ben flipped him off.

Jake grinned and patted him on the shoulder. "Love you too, bro."

Ben raised an eyebrow at him. "Yeah, love you, bro."

Isn't bro love sweet?

"Well, we're all here, thank the gods," I said. "In spite of it all, the five of us managed to survive. More or less intact."

"We have another surprise for you," Hutton said. "Actually, two surprises. One big, one *really* big."

"Which one do you want first?" Jake asked.

"I don't want to have to choose," I said. "That would be like choosing between you guys."

"We would never ask you to do that," Jake said. "I mean, everyone knows I'm your favourite already." He grinned.

"I don't have a favourite," I said firmly. "I will kick your ass is just as hard if you piss me off. Now, will someone please show me what you guys are up to?"

Silence fell for a moment.

Hutton broke it, speaking gently. "The big thing is actually at the IVF clinic," he said. "When I was going through Dagen's shit, I found a record of where they took your eggs."

"It's totally up to you if you ever decide to use them," Jake said softly. "We all agreed not to pressure you."

All of the guys murmured their agreement.

I took a moment to process that. So Dagen wasn't completely full of shit. Just mostly.

"Thank you," I said finally.

I honestly had no idea how I felt, or whether I would ever use them. It was good to know they were there if I wanted to. It felt like another victory over Dagen. Something he tried to take, but in the end he didn't. My only regret was that I didn't ask him why he bothered to keep the eggs in the first place. It was probably some kind of mind game he wanted to play. Now he would never be able to.

"What's the other surprise?" I asked. I was already feeling somewhat overwhelmed at this point anyway.

Overwhelmed in a good way. I couldn't ask for much more than they already gave me.

"It's in the bedroom," Ben said.

Okay, I should have seen that coming. Four horny guys wanted to give me something in the bedroom.

What a shock.

"It's not what you think," Cooper said quickly. He knitted his brows. "Well it is, but it isn't."

"Didn't you say you went to university?" Jake teased.

Cooper flipped him off.

Jake pretended to huff. "Remember when they respected me?"

"Nope." Hutton grinned.

Now it was Jake's turn to give him the finger. "Fuck off, bro."

I raised my eyebrows at him. That was a big step up from 'traitor.' Frankly, all this bro love was turning me on.

I grabbed Ben's hand. "So, what did you want to show me in the bedroom?"

He smiled and walked beside me.

We stopped in the doorway.

I gaped. "Holy shit."

My bed was gone, replaced by one wide enough for about ten people to sleep.

"Yes! Now I have room for all those pet cats I was going to get." I grinned.

"As long as they're tigers shifters and aren't assholes," Jake said. "Lions would be okay too."

"You don't think four guys is enough?" I asked.

"I think," Jake said slowly, "that we love you and want you to be happy. Whatever it takes to make that happen, we're okay with it."

"We also put some smaller beds in the other bedrooms in case you want to be alone," Ben said.

"I do like to spread out sometimes," I said. Maybe not *this* much though. All five of us could share the bed and not touch each other. "I'd like to see how comfortable it is. Who wants to join me?"

Predictably, we all kicked off our shoes and lay down together.

Ben snagged a spot on one side of me and Jake on the other. Hutton and Cooper both lay on the other side of Ben.

I wriggled down into the mattress. "This is exactly the right combination of not too hard and not too soft." It didn't surprise me at all they nailed that. I was very particular with the mattresses I slept on. After spending ten years on a narrow, almost flat foam one, I swore I would never be uncomfortable like that again. In this department, I was more like a domestic dog than a wild wolf, and I was okay with that.

Life was too fucking short to be uncomfortable.

"That's funny," Jake said. "I am also the perfect combination of not too hard and not too soft."

I rolled over and raised an eyebrow at him. "Where are you soft?" I poked him in the chest with the tip of my fingernail. "You feel like a rock to me."

He smiled. "I'm just a soft puppy dog on the inside. At least where you are concerned."

I smiled back. "That's true." There was nothing he wouldn't give me or do for me if it made me happy.

Same for the other guys. That went both ways. If they needed me to move heaven and earth, then I would do it. At least I could rock their world for a little while.

I scooted over to press my mouth to Jake's. Just lightly at first, then with more tongue and teeth and heat.

Before he could even touch me or catch his breath, I worked my way down his body, caressing through his clothes. I finally stopped at the top of his jeans. I eased the button loose and slid down the zipper before I tugged the front down his thighs. I took pity on his thick erection, by also pulling down the front of his bright green underpants. I even ignored the fact he had small turtles printed on the front of them.

Cute.

And then I found myself face to tip with his cock. My heart started to race and sweat broke out on my palms.

"El, you don't have to do that," he said softly. "I know it's hard... I mean, difficult." It was certainly *hard*. "I understand."

"We all do," Ben said. "None of us will ever ask you to do anything you don't want to do."

That was good, because I was notoriously stubborn. But this...

"I want to," I said, my voice soft but firm. It was something I enjoyed doing and I wasn't going to let anyone take it away from me anymore.

That didn't mean I dove straight in though. I gripped the base of his shaft and started to run the tip of my tongue feather lightly over the side of Jake's cock.

I loved the shiver that passed through him at that slight touch. I missed that. Everything I did with these guys made me feel powerful, like a goddess. But in this, I felt like I was in complete control.

One of the guys moved around behind me, unfastened my skirt and started to slide it down my hips.

I lifted myself up to help them, not even caring that I had no idea which of them it was.

My panties followed. A large hand gently bent my knee and slid in between my thighs to caress my clit.

I circled the tip of Jake's cock, tasting his precum and the salty warmth of his skin. I looked up at him and saw him watching me.

His eyes were filled with a combination of concern, desire and love.

I knew he wanted me to take him deep into my mouth, but not if it was something I would regret.

Since I couldn't imagine a universe in which I would regret sucking any of them off, I did the former. I closed my mouth around as much of his length as I could fit without choking. And then a little more. I ran my tongue up and down him and then started to suck while my hands caressed his balls.

At the same time, whoever was behind me slipped a finger inside me. Then another. And another.

Judging by the feeling of calluses against my skin, it was Hutton. He had the roughest, but at the same time, gentlest hands. He circled my clit with his thumb while he massaged inside my body with his fingertips.

Ben moved down the mattress and started to unbutton my blouse and unhook my bra to let my breasts fall free. I lifted first one arm, then the other so he could pull straps and sleeves out of the way.

He looked me in the eyes and smiled before he started to lick and suck my breasts and nipples. Obviously he remembered from when we still had the bond, that I loved this more than almost anything.

He didn't seem to mind it too much either.

I glanced back up at Jake to see he'd closed his eyes. He didn't look worried anymore. That expression was replaced with one of ecstasy.

I closed my own eyes and let the sensations from Hutton's fingers course through me. I found a rhythm of caresses and sucks and licks that drove me closer and closer before I fell into oblivion. I had to take my mouth off Jake's cock so I could breathe and let out a series of soft moans, while I came. Before I was even back down to earth, I latched back on and sucked harder than ever.

Tender hands pried my legs open a little further, and a warm, pierced cock slid into my body. Definitely Hutton.

"There's lube in the drawer over there," Hutton said.

I wasn't sure who he was speaking to until I heard Cooper say, "Are you sure?"

My eyes widened. Holy shit. Just thinking about Cooper

fucking Hutton's ass, while Hutton fucked my pussy almost made me come again.

I looked over to Ben. His eyebrows were raised, but that was the only sign he'd heard. He was obviously not going to judge them any more than I was.

I glanced up at Jake. To my surprise, he'd propped himself up on his elbow and seemed to be watching the other guys.

He must have sensed me looking, because his gaze turned to me and he shrugged one shoulder.

I wondered if he would be into that. That thought made me suck harder.

Jake groaned and rolled his hips, pushing his cock so deep down my throat I could barely breathe. I took in every millimetre and sucked faster.

Hutton's slow thrusts stopped for a few moments. I pictured Cooper's fingers smearing lube onto his rear hole. When he started to move again, it was more careful, slower. I knew, without looking, that Cooper had slid inside him.

Holy gods.

Apparently Jake agreed with that, because a shudder passed through his whole body and he came, spilling hot cum deep into my mouth.

I swallowed, savouring the taste on my tongue. He really was delicious.

I let his cock go and glanced over my shoulder. Sure enough, Cooper knelt behind Hutton, who was lying behind me. All three of our hips were moving in perfect rhythm.

I turned my face back toward Ben. He hadn't stopped spoiling my breasts since he started.

He stopped now, to look up at me questioningly.

"Can I have your cock in my mouth?" I asked softly.

"Any time," he said. Jake moved over to let him in. He slowly, gently slid his curved cock between my lips.

The taste and feel of him was different to Jake's. Just as tasty, but with a flavour that was uniquely Ben's.

I barely started sucking him when Hutton gasped and thrust a little harder and faster into my body.

"Oh, gods," he ground out. "Fuck, fuck, fuck. Yeah..." He filled my pussy with his warm cum. He panted, then mercifully pulled Cooper down to the end of the bed where I could see them. And watch. And enjoy the sight of Hutton lying on his stomach while Cooper knelt between his thighs.

Jake moved around behind me and slipped his hand between my wet thighs. He circled my clit with his fingertips, while his other hand traced lines over my bare ass. He had me panting in a matter of moments.

When I came again, I clamped my lips down on Ben's cock, drawing an orgasm out of him too. At the same time, Cooper thrust a couple of more times into Hutton's ass before he joined us in orgasmland.

I swallowed down Ben's creamy juices before I came down from the most intense, wonderful orgasm I ever had.

I lay there for a long while before I slid my mouth off his cock. Jake took his hand away from my pussy and gave a long, contented sigh. Ben and Jake relaxed on either side of me. Hutton and Cooper lay on the other side of Ben, and cuddled.

Everyone snuggled in closer, like we were a litter of content, milk drunk puppies.

"I love you guys," I whispered.

"I love you too," they said back, more or less in unison.

I sighed with contentment and snuggled down a little deeper. What in the world could be better than being naked in bed with the four hottest, sexiest, smartest, most loving guys in the entire universe?

I couldn't think of a single, fucking thing.

About the Author

Maggie Alabaster writes reverse harem and, paranormal, sci-fi and fantasy romance.

She lives in NSW, Australia with one spouse, two daughters, one dog, and countless birds.

Sign up for my newsletter! Sign Up!

Join my reader group! Join here!

Follow me on Bookbub! Click here to follow me!

Check out my website- www.maggiealabaster.com

Also by Maggie Alabaster

Dark Masque

Book 1 Bait

Book 2 Prey

Book 3 Trap

Saving Abbie

Book 1 Pitch

Book 2 Pound

Book 3 Session

Book 4 Muse

Book 5 Rhythm

Book 6 Encore

Novella Venomous

Ruthless Claws

Book 1 Ivory

Book 2 Crimson

Book 3 Elodie

Harmony's Magic

Book 1 Summoned by Fire

Book 2 Summoned by Fate

Book 3 Summoned by Desire

Shifter's Vault

Book 1 Discarded

Book 2 Deceived

Book 3 Disgraced

My Alien Mates

Book 1 Star Warriors

Book 2 Star Defenders

Book 3 Star Protectors

Academy of Modern Magic

Book 1 Digital Magic

Book 2 Virtual Magic

Book 3 Logical Magic

Complete Collection

Summer's Harem

Book 1: Shimmer

Book 2: Glimmer

Book 3: Flicker

Complete collection

Short reads

Taken by the Snowmen

Jingle All the Way

Also by Maggie Alabaster and Erin Yoshikawa

Caught by the Tide

Book 1–Pursued by Shadows

Book 2 Pursued by Darkness

Book 3 Pursued by Monsters

www.ingramcontent.com/pod-product-compliance
Lightning Source LLC
Chambersburg PA
CBHW020239120726
47904CB00001B/25